STALKED IN THE NIGHT

CARLA CASSIDY

COLTON STORM WARNING

JUSTINE DAVIS

MILLS & BOON

First Published in Great Britain 2020
by Mills & Boon, an imprint of HarperCollins*Publishers*
1 London Bridge Street, London, SE1 9GF

Special thanks and acknowledgement are given to Justine Davis for her contribution to *The Coltons of Kansas* series.

ISBN: 978-0-263-28052-4

1020

MIX
Paper from responsible sources
FSC™ C007454

This book is produced from independently certified FSC™ paper to ensure responsible forest management.

For more information visit: www.harpercollins.co.uk/green

Printed and bound in Spain
by CPI, Barcelona

STALKED IN THE NIGHT

CARLA CASSIDY

Chapter One

Eva Martin used the tip of a shovel to poke at the mutilated dead cow on the ground before her, and then she turned and stared up at the tall, uniformed man standing next to her.

Sheriff Wayne Black took off his hat and wiped his sweating face and head with a handkerchief. The month of August in Dusty Gulch, Kansas, could be sweltering, and even though it was only midmorning, the temperature had already reached into the nineties.

Eva had a burn in her chest that had nothing to do with the heat of the day. It was the slow burn of anger, coupled with more than a whisper of fear.

"Wayne, this is the third mutilated cow I've had in as many weeks, and I'm sure if I check my mailbox right now, there'll be another threatening note for me inside."

Wayne swiped the sides of his face once again and then plopped his hat back on his head and gazed out into the distance. "Well, then I guess we'd better check out your mailbox."

As he got back into his patrol car, Eva placed the shovel on the ground next to the dead cow and then mounted her horse, Thunder, and galloped ahead toward the mailbox at the end of the lane to her house.

Her heart beat in her ears almost as loudly as Thunder's hooves against the hard ground. Somebody was targeting her, and she had no idea who it might be. And what frustrated her as much as anything was that she didn't believe the sheriff was taking any of this seriously enough.

In a town practically owned by the powerful Albright family, she knew Wayne saw her as nothing more than a pesky gnat to be swatted away. Wayne Black was Justin Albright's man, and she was definitely not a fan of the Albrights. She'd never pretended to be.

She got to the mailbox first and then waited for Wayne to pull up and get out of his patrol car. She opened the mailbox, and just as she'd suspected, there was a plain white envelope addressed to her in bold black block lettering.

Even though she had received two notes before, her heartbeat accelerated and her chest tightened as she grabbed the envelope from the mailbox. She opened it and fought off a small shiver as she read, "Whore—get out of town."

"That's pretty much like the last two," Wayne said. She held the note out to him, but he didn't take it from her. "I don't need it. I've got the other ones to work with."

"So, what are you doing about this?" Eva asked. "Wayne, you should know I can't afford to lose a cow a week, and these notes definitely seem like a threat to me."

"I know, and I'm investigating it. I promise I'll call you once I have any information to give you."

To her dismay, but not her surprise, he immediately got back into his patrol car and waved to her as he drove away. "He'll call me—yeah, right," she said to her horse.

It had been two weeks since she'd found her first dead cow in her pasture. The cow's throat had been slashed and the heart had been cut out. That day she had also received the first note.

Wayne had come out both previous times and had promised both an investigation and a phone call to tell her what the investigation had found. So far there had been no follow-up phone calls, and she had a sneaking suspicion there had not been much of an investigation.

If she was part of the Albright family or was one of the people in town who kissed Justin Albright's ring, she was certain Wayne would be turning himself inside out to solve these crimes.

She remounted Thunder and headed toward the barn in the distance. She hated to call Harley, one of her ranch hands, and tell him he had to dispose of yet another dead animal.

Still, despite the discovery of another dead cow, as she rode back she couldn't help but feel a small sense of pride. Although a bit skittish, the rest of the herd was all healthy, and when the time came, the sale of them should refill her bank account—which was running dangerously low.

The large garden by the house was still yielding plenty of fresh vegetables, and her chickens were laying enough eggs that she was selling them to the locals.

Her father would have been proud of her and all her hard work to stay on the land he had loved, the land he had worked on all his life. Eva's mother had died when she was eight years old. It had just been her and her father after that. They had been both partners and best friends.

It was difficult for her to believe that he'd been gone for almost ten years. He'd died of a heart attack out in the pasture while he and Eva had been putting out hay for the cattle.

And then there had been Andrew. Her heart squeezed tight as memories of her husband flashed through her head. Andrew had been one of the kindest, most gentle men she'd ever known, and not a day went by that she didn't think of him and miss him.

Once she got back to the house, she made the call to Harley and then headed for a quick shower. Even though it was only midmorning, she felt grimy and like the odor of the cow's death clung to her.

She finished showering and pulled on a summer shift in shades of blue and violet and then went into the kitchen and made herself a cup of coffee.

She sank down at the kitchen table and drew in a deep breath. Aside from being ticked off by a sheriff she didn't believe was taking the dead cattle and the notes all that seriously, for the first time since her father had died, she was truly afraid.

Who was behind the mutilated cattle and the threatening notes? The whole thing was so sick. Why the taking of the cows' hearts? Was it part of some sort of ritual practiced by some group of nuts in this area? Was it the work of a single person? Why was she the target of such madness?

Her gaze landed on a picture hanging on the far wall. The young boy in the photo was so handsome, with his mop of dark hair and a bright smile that warmed everyone around him.

Her heart squeezed even tighter. She had to stay strong for nine-year-old Andy. Her son was what kept her going, the boy who filled her life with such sunshine and love.

The last thing she wanted was for him to see her fear. She didn't want him to know about the notes or the dead cows. Andy was an innocent child, and she didn't want him to have to deal with any adult issues. He'd already had to deal with far too many.

Three short knocks on her back door announced Harley's arrival. "Come in," she yelled.

Harley Graham had worked as a ranch hand for her for the past seven years. He was older and seasoned and had become both a good friend and mentor. He stepped into the kitchen, and she motioned him toward the coffee maker.

Neither of them spoke until he'd poured his coffee and then joined her at the table. He swept his brown cowboy hat off his head, exposing shaggy gray hair, and set it down in the empty chair next to him.

He gazed at her for a long moment and then shook his head ruefully as deep frown lines cut across his weathered forehead. "Bad business going on here," he said. "Was it the same as last time?"

She nodded. "The heart was cut out."

"And did you get another one of those notes?"

She motioned to the piece of paper folded up next to her on the table. "Same kind of thing…leave town…blah, blah."

Harley's frown deepened. "You called the sheriff?"

She nodded. "He came out."

"And what did he have to say?" Harley took a drink of his coffee.

"The same thing he said the last two times…he's investigating and he'll be in touch."

Harley snorted. "That man isn't capable of investigating his way out of a paper bag. The only reason he's sheriff out here is because he's Albright's yes-man. And speaking of the Albrights, did you hear the latest news?"

"What news?" she asked curiously.

"Rumor is old man Albright died sometime early yesterday evening."

Eva stared at him in stunned surprise. Justin Albright was gone? The powerful monster who had forever changed the course of her life had died?

She didn't even know how to feel about it. A curious numbness overtook her. She'd never prayed for the old man's death, but if she was honest with herself, she certainly felt no grief at his passing.

"I wonder how much will change around here with him gone," she finally managed to say.

"I've heard his son David is a fairly decent man. Don't know much about the older son, since the whole time I've been here in Dusty Gulch he's apparently been off someplace in Europe."

"Italy. He's been in Italy running the family's wine business," she replied. Despite the heat of the day, she wrapped her fingers around her cup, seeking warmth for her fingers that had suddenly turned cold.

"What's his name… Jack?"

"Jake," she replied. Even saying his name aloud twisted a ribbon of apprehension and a million other emotions in the pit of her stomach.

"I suppose he'll be flying in for a funeral. Wonder if, as the eldest son, he'll decide to stay on here in town." Harley took another big drink of his coffee and then stood. "Oh well, Albright business is none of my business. I'll just head out of here and take care of that dead cow." He placed his cup in the sink.

"Thanks, Harley. I really appreciate it."

"I'll check in with you later." With a slam of the back door, he was gone.

Eva took a drink of her cooling coffee and tried to keep her thoughts away from Jake Albright. However, it was impossible. Memories of him now blew through her brain like a hot wind that whispered of a wild desire and a certain kind of madness.

It had been the madness of youth and first love, and a depth of passion and desire she'd thought she couldn't live without…until it had all been stolen away.

Over the years she had occasionally seen pictures of him in the society pages of their weekly newspaper. *Jake Albright, wine mogul, shares his birthday or whatever with an Italian model or popular actress or heir to a fortune.* The women had all looked beautiful and polished in a way only money could buy.

She finished her coffee and jerked herself out of the chair and to the sink. She refused to waste another minute of thought on Jake. Just as she was certain he'd never wasted more than a minute of thought about her when he'd left her and Dusty Gulch far behind.

Besides, she was perfectly satisfied alone on her ranch with her son. Andy was all that was important to her, and she didn't need or want any part of Jake or any other man in her life. Hopefully he would fly in for his father's funeral and then be on the next plane back to Italy and she'd never have to see or speak to him again.

JAKE WALKED THROUGH the front door of the mansion where he'd been born, although he certainly felt no sense of homecoming. This big house had never held the warmth of a real home. He'd been raised by a parade of nannies and an autocratic and cold father, and now that man was gone forever.

Justin Albright had been a stern, distant father, but Jake had loved his father deeply and mourned his passing. Now there was no more time for him to get closer with his father, who had died of a sudden, massive heart attack.

He set his suitcase down just inside the front door and went in search of his brother. He found David with his wife, Stephanie, and their five-year-old son, Richard, eating lunch at the table in the elegant dining room.

"Hey, man!" David exclaimed at the sight of Jake, and both he and Stephanie rose from the table. David pulled him into a quick hug and then released him. "Why didn't you call us to let us know when you were getting in? We could have picked you up from the airport."

The Dusty Gulch airport was little more than a single runway used mostly by crop dusters and small planes. There was no outbuilding except a huge shed where some of the locals kept their planes.

"I caught a ride with Lionel," Jake replied. Lionel Watkins was the pilot of the private jet the Albright family used. "Sit down and finish your meal."

"Have you eaten?" Stephanie asked. "I can get Cookie to bring in another plate."

"Thanks. That would be great." Jake sat next to his nephew as Stephanie disappeared into the kitchen. "How are you doing, big guy?" he said to Richard. The dark-haired boy smiled and ducked his head shyly.

Stephanie came back to the table, and a moment later Cookie came into the room with a plate and silverware for Jake. She laid it down before him and then he rose and gathered the chubby woman into his arms for a loving hug.

Carol Simon, aka Cookie, had not only been the Albright cook for thirty years, she had also been a surrogate mother to Jake since his mother had died when he'd been six.

During his childhood there had been many mornings when he'd sneaked into the kitchen and sat at the counter to eat a piece of cinnamon toast while Cookie prepared breakfast for the family. They would talk about anything and everything, and she'd been a warm and loving presence in his life.

"I've missed you, Cookie," he said as he released her.

"Ah, go on with yourself." Her smile moved her plump cheeks upward into a warm smile. "Now, sit and eat. You look like you need some fattening up with some of my good food—stick-to-your-ribs cooking instead of all that foreign junk you've been living on."

Jake laughed and resumed his seat at the table. Despite the levity of the moment, the conversation quickly turned more somber as they discussed the plans for their father's funeral in three days.

"Dad already arranged everything in the event of his death," David said. "We have an appointment with Paul tomorrow at noon for the reading of the will and then at four we're to meet with Aaron at the funeral home to make sure everything is ready for the funeral at ten on Sunday morning."

Jake nodded. "I'll be available for whatever."

"I had the staff ready your suite for you. How long do you intend to stay?" Stephanie asked.

"I'm here to stay for good," Jake replied. He saw the surprise not only on Stephanie's face but on his brother's as well. "I've been planning on making the move back here for some time. The winery is running smoothly with the managers that are in place. I'm no longer needed there for the day-to-day running of anything, and I've been homesick."

"So, what are your plans?" David asked.

Jake laughed. "I've only been here for less than an hour. To be honest, the only plan I have right now is to freshen up a bit and then head into town and take a look around."

"You'll see a lot of changes have occurred in the past ten years," David said. "We have a new bakery and ice cream parlor on Main and a lot of other businesses that have opened up."

"We even have a ladies' shoe shop," Stephanie said.

Jake smiled teasingly at his sister-in-law. He'd always liked Stephanie. She had gone to high school with Jake and David, but they hadn't started dating until several years later. With her light blond hair and steel blue eyes, she appeared cold and haughty, but nothing could be further from the truth. She was a sweet person with a good and giving heart. "A women's shoe store…wow, Dusty Gulch has definitely arrived," Jake teased.

They all laughed and finished with lunch. Minutes afterward, Jake climbed the main staircase to his suite of rooms in the left wing of the house.

He'd grown up in the suite that included a living area with a fireplace, the bedroom and bathroom. The walls were a pale gray and the furniture was black. There were two leather chairs facing the fireplace and a small sofa against one wall.

He went into the bedroom, where a spread of various shades of gray covered the king-size bed. It had been here in this room where he'd dreamed and planned his future, and it had been in here he'd wept when those dreams had all fallen apart.

His suitcases were already there and awaited his unpacking. He took a quick shower and shaved and then pulled on a pair of jeans and a black polo shirt. He then headed back down the stairs.

David had disappeared into their father's office, and Stephanie was in the kitchen lingering over a cup of coffee. Jake grabbed his truck keys off the key holder where they'd always been held in the kitchen.

"David had your truck serviced this morning, so it would be ready for you," she said.

"That was thoughtful of him," Jake replied. "I appreciate him taking care of my baby while I was gone." His "baby" was the black pickup truck with all the bells and whistles he'd received ten years ago from his father upon his graduation from high school. He'd barely had a chance to enjoy it before he'd left for Italy.

More than that, the truck had been a promise from his father that he would eventually run the ranching portion of the Albright estate, something he'd dreamed of doing since he'd been a young boy.

But that had been before his life had fallen apart. That had been before *her*. Even though it had been ten years since he'd seen her, been with her, thoughts of her still shot a hot wave through his body. He was never sure whether it was the burn of a rich anger he'd never gotten over or the white-hot fever of a desire that had never burned itself out.

"Should I expect you back here for dinner?" Stephanie asked, pulling him from his wayward thoughts.

"No, I'll just grab something while I'm out, but tell

David I'll be ready for the appointment at the lawyer's office at noon tomorrow."

"I'll tell him," she replied. "And enjoy your first day home."

"Thanks, Steph. I'll see you later."

Jake stepped out the back door and drew in a deep breath of the August heat. It smelled of pasture and hay and cattle. It was a welcome scent. He'd never wanted to be in Italy working for the family winery. His heart had always been here in Dusty Gulch. But, when his father had insisted he go, Jake had believed there was nothing left here for him, and all he'd wanted to do was escape.

Times had changed. Justin Albright was dead, and Jake's grief was deep for the man he'd admired and loved and desperately wanted to please. His grief came from the fact that he would now never gain the closeness he'd wanted with his father. He'd always thought there would be time for him and his father, but time had run out.

He headed toward the garage in the distance. Once there he got into his pickup and headed out. He followed the drive around to the front of the house, where he had a view of the small town below…a town nearly owned by the Albright family.

He had no idea how his father might have divided things up between him and his brother. Hopefully David would be agreeable to letting Jake take over the ranching business and David would be kept busy with the real estate and any other business.

When he reached the bottom of the hill, instead of turning left to head into town, he turned right and headed in the direction of Eva's place.

He knew going to see Eva Taylor, now Eva Martin, was a foolish thing to do. He'd been seventeen years old and she'd been sixteen when they'd first begun dating. Eventually they had shared an explosive love affair. She'd been his first lover and he had been hers. That had been over ten years ago.

In those ten years, she'd married and had a child and was now a widow. He had no idea why he wanted to see her again, but as he drew closer to her small ranch on the outskirts of town, the nerves in his chest bunched and tightened.

He didn't know why he suddenly felt so tense. She'd really been nothing more to him than a first love...a high school sweetheart. Maybe he just needed to see her again in order to stamp closure on the fiery relationship that had haunted him over the years.

As he pulled down the long lane that was her driveway, he saw the ranch house looked much the way he remembered it. Painted white with dark green shutters and trim, this place had been where he had spent much of his teenage years.

Spending time here with Eva and her father, Tom, had felt like home. Tom had welcomed him like a son, and there had been much warmth and laughter and caring in this small ranch house.

He pulled up and parked, and his gaze swept the area. Although the house appeared to be in good shape, her barn and some of the other outbuildings were weatherworn and begged for paint and some repairs.

Was she struggling financially? It must be hard for a single woman with a son to keep a ranch up and running. He knew they had struggled with money issues when her father had been alive. *None of your business*, a small voice whispered in his head.

He got out of his truck but stood hesitantly by the driver's door. What in the hell was he doing? He shouldn't have come here.

Ten years ago she'd broken up with him, and she had never indicated that she'd regretted her decision. She'd moved on with her life and had probably never given him a second thought.

He was just about to return to his truck and drive away when the front door opened and there she stood.

Clad in a sleeveless summer dress and with her long black hair falling down beyond her shoulders, her beauty nearly stole his breath away.

Her violet-blue eyes were widened in surprise. "Jake," she murmured. "Wha…what are you doing here?"

"I just thought I'd stop by and visit an old friend," he replied. He gestured toward the door. "Can I come in? Maybe get a cup of coffee?"

She hesitated for a long moment, and once again he wondered what in the hell he was doing here. She was even more beautiful than she had been ten years ago, but she definitely didn't appear overjoyed to see him again. And why should she? He was probably nothing more than a distant memory in her mind.

She'd married her husband months after Jake had left town. She'd had his child. Jake had been nothing more to her than a high school boyfriend. But high school had been over a long time ago.

She finally opened the door wider to allow him entry. As he swept by her, he couldn't help but notice the scent that wafted from her. It was the same perfume she'd worn years ago, a spicy, slightly floral scent that instantly heated his blood.

And that's when he knew exactly why he was here.

He wanted her. He'd never stopped wanting her. And he believed the only way he could really move on from her was to have her one more time.

Chapter Two

Eva led Jake through the living room and into her kitchen, where he sat at the square wooden table. She went to her coffee maker to start a pot.

She felt as if she was in some kind of shock. Suddenly her body felt too warm, and yet her brain was frozen. The last person on earth she'd expected to see here was Jake Albright, and the surprise of him being here had definitely thrown her for a loop.

As she measured the coffee, she was acutely aware of his gaze on her. What was he doing here? Why had he come? What did he want from her? It felt so surreal to have him in her home…at her table after all these years.

Thank God Andy was still at school. There was no way she wanted her son to have anything to do with Jake Albright. As far as she was concerned, the Albrights' wealth and power-wielding ways had always tainted everything around them.

As the coffee began to drip into the carafe, she finally turned to face him. "What are you doing here, Jake?" She remained standing at the counter.

"I got into town earlier, and I thought about you and decided to stop by and catch up with you." He smiled at her, a slow, sexy rise of his sensual lips that had once weakened her knees. She steeled herself against any emotional response to him.

He had a strong jawline and sculpted features that still made him the most handsome man she had ever known. For a moment there was a long, awkward pause between them.

"I was sorry to hear about your father's death," she finally said, breaking the uncomfortable silence.

A sharp grief splashed over his handsome face. It was there for only a moment and then gone. "Thanks, and I was sorry to hear about your father and your husband. That's a lot of loss for one person to deal with."

"I got through it." She turned around and poured them each a cup of coffee and then joined him at the table. She sat close enough that she could smell him…the scent of clean male with a hint of shaving cream and a fresh-scented cologne.

She still didn't know why he was here. The last time they'd seen each other, they certainly hadn't parted as friends. Rather it had been an emotional time that had ended in acrimony on his part.

"So, how long are you in town for?" she asked and cast her gaze just slightly over his head.

The last thing she wanted to do was gaze into his eyes. Jake's eyes had always been seductive. Dark as night and with long, thick black lashes, there had been a time when she'd easily fallen into the sweet seduction they offered.

Not now.

Not ever again.

"I've been homesick for quite some time, so now I'm in town to stay," he said.

"Oh," she replied, both surprised and dismayed by his response. She'd hoped he'd be on a plane back to Italy as soon as his father was buried. Life had been easier on her without Jake Albright being in town. She certainly didn't want to be reminded of her past mistakes and the secret she needed to keep from him forever.

He leaned back in the chair. He was a tall man with lean lines, but muscled biceps bulged out from beneath his short shirtsleeves, biceps that spoke of an understated strength.

Even as a teenager Jake had possessed a presence that demanded respect. He'd been a leader, never a follower, and he'd had a self-confidence even then that had been appealing. It was as if he owned the air around him. She realized he had that same kind of presence still.

"So, tell me how things have been going around here. The house looks just like I remember it."

"I've managed to keep it up okay, but the barn needs some major repairs. I'm hoping to get on that as soon as possible," she replied.

His gaze landed on the picture of Andy hanging on the wall. "Is that your son?"

Her stomach muscles tightened, and her throat closed up. "Yes, that's Andy," she finally managed to say. She was grateful her voice sounded perfectly normal.

"He's a good-looking boy. He looks a lot like you," he replied and then, to her relief, he looked out the nearby window. "Business is good?"

"We're getting by," she replied and then frowned. The note she had received that morning was still in the middle of the table, and as she stared at it, a faint chill once again filled her body.

She released a deep sigh. "But somebody is not too happy with me right now."

"What does that mean?" One of his dark eyebrows rose slightly.

"Every week for the last three weeks, I've found one of my cows dead and mutilated in the pasture."

His eyes narrowed, and he sat up straighter in the chair. "What do you mean? Mutilated how?"

"Their throats were slashed and then the hearts were removed."

He stared at her. "What the hell?"

She reached out and picked up the note that had arrived that day and tossed it to him. "And each time I've found a dead cow, I've also received one of these in my mailbox."

She watched closely as he read the note. She wasn't sure why she'd told him about all this. Maybe because it was much easier talking about dead cows and threatening notes than discussing anything that might have happened between them in the past.

His jawline tightened as he dropped the note back on the table. "That's one nasty piece of work. What does Wayne say about all this? Surely you've called him."

"I called him the first time I found a cow down in the pasture and a note in my mailbox, but he hasn't had much to say about it all." She told him about the sheriff's visit that morning and the two times he'd been out before.

"This morning all he seemed really bothered by was the heat," she said.

"It's August in Dusty Gulch. Wayne is a native here, so the climate can't come as a big surprise to him. He's still got to do his job even if it's hot and uncomfortable. Do you have any idea at all who might be behind this?" he asked.

She shook her head. "I really don't have a clue."

"Have you dated anybody recently and broken up with them?" he asked.

"I haven't dated anyone at any time since my husband's death," she replied. "I have no interest in dating. I have my son and my ranch, and that's all I want and need in my life." She raised her chin slightly. "I haven't had any real issues with anyone and can't imagine why somebody is doing this to me."

"Sounds to me like you need for Wayne to step up his game and find out who is behind all this," he replied.

She released a small, dry laugh. "That goes without saying." She sobered quickly. "I've been having some trouble with some teenagers."

"What kind of trouble?" Jake asked and then took a sip of the cooling coffee.

"A bunch of them have been sneaking out here pretty regularly to use my barn as a party place late at night. I've caught them a couple of times and have chased them off, but I do wonder if maybe they're responsible for the notes and the dead cows as some form of revenge against me."

"Did you tell that to Wayne?" he asked.

"I did. I even gave him a couple of names of the kids, but I'm not sure he did any follow-up." She glanced at the clock on the wall, wanting Jake gone before Andy came home from school.

"I'll give Wayne a call and see if I can light a fire under him."

"Thanks, I would really appreciate that." She got up from the table, hoping he would take the hint and leave. Despite their fairly easy conversation, she was still uncomfortable in his presence. To her relief he got up as well, and together they walked to the front door.

"It was nice seeing you, Jake," she said.

He took a step closer to her. "It was good seeing you, too, Eva. You're even more beautiful than I remember." He lifted his hand, as if to stroke her hair, and then quickly dropped it back to his side.

For just a brief moment, their gazes locked, and in the depths of his dark eyes she saw something that half stole her breath away. It was something she remembered from those summer days and nights so long ago…a fiery desire that threatened to pull her in.

Shocked, she quickly took a step back from him and broke the eye contact. "I guess I'll see you around."

"Oh, you'll definitely be seeing me, and I intend to call Wayne as soon as possible and find out what's being done as far as these crimes against you."

"I really appreciate that."

"Can I get your phone number?"

She wasn't thrilled with him having her number, but if he was going to speak with Wayne on her behalf, then he should probably have it. She grabbed her cell phone, and he punched his number into hers and then set her up in his contact list.

"I'll call you after I speak with Wayne. I'm driving into town right now and will try to catch up with him."

"Thanks, Jake."

With a final last look at her, he was gone. She closed the door and leaned against it. For the first time since he'd walked into the house, she felt as if she could finally draw a full breath.

She hadn't ever expected to see him again—here in her house or anywhere else. More than that, she hadn't expected the emotions the very sight of him had evoked in her.

An unexpected desire had punched her in the stomach the minute she had seen him. A desire coupled with a deep yearning for what might have been. And would now never be.

She still wasn't sure why he'd stopped by to see her. However, she did appreciate him talking to Wayne, because she knew having an Albright behind her would make the sheriff take things far more seriously.

But that was all she wanted from Jake Albright.

He was dangerous to her. He was dangerous to the life she had built here with her son. He had the money and power to destroy her, and she feared that's exactly what he would do if he ever found out Andy was his son.

AT EIGHT THIRTY the next morning, Jake got in his truck to drive back to Eva's. The day before he'd had a long talk with Wayne Black about what was going on at Eva's ranch. He'd let Wayne know that he wanted Wayne to keep him informed not only about anything else happening there, but also about exactly what Wayne was doing to investigate.

Wayne had called him earlier this morning to tell him that Eva had found two more mutilated cows in her pasture. Jake was meeting Wayne there to see for himself what exactly was going on.

He couldn't help the way his nerves grew taut as he thought of seeing Eva again. He'd realized yesterday that she was still a fire in his blood. Despite the years that had passed and all of his dating when he'd been out of the country, Eva had always been in the back of his mind, somehow keeping him from moving on in any meaningful way with any other woman.

He needed to possess her one last time to hopefully

get her out of his head, out of his blood forever. His junior and senior years in school had been spent loving Eva, and he'd believed at the time she loved him back.

Hell, they had even held a mock wedding ceremony in the hayloft of her barn, where they had pledged to marry for real as soon as she graduated from high school. He had truly believed that she would be the woman in his life forever, that she would be his legal wife and have his children.

He would never love her again. She'd hurt him so badly. He would never forget that she'd betrayed the love he thought they'd once shared. One evening without any warning, she'd just told him she didn't love him, that she didn't want to see him anymore.

He could never forget that within months of breaking up with him she'd married Andrew Martin, a ranch hand who had worked for her and her father. Had she and Andrew been seeing each other while Jake had been wrapped heart and soul with her?

It was a question that had haunted him for all these years. What had he been lacking that a quiet ranch hand had to offer her? And why, after all this time, did it even bother him?

That was then and this was now, he reminded himself as he pulled into her long driveway. He parked and got out of his truck, then started toward the house but stopped as he saw her out by the barn.

She was in the process of saddling up a horse but paused as she saw him approaching. She was clad in a pair of jeans that fit tightly on what he knew were slim hips and long, shapely legs. Her blue blouse was a gauzy material that looked both cool and sexy as hell, and her long black hair was in a thick braid down her back that he immediately wanted to undo.

"I didn't expect to see you this morning," she said in greeting.

"Wayne called me and told me you have two more dead cows. Same thing as before?" As he drew closer to her, the faint breeze blew the familiar scent of her to him.

She nodded. "Although the note was a little different this time." She pulled the note from her back pocket and handed it to him.

He frowned and opened it to read, "Get out of town, bitch, or die." He handed it back to her as a rich anger swept over him. Whoever was responsible for this was not only messing with her livelihood, but more egregiously, they were terrorizing her. She had to be frightened by the notes, and this one was a definite escalation from the last one.

"Wayne better get some answers on this," he said tersely. "This isn't just a nasty note—this one is definitely a threat."

"Oh, he'll take it all more seriously now," she said with obvious confidence.

"Why do you sound so sure about that? You haven't felt like he was taking it seriously before now."

"I didn't have an Albright standing with me before now," she replied.

"That shouldn't make a difference," he replied.

"Oh Jake, surely you aren't still so naive. You have to know your name wields a lot of power in this town." She reached down and grabbed the saddle at her feet and swung it up and over the horse's back. "It's always been that way."

"I guess you're planning on riding out into the pasture when Wayne gets here. Do you have a spare horse I could borrow?" he asked.

He didn't want to think about what she'd said about him being naive. Still, it wasn't right that his being here with her would make Wayne take the case more seriously. The sheriff should take every crime that happened in this town seriously, and he definitely should have been taking this seriously all along.

She disappeared into the barn and moments later returned with a large black mare who had a white marking on her nose that looked like a lightning bolt.

"This is Lightning," she said.

"Very appropriate name," he said with a grin. He gestured toward her big dark mare. "And I suppose she's Thunder."

She returned his smile. "That's exactly right." Her beautiful smile lasted only a moment and then was gone. "The gear is in the second stall on the right. Help yourself to whatever you need."

By the time he grabbed what he needed and returned, she was already mounted on the back of her horse. For the next few minutes, he got his horse ready, and then he mounted as well.

"Seems like old times," he said, remembering how much they had always enjoyed horseback riding together in the past. They'd get out of school and then ride horseback on the ranch until it was time for her to start cooking dinner.

She looked out in the distance. "Those carefree days of youth are long gone," she replied. "And we'll never get them back."

He wasn't sure if he was imagining it or not, but her words sounded like a warning to him. But, before he could reply to her, two men came from around the side of the barn on horseback.

"Jake, this is Harley Graham, my foreman for the last seven years, and Jimmy Miller, who has worked for me for the past year," she said. "And this is Jake Albright. He's here to help with Sheriff Black."

"That man definitely needs some help," Harley, the older of the two, muttered halfway beneath his breath. "And it's nice to meet you, Mr. Albright."

"Jake," he replied. "Please call me Jake." Harley looked like a man who'd worked in ranching his whole life. His face was weatherworn, and there was a quiet confidence about him.

Next to Harley, Jimmy looked like a young pup. Shaggy blond hair peeked out from beneath his black cowboy hat, and his bright blue eyes held an eagerness to please.

"Harley and Jimmy found the two cows this morning," Eva explained to Jake.

"Bad business going on around here," Harley said. "Somebody out there is trying to destroy Eva."

"Between all of us, we won't let that happen," Jake replied forcefully.

They all looked toward the road at the sound of a vehicle approaching. It was Wayne. He pulled up and parked and then left his car running and stepped out. "Looks like we're all ready to go," he said, as if he had been the one waiting for all of them. "You lead and I'll follow."

Eva looked at Harley, who gave a curt nod and then galloped away. The others quickly caught up with him as Wayne took up the rear in his car.

Jake rode just behind Eva, admiring her form in the saddle. He'd forgotten how good she looked on the back of a horse, like she'd been born there. Her slender back was straight, and her hips rolled easily with the horse's gait.

As always the smells of pasture and cattle were welcome to Jake. They rode past the pond where he and Eva had often fished together. He forced back the memories that threatened to erupt in his head.

He looked ahead and frowned. He could now see the two downed cows on the ground. The scent of blood and death hung in the still, hot air, and two buzzards circled lazily in the sky above.

They all dismounted next to the big animals and waited for Wayne to leave his car and join them. There was no question the cows' throats had been slashed, and there were bloody, butchered holes in their chests.

What in the hell was going on here? Who was behind this kind of madness? The taking of the hearts was particularly heinous. Why were they targeting Eva, and how much danger was she really in?

They all dismounted, and then Jake turned to look at Wayne. "What are you doing to find out who is responsible for this?"

Wayne shifted from one foot to the other. "This has been a tough thing for me to investigate. There have been no weapons left behind and no real clues for me to work with."

"Eva told me she mentioned some teenagers to you. Have you questioned them?" Jake asked.

"I really haven't had a chance yet," Wayne confessed.

"Get a chance today, Wayne. The note Eva got this morning is definitely a threat." Jake spoke forcefully.

He and Wayne had gone to high school together. Jake had always liked the man, but Wayne had been lazy in high school, and that trait seemed to have followed him into adulthood. Jake didn't want Eva to be a victim of what Jake suspected was Wayne's usual lethargy.

"I'll get on it as soon as I leave here," he said. He looked at Eva. "Is there anyone else you can think of that might have a grudge against you?"

Eva frowned. "I've been thinking about it, and I guess you might want to question Ben Wilkins."

"Who is he?" Jake asked.

"He's a ranch hand I had to fire about six months ago," she replied. "He's a heavy drinker and more often than not didn't show up for work. I thought we'd parted ways amicably, but who knows."

"I think he's working on the O'Brien spread now, although I haven't seen him around town lately. If I can find him, I'll have a chat with him as well," Wayne said.

"I just want all this to stop," Eva said. "I can't afford to lose my cattle, and nobody is going to make me leave town." She raised her chin. "This is my land, and nobody is going to terrorize me off it."

"You know you have our support," Jimmy said fervently. "I'd never let anything happen to you, Eva."

By the look in Jimmy's eyes as he gazed at Eva, it was obvious the young pup had a big crush on his boss. As long as he stayed in his own lane and didn't get in Jake's way, there would be no problem.

The group broke up. Wayne drove off with a promise to come back later that evening, and Eva and Jake headed back to the barn, leaving Jimmy and Harley the distasteful duty of taking care of the dead cows.

As much as Jake would have loved to stay with Eva, by the time they unsaddled the horses and put them back in their stalls, it was time for him to head back home and get cleaned up for the appointment with his father's lawyer.

"Thanks for coming out this morning," she said as she walked him to his truck.

"Eva, I intend to be here for you until Wayne has solved this and somebody is in jail."

"That's really not necessary. I'm sure Wayne is going to step up and do his job," she replied. "I appreciate what you've done, but you're officially off the hook now."

She had no idea how badly he was on her hook, how much he wanted to taste her lips once again and feel her lithe body against his own. He wasn't about to walk away from her before he got what he wanted.

And since he had left Dusty Gulch all those years ago, Jake Albright always got what he wanted.

Chapter Three

As Eva finished up her morning chores, she tried to keep her mind off Jake. She hoped he wouldn't come around anymore. Just the sight of him stirred up too many memories, ones that were both exquisite and splendid and others that were too painful to entertain.

She ate a light lunch and then decided to put on some tomato sauce for spaghetti and meatballs for dinner. Even though the hot weather called for cold salads and sandwiches for the evening meals, Andy loved her spaghetti and meatballs. She tried to make it for him fairly regularly.

There had been a time when she would expect Jake to share the evening meal with her and her father. Her father had adored Jake and had treated him like the son he'd never had. She had loved the relationship the two had shared. It had killed her to end things with Jake not only for herself, but for her father as well.

He'd never asked her what had happened between her and Jake. She supposed he supported whatever decision she made in her dating life, and her father had respected her privacy on the matter.

She wasn't that girl anymore…the young girl who had

believed anything was possible with love…that anything was possible with Jake.

The life choices she'd been handed had been decisions that had been necessary but difficult. They had been decisions she'd had to make with her head and not with her heart.

Other than the joyous birth of her son, her life had been built by moments of quiet contentment and respect for the man who had offered to marry her in order to give Andy his name.

Andrew Martin had been the one who had helped her through her grief over her father's unexpected death. That had been a time of fear…of complete uncertainty.

Jake was gone, and she'd been a pregnant eighteen-year-old with a ranch that was failing. Andrew had stepped in with an offer of marriage that had benefited them both at the time. And in the end, he had left her a life insurance policy that had helped her stay afloat around the ranch and put some money away in a college fund for Andy.

As the scents of garlic and tomatoes filled the kitchen, she sank down at the table and wished her father was alive. She needed to talk to somebody and say that the note today had frightened her even more than the others. *Get out of town, bitch, or die.* Who could possibly entertain such utter hatred toward her?

She'd always kept a pretty low profile. She stayed busy working on the ranch and raising Andy. She went into town only when she needed supplies or if Andy had some activity, and she was always pleasant to the people she encountered.

So, who was behind all this? Although she took the

death of her cattle very seriously, she wasn't sure how seriously to take the personal threats indicated in the notes.

Nasty notes couldn't hurt her. However, would the person writing the notes escalate and try to physically harm her? Kill her? She got up and stirred the sauce as troubling thoughts continued to fire through her brain.

Nobody had shown any interest in wanting her ranch. Nobody had stepped forward to offer to buy the place. She'd had no indication about anyone being interested in getting this land away from her. Her father had bought all these acres when he'd been nineteen years old, and he'd built the house they now lived in. Nobody was ever going to force her off this land.

So why was somebody obsessed with her leaving town?

At four o'clock she left the house and walked down the lane to the main road where the school bus would drop Andy. Even though it was only mid-August, school had started the week before due to the many snow days the kids often had off in the winter. As always, all bad thoughts fell away from her mind as she anticipated seeing her son.

The bus pulled up and Andy jumped off, his wide smile immediately contagious. "Hi, Mom. I got an A on my spelling test and can I spend the night with Bobby tonight? It's Friday night so we don't have school tomorrow. We already talked to his dad and he said he could pick me up and we'd go out for pizza for dinner and then we can rent a movie."

"Congratulations on the spelling test," she said and grabbed his hand to hold as they headed back to the house. "And you know I'll have to check all the details with Bobby's father. I'll have to make sure you and

Bobby don't have him tied up somewhere and are forcing him to meet your demands."

Andy giggled. "You're silly, Mom."

"I'll still need to speak with Bobby's father," she replied, her heart warmed by her son's laughter.

"He said you can call him as soon as I get home from school. Bobby and I want to rent a scary movie tonight."

"Then I'm glad I won't be there with you. You know how much I hate scary movies."

"That's 'cause you're just an old fraidy-cat," Andy replied with a giggle.

"Oh yeah?" Eva released his hand and proceeded to tickle him.

He howled with laughter and took off running toward the house with her following in hot pursuit. "I made you spaghetti for dinner," Eva said once they were inside.

Andy frowned. "I guess I could stay and eat dinner here before going to Bobby's."

"Don't be silly. You can always have the spaghetti tomorrow night. You go pack your overnight bag and I'll give Bobby's father a call."

"Thanks, Mom. I love you," he said and then zoomed out of the kitchen and down the hallway toward his bedroom.

At five thirty Robert Stephenson pulled up with his son, Bobby. Bobby bounced out of the car, and the two boys bumped shoulders and then high-fived each other.

Robert was a handsome man with sandy brown hair and green eyes. Tragically, he had lost his wife three years ago to cancer. Eva never worried about Andy spending time at the Stephenson house. She knew Robert had rules and a parenting style that closely mirrored her own.

"Hi, Eva." He greeted her with a warm smile.

"Hey, Robert, are you sure you're ready for this?" She gestured toward the two energetic boys who were dancing around each other and fake fighting.

He laughed. "I think I can handle them. Maybe one evening the four of us could go out for some pizza together."

This wasn't the first time Robert had mentioned an outing including her. "Right now I'm staying really busy, Robert. It's really hard for me to get away."

She'd sensed that the man had a romantic interest in her. She wasn't interested in him, but she also didn't want to say or do anything that might mess up the boys' friendship.

"But Eva, everyone needs a break once in a while," he chided. "You know the old saying about all work and no play."

"I know, and maybe we can plan something sometime in the future," she replied noncommittally.

"I'd really like that," he replied. "Now, what time do you need your son home tomorrow?"

"Whatever time is convenient with you. I should be here all day."

Within minutes they were gone, and Eva was alone in the house. She ate spaghetti for dinner and then put the leftovers in the fridge and cleaned up the kitchen. Once that was done, she went into the living room and sank down on the sofa.

With a deep sigh, she reached up and unwound the braid in her hair, then used her hairbrush to stroke through the long strands.

It had been a long day, starting with the discovery of the two dead animals and the new note. She was exhausted not from any physical activity she'd done during the day, but rather from the simmering fear that buzzed continuously inside her head.

She'd never felt afraid here. She kept her father's shotgun loaded and in a gun safe in her bedroom, but she'd never had to take it out. Tonight, however, the silence of the house pressed in all around her as she thought of the notes she'd received.

She got up and checked to make sure the front door was securely locked and then went to the back door and did the same thing. Being a single woman with a young son, she had invested in good locks on the doors and windows when Andrew passed away.

The place didn't have central air, although she had air-conditioning units in the windows of the living room and both bedrooms. She only ran the one in her bedroom when it was really hot and there was no breeze coming into the second window in her room. Eventually she'd love to get central air, but right now that wasn't in her limited budget.

She closed and locked the windows in the kitchen and then returned to the sofa and turned on the television to fill the quiet.

It was a few minutes after eight when her phone rang, and she saw by the identification that the caller was Wayne. "Is it too late to make a house call?" he asked.

"Not at all, what's up?" she asked.

"I just wanted to come by and update you with what I've learned today. I'll be out there in about twenty minutes or so."

"Okay, see you then," Eva replied. She got up and reopened the kitchen windows to allow in the light evening breeze and then put on a pot of coffee.

She hoped the sheriff was bringing some answers. God, she hoped he was coming to tell her he'd identified the guilty person and that person was now behind bars. That was the only thing that would both answer her questions and halt the simmer of fear that had burdened her since the first cow and note.

About twenty minutes later, with the sun dipping low in the sky, Wayne arrived with Jake following in his truck right behind.

She was definitely not happy to see Jake, who was spending far too much time and energy in her business. And yet she had to confess she was grateful he'd initially gotten involved, since it had obviously lit a fire under Wayne's backside. But it was now time for him to go away.

"Wayne." She opened the door wider to allow in the lawman. "Jake, I didn't expect to see you here again."

"Expect to see me around here a lot," he replied as he followed Wayne through the living room and into the kitchen.

Now that's so not happening, she thought to herself as she followed them into the kitchen. But she couldn't exactly set Jake straight in front of Wayne. She would definitely speak to Jake once Wayne left.

"Ah, I smell fresh-brewed coffee," Wayne said as he sank down at the table.

"I know how much you like your coffee, Wayne," she replied. No matter the time of day or night, she rarely saw the man around town without a cup of java in his hand.

"None for me," Jake said.

She poured Wayne a cup and then joined the two men

at the table. "I hope you have some good news for me, Wayne," she said.

He winced. "Well, I wouldn't go that far," he replied. "I just wanted to catch you both up on what I've done today." He shot a quick glance at Jake and then looked back at her. "I want you to know I'm taking this all very seriously."

"Then what do you have for us?" Jake asked.

When did she become "us" with Jake Albright? She tried not to look at him, even though she was acutely aware of him. His presence made the room feel too small and without enough air to get a full breath.

Wayne rose just enough to pull a notepad from his rear pocket. He opened it and flipped the pages in obvious self-importance. "The first person I spoke to this afternoon was Griff Ainsley."

"Who is he?" Jake asked.

"He's one of the teenagers who have been using my barn to party in," Eva explained. She'd given Wayne Griff's name after the first dead cow had been found. "He's a mouthy, disrespectful boy who has been in my barn with his friends more times than I can count. He seems to be the ringleader of all of them."

"So, what did he have to say?" Jake's jaw muscle tightened.

Wayne's cheeks dusted with color, and he kept his gaze on the notepad on the table in front of him. "He said Eva was a crazy woman. He told me that he and a couple of his friends had come out here at the beginning of the summer to see if Eva needed any part-time help. But she greeted them all with a gun and screamed at them to get off her property or she'd shoot them. After that he said he'd stayed away from here."

"He's such a liar," Eva replied sharply. "That certainly never happened, and the kids were out in my barn as recently as two weeks ago. I cleaned up the trash they left behind, like I always have to do. I'll admit I've confronted them before and I've screamed at them all, but never with a gun."

"So, what was his alibi on the nights that Eva's cattle were killed?" Jake asked.

"He was in bed asleep, and his parents backed him up." Wayne finally looked at Eva.

"Are they the kind of people who would lie for their son?" Jake leaned forward in his chair.

Wayne hesitated a long moment and then finally replied, "Yeah, they'd probably lie for him. He's their only kid. He's also the high school's star quarterback, and they're very proud of him. They definitely wouldn't want him to get in any trouble."

"So we don't know if this is the work of a bunch of teenagers or not," she replied flatly.

"Not at this point. I also don't think Ben Wilkins is responsible, either," Wayne said.

"He's the ranch hand I fired six months ago," Eva reminded Jake. "Why do you think he isn't responsible?" she asked Wayne.

"He quit the O'Brien ranch about two months ago and moved to Makenville," Wayne replied, referring to a nearby small town.

"That's only a twenty-minute drive from here," Jake said. "He could easily drive here, wreak havoc on Eva's ranch and then drive back. Did you interview him in person?"

"I didn't get a chance today, but it's on my to-do list for tomorrow." Wayne took a drink of his coffee.

"What about the notes? Have you been able to pull any fingerprints from them?" Jake asked.

"Not in the two I've checked so far. There were a few on them, but I'm guessing they were Eva's."

"You're guessing?" Jake looked at Wayne in disbelief. "Have you taken Eva's fingerprints so you can rule hers out?"

"Uh…not yet. Eva, maybe you can stop by the office sometime tomorrow and we can get that done," Wayne replied.

"I'll be glad to," Eva said. Finally something was being done. Even though Wayne hadn't brought any real answers with him, she did believe now he would do anything in his power to find the guilty person or persons. If nothing else, he wouldn't want to displease Jake.

Wayne took another drink of his coffee and then tucked the small notepad back into his pocket. "Right now I don't have a lot to go on, but I intend to keep digging for answers."

"I would expect nothing less from you, Wayne," Jake said. "Whoever is behind this needs to be caught and thrown into jail."

Wayne finished his coffee and then stood and looked at Eva. "I promise you I'm going to stay on top of this, but if you think of anyone else who could be doing this to you, you need to contact me immediately."

"I've twisted and turned my brain inside out trying to think of anyone who might have an issue with me, but other than the names I gave you, I can't think of anyone else." Eva and Jake also got up from the table, and the three of them headed back to the front door.

"I'll check in with you tomorrow after I've spoken to some more people," Wayne said.

She turned on her porch light, and they all stepped out of the house. “Thanks, Wayne,” she said. “I’ll probably be in sometime tomorrow afternoon to get my fingerprints taken.”

“That works for me,” he replied.

She watched as Wayne got into his car, and then she turned to look at Jake, who seemed to be in no hurry to head out. “I appreciate your help in this, Jake. But I told you this morning there’s really no reason for you to be involved with this anymore.”

“But Eva, I intend to stay involved.” He took a step closer to her, and every muscle in her body tensed. “I’m worried about you, and I intend to be here for you until I know there’s no more danger to you.”

He took another step closer, now invading her personal space and bringing with him his familiar scent. “It’s just been notes left in the mailbox and nothing more dangerous than that,” she replied.

“But we can’t know what might happen next, and that’s what has me worried for you.” His gaze bored into hers, and for a moment she couldn’t breathe. “Right now it’s just notes.”

He looked at her now the same way he had then… when she’d been sixteen years old and they had been madly, crazy in love. His dark, sinful eyes beckoned her forward, to take the last small step between them and fall into his arms.

For just a brief, insane moment she wanted to fall. She wanted to be in his strong arms and feel his lips on hers. She remembered the magic, the all-consuming passion they had once shared, and there was a part of her that wanted to feel that again.

“I want you, Eva. I’ve never stopped thinking about

you." His deep voice shot a wave of heat through her. Before she knew what was happening, he opened his arms and she fell into them as she parted her lips to receive his kiss…it was a fiery kiss that she'd desperately wanted.

It was still there…the desire that he'd always been able to evoke in her. It shocked her, and before he could deepen the kiss any more, she stumbled back from him.

"Jake, I'm not interested in going backward. Our past is gone and there's no place for you in my life now," she said.

His dark gaze held hers, and then his mouth moved into his sexy smile. "That's not what our kiss just told me. Good night, Eva."

Before she could say anything in response, he was gone, swallowed up by the darkness outside the illumination of the porch light. She went into the house and collapsed on the sofa, her body still warmed by the kiss they had shared.

She'd known Jake was a danger to her because of the secret of Andy, but she'd never dreamed that he'd be a danger to her because of her own desire for him.

She needed to stay away from him. Right now he felt as dangerous to her as the person who was mutilating her cattle and leaving the hateful notes.

She had once loved Jake Albright with all her heart and soul. He'd not only been her lover but also her best friend. She hadn't cared one bit about his family's money and power. She had loved the sweet, gentle boy who had aspired to ranch and love her forever.

The truth of the matter was she didn't trust herself with Jake. She had loved him ten years ago, and she was shocked to realize now that she had never really fallen out of love with him.

SUNDAY AFTERNOON JUSTIN ALBRIGHT was laid to rest. Most of the townspeople showed up to pay their final respects, but Jake had never felt so alone.

As he stared at the flower-adorned coffin and listened to the preacher drone on, extolling Justin Albright's life, all Jake could think about were the years he'd lost with his father.

Even though his father had flown to Italy to visit Jake several times over the years, it hadn't been enough for Jake to feel the closeness he'd yearned for. And now would never have.

David and Steph stood next to him, but Jake wished Eva was beside him. Eva knew how much he'd loved his father, how badly he'd wanted a deeper, more meaningful relationship with the man he'd admired and loved. Eva would understand the depth of grief that now pierced through him.

The funeral seemed to last forever, and once it was over, dozens of people descended on the house with food and more condolences. David and Steph were gracious hosts, while Jake felt disconnected from everyone. He hung around for about an hour, and then he changed out of his suit and into more casual clothes and sneaked away to the stables.

He saddled up and then took off riding across the pasture, hoping to escape some of the grief that clung to him. His thoughts were scattered as the sun beat down hot on his shoulders. He rode hard and fast until he reached a large shade tree, where he pulled up and dismounted.

From this vantage point, he could see the herd of cattle in the distance. His father's will had left everything divided equally between his two sons, with an additional amount of money set aside for any grandchildren. He'd been grateful that David had agreed to let him run the ranching business and continue to manage the winery and David would take care of all the other businesses.

Jake had already spoken to David about potentially putting the winery on the market. They could sell it at an enormous profit and get out of the wine business altogether.

Running the ranching side of things was all Jake had ever wanted to do. He felt a real affinity for the land. There had been one man who had understood exactly how Jake felt, and that had been Eva's father.

He wished he'd been in town when Tom Taylor had died. He wished he'd been here for Eva, but instead he'd been in Italy, and apparently Andrew Martin had been the man who had helped Eva with her grief.

According to what he'd heard, it had been soon after that when Andrew and Eva had gotten married and not long after that she'd been pregnant.

Jake still had questions about that time. One night Eva had professed her deep and abiding love for him and they'd been planning their future together, and the next night she'd told him she didn't care anything about him and she never wanted to see him again.

She'd indicated that they couldn't go back in time, and while Jake would like some answers, he didn't want to go back for anything other than making love with her one last time. She might act like she's immune to him now, but the brief kiss they had shared told him much differently.

There was still something there between them, something burning hot and wild, and he couldn't wait to explore that again. He would never forget how she'd broken his heart, but he had no intention of ever giving her his heart again.

Still, he was very concerned about the fact that somebody was targeting her. The dead cattle and the notes worried him, and from what he'd heard around town so far, she didn't have anyone to support her other than her two ranch hands.

With Eva still on his mind, he saddled up and headed back to the stables. He'd been gone long enough that all the well-wishers were gone from the house.

He showered and changed clothes and, feeling too restless to just hang around the house, he grabbed his truck keys and headed into town with no particular destination in mind.

Once he was on Main Street, he parked and took off walking at a leisurely pace in an attempt to get rid of the restlessness that had plagued him since the funeral. David had been right—the small town was growing, and there were many new businesses open since the last time Jake had been here.

It was past the dinner hour and not too many people were on the sidewalks, but the few who passed him nodded or offered their condolences about his father.

He smiled as he saw Benny Adams approaching from the other direction. Benny had been one of Jake's best friends in high school. "Hey, man," Benny said as he pulled Jake into a bear hug. He released him and took a step back. "I wanted to talk to you at the funeral today, but there were so many people around I couldn't get to you. I'm so sorry about your father."

"Thanks," Jake replied.

"So, what are your plans now that you're back?"

Benny asked. "Are you going to hang around for a while before heading back to Italy?"

"I'm staying here for good. I've had enough of being on foreign soil. But tell me about you. Have you married? Do you have a family?"

"Yeah, I married Lori right out of high school." Benny grinned. "You know how that girl drove me crazy during our senior year—well, she's still keeping me crazy." Benny laughed.

"That's terrific. You have kids?"

"Yeah, two. I've got a boy who is six and a three-year-old daughter who Lori and I are convinced is the spawn of Satan. In fact, I'm on my way to the grocery store because the spawn of Satan wants chocolate milk before bed."

Jake laughed. "I'd love to get together with you and your family for dinner one night."

"Sounds good to me. What about you? From what I've seen in the occasional newspaper clippings, you look like you've been busy dating a lot of hot women and living it up in Italy. Any one of those women get you to the altar?"

"No, I'm still footloose and fancy-free."

"I'm going to hold you to that dinner. Lori is a great cook, and we'd love to have you over to our place."

"Just tell me when and where and I'll be there," Jake replied. The two men exchanged information, and then Benny hurried on down the sidewalk toward the grocery store.

Jake watched until he disappeared into the store. So, Benny had married his high school sweetheart and had a family. It was what Jake had once hoped for with Eva. He'd once believed that by now he'd be long married to her and they'd have a couple of children.

He sighed and continued down the walkway. He was just about to pass by an ice cream parlor when he halted in his tracks. Seated inside at one of the high round tables were Eva and her son, Andy.

Suddenly he had an overwhelming hankering for a strawberry ice cream sundae. He pushed open the door and entered the shop. "Eva," he greeted her. "And you must be Andy," he said to the young boy. "Hi, my name is Jake. I'm an old friend of your mother's."

"Cool, it's nice to meet you, Mr. Jake," the boy replied with a bright smile.

"I certainly didn't expect to see you here," Eva said, her gaze simmering with a hint of anger.

"I felt a little restless after all the events of the day and decided to come into town," he replied. "I was just passing by and thought I'd get some ice cream."

The anger in Eva's eyes softened. "I'm sure today was a difficult one for you," she said. She looked at her son, who appeared curious. "Jake's father died, and the funeral for him was today."

"I'm sorry, Mr. Jake," Andy said with sadness in his eyes…eyes that were shaped just like his mother's. "My dad died when I was only three years old. I don't remember being sad, but I'm sure I was, and I'm sorry if you feel sad."

"Do you think I'd feel better if I got some ice cream and sat here with you and your mom for a few minutes?" Jake asked.

"Maybe," Andy replied. "Mom and I are pretty nice."

"Then I'll just go get me some ice cream and be right back." Jake knew he was being a bit manipulative in forcing Eva to either make a scene in front of her son or accept his presence gracefully. But surely it couldn't hurt for them all to enjoy some ice cream together.

He got a strawberry sundae and then rejoined Eva and her son at their table. "So, what are the two of you doing out and about on a Sunday evening?" he asked.

"We're celebrating an A on a difficult spelling test," Eva said with a look of pride at her son.

"So, you're not only a handsome boy, but you're smart as well," Jake said. "What do you want to be when you grow up?"

"I want to raise cattle and work on the ranch just like my mom," Andy replied. "But Mom says I've got to get my education before she turns things over to me."

"That sounds like good advice to me," Jake replied.

"What do you do, Mr. Jake?"

"I've been away for a while, but now I'm going to work on my family ranch and raise cattle."

"Cool," Andy said.

"Do you like to fish?" Jake asked.

"I've never been," Andy replied.

"What? There's a big pond right there in the pasture near your house and you've never fished in it?" Jake looked at Eva in surprise. Andy shook his head.

"It's one of those things we've just never made time to do," Eva said with a touch of guilt in her voice.

"Maybe I could take you fishing when you get home from school tomorrow if your mother agrees," Jake said.

Andy's face lit up with excitement. "Mom?"

"I guess that would be okay," she said, but her eyes communicated something far different than okay. They indicated to him that she was ticked off, but he was hoping that by tomorrow she'd have forgiven him. What could be wrong with taking a boy fishing? Especially one who had never been fishing before in his life?

The plans were made, and then the three of them left the ice cream parlor together. "Do you feel better now, Mr. Jake?" Andy asked.

"I believe I do. Thank you for letting me spend some time with you and your mom," Jake replied.

"You can always spend time with us," Andy replied with a big smile.

"We'll start tomorrow with that fishing date."

"Go ahead and get in the truck, Andy," Eva said.

He ran to a red pickup parked in front of the shop, and Eva turned to Jake.

"Have you heard anything new from Wayne?" he asked, hoping to circumvent the tongue-lashing he suspected he was about to receive from her.

"No, and don't think I'm going to get distracted by you asking me that. If you think you're going to somehow get closer to me by getting closer to my son, you'd better think again." Her eyes snapped with anger as her chin rose. "Andy isn't some pawn in whatever game you might be playing."

God, she looked so beautiful in her mother-bear ire. "Trust me, Eva, I'm not playing a game, and the last thing I'd ever want to do is hurt your son."

"I'm warning you, you'd better not, Jake."

"I'm just taking him fishing, Eva. Don't make it a bigger deal than it is."

"Just remember what I said. I don't want him hurt." She gave him no chance to reply but rather turned and walked to her truck.

Instead of the restlessness that had filled him before, he was surprised by a wave of heartache that pierced through him. In another life and time, Andy could have been his son.

Andy should have been his son with Eva. Jake would have taken his son fishing. He would have taught him how to tie a rope and make a lasso. He would have spent time with his son and created the male bonding relationship that a father and son should have.

He wouldn't have spent his time behind a desk, consumed by profit and loss statements and making more and more money, like his father had done.

With a deep sigh, Jake got into his truck, a strange wistfulness riding with him all the way home.

Chapter Four

Eva woke up the next day in a foul mood. The cause of that mood? Jake Albright. She didn't like the fact that he was attempting to worm his way into her life by going through her son. It hadn't helped that Andy had been beside himself with excitement about the fishing date over breakfast.

He'd asked her about bait and different kinds of fish, and each question had only made her feel more guilty for not taking the time to take him fishing before now.

At least there had been no dead cows discovered this morning and no threatening notes in the mailbox. There was also no trash in the barn, indicating none of the kids had partied there the night before.

Of course, it had been a Sunday night and they all did have school today. But they had partied on school nights in the past. Unfortunately, the barn was too far away from the house for her to hear them whenever they arrived in the night.

The only times she'd caught them were when she'd stayed awake and sat at the front window. The idea that Griff would say she had ever greeted the teenagers with a gun was absolutely ludicrous.

She did have a big stick she kept in the hallway closet,

and she had carried it with her into the barn when the kids had been there for her own protection. But that stick was a far cry from a gun.

It wasn't that she was a big party pooper—she just didn't want a bunch of kids drinking and whatever else in her barn. First of all, they were trespassing, but equally important, she was afraid somebody was going to get hurt eventually. Not only would she feel terrible if one of them were injured, but she also didn't need the liability such an accident might cause.

At three o'clock she sank down at her table with a fresh cup of coffee. As her gaze landed on Andy's picture, a whirlwind of thoughts shot through her head.

She knew her son yearned to have a strong male figure in his life. It was the one thing Eva hadn't been able to give to him. After Andrew died, she hadn't wanted to date anyone. Her sole focus had been the ranch and her son. And nothing had changed since then. She still didn't want to date.

But she did wish Andy had a male in his life who could give him a man's perspective on life, a man who would take him fishing and to rodeos. She'd tried to be both mother and father to her son, but she knew there was no way she could make up for the lack of a father figure.

She certainly didn't want that person to be Jake. It had been the Albright power that had torn her and Jake apart, and she couldn't forget that now Jake had that wealth and power.

Thank God Andy had her features. She'd feared Jake and her son meeting, but Jake didn't seem to have any suspicions about Andy's paternity.

Eva had only lied to her son once, and that was when

she'd told Andy his birthday. She'd moved Andy's birthday celebrations back three months in order to keep the secret of Andy being Jake's. Thankfully nobody in town had ever questioned it, and everyone believed Andrew was Andy's father. The only person who had known the truth was Andrew.

She would go to her grave with the secret of Jake being Andy's father. Just as she would go to her grave with the secret of what part Justin Albright had played in their breakup.

She knew how much Jake had loved and adored his father, and she would never tell him anything that would take that away. Even after all these years, she still cared enough about Jake not to do that to him.

The crunch of gravel announced the arrival of the devil himself. Andy wouldn't be home for another twenty minutes or so, and if Jake thought he was going to spend those minutes with her, then he had another thought coming.

She opened her front door as he got out of his truck. "Andy won't be here for another twenty minutes. Feel free to hang out here by yourself."

His eyes twinkled with amusement. "What's the matter, Eva? Afraid to spend a little time with me?"

"Of course not," she replied, instantly heated by his taunt. The minute she stepped out on the porch and closed the door behind her, she realized she'd given him exactly what he wanted.

"Beautiful afternoon for a little fishing," he said as he gestured to a tackle box, a cooler and two fishing rods that were in his truck bed. "You and I used to catch some big catfish out of your pond. Remember how we'd sit together on the little dock with our poles in the water as the sun set?"

His smile seduced her to remember that time with him, when they'd talked about everything from a simple wedding in the barn to what they would name their kids.

There was no way she was letting him into her head. "There should be plenty of big catfish left in the pond, since it hasn't been fished for years."

"Your son seems like a good kid," he replied.

"He's an awesome kid." As always, a wealth of pride rose up inside her as she thought of her son. "He's been a real joy from the moment he was born."

"You've obviously done a great job with him."

For a moment the warmth of his gaze felt welcome. She'd been alone for so long, and as she looked into his eyes, she remembered not only the love of the boy he had been, but also that he'd once been the keeper of her secrets and the builder of her dreams.

The rumble of the school bus approaching in the distance snapped her out of the momentary lapse. "That will be Andy now." She began walking down the lane, and Jake fell into step beside her.

"I ran into Benny last night," he said. "Do you ever hang out with any of the old gang from high school?"

"I really don't have time to hang out with anyone." When she'd learned she was pregnant, she'd stopped seeing all her friends from school for fear they would know she was carrying Jake's child. Then there had been a baby to care for, an ill husband and her father's death.

Before Jake could ask her any more questions, the bus pulled to a halt and Andy got off. He hurried toward them, sheer excitement shining from his eyes and a happy bounce to his steps.

"Mr. Jake, you're here!" Andy smiled up at Jake.

"Well, of course I'm here. We have a fishing date," Jake replied as the three of them headed to the house. "Did you forget about that?"

"Heck, no. I just wasn't sure you'd really come," Andy replied. "But I want to catch a big fish."

Jake laughed. "And I want you to catch a big fish."

Eva's heart squeezed tight as she watched the interplay between her son and Jake. It was obvious Andy already had some hero worship going on.

She feared this relationship. She didn't want Andy to get attached to a man who would never have a place in her life. But it was too late to stop this afternoon of the two of them fishing together from happening.

"I've got bottles of water in the cooler, along with a container of big, fat worms," Jake said when they reached his truck.

"Worms?" Andy nodded his head. "Mom told me that worms are the best bait for catching a big catfish."

"Your mom is right. That's the best bait for catching a big fish," Jake replied. "Are you going to be able to put a wiggling worm on a hook?"

"Of course," Andy replied confidently. "I'm not a wimp."

Jake laughed and reached out and ruffled Andy's hair. "I knew you weren't a wimp the first time I saw you." Andy beamed up at Jake.

"Then I guess I'll see the two of you later," Eva said.

She watched as the man who had once owned her heart and the boy who held her heart completely got into the truck and drove down the pasture lane toward the pond. For a brief moment, she wanted to run after them.

She wanted to sit on the edge of the dock with them.

Fishing wasn't just about catching a big one. It was sitting together and talking quietly about anything and everything that popped into your head.

It was relaxing and talking and laughing together and building stronger bonds with the people who shared the dock with you. It was about a couple hours in time where nothing was important and worry was near impossible.

With a sigh, she turned and headed back to the house. The last thing she needed or wanted was to spend any more bonding moments with Jake.

She had spent the last ten years not only being angry with his father but also harboring what she knew was a bit of irrational anger toward Jake. Even though she had been the one forced to break up with him, he hadn't fought for her. He hadn't tried to change her mind. Instead he'd been on the next plane to Italy, and as far as she knew, he had never looked back.

After that, she'd always wondered if she'd been nothing but the cliché of a rich boy's toy for a couple of summers of sex. And in that hurt was the desire to keep herself in a place where he could never, ever hurt her again.

Instead of heading directly into the house, she went around to the back and picked a handful of big, ripe tomatoes to slice up for sandwiches for dinner.

As she worked, dark clouds began to gather in the southwestern sky, and the air thickened with additional humidity. She hoped the fishing didn't get interrupted by a pop-up thunderstorm. They could be fairly common at this time of year.

She carried the tomatoes through the back door and placed them in the kitchen sink to wash. Although it wasn't her intention for Jake to eat dinner with them, she had plenty of ham and cheese in case Andy insisted his fishing buddy share the evening meal of sandwiches and chips.

The clouds had thickened even more, making for a false twilight, but so far there had been no lightning, thunder or rain. However, the wind had definitely picked up.

Her father had always told her the fish bit best when it was cloudy, and she hoped Andy was pulling out fish left and right.

A loud bang sounded several times from the front of the house. She hurried into the living room and peered out the front window. She saw nothing amiss.

The wind had probably found that loose shutter outside her bedroom window and smacked it against the house. She made herself a mental note to hammer it down in the next couple of days. She returned to the kitchen and busied herself by setting the table for two.

She flipped on the kitchen light to ward off the darkness caused by the clouds overhead, grabbed a soda from the fridge and then sat at the table to wait for the fishermen's return.

What were Jake and Andy talking about while they sat on the dock together? Was her son sharing thoughts and emotions with Jake that Andy hadn't shared with her? She shook her head to cast these thoughts out of her head, knowing she was being foolish.

She hoped that if Andy had some questions or issues he wasn't comfortable asking his mother, then he would ask those questions of Jake. She trusted Jake to give her son good answers to whatever Andy might ask.

She wasn't sure how long she'd been sitting when,

to her surprise, Jake's pickup pulled to a halt in front of the back door.

The two entered the kitchen. "Mom, I caught four big fish," Andy said, his eyes twinkling with excitement. "It was so cool. I had to fight to reel them in. Right, Mr. Jake?"

"Right," Jake replied. There was a tension radiating from Jake—a troubling tension. Had something happened with Andy? Had he misbehaved or back talked? Even as she thought it, she couldn't believe her son would ever be that kind of boy.

"But we let them go," Andy continued. "Mr. Jake said to let them go so they can get even bigger and we can catch them again. Catch and release, right, Mr. Jake?"

"That's right," Jake replied.

"Did you behave for Mr. Jake?" Eva asked her son.

"He did," Jake replied and smiled, but the smile didn't quite reach his eyes. "He turned out to be a terrific fisherman. And now why don't you go into the bathroom and wash up?"

"Okay." Andy raced out of the kitchen.

The minute he left, Jake turned to Eva, his gaze dark. "We need to call Wayne."

"Why? What's happened?" Her heart skipped a beat.

"One of your missing cow hearts has shown up."

A gasp escaped Eva. "What? Where?" Fear sizzled through her veins.

"Hanging from your front porch rail."

Eva stared at him in horror. Now she understood why he had driven around to the back door. It had been in an effort to keep Andy from seeing anything disturbing.

"Before we call Wayne, let me make Andy a sandwich and get him settled in his bedroom," she said.

"We should call him before it starts to rain," Jake replied. "The clouds have definitely thickened up."

"Just give me five minutes." Eva quickly made Andy a sandwich, added potato chips to his plate and had it ready by the time he returned to the kitchen.

"You can eat in your bedroom and play your video games until bedtime," she told him.

"Really?" Andy took the plate from her. "You never let me play my games on a school night."

"Tonight is the exception to the rule," Eva replied.

"Cool. Thank you, Mr. Jake, for taking me fishing. I hope we can do it again soon," Andy said.

Jake smiled. "We'll definitely do it again soon."

Andy took his plate and then disappeared into his bedroom. Eva headed for the front door, with Jake close behind her. Her heart beat the rhythm of dread as she anticipated what she was going to see.

The minute she stepped out on the porch, the wind whipped her hair around her head, and a bolt of lightning split the darkness of the clouds.

Even though she'd thought she was mentally prepared, she wasn't. There was no way she could have prepared herself for what she saw.

The cow's heart was stabbed through with a knife and dripped with blood. A note was next to it, appearing to have been written with the blood from the heart.

"Die, bitch."

It was a grotesque sight, made more horrifying by the fact that the person who threatened her had sneaked so close…had been bold enough to invade her personal space by coming up onto her porch.

She jumped, and a small cry escaped her lips as thunder boomed overhead. Jake threw his arm around her shoulder and pulled her close. Instead of pulling away from him, she leaned closer into him.

"Die, bitch." The words echoed in her head over and over again as she stared, almost mesmerized by the note next to the horrible bloody heart.

"Come on, let's get inside and call Wayne," Jake said gently and tightened his arm around her.

With her heart still pounding and fear tightening her stomach muscles, she prayed that this time Wayne would find something that would identify who was behind these attacks…before whoever was behind it made good on the threat.

JAKE STOOD ON the porch with Wayne and his deputy, Phil Barkley. Jake had insisted Eva stay in the house with her son while the men took care of the evidence gathering. There was no reason for her to see this atrocity again.

"That had to have been frozen," Jake observed as Phil took photos of the heart.

"Maybe, although it's sick to think about somebody… anybody in Dusty Gulch tearing the heart out of an animal and then putting it in their freezer," Wayne said. "It's hard to believe somebody in Dusty Gulch is behind any of this. It's the sickest thing I've ever seen."

"I just want to know who is targeting Eva and why," Jake replied.

"Let's hope this time the person made a mistake. Hopefully I can get something from the knife that was left behind," Wayne replied. "It's got a nice carved handle."

"Looks like it's handmade," Jake observed. "You know anybody who does that kind of work around here?"

"Not off the top of my head," Wayne replied. "But I'm not much of a knife guy."

"At least the rain held off," Jake said. Lightning had split the night sky and thunder had boomed overhead, but there hadn't been a drop of rain so far.

He watched as Wayne and Phil pulled on plastic gloves and then removed the knife and two ordinary nails that held the note in place. They then caught the heart as it fell into a plastic evidence bag. The knife, the nails and the note were also bagged as evidence, and then Phil left with the items.

Jake and Wayne spent the next twenty minutes walking the area around the porch and looking for anything that might provide a clue as to the identity of the perpetrator. However, they found nothing. Unfortunately the ground was too dry to give up a single footprint or tire track, and they didn't even know in what direction the perp had come from.

"I need to get back inside to Eva," Jake finally said.

"I'll head in with you. I need to get an interview with her on the record," Wayne replied. "I want to do everything strictly by the book, so when we catch this creep, the district attorney can put him away for a long time."

Together the two men went back into the house, where Eva sat on the edge of the sofa. She jumped up as they came in. "I made coffee," she said. Jake eyed her worriedly. Her eyes were slightly glazed, and she was pale. She appeared small and more vulnerable than he'd ever seen her. "Let's go into the kitchen, and I can get Wayne a cup of coffee."

She led the way, and as the two men sat at the table, she got Wayne a cup of the fresh brew and offered Jake a soda, which he declined.

Finally the three of them were seated, and Wayne took out his notepad and a small recorder. "Do you mind if I record your statement?" he asked.

"No, not at all," Eva replied.

"I just can't believe somebody had the nerve to do this while I was here," Jake said.

"Unless you specifically told somebody, nobody would have known you were here. Your truck was down by the pond and wouldn't have been visible from the road or the house," Eva said.

Jake was grateful to see a bit of color returning to her cheeks, and her gaze was becoming more clear and focused. "I didn't tell anyone I was coming here," he replied.

Wayne turned on his recorder and focused on Eva. "Do you have any idea what time this happened?"

"I'm not sure, but I heard a couple of bangs coming from the front of the house around six o'clock or so. I thought it was the wind banging one of the shutters that are loose." She frowned. "I looked outside, but I didn't see anything. If only I'd come all the way out of the house immediately when I heard it, maybe I could have caught the person."

"Thank God you didn't run out of the house," Jake replied. "Who knows what might have happened if you'd encountered the person?" The very thought of Eva interacting with the perp clenched Jake's stomach muscles and made him feel ill.

Minutes later, after Wayne had asked all his questions, Eva and Jake walked the lawman to the front door. "Hopefully the knife is going to be the key in breaking this case wide-open," he said. "It's unusual, and I'm going to home in and see what I can learn about it. I'll be in touch in the next day or two to let you know what we find out."

"At least Wayne seems to be stepping up his game," Jake said when Wayne was gone. "Where is Andy?"

"He's sleeping. I think all the heat and excitement of fishing completely wore him out. I tucked him into bed while you and Wayne were outside. I just hope Wayne really can figure something out from the knife," she replied and then collapsed onto the sofa. To his surprise, she patted the sofa next to her. "Will you sit with me for a while?" There was a soft plea in her eyes that let him know she was still frightened.

"Of course. I should just move in here to keep you safe." He sank onto the sofa next to her.

She released a small laugh. "Jake, I asked you to stay for a little while, not to move in with us." Her laughter faded. "This whole thing is frightening, but the locks on my windows and doors are good ones, and I have a big stick and a shotgun in case I get really scared about somebody coming inside the house."

That moment of vulnerability she'd displayed earlier was gone. However, he knew she must be entertaining residual fear in the fact that she'd asked him to hang around for a while longer. If nothing else, the note written in blood had to have terrified her. It had certainly scared the hell out of him for her.

"It was fun taking Andy fishing for his first time," he said, knowing that talking about her son would ease some of her anxiety. "He was so excited about everything. He baited his own hook like a champion, and by the time we left the pond, he was casting out like a real pro."

A whisper of a smile curved her lips…lips that even

under these circumstances he wanted to cover with his own. "I appreciate you taking him. I should have taken him a long time ago, but it was just one of those things that I kept putting off."

"So, tell me about your husband. Were you happy in the marriage?"

She hesitated a moment and then nodded her head. "Yes, I was happy. Andrew was one of the most gentle and truly good men I've ever known."

Jake's heart quickened slightly. "Eva, I just need to ask…were you seeing him while we were dating?"

Her eyes narrowed. "Do you really believe I'm the kind of woman who would do something like that? You do me a disservice by even asking that. The answer is no. At that time Andrew was just a ranch hand I occasionally saw working out in the pastures. And then my father died."

Her eyes filled with sadness, and she took a moment before continuing. "I was eighteen years old and utterly lost in my grief. I didn't know anything about how to run this place, and I felt so alone. Andrew stepped up and not only helped me through my grief, but also taught me what I needed to know about running this place and surviving here on the ranch my father had loved."

"I wish I had been here to help you with your grief," he replied. How he wished he had been the one she'd leaned on and cried to, how he wished he'd been the one she'd depended on during that terrible time in her life. "So, why did you break up with me, Eva?"

She released a deep sigh. "Does it really matter now? I told you before, Jake, I don't want to rehash the past. It's over and done with, and we can't go back and rewrite history. Besides, I'm far more concerned about my future right now."

Her response didn't answer his question, but she was right. In the grand scheme of things, what did any of it really matter now? It was obviously his problem that he hadn't quite been able to get over her. Maybe by spending more time with her now, he'd realize they had never been meant to be together.

"I saw pictures of you on dates in Italy. None of those beautiful women managed to tie you down?" she asked.

"No, I wasn't even particularly serious with anyone over the last ten years. I found most of those beautiful women exceedingly boring."

A small laugh escaped Eva. "I find that hard to believe."

"It's the truth," he protested with a laugh of his own. "I really had nothing in common with any of them. They saw me as an heir to a fortune, but when I tried to tell them about my desire to ranch in Dusty Gulch, Kansas, their eyes glazed over and they stopped listening to me. It's hard to build a relationship with somebody when you can't talk about your real hopes and dreams."

He'd wanted to feel the same deep connection…the same passion for another woman that he'd once felt for Eva, but so far he hadn't found it with anyone else.

He suddenly realized how close they sat to each other, close enough that he could smell the spicy scent of her. He could feel the warmth of her radiating toward him—a warmth that had always both comforted and excited him at the same time.

Their gazes locked, and he felt himself falling into the beautiful violet depths. He was eighteen years old again, and in his eyes she was the most beautiful girl in the entire school, in the entire world.

Her long hair held the sheen of fine silk, begging him to stroke his fingers through the thick strands. His chest tightened, and he leaned closer to her.

Her eyes darkened, and she released a small gasp and sprang to her feet. “It’s been a long day, Jake. I really appreciate you hanging out for a little while, but I’m fine now and I think it’s time for us to say good-night.”

Jake got up from the sofa, feeling as if he was reluctantly leaving behind a wonderful dream. “Are you sure you’ll be all right? I could always bunk right here on the sofa for the rest of the night.”

“Thanks, but I’ll be fine.” She walked with him to the front door. “Now that the initial shock is over, I’m okay.”

“You’ll call me if anything else happens or if you just get frightened?” he asked. She hesitated a moment and then nodded.

He lifted her chin with his fingers so he could look one last time into her beautiful, long-lashed eyes. “Promise me, Eva,” he said.

“I promise.” She stepped back from him. “Good night, Jake.”

He told her good-night and then stepped out on the porch. She closed and locked the door behind him. His gaze shot directly to the place where the heart had hung.

Was somebody just terrorizing her with no desire to actually harm her? His hands tightened into fists at his sides. Who was doing this to her? Why would anyone do this to her? Would this escalate into something deadly?

There was no question that he was worried about her. However, he didn’t believe anything more would happen tonight. He left the porch and headed for his truck.

It had been a long day, with lots of emotions to process. He'd truly enjoyed his time with Andy. The boy was bright and funny and had been eager to please. It was obvious he longed for a father figure in his life and missed the father he could barely remember.

Jake got in his truck but remained sitting without starting the engine as his tangled thoughts attempted to unwind. He'd seen the heart the minute he had pulled up toward the house and had immediately detoured around to the kitchen door in hopes that Andy wouldn't see the monstrosity. He didn't want Andy's memory of his first day fishing to be tainted. Hell, he never wanted a kid to see something like that.

He'd come here initially because he'd wanted to make love with Eva one more time…because maybe he'd wanted a bit of revenge on her for breaking his heart so many years ago.

But tonight something had changed in him. His desire for her was still there, as strong as it had ever been. But as he'd talked about sharing hopes and dreams, he'd remembered that he'd had that with Eva.

He still loved her. He was still in love with her. There was no doubt in his mind that she had loved him once. He didn't know exactly what had gone wrong between them, but none of that mattered now.

More than anything, he wanted to keep her safe from any and all danger—and he wanted her to love him again.

Chapter Five

"That kind of knife is sold at a couple of convenience and cigarette stores around the immediate area," Wayne explained. Lines of exhaustion creased the lawman's face, the lines made more prominent by the morning sun that danced through Eva's kitchen windows.

"We got lucky in that they are handmade by a man named Riley Kincaid, who lives out on a ranch about twenty miles from here. Unfortunately, I haven't had a chance to follow up on any of this, because old man Brighton was murdered in his sleep last night."

Both Eva and Jake released gasps of surprise. "How?" Jake asked.

"What about his wife? Is Sadie all right?" Eva leaned forward, horrified by this news. Walter Brighton and Sadie were fixtures around town. They had been married for fifty years, and they took afternoon walks together in town and greeted each person they passed with warmth. They often sat on the bench in front of the post office or could be seen having an early dinner at the café.

"Sadie is fine, but needless to say, she is very shaken up by this," Wayne replied. "Walter was stabbed sometime in the middle of the night while he slept."

"Where was Sadie when all this happened?" Jake

asked. He looked so handsome this morning, clad in a navy blue T-shirt and a pair of jeans.

"Apparently Sadie slept in one of the other smaller bedrooms in their house due to Walter's loud snoring. She didn't see or hear anyone. She found Walter just after sunrise this morning when she went to wake him for the day. My point is right now all my men are assigned to the murder case, and I need to get back over to the scene of the crime as soon as possible. And that means it's going to be some time before I can speak to Riley Kincaid or follow up on any of the stores that sell the knife." He shook his head ruefully. "I'm sorry, but I've got to focus on this murder case right now."

"Wayne, we completely understand. How about Eva and I check out the convenience stores that sell the knife and speak to this Kincaid guy?" Jake asked.

Wayne sighed in obvious relief. "It would be real helpful if you two did the initial legwork," he said. "We need to find out who might have bought one of those knives recently. It looked brand-new. Unfortunately there were no prints on it, but if you remember, Jake, it had a wolf carved into it."

"Trust me, I remember," Jake replied.

"We'll see what we can find out by talking to these people," Eva said. Although she was ambivalent about spending any more time alone with Jake, the bloody heart and the new note had truly frightened her.

She would dance with the devil if it brought her closer to discovering who was behind the threats. And in this case, her devil was Jake.

She knew he could get answers where she might not be able to. His name not only commanded a lot of respect, but also a bit of fear. Storekeepers would speak to him because the Albrights owned most of the stores. Yes, she would dance with him in this investigation, but she couldn't let him in on a personal level.

Last night had proven just how dangerous he was to her. There was a part of her that ached with desire for him, a place that wanted to go back to that simpler time when they were just two teenagers madly in love with each other.

But going back in time wasn't possible, and having any kind of a personal relationship with Jake wasn't an option. She needed him right now to be her partner in helping to solve the mystery of the threats against her. But that was all she needed him for.

"I'll warn you, from what I hear this Kincaid fellow is a bit of an eccentric old coot." Wayne gave them Kincaid's address and then stood from the kitchen table. "All I ask is that you keep track of who you talk to and what they say. As soon as we get on top of this murder case, I'll have everyone in the station working on who is terrorizing you, Eva."

"Thanks, Wayne." Eva and Jake walked him to the front door. There was no question Eva was disappointed that Wayne couldn't get his men to investigate her case right now. But she certainly couldn't blame him for needing to investigate a murder that had just taken place the night before, and she knew how small Wayne's department and resources were.

"Want to take a ride?" Jake asked the minute Wayne had left.

"Where are we going?" she asked.

"How about we go talk to an eccentric old man about a knife?"

She nodded. “I’m in, as long as I’m back here by three forty-five or so when Andy gets off the bus.”

“Then let’s see how much investigating we can get done before then.”

Minutes later they were in Jake’s truck. The scent inside the cab cast her back in time—the pleasant smells of leather polish, his fresh-scented cologne and the familiar aroma that was in all her memories as just being Jake’s.

Before they’d left her house, she’d grabbed a notebook in order to keep track of whom they spoke to and what they were told. She wanted to provide a clear and complete record for Wayne to use when he followed up.

“I can’t believe Walter was murdered,” she said once they were underway. “I can’t even remember the last time Dusty Gulch had a murder. And who on earth would want to hurt poor Walter?”

“I wouldn’t have a clue. Hopefully Wayne will be able to solve it quickly,” Jake replied.

“I can’t imagine who he’ll even find as a suspect. I’ve never heard of Walter exchanging cross words with anyone.” Just like she really didn’t have a clue who any real suspect was in her own case.

It bothered her that the person who was terrorizing her could be somebody she saw often, somebody who smiled at her and was pleasant to her and yet hid this kind of evil hatred toward her.

Jake rolled down his window partway even with the air conditioner blowing from the truck vents. Immediately the scents of dusty heat and pastures filled the truck’s interior.

“Ah, I missed the smell of the pastures while I was away,” he said. “I also missed this scenery.”

"But I've heard wine country is quite beautiful," she replied.

"Oh, it is, but it wasn't the sights or smells of home." He drew in a deep breath. "Now this looks and smells like home."

She wanted to ask him why he had flown to Italy the day after their breakup, but she knew the answer. His father would have orchestrated that to keep the two young lovers as far away from one another as possible. And Jake would have done anything to gain his father's approval.

"If you were so homesick, why did you stay away for so long?" she asked. Even in profile he was an extremely handsome man. She turned her gaze away from him and instead gazed out the front window.

"My father depended on me to run the wine business. He trusted me, and I didn't want to disappoint him. He thought I needed to be there and so I stayed, but I'm glad to be back here now."

"I have to admit, I'm glad you're here now. Otherwise Wayne would still be giving me the runaround," she replied.

"Wayne's not a bad guy—he's just lazy and needs somebody to push him occasionally," Jake replied.

"He'll have his hands full now with the murder." Eva shook her head. She still couldn't believe somebody had murdered Walter in his sleep.

For a few minutes, they rode in a comfortable silence. Hopefully Riley Kincaid kept a record of what stores carried his knives and who might have bought them directly from him. And hopefully one of those names was the person who was tormenting her.

"Tell me more about your husband."

She turned to look at him, surprised by his question. "What do you want to know about him?"

"Was he good to you?"

Eva's heart squeezed tight as she thought of Andrew. "He was very good to me."

"I'm glad. I heard he died of pancreatic cancer. That must have been very tough on you."

"It was. It's a brutal disease." It had been torture to watch Andrew suffer. In the end she'd been grateful that he'd finally passed to escape the ravages of the cancer. She'd been holding his hand when he'd finally taken his last breath.

"I'm so sorry you had to go through that," Jake said.

"I knew he was sick when I married him. Part of our arrangement was that I would be there for him to the end so he wouldn't have to die all alone. His parents were dead and he had no siblings. He really had nobody in his life except me."

"You said it was part of your arrangement." Jake shot her a curious look, and Eva cursed herself for saying as much as she had. "What do you mean by an arrangement?"

"Nothing," she replied quickly. "I just meant that when you marry somebody, you take a vow to be there in sickness and in health."

Thankfully that seemed to end his curiosity. He slowed the truck as they approached the turnoff on a narrow, two-lane country road. "This guy definitely lives out in the middle of nowhere."

"I wish somebody had been able to give us a phone number so we could call ahead to let him know we're coming," she replied. Wayne had told them that he had no phone contact for the man. He had a primitive web page up showcasing his knives but only an email address for contact.

"Let's just hope he got the email we sent," Jake replied. Before they had left her house, she had emailed Riley to let him know they were coming. Unfortunately there was no way for them to know how often the man read his email.

Once again they fell silent, although this silence felt charged with energy. She wasn't sure what Jake was feeling at the moment, but there was definitely a slight edge of desperation that tightened her chest.

She'd been living with her own personal nightmare for the past three weeks. From the moment she'd found her first dead cow and the first note in her mailbox, there had been a chill deep in her bones that grew colder with each new discovery. She was desperate for answers and hoped the knife maker would have them for her.

Jake pulled the truck to a halt and peered down the road that led to their right. Calling it a road was a stretch—it was little more than a dirt path through trees that encroached on either side.

"I think that is the driveway," he said.

"It looks more like a deer trail," she replied.

He turned into it and instantly hit a big pothole. "It's a bumpy deer trail. Hold on to your seat."

He had to crawl down the road as he attempted to miss the worst of the bumps. He also had to swerve slightly to avoid hitting a rabbit and then several squirrels that scurried across the road in front of them.

The air coming in through his window, rather than smelling of sweet pastures, now smelled of something dark and mysterious. The morning sunlight disappeared, trapped by the canopy of thick tree branches overhead.

"Nervous?" Jake asked, obviously picking up on her anxiety.

"Nervous," she admitted. "And eager. I'm really hoping in the next few minutes we'll get the answer I need to make all this craziness stop. I need to know who is doing all this to me and why."

"That would definitely be a good thing," he replied. They broke into a small clearing, and he stopped the truck in front of a weathered wooden gate spray-painted with the words No Trespassing.

In the distance a small ramshackle cabin sat next to an outbuilding that was almost the same size. A large blackened chimney rose up from the outbuilding.

Old tires, colorful wind whirligigs and a couple of old toilets sporting arrays of flowers growing from them littered the front yard. It was hard to believe the answer to the mystery might lie in the little cabin.

They got out of the truck and approached the gate to the sound of birds singing in the trees and the rustle of animals in the nearby brush.

Jake reached out to open the gate. A gunshot sounded, and the bark on the tree near where Eva stood splintered from the force of a bullet hitting it.

"Get down," Jake yelled at her. He tackled her to the ground and threw his body over the top of hers as the scent of imminent danger filled her head.

EVA'S HEART BANGED with fear and the shock of nearly being shot. What was happening? Why had the person in the cabin nearly hit her with a bullet? Jake's body covered hers, his heart hammering almost as quickly as her own.

"You okay?" he asked softly. His eyes were as dark as night and narrowed with a sharp focus.

"I… I'm okay," she replied.

Jake rose up a bit, his gaze going toward the cabin. Eva clutched at his shoulders, afraid if he rose up any more he'd catch a bullet in his head. Why on earth had they just been shot at? What was going on now?

"Riley Kincaid," Jake yelled. "We're here to ask you some questions about your knives."

"You can't fool me," a deep, raspy voice shouted back. "You look like some of those government tax people. You got the stink of tax agents, and you ain't coming in here and messing in my business. Go away and stay off my property."

"We aren't tax agents," Jake yelled back. "We have nothing to do with the government. She is Eva Martin and I'm Jake Albright. We just need to ask you some questions about your knives."

"Albright?" There was a long pause. "Are you Justin's boy?"

Jake slowly rose to his feet and motioned for Eva to stand just behind him. Her legs were still shaky, and her heart still beat far too quickly. At least they were standing up and no bullets had followed the one that had scared her half to death.

"Yes," Jake replied. "Justin is my father."

Eva held her breath. The man with the gun might not be a fan of the Albrights. Maybe he hated them and would shoot at them again, and standing here they both made perfect targets.

Riley Kincaid stepped out onto the porch. He was a

tall, thin man clad in a pair of worn jeans and a dirty white T-shirt. Frizzy gray hair fell to his shoulders, and he held a rifle in his hand. "Well, why in the hell didn't you say so in the first place? Come on in."

Jake threw his arm around her shoulders and then opened the gate. Together they advanced toward the weatherworn cabin. She released a sigh of relief as Riley leaned the gun against the porch rail.

"So, you're Jake Albright," Riley said. "Your daddy speaks well of you." He grinned, exposing a missing front tooth. "That man loves my knives."

"Unfortunately, he passed away several days ago," Jake replied.

"Well, that's a damn shame." Riley frowned and then grinned once again. "Even with all his buckets of money, he always tried to talk me down on the price of my knives. We'd haggle for an hour or so before he'd finally pay me what I wanted. Sometimes I'd knock off a couple of dollars just to make him feel better about it."

"We'd like to ask you some questions about people who have bought your knives," Jake said.

"Well, come on inside and we'll talk."

The living room/kitchen was obviously Riley's work area. Two pieces of plywood were set up like workbenches, each of them holding knife handles in various stages of completion. Wood shavings and dust covered the floor.

"Have you seen any of my knives?" he asked.

"Only one," Eva replied.

"Let me show you some of them," he said and led them to the workbench. It was obvious the man was very proud of his hand-carved handles, as he should be.

The handles held the images of birds and dogs and all kinds of wildlife.

They were all absolutely exquisite, except one that instantly sent her heart racing and her hands trembling. The handle had the carving of a wolf on it. Even though it wasn't exact, the knife looked very close to the one that had been stabbed through the heart left hanging on her porch railing.

Although Eva was eager to get to the matter at hand, and despite the fear that the wolf knife brought back to her, she couldn't help but admire the obvious talent Riley had in carving something beautiful into a simple piece of wood.

"These are all so beautiful," she said.

"If you want, I can show you my setup in the outbuilding. That's where I make the blades. They're all good and balanced and very sharp," Riley said.

"Thanks, but what we really need is some answers from you," Jake said.

"Then let's sit and talk," Riley replied.

There was only a worn recliner in the work area. He led them to a small kitchen table, where they all sat. "Can I get you something to drink? Or maybe a little snack?"

"No, thank you," Eva replied. She couldn't imagine what the man would provide as a little snack. But she couldn't help but notice the cockroaches that scurried across the kitchen counters. The fact that they were active even in the daytime let her know his roach problem was huge. She definitely had no appetite to eat anything he might prepare for them.

"Thanks, but we're good," Jake said. "What we'd like to find out is if you keep records of who buys your knives."

"I've got records of who buys from me directly, but

they're sold in three different stores, and once a month or so I go in and they pay me for the knives I've sold, but I don't get no names from them."

"Could we have a list of who you've sold to directly?" Jake asked. "We're especially interested in the ones that have wolf handles."

Riley narrowed his pale blue eyes. "Are you sure you're not working with the damned tax people?"

"I promise you we aren't," Eva said and then proceeded to tell him about why they were interested. She explained to him about the dead cows and then the heart hung on her porch by one of Riley's knives.

"Now that just ticks me the hell off," Riley said when she was finished. "My knives are meant to be collectibles, not to be used for such evil intent." He rose from the table and disappeared into what Eva presumed was a small bedroom.

Anxiety still fired through Eva. To her surprise Jake reached across the table and took one of her hands in his. He cast her a reassuring smile. She shouldn't have been surprised by his gesture. He'd always been able to read her mind, to read her moods.

As Riley returned carrying a spiral notebook, Jake released her hand and sat up straighter in the chair, obviously as eager as she was for any information Riley could give them.

"How far back you want me to go? I've been selling these knives in the stores and from my website for the past five years or so." He opened the notebook, which displayed surprisingly pretty and neat handwriting.

"We're really interested in the ones with wolf handles," Jake said.

Riley frowned. "I didn't keep records of what was on the knife handles, and the wolf knives are really popular."

"Then let's start with a year ago and see if any of the names you have ring a bell," Jake said.

"You tell me, girlie, if you recognize one of these people," Riley said to Eva. "I want to know who disrespected my knife by doing something so wicked to you."

Eva had never been called "girlie" in her life, and normally she'd be offended as hell by the term. But she knew Riley hadn't used it to diminish her. Besides, she was here for answers, not to get all riled up about political correctness.

"Do you know how many knives Justin Albright bought from you?" Eva asked. If Justin hadn't been sick when her whole ordeal had started, she would have suspected he was behind the attacks on her.

She would have thought that he believed Jake was getting homesick enough to return and he'd tried to drive her out of town before Jake returned home. But Justin Albright was dead and the threats were ongoing.

"I believe he bought ten in total."

Eva turned and looked at Jake. "Do you know where those knives are?"

"I don't know right now, but I'll find out before the day is over," he replied.

She knew Jake's father wasn't responsible, but maybe it was possible one of his knives had been stolen and used. She didn't want to leave any stone unturned in trying to find out who was responsible for her fear.

Riley began to read off the names of his customers. With each one he mentioned, Eva's hope that she might find an answer here began to wane. The names were unfamiliar to her.

"Griff Ainsley," Riley said, and the name caused all the hairs at the nape of her neck to rise up.

"Your high school barn partier," Jake said.

She nodded. Was it possible this was all the work of a bunch of teenagers? Could kids really be this evil? She just found it so unbelievable. Had the knife Griff bought been the same one that had stabbed through a cow's heart?

Riley continued to read off names. When he read the name Carl Robinson, Jake frowned. "Do you know Carl?" he asked her.

"No, I don't know him. Why?"

"He works as a ranch hand for us."

"Since I don't even know him, I think it's safe to say he isn't our man," she said.

Riley continued, and another name he read off surprised her. "I know him." She straightened in the uncomfortable wooden chair. "Robert Stephenson is Bobby's dad, and Bobby is Andy's best friend."

"You ever have any issues with him?" Jake asked.

"No, on the contrary—he's always been very pleasant to me. He's mentioned several times that he'd like the boys and him and me to go out for pizza or ice cream."

"And are you interested in doing that?" Jake's eyes bored into hers.

Her face flushed with warmth. "No, I've told you I'm not interested in forming any kind of a romantic relationship with anyone."

Riley laughed and clapped his knee in glee. "I would have sworn you two were lovers. Hell, there's enough tension between you to light a fire."

Eva's cheeks warmed even more. "We're just old friends," she replied.

Riley laughed again and winked at Jake. "She might say that now, but nobody knows what the future might bring."

Jake looked at Eva, and his lips slid into his damned sexy, knowing grin. She frowned back at him. She was determined that she would never have a romantic relationship with him again.

If she had a life to live, it was one that couldn't have Jake Albright in it.

Chapter Six

"We should be able to go to the last convenience store before heading out to get you home for Andy," Jake said. He glanced over to Eva, who had fallen quiet as the frustrating day had worn on.

"If this one is like the last two we visited, it won't be any help," she replied dispiritedly.

Riley had given them the locations of the three stores that sold his knives. Unfortunately the stores hadn't kept the names of the people who had bought knives. The only way they might get any information was if somebody used a credit card for the purchase, but in that case Jake and Eva would have to have a warrant.

"Don't get discouraged," Jake said. "At least we have two more names than we did."

"I can't believe that Robert Stephenson would do all this to retaliate against me because I wouldn't go out for pizza with him and the boys," she replied dryly.

"You can never be sure what goes on in somebody else's mind. I mean, somebody killed Walter, for crying out loud. There can be all kinds of craziness, mental illness and just plain evil that people can hide from everyone."

"Jeez, that's encouraging," she said.

"We'll get him, Eva. We'll figure out who is doing this to you and we'll put his butt in jail." He could tell his words did little to assuage the depression that was slowly taking hold of her.

"Maybe I should have just sold out and left town when I received that first threatening note," she said softly.

He shot her a look of surprise. "This can't be Tom Taylor's daughter speaking right now. Tom, who loved his land and envisioned it being passed down from generation to generation."

She released a tremulous sigh. "You're right. I need to stay strong, if not for myself, then for Andy. The ranch is his legacy. It's all I have to give him. I'm just discouraged and more than a little bit tired right now."

He reached out and captured her hand with his. "Then I'll be your strength when you're tired." He released her hand. He wished they weren't in his truck but rather standing in her living room so he could pull her into his arms and hold her tight.

The third convenience store was like the other two. They could get no information from them and were told to come back with a warrant.

"At least we've done the preliminary footwork for Wayne," Jake said as they headed home. "Let's just hope Wayne solves the murder case quickly and can focus his full attention back on this."

"We'll see if the two we know of who bought knives still have them in their possession," she said. "And I'd definitely like to be there when he talks to Griff again. That little creep has already lied to Wayne about me. I want to be there to call him out if he tries to lie again."

He shot her a quick grin. "Now that's the strong and amazing Eva I know."

She fell silent once again and stared out the window as if lost in thought. There had been a time when he could easily guess what she was thinking and feeling. But at the moment he had no clue what thoughts were whirling through her brain.

She looked so beautiful, clad in a pair of tight jeans and a sleeveless red blouse that showcased her full breasts and slender waist.

He clenched his hands tighter on the steering wheel. He wanted to get lost in the scent of her hair, to feel the silkiness of her skin against his own. There was no question he wanted her physically, but he wanted more.

He wanted every thought in her head and every dream she might entertain. He wanted her laughter and her tears, her hopes and her fears. He'd missed the last ten years of her life, but he wanted her from this time on and forever. And he wanted the person who was terrorizing her caught and thrown into a jail cell to rot.

She remained quiet until he parked back in front of her house. "I'll call Wayne and tell him what we found out," he said when they were out of the truck.

"Thanks. I'll hope to hear from him in the next couple of days, and I'll talk to you then." It was obviously a dismissal.

He looked at his watch. "It's just about time for Andy's bus to come. Mind if I hang out and say hi to him?"

He saw the hesitation in her eyes, but after a moment's pause, she said that would be fine.

They fell into step together as they walked down the lane to where the bus would stop. When they reached her mailbox at the end of the long driveway, she opened it and reached inside and grabbed a couple of envelopes.

"Any nefarious notes?" he asked once she'd flipped through all of them.

"No, just a handful of bills," she replied and frowned.

"Eva, how are you doing financially?"

Her shoulders visibly stiffened. "I really don't think that's any of your business."

"I just thought if you needed a bit of a loan or anything, I could always help out."

"I don't need or want any of your money, Jake," she protested. "I've never wanted anything to do with your money."

"I know that. I just want you to know if you ever get in a bad place, I'm always here for you," he replied. He took a step closer to her. The sun sparkled in her hair, and his head filled with the memories of making sweet, hot love with her.

She gazed up at him, and in her eyes he saw those memories were there, burning bright within her. "Eva," he murmured softly. But her eyes suddenly cooled.

"I know the Albrights have always been wealthy enough to pretty much buy whatever they wanted, but Jake, you can't buy your way back into my life," she said.

"Eva, that certainly wasn't my intention…" His protest was lost to the sound of the school bus arriving. It stopped by the drive, and the doors opened for Andy to get off. Any further talk between them was lost.

"Mr. Jake." Andy greeted him with a wide smile. "Are we going fishing again today?"

"Not today." Jake grinned and ruffled the boy's dark hair. "But we'll plan to go again real soon."

"You want to come in and have a snack with me? Mom usually makes me a snack before I start doing my homework. Maybe if you stay, Mom will give us cookies instead of dumb old carrot and celery sticks."

Eva laughed. "Carrot and celery sticks are good for you."

"Yeah, but cookies are just good," Andy quipped back.

Eva and Jake both laughed. "How was school?" Jake asked as they headed back toward the house. He was concerned about how Eva had taken his offer to help her. He'd certainly not intended for her to think he was trying to somehow buy her, but this was a subject for them to discuss at another time.

"It was good." As Andy talked about his day, a warmth rushed through Jake. This was what life was all about…walking children home from school…listening to them share their days and smiling over their heads at the woman you loved.

He wanted this, not just for now, but for forever. He could easily love Andy, who had no father and was a part of Eva. He wanted to make more babies with her and build a life with her.

However, first he had to make her want that same thing with him. The only thing she was offering him at the moment was cookies and milk.

Patience, he told himself. He had to be patient even though he wanted all of her now. His chest tightened as he thought of everything that had happened.

The most important thing right now was making sure they got the perpetrator who was tormenting her behind bars. That needed to happen before the creep got a chance to hurt or kill Eva.

Leaving the heart on her front porch was definitely an escalation. What concerned Jake the most was if the person escalated even more, there was no way to guess what he might do next.

THE NEXT MORNING Eva waved goodbye to Andy as the school bus whisked him away. The heat had abated somewhat overnight, but a stiff wind blew, screaming around the sides of the buildings and driving Eva just a little bit crazy.

She walked back to the house, but before she got inside, Wayne's official car turned into her drive, followed by Jake's pickup.

Jake. He'd been on her mind all night. He'd even occupied a prominent role in her dreams…dreams that were filled with passion and desire and the memories of what once had been between them.

Watching him interact with Andy made her want things she couldn't have. She wanted Jake, but she could never, would never have any kind of a future with him.

All she wanted right now was answers, and hopefully Wayne had brought some with him. She was surprised to see him, since he and his men had a murder case to solve. She watched as the two vehicles parked and the men got out.

"Morning, Eva," Wayne said in greeting. "I hope you have the coffee on."

"As a matter of fact, I do." She nodded to Jake and then opened the front door to allow them in. "Wayne, I didn't expect to see you so soon. What about Walter's murder case? I thought you were all tied up with that." She poured them all a cup of coffee and then joined them at the table.

"The murder has been solved. Sadie confessed to it late last night," Wayne replied.

Eva gasped in stunned surprise. "What? Sadie killed her husband? My God, is this some kind of a joke?" She couldn't imagine the sweet old lady hurting a fly.

Wayne nodded. "No joke. She said she was sick of him bossing her around, and she was disgusted by his snoring every night and her not being able to enjoy the master bedroom. She hated the way his dentures clicked and how his ears were so hairy and he refused to let the barber clean them up." Wayne shrugged. "She said she just snapped. She got up in the middle of the night, grabbed a knife and stabbed him."

"I would never have guessed that Sadie was capable of such a violent thing," Eva replied.

"Oh, we were pretty sure it was Sadie right from the get-go," Wayne said. "Mainly because there were no signs of forced entry and the knife she used was right from the kitchen countertop. It was just a matter of time before she finally confessed that she'd done it."

He took a long swig from his coffee cup, and then continued, "Anyway, Jake has caught me up on what you two found out yesterday from Riley Kincaid, and he mentioned that you'd like to come along when I question Griff once again."

"Definitely," Eva said forcefully. "Just thinking about the lies that kid has already told about me makes my blood boil."

"If I take you along for the interview, you'll have to keep your temper in check," Wayne warned her with a frown.

"Oh, don't worry, I promise I'll behave," she replied. "So when are you going to go talk to him again?"

"As soon as I have another cup of your coffee," Wayne replied.

She frowned. "Isn't he in school right now? Don't you have to wait and question him with his parents in attendance?"

"Actually, since last time he interviewed the kid, Wayne learned a very interesting fact," Jake said. "Griff is eighteen years old. He's legally an adult."

"And so that means I can question him all I like until he asks for a lawyer. Now…about that second cup of coffee?"

Eva poured him another cup. "What about the convenience stores that sell the knives?"

"I'll be writing up warrants tonight and taking them to Judge Himes first thing in the morning. At least we should be able to take a look at credit card transactions and get the names of all the people who bought those knives on credit. Unfortunately there's no way we can know the names of anyone who paid cash in the stores."

"And what about Robert Stephenson? I'm sure you're intending to talk to him as well," Jake said.

"Sure, but Robert is an upstanding man in the community. Besides owning a successful insurance agency, he's also on the town council," Wayne said. "I just can't imagine him having any part in this."

"And Sadie was just a sweet old woman," Jake said dryly.

"Point taken." Wayne drained his coffee and then stood. "So, are we ready to take a trip to the high school?"

"Just let me grab my purse," Eva said.

"If you want, Eva, you can ride with me," Jake offered. "As I remember, parking was always difficult at the high school. Of course, the last time I parked there was ten years ago."

"Nothing much has changed in the last ten years," Wayne replied. "It's still hard to find open parking spaces because so many of the students drive to school."

Minutes later Eva was in Jake's truck, and they followed Wayne's patrol car into town, where the junior high and high school buildings were located just off Main Street. Andy's grade school was on the opposite end of Main.

Like Jake, Eva hadn't been back to the high school for the past ten years. Walking inside to the smell of cafeteria food and the faint odor of the locker rooms, she was struck with a wave of nostalgia so strong it nearly weakened her knees.

It had been within these walls that she had fallen head over heels in love with Jake. He'd walk her to her classes, and they'd talk until the bell rang and he'd have to hurry off before he was tardy for his own class.

After he graduated, when she was still a senior, they'd planned it so he could sneak in a back door for stolen kisses and sweet-talk with her during the days. It had been the happiest time in her entire life.

As they stood in the office waiting for Griff to be brought in, she hazarded a glance at Jake. She was shocked to see him staring at her with the heat of yesteryear burning bright in his eyes.

Would they have made it together if his father hadn't interfered? Would they have really gotten married and lived happily ever after? There was no way to know now. She forced her gaze away from him.

At that moment Griff swaggered into the office and pulled himself up short at the sight of the three of them waiting for him.

"Hey, what's going on here?" he asked indignantly.

"What's she doing here?" He narrowed his brown eyes as he gazed at Eva.

"Mrs. Pritchard, would it be possible for us to use the privacy of your office for a little while?" Wayne asked.

"Of course." The school principal led them to a nice-size room with a large desk and six chairs against the wall.

Wayne quickly rearranged the chairs so Griff sat facing the three adults. Griff was a big, good-looking guy with short blond hair and a confident air that Eva was sure made him very popular with the girls and a leader among the boys.

"What's going on?" he asked the moment Wayne closed the door and then turned to face him. "Why do you want to talk to me again?"

"We just have a few more questions for you, Griff," Wayne said.

"You already asked me questions, and I can tell you I got no more answers for you."

He smirked, and Eva wanted to pinch his impertinent head off his sturdy neck. It was obvious Griff had little respect for Wayne or the other two adults in the room.

"We understand you bought a knife from Riley Kincaid about six months ago," Wayne said.

The smirk on Griff's face quickly disappeared. "Yeah, so what? That's not against the law."

"They are fine-looking knives," Jake said.

"And who are you?" Griff asked.

"My name is Jake Albright."

Griff's eyes darkened. "Albright…why are you here? What do you have to do with anything?"

"I'm here because Eva is a close friend of mine and I

understand you like to party in her barn uninvited," Jake replied. There was a steely strength in his tone.

"I don't know what you're talking about," Griff replied and looked down at his feet.

"We both know that isn't true," Eva said evenly.

"What kind of animal was on your Kincaid knife?" Wayne asked.

Griff frowned. "I don't know… I think it was a wolf or a leopard."

"Which was it?" Jake asked. "A wolf or a leopard?"

"I said I don't remember." Griff's tone held obvious irritation.

"Where's your knife now, Griff?" Wayne asked.

Griff looked at Wayne in surprise. "My knife? Uh… I don't know where it is. I lost it somewhere."

Wayne frowned. "When, exactly, did you lose it?"

Griff shrugged. "I don't know, a couple of months ago. What's the big deal?"

"The big deal is somebody stabbed a cow's heart into my porch railing using one of Kincaid's knives," Eva said.

Griff's eyes widened and then narrowed. "I have nothing to do with that," he exclaimed. "A cow's heart? That's totally disgusting."

"Then where is your knife?" Eva asked. "It's very coincidental that you don't have the knife you bought and Wayne now has one in evidence. Too bad you don't remember where you lost it."

"I did lose it." Griff looked frantically at Jake and then at Wayne. His cheeks grew red. "Okay, some of us sometimes have had parties in her barn. The last time I remember having the knife was at one of the parties, and when I got home I realized it was gone."

"So, you think your knife is someplace in Eva's barn?" Jake asked.

"I think so," Griff replied. He shifted in his chair, obviously uncomfortable. "Can I go back to class now? I had nothing to do with stabbing a cow's heart. That's messed up, and I swear I don't know anything about that."

Wayne looked at Jake and Eva and then back at Griff. "We may be back with more questions, Griff."

Eva stood. "And stay the hell out of my barn."

"What do you think?" Wayne asked a few minutes later when they were outside the school.

"I think he's a sly little creep," Jake replied.

"Do you think he was telling the truth about the knife?" Wayne asked.

"I don't know what to believe, but if that knife is in my barn, I'll find it," Eva said.

"Eva and I can both search the barn so you can work on getting the warrants ready for the convenience stores. You'll stay in touch?" Jake asked.

"Of course," Wayne replied. "And you let me know right away if you find that knife."

He returned to his patrol car, and Jake and Eva got back into the truck. "If Andy ever shows evidence that he's turning into a Griff, I'll lock him in his room for the rest of his life," she said.

Jake laughed. "Trust me, Andy doesn't have an ounce of Griff in him, because he has a mama who is raising him with the right morals and values."

"I hope so," she replied. "I sometimes worry that I'm being too hard on Andy, and then I worry that I'm being too soft on him."

"I think that's normal," Jake replied with a small laugh. "You are an amazing mother, Eva."

"Thanks." She stared out the window. And Jake would be an amazing father. But it was too late for that. If he discovered now that Andy was his son, he would hate her for the years lost. And in his hatred, with his power and money, he could take Andy away from her forever.

Chapter Seven

Eva's barn held the horses' stalls and square bales of hay stacked in the back and hundreds of memories that immediately assailed Jake when they walked inside.

She led him to the back of the barn. "This is where I usually find the most trash after one of their parties," she said. "If Griff lost his knife in here, then it's either in this area or upstairs in the loft. I usually find trash up there, too."

He looked around the hay-covered floor and then back at her. "Then we'll start our search here." He grabbed a pitchfork from the corner and began to move the hay on the earthen floor to one side. She got a lawn rake and began to do the same.

He tried to focus on the task at hand, but he couldn't stop the memories that rushed through his brain. It had been here, in this general area, that he and Eva had given their virginities to each other.

That night she had sneaked out of the house with a blanket to meet him in the barn. He'd brought a kerosene lantern that had provided a cozy glow. It had been a night of sweet exploration and discovery and had led to many more passionate trysts in the barn.

They now worked together, the only sound in the barn

their tools scraping against the floor. He shot her several surreptitious looks, wondering if she was thinking about their past lovemaking, too.

It was impossible to tell what she was thinking at the moment. Her face was devoid of any expression, and she swept the hay with swift, almost angry strokes.

It didn't take long for them to clear the hay from one area and then sweep it back where it belonged. She frowned and leaned against the rake handle.

"This is like literally hunting for a needle in a haystack," she said in obvious frustration. "And we don't even know if Griff was telling the truth about losing the knife in here. For all we know, it was his knife stabbed through that heart."

"You're right, but we need to check in case he was telling the truth. Let's take a quick look around the loft and then we can call it a day," he suggested.

She nodded, and a moment later he followed her up the ladder to the loft. Up here there were more stacks of hay. This area also held a wealth of memories.

It was here that he and she had conducted their very own solemn mock marriage ceremony. They had pledged their hearts and souls to each other, vowing to make the marriage real as soon as she graduated from high school in two months' time.

He looked at her now, with the heat of his thoughts burning inside him. At the same time, her gaze met his. For a moment time seemed to stand still.

He slowly leaned his pitchfork against a stack of hay and took a step toward her…and then another. She didn't back away from him, and that's when he knew she was caught up in the memories as well.

"Eva," he said softly. He reached out and took the rake

from her hand and leaned it against another bale of hay. She stood as still as a beautiful statue.

"Sweet Eva." He reached out and dragged his fingers down the side of her face. She closed her eyes and turned into his caress, giving him the courage to gather her into his arms.

"Do you remember, Eva?" he whispered softly into her ear. "Do you remember how it was between us?"

She opened her eyes, and her lips parted in invitation. That's all he needed. He covered her mouth with his as his arms tightened around her.

Immediately he was half-crazy with the smell of her, with the feel of her soft breasts against his chest and the length of her legs along his own.

Her mouth opened wider to allow his tongue entry, and he took full advantage, swirling his with hers as his pulse accelerated. She was hot in his blood. She always had been, and nothing had changed.

She leaned into him, and one of her arms crept up so her fingers could toy with the hair at the nape of his neck. He moved his lips down the side of her jaw, and she leaned her head back to give him full access to her throat.

Tangling his hands in her thick, silken hair, he couldn't hold back the groan of desire that escaped him. His body had spent the last ten years missing hers, and now to have her back in his arms was beyond wonderful.

"Tell me that you've thought about this…about us over the years," he said. He leaned back slightly so he could see her features.

Her eyes were the deepest violet of dusk and shone with a hunger that nearly stole his breath away. "Yes… yes, I've thought about this." Her voice was barely audible, as if she was reluctantly admitting to a sin.

She stared at him for another long moment, and then she pushed away from him and stepped back. "But I'm not sixteen years old anymore, and I'm not about to have sex in a hayloft with a man who walked out on me ten years ago."

Desire was replaced with stunned surprise. "I didn't walk out on you, Eva. You pushed me out. You told me you were through with me, that you didn't love me anymore."

Her cheeks flushed with color. "Well, you certainly didn't stick around to fight for my love. As I remember, the next day you were on a plane to Italy, and you never looked back."

He raked a hand through his hair and frowned. "Eva, you gutted me that night. I couldn't even think straight. You pulled the rug out from under my life and the future I thought we'd have together."

He paused a moment, his breath caught in his chest as old, painful emotions threatened to overwhelm him. "Eva, did you really think I was going to just hang around here and watch you date other guys? I would have gone totally insane."

For a long moment, their gazes remained locked, and then she looked away and released a tremulous sigh. "I'm sorry about the way things worked out between us, Jake. But we were both so young."

She sighed again and then grabbed both the pitchfork and rake in her hand. "I'm done. Let's get out of here."

He took the tools from her and followed her down the ladder. Once again he leaned the pitchfork and rake in the corner and then turned to look at her.

"Eva, I never stopped loving you."

"Jake, you were in love with a young teenage girl.

I'm not that girl anymore." Her gaze drifted to a place just over his head. "You need to get over the past. Jake, I'm never going to fall in love again. I have no intention of ever marrying again." Her gaze met his once again. "Don't love me, Jake. It's a total waste of your time."

She walked out of the barn, and he slowly followed behind her. He wished it were that easy, that he could just shut off all his emotions where she was concerned.

Had her marriage been so bad that she never wanted to marry again? Or had her marriage been so good she didn't want to try again with anyone else? Were her memories of loving her husband enough to keep her happy for the rest of her life?

"Eva, you can't deny that there's still something between us," he finally said.

"Lust," she replied tersely. "I won't deny that there is a strong physical attraction between us, but that's all it is, and it's something I certainly don't intend to explore."

"That's not the message you were sending to me a few minutes ago," he replied.

Her cheeks flushed a deep pink once again. "And that won't happen again. Jake, I've moved on. I've got enough chaos in my life right now, and I don't need any more."

"I'm sorry, Eva. The last thing I want to do is make your life more difficult." A bit of guilt swept through him. She was right. She had a crazy person after her, and he had been just thinking about his own wants and needs. Totally selfish on his part.

"Let's just move on." She looked away from him again. "And now I've got things to do before Andy gets home from school."

"You'll let me know if you hear anything from Wayne?"

"Of course I will," she replied.

Jake got in his truck and headed home. He'd been foolish to believe that Eva would be open to having a relationship with him right now.

She had a crazy person killing her cattle and making threats on her life. She had no idea who might be a danger to her and how that danger might play itself out.

He was sure she was in no state of mind to think about romance or relationships right now, and he'd been a selfish fool to express his feelings for her at this point in time.

Still, he couldn't imagine that a beautiful, vibrant twenty-eight-year-old woman would completely close herself off from love for the rest of her life. Eventually Andy was going to grow up and move on with his life, and he couldn't imagine Eva would want to be all alone forever.

He'd wait and hope that the perp was caught soon, and then all bets were off and he intended to pursue Eva and make her see that they were really meant to be together forever.

"WE HAD A portion of the fence down on the west side of the pasture this morning," Harley said to Eva.

Jake had left minutes before, and Harley had appeared at the kitchen door. She now sat facing him across the kitchen table. "How did that happen?" she asked.

"Looked to me like it was intentionally pulled down. Thankfully no cattle got out, the fence wasn't damaged and Jimmy and I were able to get it back up."

Eva released a deep sigh. "I swear, if it's not one thing, then it's another."

"At least there were no dead cows this morning," Harley replied. "I can deal with a downed fence."

"Thank goodness for small favors," Eva replied dryly.

"Any news from Wayne on solving this whole mess?"

"Not much, but I have to admit he's working hard on it. Of course he got thrown off for a day with Walter's murder."

Harley frowned. "Hell of a thing, wasn't it? Who would believe that Sadie had that kind of rage pent up inside her? I guess you just never know about people."

"I still find it hard to believe," Eva replied.

"At least it was a quick solve for Wayne."

"Yeah, he said he knew it was Sadie from the very beginning. It was just a matter of how long it was going to take her to confess."

"On a happier note, the herd is looking really good. All of them are nice and healthy."

She flashed a smile to Harley. "Thanks for a bit of good news for a change."

Harley stood. "Well, I just wanted to let you know about the fence. Jimmy and I intend to ride the fence line at dusk tonight to make sure there are no more problems, and we'll check it all again around dawn."

"That's going above and beyond," Eva replied. Neither Jimmy nor Harley lived on Eva's property, and their chores were usually done by five or six in the evening, and they went to their homes. If they intended to be here until dusk tonight, that meant they would be working late.

"We don't mind. We both want to do what we can to help you. We understand these are unusual circumstances. Hopefully Wayne will make the arrests that need to be made in this case and things will get back to normal around here."

Eva got up and walked with him to the back door. "I've almost forgotten what normal is around here."

"Keep your chin up, Eva. You'll get through all this," Harley said with a reassuring smile. "You're as tough as they come."

"Thanks, Harley."

When Harley left, Eva got busy with the daily chores. She tried desperately not to think about what had happened between her and Jake earlier in the barn.

She couldn't allow anything like that to ever happen again. Her desire for Jake was definitely her weakness, and it was a weakness she couldn't afford.

There was a part of her that knew she was being unfair in wanting him to help and support her through the darkness and uncertainty of the danger she found herself in and not wanting any of his other emotions involved.

However, fair or unfair, that was exactly what she wanted and needed from him. She hadn't realized until now how truly isolated she'd become from any other people who might support her through this ordeal. Other than her two ranch hands, she really had nobody else in her life.

Until now…until Jake.

She'd been so busy working to survive, working to keep her ranch so her son would have something for himself when he got older, that she hadn't made any real adult friendships.

When this was all over, maybe it was time she tried to rectify that. There had been times in the past when one of Andy's friends' mothers had invited her for coffee or a quick lunch at the café or drinks in the evening, but Eva had always declined those invitations, telling herself she didn't have time for socializing. And yet she couldn't regret that she'd spent every spare moment when she wasn't working around the ranch with her son.

At least she'd made it clear to Jake that he had no future with her. If he wanted to continue to support her through everything, then he was forewarned that there was nothing else in it for him.

By the time Andy got off the school bus, she'd successfully put all crazy thoughts of Jake, and any other negative thoughts, out of her head. It was impossible to sustain the simmer of fear every minute of every hour of every day. If she allowed her fear to completely consume her, then she'd go mad.

"We have to do the egg deliveries tonight, Mom," Andy said as they walked back to the house from the bus stop.

"I know. All you need to do is package up the eggs and I'll drive you…unless you'd rather me package up all the eggs and you drive me."

Andy laughed. "Mom, you're a silly goofball. You know I can't drive."

"Oh, that's right. I forgot for a minute." As always Andy's laughter warmed her heart. "We'll eat dinner and then head out. In the meantime, you get the deliveries ready to go while I get the meal on the table."

It was just after five thirty when she and Andy got into her pickup to make the rounds of the deliveries. They had six houses to go to this evening, and then Saturday they would make deliveries to half a dozen more people.

Eva didn't give her son an allowance. Instead he earned his money with his egg business. He fed the chickens in the mornings, cleaned out their coops, gathered eggs and then he sold them. She took a percentage of the money he made to buy cartons and feed so he would learn that there was a cost to profit. He had a little record book and was diligent in writing in it after each delivery date. She considered the process a teaching tool, and he was proud of earning the money he got to spend.

She watched him now as he returned to the truck after making his final delivery of the night. "Mrs. Edwards wants four dozen eggs next week instead of two," he said with excitement. "She said she's got family visiting and they all love her deviled eggs."

"That means a little more money in your pocket next week," Eva replied. "Can I tell you a little secret?"

"Yeah, what secret?" Andy looked at her curiously.

"Mrs. Edwards makes the worst deviled eggs I've ever tasted," Eva said.

Andy giggled. "Really?"

"Really. She brought them to the little buffet we all put together after the last school fair, and they were yucky."

Andy giggled again. "At least she's buying extra eggs next week. I was thinking maybe we could celebrate by getting ice cream on the way home," Andy said. "I'll treat you with my own money."

"Hmm, that sounds like an offer I can't resist."

Minutes later they were seated in the ice cream shop with sundaes before them. "Mom, can I ask you a question?" Andy swirled his spoon through his hot fudge.

"You can always ask me anything," she replied.

"When did you know Mr. Jake before?"

"What do you mean?" she asked, not sure she understood.

"He said he was an old friend of yours, but I never saw him before."

"He was my best friend when I was in high school," she replied.

"So, what happened? Why didn't you stay best friends?"

"He went away for work, and then I got married to your daddy and Jake and I just lost touch with each other. Why all the questions?"

"I was just wondering," Andy replied. "I like Mr. Jake a lot. He was so nice to me when we went fishing together."

She wanted to tell her son not to get too attached to Jake, that ultimately he wouldn't be in their lives for long. But of course she didn't say any of that.

In any case, before she could reply, the door to the ice cream parlor swung open and Robert Stephenson and Bobby came in.

Bobby rushed over to where they sat, and the two boys high-fived each other in greeting. "We were just walking by and saw the two of you in here," Robert said. "Mind if we join you?"

"Not at all," Eva replied, although she felt slightly uncomfortable knowing that Robert was on the list of people who had bought a knife from Riley Kincaid. She had no idea if Wayne had spoken to him about it yet or not.

Robert and Bobby got their ice cream and then settled at the table with Eva and Andy. As the boys chattered together, Robert smiled at Eva. "You look really pretty tonight, Eva. Red is definitely a good color for you."

"Thank you," she replied, even more uncomfortable beneath his intense gaze.

Thankfully Andy and Bobby began speaking with the adults about plans for a sleepover the next weekend. Even though it was Eva's turn to have the boys at her house,

Bobby wanted Andy to stay at their home because the two boys had a big puzzle they were working on together that wouldn't transport to Eva's place.

By the time the arrangements had been made, Eva and Andy were finished with their ice cream. "It was nice seeing you, Robert," Eva said as she and Andy got up from the table.

"It's always a pleasure to see you, Eva," he replied.

"Bobby's dad likes you," Andy said when they were back in the truck and heading home. "Bobby told me his dad wants to take you out on a date. If you two got married, then Bobby and I would be brothers."

"Whoa, that's not going to happen," Eva replied. "Bobby's dad seems like a very nice man, but I'm not going to go out on a date with him, and I'm definitely not going to marry him."

"Maybe you could marry Mr. Jake instead. Then he'd be my dad. That would be so cool. I know you like him and he likes you, and I really, really like him."

Eva's heart squeezed tight. "Andy, I can't just marry somebody to give you a dad. There's a lot more to a marriage than that."

"Okay, if I can't have a dad, then could we get a puppy?" He looked at her appealingly.

Eva laughed with more than a little bit of relief. "Now, that's something we can definitely think about."

An hour later Andy was tucked into bed and Eva wandered the house restlessly. It had been a long day, but she wasn't even close to being ready for bed.

She finally grabbed a house key and a cell phone she kept for Andy. She crept into his bedroom and placed the phone on his nightstand. She stood for a long moment just watching him sleep.

She had fallen in love for a second time in her life the moment Andy had been placed in her arms after birth. He'd been a beautiful, good baby who rarely fussed. His presence in the house had brought great joy to a dying man.

Despite being sick, Andrew had tried to be a present father who had played with Andy and had often read bedtime stories to him. He'd helped Eva with the nighttime feedings and had been thrilled when Andy's first word had been *dada*.

The questions Andy had asked about her getting married again so he could have a dad had broken her heart, but that was the one thing she couldn't give him.

Turning away, she left the room and made sure she had her own phone in her pocket. She locked up the house and stepped outside.

The warm night air wrapped around her, and the sky was filled with a million stars. It wasn't unusual for her to leave the house at this time in the evening to check on the horses or finish up some chore or another. If Andy awakened, he knew where she was, and he had the phone to call her.

Tonight not only did she want to give her horses a treat, but she also wanted to spend some more time finishing checking the loft for Griff's knife. If it was up there, she was determined to find it. She just didn't know if Griff had been telling the truth about it or not.

At least she wasn't worried about Griff and his friends showing up unexpectedly to party in the barn—not with Griff knowing Wayne had him in his sights.

She opened the barn door and flipped on the light switch. Nothing happened. "Damn," she muttered beneath her breath. Apparently the lightbulb had burned out, and that particular bulb was a real pain in the neck to replace.

Because the bulb burned out on a fairly regular basis, she kept a flashlight hanging from a hook on the wall just beneath the light switch.

She grabbed the flashlight and flicked it on, shooting a path of illumination ahead of her. She didn't intend to change the bulb tonight, and that canceled out her plan to do any further search for the knife in the loft. But she could still feed the horses some treats before heading back to the house.

The horses seemed restless, sidestepping in their stalls, and as she drew closer to them, she caught a whiff of something that had no business being in a barn. It was the smell of gasoline.

Her stomach clenched, and her adrenaline shot up. She guided the light all around the area in an attempt to find the source. She took another couple of steps forward and then screamed as a dark figure lunged out of the darkness toward her.

The person wore a ski mask and had a pitchfork in his hands. "Wh-who are you? Wh-what do you want?" she asked, her heart nearly exploding in her chest. Her entire body went cold with a deep terror she'd never felt before.

He didn't answer. He stood before her for a long moment and then rushed forward and stabbed the pitchfork at her. She screamed and stumbled backward in an attempt to get away from him. He continued to advance on her, and with a sob of terror she turned to run.

Nobody knew she was out here, and there was nobody to hear her frantic cries for help. *Die, bitch.* The words on the note screamed over and over again in her head.

The flashlight slid from her hand, hit the floor and

immediately went out. She headed toward the door in the distance as fast as she could, aware that he was right behind her. Sheer horror ripped through her. Her breaths escaped her on painful gasps.

He was going to kill her. There was no question in her mind that his intent was to murder her. If he caught her, he was going to use the pitchfork to take her life in a painful, horrid way. In her frantic desire to escape…she tripped.

She slid across the floor on her stomach, all the while struggling to get back up on her feet. She looked behind her just in time to see the pitchfork tines coming down. With another scream, she rolled, and the sharp tines thudded into the floor right next to her body.

As her attacker yanked at the pitchfork, she made it to her feet. However, before she could completely get away, the attacker hit her with the tines in her lower leg, piercing her with excruciating pain.

She hit the floor on her hands and knees. She scrabbled forward, sobbing and terrified that the pitchfork would strike her again, this time in the back. Instead, nothing happened. Rolling over on her back, she realized her attacker was gone.

"Mrs. Eva?"

The familiar voice came out of the darkness by the barn door. "Oh my God…what happened? Mrs. Eva… are you okay?"

"Jimmy? Jimmy, is that you?" Sobs escaped her, sobs of both pain and relief.

"It's me, Mrs. Eva." He ran to her side and crouched down next to her.

"Please…help me up," she cried. Had the attacker heard Jimmy's approach and run off? Or was he still hiding out somewhere in the barn? "Please, Jimmy, get me out of here right now."

She could scarcely think straight. "Did you see him? H-he was in the barn, and he attacked me with the pitchfork."

"I'm sorry, I didn't see anyone," Jimmy replied. "I just heard you scream, and I knew something was wrong."

Fear still torched through her, along with the pain in her leg. Jimmy helped her to her feet and slowly walked with her to the house.

Tears half blinded her as she fumbled to unlock the front door. When it opened she almost fell inside. "You're hurt," Jimmy exclaimed, as if noticing the blood on her pants leg for the first time. "What can I do to help?"

"Call Wayne," she managed to gasp through her tears. "And check out the barn. I thought I smelled gasoline in there. But be careful. Whoever attacked me might still be there."

"Don't worry about me, Mrs. Eva. If anyone is out there, I'll shoot the bastard first." Jimmy pulled his gun from his holster. "Are you sure you don't want me to stay here with you?"

"No, I'll be fine until Wayne gets here." With her thoughts still so jumbled in fear, she didn't want anyone in the house with her unless it was Wayne. She couldn't believe what had just happened to her.

Once Jimmy stepped back outside, she locked the door behind him and hobbled into her bedroom. She got her shotgun from the gun case and then returned to the living room. Tears of pain, of fear, still coursed down her cheeks.

She felt as if she was trapped in a nightmare or had entered some kind of horrible twilight zone. She couldn't believe somebody had attacked her. She turned her leg to try to look at her wounds.

"Mom?" Andy appeared in the living room doorway.

She quickly swiped at her cheeks. "Go back to bed, Andy."

"But Mom, you're bleeding." His eyes were wide and alarmed as he looked first at the blood on her jeans leg and then at the gun she had leaning up next to her. "What's happening? Mom, what's going on?"

"Honey, what I need for you to do right now is go back to your room. I'm okay, and everything is going to be fine." Dear God, she didn't want her son to see her this way. "The sheriff is coming to talk to me, and I need you to go back to your room and close the door and go to sleep."

Andy eyed her worriedly for another long moment and then did what he was told and went back to his room.

She needed to clean up her leg, but at the moment she couldn't move as an icy chill filled her heart and soul. She still felt as if she were in a nightmare. But unfortunately this wasn't a dream. It was reality, and the truth of the matter was somebody had just tried to kill her.

Chapter Eight

Jake poured himself a shot of scotch from the mini-bar and then sank down on the sofa in his suite. He grabbed the remote and turned on his television. Tonight he needed a distraction from his thoughts. It had been a long, emotional day, and even now he couldn't seem to shrug off thoughts of Eva. He was hoping a silly sit-com would empty his mind or at least make him sleepy.

He'd just found what he intended to watch when his cell phone rang and Eva's name came up on the caller identification. Why would she be calling him? Maybe she'd heard some news from Wayne?

"Eva?" he answered.

"No, it's me. It's Andy. Mr. Jake, my mom is bleeding on her leg and she's crying. Maybe could you come over here?"

The boy's voice shook with obvious fear, and his words shot an equal amount of apprehension through Jake. "I'm on my way, Andy. I'll be there as quick as I can."

"Okay," Andy replied with obvious relief. "Thanks, Mr. Jake."

Minutes later Jake was in his truck and driving as fast as possible to Eva's ranch. She was bleeding? Had she somehow cut herself? Jake should have asked Andy more questions, like where she was bleeding from? What had happened to her? How badly was she hurt?

He stepped on the accelerator to go even faster, grateful that there was little traffic to get in his way. His heart beat a frantic rhythm. Why hadn't Eva called him herself? Was she too incapacitated to make a phone call?

What in the hell had happened?

It seemed like it took him forever, but he finally pulled up in front of her place, cut his engine and jumped out of his truck. He raced to the door and banged on it. "Eva… Andy, it's me. Open the door."

After a long moment, the door opened and Eva collapsed into his arms. He held her tight as she sobbed into the crook of his neck. Thank God she wasn't hurt so badly that she hadn't been able to get to the door and into his arms. But she was obviously hurt, because she was weeping and clinging to him.

He let her cry for a few minutes and then pulled her arms from around his neck, leaned back and looked at her. "Eva, what happened?" he finally asked. Her eyes were dark with unmistakable fear.

He led her to the sofa, and it was then he saw the blood on the back of the lower leg of her jeans and the shotgun leaned against the corner of the couch. "You're bleeding. Honey, what happened?" he repeated.

"Wh-what are you doing here?" She spoke between barely suppressed sobs.

"Andy called me. He sounded scared and he told me you were bleeding and crying. What happened to your leg?"

"I was attacked by a man with a pitchfork in the barn

and I… I think…no, I know he…he meant to kill me." She began to cry once again.

Between her tears, she told him what had happened from the time she had entered the barn to when Jimmy had helped her back to the house. When she was finished, a rich rage coupled with a chilling fear lodged in his chest.

"Let's take a look at your leg," he said. At least she was able to walk.

He knelt down in front of her, and he rolled up her jeans leg so he could get a look at the puncture wounds. There were two, but thankfully they had mostly stopped bleeding. "Maybe we should get you to the hospital to get these checked out."

"No, that's not necessary," she protested. "They hurt, but I don't think they're as deep as I originally thought. I was scurrying across the barn floor as fast as I could, and so I guess he only got a quick, glancing jab into me."

The vision her words created in his head once again filled him with a deep anger. Dammit, who was this person and why would he want to hurt Eva?

"Let me get a warm cloth so we can clean you up. Do you have some antibiotic cream?"

"There's a medical kit in the hall closet, and there's some antibiotic cream in it," she replied.

He stood, but before he could walk to the hall closet to get a cloth, Wayne showed up.

Jake let the lawman into the house, and while he began to question Eva, Jake got the washcloth and the medical tin box and then sat next to Eva to wipe the blood off the wounds and get some antibiotic cream on them.

As she recounted to Wayne what had happened in the

barn, his fear for her once again tightened his chest. "Did you get a look at the person?" Wayne asked. "Anything that might help identify him or her?"

"I'm pretty sure it was a male by the brief view I had of his size. But he wore a ski mask, and I couldn't begin to identify who he was. The barn was dark, and I only had a minute before I lost the flashlight."

Jake finished tending to her leg and then returned to sit beside her. "I was so stupid," Eva said angrily. "With everything that's been going on, I should have never gone out to the barn by myself after dark. When the light didn't work, I should have immediately turned around and run to the house."

"Can you tell me anything else about the attack or your attacker?" Wayne asked.

"It all just happened so fast." She raised a hand to her temple and rubbed it as if trying to alleviate a headache. "He seemed to come out of nowhere. Other than believing it was a male, I can't think of anything else. I'm sorry. I… I was just so afraid."

"It's all right, Eva…take your time," Jake said. All he really wanted to do was draw her back into his arms once again until he knew there was no more danger to her and no more fear inside her.

"I really believe he would have killed me if Jimmy hadn't shown up when he did," she replied. "I sensed a hatred coming from him. At one point if I hadn't rolled away in time, the pitchfork would have struck me in my back. Why does somebody hate me enough to kill me?"

Jake frowned. "What was Jimmy doing out around there at this time of night?"

"I… I don't know," Eva replied with a frown of her own. "Harley told me earlier that he and Jimmy were going to check the fence line around dusk, but dusk was a long time ago."

"Where's Jimmy now?" Wayne asked.

"I sent him back to the barn. Right before the attack, I thought I smelled gasoline."

"Gasoline?" Another alarm shot off in Jake. It would take very little to set a fire that would destroy not only the barn, but also the horses that were inside.

"I'll call in some men to check out the barn. Do you mind if I bring Jimmy in here to ask him some questions?" Wayne asked.

"That's fine," Eva replied.

Jake was definitely interested in finding out why Jimmy had been hanging around the barn at this time of the night. Although he was grateful the attack had been stopped before Eva had gotten hurt even more, he also found it damned odd that Jimmy had been there at all.

As Wayne stepped outside to get Jimmy, Jake put his arm around Eva and pulled her closer against his side. He could feel small tremors shaking her body, and he hated that she was obviously still so afraid.

"Could you do me a favor?" she asked.

"Of course," he replied.

"Would you go check in on Andy? He saw me when I was crying, and he noticed I was bleeding. I know he's probably in there scared to death right now."

"I'll go talk to him." Jake got up and went down the hallway to Andy's room. He knocked softly and then opened the door.

A night-light illuminated the room enough that Jake could see that Andy was wide-awake. "Mr. Jake," he said and sat up.

"Hey, buddy, how are you doing?" Jake walked over and sat on the edge of the bed.

"I'm okay, but is my mom okay? She was bleeding and she got out her gun."

"She's just fine."

"I heard Sheriff Black here. What happened to my mom, Mr. Jake?"

Jake hesitated a moment before replying. He decided the boy deserved the truth instead of some made-up story. "Somebody bad was hiding in the barn and tried to hurt your mom," Jake explained. "But I'm going to make sure nothing like that ever happens again. Now, what you need to do is get to sleep. You have school tomorrow."

"Maybe I shouldn't go to school." Worry still laced Andy's voice. "Maybe I should stay home to help protect my mom."

Jake smiled at him. "Andy, your job is to go to school, and you need to let the grown-ups take care of your mother. Now everything is fine for the night, so you need to get to sleep."

"Thanks, Mr. Jake." Andy settled back in the bed, and then Jake pulled the sheet up around the boy and leaned down and kissed him on the forehead.

"Stop worrying, Andy. I promise you that everything is going to be just fine."

"I'm glad you came."

"I'm glad I'm here, too. I'm glad you thought to call me. Now, get to sleep." Jake got up and left the room.

He returned to Eva's side just as Wayne led Jimmy into the house. Jimmy immediately looked at Eva. "Are you all right, Mrs. Eva?"

"I will be," she replied.

"I'm so sorry you got hurt. I wish I'd gotten to you sooner." He looked at her mournfully.

"Why were you here at all?" Eva asked.

"I just thought I'd hang around a little later than usual and keep an eye on things. I know somebody has been causing you bad problems, and I just figured I'd check things out before heading home and going to bed. I was hoping to catch somebody causing trouble for you so it would all stop."

"Did you see the perpetrator?" Wayne asked.

"No. All I saw was Mrs. Eva on the floor. I wish I had seen him. I wish I'd caught him," Jimmy exclaimed.

As Wayne continued to question Jimmy, Jake's mind whirred with a dozen emotions. His heart ached with Eva's fear. He was afraid for her, too. He was also enraged by what had happened and angry that a nine-year-old boy had the burden of being afraid for his mother's welfare.

He was also suspicious of Jimmy's story. Had the man orchestrated the attack on Eva and then rushed in to be a hero? The young man looked at Eva as if she hung the sun each morning. There was no question he had a crush on Eva. Had he attacked her and then "saved" her?

Jake spoke those suspicions aloud once Wayne sent Jimmy home. By that time Wayne's men had arrived to check out the barn.

"Those same thoughts about Jimmy crossed my mind, too," Wayne admitted. "At this point everyone is a suspect. It's too bad Eva didn't see the perpetrator and Jimmy at the same time."

"I just assumed the attacker heard Jimmy's approach and ran away, and then Jimmy showed up," Eva replied.

"But you didn't see which way he ran, right?" Wayne asked.

"I didn't," she replied.

"And you didn't see exactly where Jimmy came from, right?" Wayne said.

Eva frowned. "I'm pretty sure he came in the main barn entrance. It's all so jumbled in my head right now."

Jake was grateful that the tremors he'd felt in her earlier were finally gone, but she still appeared small and achingly vulnerable. Once again Wayne left to go out and check with his men in the barn.

As he stepped out of the house, Eva released a weary sigh. "I can't believe this happened. I feel like I'm in a nightmare, and no matter how hard I try I can't wake up."

Jake tightened his arm around her. "I'm just grateful you weren't hurt even more. This could have had a tragic ending."

"Was Andy okay?" she asked.

"He was worried about you, but I told him to leave the worrying to the grown-ups and that you were going to be just fine."

"Thank you, Jake." She released a shudder. "The man wanted to kill me. I believe he really wanted to kill me." She crossed her arms in front of her so she was hugging herself. "I… I didn't really think it would come to this… that the written threats would become a physical reality."

"I had certainly hoped it wouldn't come to this," Jake said. "But now we know just how serious the situation is."

Eva leaned her head back against his arm and closed her eyes. He gazed at her face and vowed to himself that he would do whatever was necessary to keep her and her son safe.

He didn't know how much time passed before Wayne came back into the house. "The deputies are still out there looking for clues, but I came back inside to tell you that it appears somebody was going to set the barn on fire."

Eva sat up straighter. "So I did smell gasoline."

Wayne nodded. "There was a small stack of hay with several pieces of kindling smothered with fuel. All it was waiting for was a lit match. Maybe it was possible you interrupted him attempting to set a fire and that's why he came after you."

"If he didn't really want to hurt her, then why attack her at all? If she interrupted him, then why didn't he just slink away into the night instead of going after her with a pitchfork?" Jake asked. "The barn was dark. No light was on. Hell, he could have hid in a stall until Eva left. So, I repeat, why go after her?"

None of them had the answer. "Have you had a chance to question Robert Stephenson about owning a Kincaid knife?" Eva asked.

Jake gazed at her in surprise. "Why would you think of that right now?"

She told them about Robert and his son joining her and Andy in the ice cream place. "He keeps kind of asking me out, and I keep rejecting him." She shrugged her shoulders. "I don't know who to trust anymore. I mean, it could be a couple of teenagers led by Griff, or the father of my son's best friend, or my own ranch hand or somebody else not even on our radar." She seemed to get smaller and smaller with each word.

"We're going to get to the bottom of this, Eva," Wayne said. "I've already taken your pitchfork into evidence. Hopefully we'll be able to pull up some prints. My men are going through the barn with fine-tooth combs looking for any evidence. Maybe he dropped something or left something behind that will help us along."

"There won't be any fingerprints," Eva replied, her voice sounding hollow. "And you won't find any evidence, either. Whoever is behind all this is really smart."

"They aren't that smart," Wayne protested. "They left a knife for us to use to identify them."

"A knife made by a man who sells lots of knives," Eva replied. She reached up and once again rubbed her temple. "I'm sorry. I'm tired and scared, and I just want this person to be caught."

Jake got to his feet and looked at Wayne. "Can you stay here with Eva until I get back?"

"Sure, but where are you going?" he asked.

"I'm going home to pack a few bags, and then I'm moving in here." He didn't give Eva a chance to protest. As quickly as the words left his mouth, he was out her front door.

He drove quickly. He hoped Eva didn't fight him on this. If she didn't agree to him moving in with her, then he would sleep in his truck outside her front door. He would camp out in her front yard so that whoever was after her wouldn't get another chance to hurt her.

When he reached the house, he was about to go up the stairs to get his things when David stepped into the hallway and stopped him. "Hey, man, what's happening? You've been like a ghost around here."

Stephanie stepped up behind David. "We were just having a glass of wine before bed. Why don't you join us, Jake? We've scarcely seen you since you've been home."

"No, I'm sorry, but I've got to go," Jake replied.

"Go where?" David asked. "Can't you sit and visit with us for just a few minutes?"

"I can't. There's been some trouble at Eva's place. I'm packing some bags and moving in there," Jake explained.

"Oh Jake," Stephanie said softly.

"What are you doing? Jake, don't you remember what happened the last time you had anything to do with her?" David said. "She broke you, man. She totally destroyed you."

"She needs me right now," Jake replied. "She's all alone in that place with her son, and bad things have been happening to her."

"Let the sheriff protect her," David replied with obvious frustration. "Jake, I don't want to see you hurt by her again. The last time she hurt you, I lost my brother for ten years."

"David, I need to do this, and if I get hurt in the process, so be it. I'm a big boy. Now, I've got to get moving." He didn't wait for his brother to say anything more, instead he thundered up the stairs to his suite.

It was true that when Jake had gone to Italy, his relationship with his younger brother had suffered tremendously. Although they had spoken on the phone and video chatted whenever possible, it hadn't been the same as spending life together on a day-to-day basis.

A half an hour later, he was again in his truck and headed back to Eva's. He understood his brother not wanting him to be involved with Eva again, but there was no way Jake was walking away from her, especially now. No matter what happened between them in the future, he would be there for her right now.

He wanted to protect her from any and all danger. Aside from that, he was hoping they could reclaim the love he believed they'd once had for each other.

This was either going to end with him planning a future with the woman he loved, or he'd suffer the second greatest heartache he'd ever had in his life.

Chapter Nine

The minute Jake got back to the house and dropped two duffel bags inside the front door, there was a part of Eva that wanted him to immediately pick the bags up and go back to his house. However, there was a bigger part of her that was still shaken and frightened and didn't want to be alone.

She figured she'd let him stay with her for the remainder of the night, and then she'd ask him to leave first thing in the morning. There was no real reason for him to move in here permanently.

"I'll get you a pillow and a blanket so you'll be more comfortable," she said to Jake once Wayne and his men were finally gone. "You can sleep out here on the sofa." She steeled herself for him to say something about wanting to sleep with her.

Instead he merely nodded. "That works for me. But I'd like your bedroom door and Andy's door open for the rest of the night. Just in case there is any more trouble. I need to be able to hear you if either of you cry out."

"Don't even tempt fate to bring more trouble here tonight," she replied wearily. "I'm too tired to deal with anything else. I'll be right back." She disappeared down the hallway to get the things for him.

She returned to the living room with a bed pillow and a throw blanket. "Does Andy know about gun safety?" he asked as he took the items from her. He gestured toward his gun, which was now on the coffee table. "I'd like to keep this here for easy access in the night."

"Andy knows his gun safety, and you don't have to worry about him touching your gun," she replied.

"That's good to know. Do you want to go straight to bed, or would you like to talk for a little while? Maybe try to decompress a little bit?" he asked.

"I think I'm ready to go to bed." She released another weary sigh. "I just want to fall asleep and try to forget what happened tonight." Even though she said the words, she knew she couldn't sleep long enough or hard enough to forget the horrifying events of the night.

"How is your leg?"

"It hurts, but not too bad. I did a stupid thing by going to the barn, and I just still feel a little overwhelmed by everything that happened tonight. I'm sure I'll feel much better in the morning."

"I hope so, and I hope you sleep well," he said.

"Thanks. I'll see you in the morning." She turned and walked down the hallway. When she got to Andy's room, she opened the door and was grateful to see that he was sleeping.

She hated that he'd seen her weeping and so scared. She hated that he'd been so frightened he had called Jake. However, she had to admit she'd sleep easier tonight knowing Jake was in the house.

Once she was in her own bedroom, she stripped off her jeans and threw them into the corner. Tomorrow they would make their way into the trash. Even if they hadn't been ruined by the pitchfork, she would have thrown them away anyway.

She then finished undressing and pulled on a cool, short, sleeveless blue nightgown. She peeked out of her room and, not seeing Jake lurking nearby, she hurried into the bathroom, where she washed her face and brushed her teeth.

For several long moments, she stared at her reflection in the mirror. What had she done to warrant the kind of vitriol, the kind of killing rage that somebody had for her? Who was behind these attacks on her? The mirror had no answers to her questions.

Minutes later she was in her bed. She curled up on her side facing the open doorway as the events of the night played and replayed through her mind.

There was no question that with everything that had been going on, she'd been incredibly brainless in going to the barn all alone after dark. But who could have guessed that a man with a pitchfork would come after her?

As her mind filled with a vision of the dark figure with a pitchfork, she shivered despite the warmth of the room. There was a well of iciness inside her that no amount of blankets could warm. It was a cold deep in her soul created from the knowledge that somebody wanted her dead. And that somebody had nearly succeeded tonight.

It had been difficult to explain to Wayne the utter hatred she'd felt emanating from her attacker. It was hard to make the lawman understand that there had been no question in her mind that the attacker wanted to kill her. He hadn't merely been trying to scare her out of the barn. She'd been running away when he'd attacked and used that pitchfork like a weapon to kill.

She finally fell asleep and into fitful dreams of being chased by a masked figure through the night. They were horrid nightmares of near death. It was with relief that she awakened as the sun was just beginning to peek over the horizon.

As she dressed, the scent of fresh coffee wafted from the kitchen, letting her know that Jake was already up. She was far more clearheaded this morning than she'd been the night before.

While she had appreciated his presence in the house last night, she felt confident in sending him home this morning. She was now forewarned that somebody wanted to do her physical harm. She would make sure she didn't make any more stupid mistakes that might put her at risk. But the last thing she needed was Jake in her personal space.

She entered the kitchen and found him seated at the table. He looked far too appealing with his sleep-tossed hair, his bare feet and clad in a white T-shirt and jeans.

"Good morning," he said. "I hope you don't mind. I made some coffee."

"Mind?" She smiled at him. "I thank you." She walked over to the pot and poured herself a cup and then joined him at the table.

"How did you sleep?" he asked.

"Actually, I had a few nightmares," she admitted after a moment's hesitation. "I was glad to wake up and escape from them."

"I'm sorry," he replied, his dark eyes expressing the sentiment. "How does your leg feel?"

"A little sore, but it's okay. How did you sleep?" she asked.

"With one eye open," he replied with an easy grin. "Actually, I found your sofa pretty comfortable."

"That's good." She figured she'd tell him he didn't need to spend another night here after she made breakfast and got Andy off to school. That way if he argued with her, they wouldn't be having the argument in front of her son.

"What do you have on tap for today?" he asked.

"The usual—chores, and I need to go into town for some groceries," she replied. "I refuse to give this person all my power. My daily life certainly can't stop because of all of this going on."

"Of course it can't," he agreed easily. "We all just have to be smarter going forward."

She released a small laugh. "Oh, trust me. I'm well aware of that." She took a couple more sips of her coffee and then got up. "Bacon and scrambled eggs for breakfast?"

"Sounds good to me," he replied.

"I'm going to start the bacon, and then I'll get Andy up for school." She pulled a pound of bacon out of the fridge and began to place the slices into a skillet.

"I'd better go clean up before Andy is up," Jake said. "Do you mind if I take a quick shower?"

"Go ahead. Towels are under the sink."

She breathed a little easier as he left the kitchen. He'd looked far too attractive seated at her kitchen table with his morning stubble on his jaw and the early-morning light shining on his dark, sleep-mussed hair.

By the time the bacon was crisp and out of the skillet, Jake came back into the kitchen, smelling of minty soap and his shaving cream. He'd exchanged his T-shirt for a navy blue short-sleeved shirt.

"I'm going to go wake Andy," she said.

"Is there anything I can do to help with breakfast?" he asked.

"Just get yourself another cup of coffee and relax. I've got this." She needed to stay busy, to keep her mind relatively empty, otherwise she'd fall back into the abject fear that she'd felt all night long.

She walked down the hallway and into Andy's room. He was sleeping so peacefully she hated waking him. But he needed to get up and get ready for school.

"Hey, buddy," she said and sank down on the edge of his mattress. "It's time to get up." She reached out and swept a strand of his dark hair away from his forehead.

His eyes fluttered open, and he offered her a sleepy smile. "Hi, Mom."

"Good morning," she replied. "Breakfast is in fifteen minutes. You need to get up and dressed for school."

He stretched and nodded. She got up and left him. He'd always been easy to get up in the mornings, and she was grateful that this morning was like all the others. However, she knew he had been awake late last night and suspected that he might be in bed a little earlier tonight.

"That didn't take long," Jake said when she returned to the kitchen.

"He's always been an easy kid to get up in the mornings." She got the bread ready to pop down in the toaster and then set to scrambling eggs in a bowl.

"There was a time it took nothing short of a bomb to get me up in the mornings," Jake said. "When I was about Andy's age, it took the housekeepers dozens of efforts to get me out of bed."

She turned and smiled at him. "You never told me that about yourself before."

He laughed. "Thankfully it was something I grew out of. I realized a real cowboy had to be up before dawn, and you know more than anything I wanted to be a real cowboy."

"And now you finally get to be the cowboy you always wanted to be," she replied.

"I do," he agreed. "Although I really won't be completely happy until I'm working on my own ranch instead of the family ranch."

"Would you want to stay around the Dusty Gulch area or head to fresher pastures?" she asked.

"Oh, I'd definitely stay in Dusty Gulch," he replied. "Now that I'm finally back here, I can't imagine living anyplace else."

She poured the eggs into the waiting skillet, and for just a few minutes a comfortable silence reigned between them. His answer to her question about living elsewhere hadn't surprised her. Even as a teenager, Jake had shared with her his love for Dusty Gulch. She'd just popped the bread down to toast when Andy came into the kitchen.

"Mr. Jake! You're still here," Andy said with delight.

"I'm going to be here for a while," Jake replied. "I want to stay here until the bad man who tried to hurt your mother last night is in jail."

"I'm so glad." Andy slid into the chair next to Jake. "If you weren't here, then I'd be really, really worried." Andy looked at Eva as she set his plate before him. "We want Mr. Jake here, don't we? We need him here, right, Mom?"

Eva stared into Andy's worried eyes and felt a sinking sensation in the pit of her stomach. How could she possibly send Jake away now, knowing his presence here made her son feel less afraid?

She would never forget the scared look on Andy's face the night before, and she never, ever wanted to see it again on his beautiful face. And if that meant Jake had to stay here, then she would swallow her discomfort for the sake of her son.

As they ate breakfast, Jake teased Andy and recounted silly times in Jake's own childhood that made Andy laugh over and over again. Eva's heart warmed, and it continued to stay warm as the three of them headed down the lane so Andy could meet his school bus.

This had been Eva's dream at one time…her and Jake together and taking care of their children. She'd once been so certain that it was what her future held. Unfortunately, it had only taken one threat from Justin Albright to change the path of her future.

She shoved these thoughts aside. They had no place in her head anymore. She would put up with Jake being in her personal space for the sake of her son, but that didn't mean she was inviting Jake anywhere near her heart.

THE MINUTE THEY returned to the house, Harley knocked on the back door, and Eva let him in. He looked in surprise at Jake, who had just sunk back down in a chair at the table.

"Good morning, Mr. Albright," he said to Jake.

"Back at you," Jake replied. "And it's Jake."

"Sit, Harley," Eva said. "I'll pour you a cup of coffee."

Harley sat next to Jake and looked at Eva. "Jimmy filled me in on what happened last night. I wanted to come in and see for myself that you were really okay."

Eva set the coffee cup before him and then joined them at the table. "As you can see, I'm fine."

"Thank God for that," Harley replied. "According to

Jimmy, you were bloody from head to toe and screaming when he found you."

"That's a bit of an exaggeration, although I was definitely screaming and crying. Whoever was in the barn managed to stab me in the back of my leg with a pitchfork before Jimmy showed up," Eva explained.

Just talking about it darkened her eyes with what Jake knew was fear, and there was nothing he would like more than to have fifteen minutes alone with the attacker. He would beat the man to a bloody pulp for what he'd done to her. He would beat him and then see to it that the person spent the rest of his life in jail. What the perpetrator had done last night was attempted murder.

"Jimmy also told me the person intended on setting a fire in the barn." Harley shook his head. "Thank God that didn't happen. As dry and windy as it's been, the entire barn would have gone up in flames in minutes. I'd sure like to know who the hell is behind all this. I wouldn't mind taking him out behind the barn and beating the hell out of him."

"That makes two of us," Jake replied fervently.

As Harley and Eva began to talk about ranch business, Jake sat back in his chair and studied the man Eva obviously depended on not only as a ranch foreman but also as a friend.

Did Harley have some kind of a secret grudge against Eva?

Harley had access to all the cattle and the barn. After seven years of working for her, he probably knew her routine. He might have been able to guess that she would go into the barn last night.

Had he at some time or another bought one of Kincaid's knives and paid cash for it? And if he had, did he still have that knife, or had he used it to stab a cow's heart into Eva's porch?

Jake frowned and stared down into his coffee cup. He didn't trust anyone right now, and that included the two ranch hands who worked for Eva.

Eva and Harley talked for another fifteen minutes or so, and then Harley left to head out to the pastures.

"I don't know what chores you have to do this morning, but the one thing I don't want you to do is get on the back of a horse and ride around in the pastures," Jake said as soon as Harley had left.

She frowned. "What harm could come from that?"

"Eva, I can't protect you if you're out in an open pasture. If somebody really wants you dead, then all it would take is a bullet," he replied. "And even though I would love for you to believe I'm a superhero, I can't stop a speeding bullet that might be aimed at your head or your heart."

She stared at him for a long moment and then stood and slammed her palms down on the table. "I hate this. I hate being afraid. I hate that my son is afraid, and I'm so angry that my entire life has been turned upside down because of some creep lurking in the shadows." Her eyes blazed with anger.

"I know, Eva, and I'm so sorry for what you're going through." He moved his hands to cover hers. "If I could fix this for you, I would." Her hands were so small and tensed beneath his. "I want this to be over as soon as possible, but right now all I can do is my very best to try and keep you safe."

He felt the tension in her hands slowly soften just before she pulled them away. "I know, and I appreciate it. Am I at least allowed a trip to the grocery store?"

He smiled at her. "I think we can manage that. I'll help you clear up the dishes, and then we can be on our way."

For the next few minutes, they cleaned up the kitchen in silence. He sensed that she wasn't in the mood for idle conversation right now. She worked with a single-minded focus to load the dishwasher and then looked up at him. "I'll go get ready to leave."

Jake went into the living room and pulled on his holster. With his gun hanging from his hip, he felt ready for almost anything…almost.

However, he didn't expect any trouble from just a simple trip into town. Once they arrived there, they would be surrounded by other people, and an attack on Eva where there were witnesses around would be stupid on the perp's part. Unfortunately it was obvious the man wasn't stupid.

His breath caught deep in his throat as she came back into the living room. She'd lengthened her already sinfully long, dark lashes with mascara, and a pink gloss covered her lips. The makeup, coupled with her bright blue blouse and tight jeans, shot his adrenaline just a little bit higher.

"I'm all ready to go," she said.

"You look very nice."

Her cheeks colored a dusty pink beneath his gaze. "Thanks."

They left the house and got into his truck, and he headed toward town. "It's a beautiful day," he said once they'd been driving for a few miles.

"Do you really want to talk about the weather?" she asked wryly.

He flashed her a quick smile. "Not really, but I was afraid of an awkward silence building up between us."

A small laugh escaped her. "And as I remember, you never did like any kind of silence to grow between us."

"I always figured if you got quiet it meant you were mad at me for something," he admitted. "And I could never stand the idea of you being angry with me for anything."

"I fully intended to probably make you angry this morning," she said.

"How so?" He looked at her curiously and then gazed back at the road.

"I had every intention of telling you to take your bags and go back home, that I was fine alone, but then Andy said he felt so much better with you in the house, and now I realize I'm stuck with you."

"Eva, why would you send me home when I'm just another layer of protection for you?" He didn't wait for her to answer. "If you had kicked me out of your house this morning, then I would have camped out in my truck outside your front door in an effort to keep you safe. I don't intend to go away until whoever is after you is in jail."

"Then we need to have rules while you're in the house," she said.

"Rules? What kind of rules?"

"First of all, you need to make sure you're out of the bathroom when it's time for Andy to get ready for school."

"That's an easy rule to follow," he replied agreeably. "What else?"

"You don't try to discipline Andy. If you have a problem with him, you bring it to me, and I'll discipline him."

"Eva, I would never overstep boundaries where Andy is concerned," he said.

"Okay, and last, you sleep on the sofa and you don't try to seduce me to get into my bed."

He laughed. "I can't help it that I'm naturally seductive." He glanced at her in time to see her glare at him.

"I'm being serious here, Jake."

"Okay, I agree to sleep on the sofa and not try to get into your bed. To be honest, I'd sleep on the floor in the hallway if I thought that would keep you safe."

"Thank you, Jake. I really appreciate you doing this, especially since Andy feels so much better with you in the house," she replied.

By that time, they had arrived at the grocery store. They were just about to go inside when they nearly bumped into a man coming out.

"Eva," he greeted her with obvious warmth and then looked at Jake. "Hello, I'm Robert Stephenson." He shifted the grocery bag in his arm and held out his hand to Jake.

"Jake Albright," he replied and shook the man's hand. So, this was Andy's friend's father…the man who had an interest in Eva and was also an owner of a Kincaid knife.

"I was just picking up some snacks for the boys' overnight next Friday," Robert said.

"You should let me contribute to the cause," Eva replied. "It's bad enough it seems lately they are always at your house instead of mine."

"Nonsense," Robert replied, his gaze lingering on her. Jake wanted to tell the man to stop looking at her like she was a tasty treat he'd like to enjoy.

"I never have any trouble with Andy," the man continued. "In fact, I consider him a good influence on my son."

Eva laughed. "That's nice to hear. And I feel the same way about Bobby."

Robert's smile turned into a frown of concern. "Sheriff Black came to my office and spoke to me yesterday. Why didn't you tell me about all the problems you've been having at your ranch?"

"Did Wayne talk to you about a knife?" Jake asked, consciously interjecting himself into the conversation.

"He did, and I showed him my knives. I have a whole collection of Kincaid knives. The handles are so intricately carved, I find them real works of art."

"How many of them do you own?" Jake wanted to know anything that might further the investigation.

"I believe right now I have a dozen."

"How did you pay for the knives you own?" Jake asked.

Robert shot him a cool look. "I explained all that to Wayne. And now I need to get these groceries home. Eva, it's always a pleasure, and it was nice meeting you, Jake."

"I want to talk to Wayne about him," Jake said once Robert was gone and he and Eva were inside the store. "What I'm concerned about is, whoever left that knife in your porch, there's nothing stopping them from buying a replacement to show Wayne."

"Jeez, thanks. You just gave me something else to worry about," Eva said dryly.

"I'm just trying to look at this from all angles," he replied. "And now, let's go buy a cake or some ice cream. I'm in the mood for something sweet."

Their moods lightened as they shopped. It was funny to him that even food brought back memories of the time when they'd been together and he'd eaten most of his evening meals with her and her father.

"Remember that time when you tried to make that soufflé?" he asked as they went up the baking aisle.

She nodded, and her eyes filled with merriment. "I'd been watching a cooking show on television and decided I wanted to start cooking more sophisticated foods."

"And when the soufflé fell flat, you cried like a baby," he replied. She'd cried in his arms, devastated by the cooking failure. "But you've always been an amazing cook."

"That's because my father was a good cook and taught me everything I know," she replied. She released a deep sigh. "I still miss him."

"I don't think grief ever really goes away. If you're lucky and well adjusted, you eventually find a small space in your heart to tuck it away into so you can keep moving forward in your life."

She smiled up at him. "Sometimes, Jake Albright, you can be a very wise man."

He laughed. "I try."

They finished buying the groceries, packed them in the truck bed and then headed for home. Jake had just left the outskirts of town when he glanced in his rearview mirror and saw a pickup truck coming up fast behind him.

Adrenaline fired through him, and he tightened his hands on the steering wheel. "Hold on to your seat. There's a pickup coming up fast on us."

Eva shot a glance out the back window and then looked at Jake. "Do you think whoever is driving it is after me?"

"I don't know," he replied tersely, his gaze divided between the rearview mirror and the road ahead. The suspicious truck kept coming way too fast, and it drew up right on Jake's bumper.

Was it going to try to ram Jake's bumper? Would the driver try to wreck Jake in an effort to get to Eva? Would somebody fire a gun at them? Certainly it was possible somebody could shoot him in order to get to Eva. He could become collateral damage. His stomach clenched tightly as he tried to anticipate what might happen.

Then the offending truck zoomed around them and kept on going.

Both of them expelled sighs of relief as the back of the truck disappeared ahead of them. "I can't believe I got so scared about a truck that was only guilty of speeding," she said.

"Me, too," he admitted. He continued to grip the steering wheel tight. The problem was there was no way for them to guess from what direction danger might come. All he knew for sure was it was coming, and he could only hope that when it came he could stop it before Eva paid a terrible price.

Chapter Ten

Eva, Jake and Andy fell into a routine that Eva found slightly threatening, because it felt so right having Jake in the house.

They ate breakfast together and walked Andy to the bus stop, and then Jake helped her with any chores she had to accomplish. Jake spoke on the phone to his brother and to the foreman of Albright ranching most afternoons while Eva did chores around the inside of the house.

They would then walk back to the bus stop to get Andy, and after that they ate dinner together. Once they finished dinner, Jake helped Andy with his homework while Eva cleaned up the kitchen. There was a lot of laughter in the house—laughter that warmed Eva's heart and made the house feel like a real home.

There had been no more dead cows, and nothing nefarious had occurred since Jake had moved in, and for that Eva was grateful. But she remained on guard, and she knew Jake did, too.

A couple of days of peace certainly didn't mean the danger had passed. Rather, it felt like a wicked countdown to something huge and awful. It was as if there was a clock ticking down to a big explosion.

They were now in the truck and headed into town to

drop Andy off for his Friday overnight with Bobby. "I don't know what I'm going to do without you tonight, Andy," Jake said. "What happens if your mom gets mean with me and you aren't there to protect me?"

Andy giggled. "Mom doesn't get mean, and even if she did, I don't know if I could protect you. She'd probably just send me to my room."

Eva and Jake laughed. This was what a real family felt like, she thought as she cast her gaze out the window. Jake filled in a space that had been missing.

It was going to be difficult when the time came for him to go home. Andy would be upset, and Eva had to admit that she would miss him, too. But this had been an arrangement built on desperate need and fear, not want, and she certainly hadn't invited Jake into her life forever.

When they reached town, Eva gave him directions to the Stephenson home. "I'll walk him to the door," Jake said when he'd parked in the driveway of the attractive, two-story home.

"Bye, Mom. I'll see you tomorrow," Andy said as he and Jake got out of the truck.

"Make sure you behave yourself, and I love you," Eva replied.

"Love you, too," Andy said.

Eva watched as the two walked up the sidewalk to the front door. She was shocked to realize father and son had the same gait. Again she thanked her lucky stars that Andy looked more like her than his father.

Robert answered the door, and he and Jake shared a short conversation, then Andy disappeared into the house and Jake returned to the truck.

"He asked how you were doing and if you were okay," Jake said as he slammed the truck door.

"That was nice of him," Eva replied.

"I don't like him. He's way too fixated on you."

Eva laughed. "Jake, he's just a nice man who wanted to go out with me."

"I still don't trust him."

"I don't trust anyone right now except you and Wayne," she replied.

"And that's the way it should be," he said.

As they drove home, their conversation turned to the ranch and her hope to start the barn renovations soon. "I'm planning on hiring Barney Jennings to come out and give me an estimate."

"Who is Barney Jennings?" Jake asked.

"He owns a construction company and has a good reputation for being fair while doing excellent work."

Jake pulled up and parked in front of her house. "How about you wait on that until everything else is resolved? The last thing I want right now is a bunch of men I don't know running around on your property."

"You're right," she replied. "The barn can wait."

Together they got out of the truck and headed inside. "How about some ice cream?" he asked. "I'll fix us each a bowl." He paused in the living room and pulled off his boots. "Ah, that's much better," he said.

"You always looked forward to taking off your boots," she said with a smile.

"Some things never change, and barefoot is always better," he replied with a smile of his own.

Together they went into the kitchen, where she sank down at the table and watched as he prepared two bowls of vanilla ice cream and then covered them with chocolate syrup. He put the bowls on the table and then sat across from her.

"There's nothing better than ice cream on a hot summer night. Hmm, this tastes delicious," she said and then slowly licked the chocolate off the spoon.

She immediately realized her mistake as Jake's gaze on her instantly heated. Suddenly there was a tension between them…a tension that had begun the moment he'd first shown up at her house, a tension that not only had to do with his obvious desire for her, but her own for him.

Her marriage to Andrew had been a sexless one. It had been ten years since she had experienced the sweet slide of a man's kisses against her skin. It had been since her last time with Jake that she had reached the heights of sexual pleasure, since she had felt the unity of complete and total intimacy.

And she suddenly realized she hungered for that now, and she didn't want it with any other man. She wanted it again with Jake.

What harm could come from making love with Jake one more time? She was determined he would never be in her life long-term, and she'd made that very clear to him. Surely if they were both on the same page, it wouldn't be such a bad thing.

She slowly licked her spoon again, her gaze holding his. "Do you have any idea what you're doing to me right now?" His voice held a deep, husky growl.

"Yes, I think I do," she replied.

He placed his spoon down. "And are you doing it on purpose?"

"Oh, definitely." Her heart beat an unsteady, quickened rhythm as he stood. He reached out and took the spoon from her fingers. He then walked around the table, grabbed her hand in his and pulled her up and out of her chair.

His arms encircled her and pulled her tight against him. The feel of his hard, muscled body against hers thrilled her. His lips crashed down on hers in a kiss that instantly stole her breath away and weakened her knees.

This was what had been missing in her life, this… this passion for another person, this passion that momentarily swept all other thoughts, all other feelings from her mind.

"Eva," he whispered against her ear when the kiss ended. "You know I want you."

"And I want you," she confessed. "But it's just this one night…just this one time. Jake, I need to know that you understand that."

"I understand," he replied, and then his lips found hers once again.

Somewhere in the back of her mind, she knew this was probably a mistake. She was breaking her own rule that he would never be in her bed again. But a bigger part of her didn't want to deny herself the pleasure of being with Jake just one more time.

This time when the kiss ended, she took him by the hand and led him down the hallway and into her bedroom. The room was warm, but a nice breeze blew in from an open window that made the temperature tolerable.

He pulled her into his arms once again, and as he kissed her, his hands caressed down her back. He cupped her buttocks and pulled her hips firmly against his. He was already aroused, and that only thrilled her more.

She finally stepped back from him and pulled her T-shirt over her head. Neither of them spoke as they continued to undress. She finished first and then slid beneath the pink-flowered sheet on her bed.

She watched as he pulled his T-shirt over his head, exposing his broad, muscled chest. He then quickly got out of his jeans and boxers. Dressed, Jake Albright was a handsome man, but undressed he was sinfully beautiful.

He joined her in the bed and pulled her to him. Being in his arms again was like heaven. She'd spent so many nights over the years thinking and remembering and fantasizing about being with him once again. She'd spent the last ten years being lonely and wanting the loving caresses of a man…this particular man.

He knew each and every place to touch and kiss to bring her the most pleasure. His lips found the area just behind her earlobe that caused small shivers to shoot through her body. "I've missed you so much, Eva," he whispered.

"I've missed you, too," she replied. Oh, she had missed this. She had missed the passion he stirred inside her, the utter desire he evoked in her, a desire that made her remember she was young and alive.

His mouth then slid down the length of her neck and moved from there to one of her breasts, where he sucked and licked her nipple. She softly cried his name as her fingers tangled in his hair.

She was lost in him…in the feel of his warm skin against hers, in the scent of him that dizzied her senses. He licked first one nipple and then the other and a welcome heat formed and swirled around in the pit of her stomach.

His hand slowly slid down her stomach and circled down across her upper thighs, where he languidly stroked.

She raised her hips, already fully aroused and gasping with the need for him. He was also aroused, and she reached down and encircled her fingers around his hard length.

He drew in a deep breath and gently pushed her hand away. “Eva, don’t… I won’t last if you touch me right now,” he said, his voice a husky half groan.

His fingers then found the center of her, and as he stroked her, she arched up to meet his touch. Heat fired through her as exquisite sensations built and built.

Her climax crashed over her, and before she could begin to recover, he moved between her thighs and entered her. Once he was inside her, he froze for a long moment, and their gazes locked.

Jake not only made love with her with his body, but also with his eyes. His eyes burned into hers with such a wealth of desire it was as if he were making love to her on a completely different, breathtaking level. She felt as if he was seeing into her very soul and reading all her secrets and dreams.

Still looking deep into her eyes, he began to slowly stroke in and out of her. She felt connected to him in a way that transcended just their physical act. She had missed this soul connection as much as she’d missed lovemaking.

They moved together like old, familiar lovers and yet with the excitement of two people who couldn’t get enough of each other. When they were finished, they collapsed back and waited for their breathing to return to normal.

She released a deep sigh into the crook of his neck, and one of his hands languidly stroked the side of her hip. “I think we just wasted two perfectly good bowls of ice cream,” she finally said.

He laughed, and it was a deep, pleasant rumble in her

ear. "This was way better than a bowl of ice cream." He leaned down and kissed her forehead.

She knew she should get up and somehow immediately distance herself from him, but she was reluctant to leave the peace and utter contentment she always found in his arms. "Tell me about your life in Italy," she said.

"What do you want to know?" He continued to stroke her hip in a lazy way that furthered her relaxation against him.

"Where did you live? What was your average day like?"

He told her about the luxury villa that he had called home and how every morning he would get up at dawn to drive to the Albright land of grapes and wine making.

"I knew nothing about growing grapes or making good wines when I arrived there. I spent the next month being walked through the operation by the manager, Enrique Bracolla, and then at night I read every book I could find about the process."

"It must have been pretty overwhelming for a nineteen-year-old cowboy from Dusty Gulch," she said.

"Oh, trust me, it was. For the first two years, I completely immersed myself in learning everything I could. I not only wanted to prove myself to Enrique, who was a great mentor and became a good friend, but also to my father. I wanted him to be proud of the man I was becoming."

"I'm sure he was very proud of you, Jake," she said softly.

"I wish I had come back home earlier so that I could have told him goodbye and maybe hear him say that he loved me." He released a short laugh. "But we both know my father wasn't exactly a warm and fuzzy guy."

The last thing she wanted to talk about was Justin Albright. Thoughts of him still brought a bad taste to her mouth, and she certainly couldn't share with Jake the depths of his father's betrayal. It would absolutely break Jake's heart to learn that his father had been such a manipulating monster.

Thankfully the conversation turned to the food in Italy. "The bread was absolutely out of this world," he said. "My cook joked that I was going to turn into a loaf of bread because I ate so much of it. But I also loved the lasagna and all the pastas there, too."

Eva laughed. "If I ate like that, I'd weigh five hundred pounds within the first couple of weeks." She glanced toward the window, where the dark shadows of night had begun to encroach. She froze, her heart seizing in her chest. "Jake, there's somebody at the window watching us," she whispered.

The man wore a ski mask, and his eyes glittered brightly, but she couldn't tell what color they were. She'd only gotten a quick glimpse of him, and she didn't want to look at him again and scare him off.

"Act natural," Jake said softly and then more loudly. "How about I bring us a couple of new bowls of ice cream?"

"Sounds good to me," she replied, thankful that her voice sounded normal instead of trembling with the fear that shot through her.

As he got out of bed and pulled on his boxers, she slid back beneath the sheet. She felt sick to her stomach knowing that the peeper had seen her naked, had possibly watched as they had made love.

"I'll be right back." Jake left the room, and then complete fear exploded in her chest. What was the man doing at her window? What did he want? And what would happen if Jake approached him?

At one time she'd been in love with Jake the boy, and she suddenly realized at that moment she was in love with Jake the man. And now the man she loved was about to confront somebody evil. She could only pray he came back to her unharmed.

JAKE HURRIED INTO the living room, where he yanked on his cowboy boots, grabbed his gun off the coffee table and then flew out the front door. Adrenaline shot through him as he slowly crept to the corner of the house. He turned the corner and continued creeping to the next corner.

He held his gun tightly, unsure what to expect. What was the person doing looking in Eva's bedroom window? Was he hoping to catch her alone in the room so he could shoot her? Break through the window and strangle her?

When he turned the next corner, he saw the man still at her window. He must have made a sound, for the man turned his head, saw Jake and then took off running.

Jake pursued, pushing himself to run as fast as possible in an effort to catch the offender. He had to catch him. He needed to know who it was and what he was doing outside Eva's window.

He followed the man into the pasture, and the darkness of night slammed down all around, making it more difficult for Jake to keep the dark figure in his eyesight.

He wanted to shoot the man, but he knew a bullet in the back of a window peeper would only get Jake a long prison sentence. It was one thing to shoot a man in self-defense, but quite another to shoot a retreating man.

Sweat popped out on his forehead, and his muscles

tried to cramp, but still he pushed forward. He had to slow down as he now had the obstacles of Eva's cattle to contend with.

"Dammit," he said on a gasp as he finally stopped running. There was no way he was going to catch the man now, and in any case, he'd lost sight of him. He leaned over with his hands on his knees as he panted from his efforts.

A wealth of frustration weighed heavily on his shoulders. He hated like hell that he hadn't been able to catch the man. He had certainly been the person they had all been looking for…the man who wanted Eva dead. All he had was a general impression of the perp. He'd been tall and with an average build, hardly enough to specifically identify him.

Finally catching his breath, he straightened, and a horrifying thought shot through his head. Had the man at the window wanted to be seen, knowing that Jake would come after him?

While Jake had been running around out in the pasture, had another man gone into the house? Had it been a scheme to get Eva all alone?

God, he'd left the front door not only unlocked but open when he'd raced out of the house. Eva had been naked in her bed, potentially a vulnerable victim to whoever might come into the house.

With all kinds of horrible visions of what could happen, what might have already happened, burning in his brain, he took off running toward the house in the distance.

Was it possible it wasn't just one person behind all the attacks? He immediately thought of Griff and his band of teenage friends. But would teenagers really set out to murder a woman because she'd objected to them partying in her barn?

Visions of news stories concerning the terrible crimes committed by teenagers flashed in his mind. Yes, it was possible teenagers could plot and carry out a murder.

None of that mattered right now. He just had to get to Eva. He ran all out, as if his very life depended on it. And it did, for if Eva was hurt or worse while on his watch, he'd never, ever be able to forgive himself.

His side hitched and his breath became gasps as he raced. His heartbeat thundered not only from his exertions, but also from fear.

As he rounded the corner to the house, he saw that the front door was shut. Was somebody right now inside there with Eva? He got to the door and found it locked. "Eva," he shouted and banged on the door with his fist.

The door opened, and she stood there, her eyes wide with fear, but she was unharmed. "Thank God." He grabbed her to him, needing to feel her in his arms to ensure himself that she was really okay.

"I was about to say the same thing," she said. "I was so scared for you."

He released her and then closed and locked the door. He led her over to the sofa, where they both sank down. She was now clad in a lightweight white robe.

"Needless to say, I didn't catch the guy," he said, frustration pressing tight against his chest.

She placed a hand on his arm. "It's okay. I'm just glad you're back here safe and sound."

"I'd rather have the man in my custody and Wayne on the way to arrest him." He clenched his hands as he remembered how badly he'd wanted to shoot the man.

"Speaking of Wayne, do we really need to call him out about this?"

"It's your call," he replied. "The man is obviously long gone, and I don't have any real details that would help identify him."

"Neither do I. I think we can wait until tomorrow and just let Wayne know this occurred," she replied.

"I definitely think we need to change some things around here," he said.

"Like what?" She looked at him curiously.

"From now on, we need to keep all windows down and locked, and the shades need to be pulled down tight. I don't want anyone to be able to look in and see where we are or what we're doing in this house."

Color crept into her cheeks. "I can't believe that creep saw me naked."

"Yeah, I don't like that, either," he replied with a touch of anger. He hated that anyone except him had seen Eva's beautiful body.

He released a weary sigh. "I need a shower. I worked up a sweat running through the pasture, but first let's get all the windows closed and locked and the shades pulled down."

Together they went around the house and drew curtains and pulled down blinds. "When you get finished with your shower, I'll take one, and then I don't know about you, but I'm ready for bed."

He'd love to ask her if she wanted to shower together, but he sensed she needed a bit of distance. Besides, they were both still processing more than a little fear.

"Why don't you go shower first," he suggested. "I know how long it takes for your hair to dry."

She nodded and headed for the bathroom. With the

sound of the water running, he once again walked around the house, rechecking windows and doors to make sure everything was locked down tight.

He had no idea why the man had window peeped. What had he hoped to gain by watching Eva's bedroom? After dead, mutilated cattle and a bloody heart left hanging from the porch rail, a window peeper seemed rather benign. So, what did it mean?

The shower stopped running, and minutes later Eva left the bathroom clad in a short, sleeveless nightgown that perfectly matched her violet eyes. She carried with her a hairbrush and a dryer.

"I can dry my hair in here," she said. She plugged her dryer into a nearby socket and then sank down on the sofa.

"I'll just be a few minutes. Needless to say, don't open the door to anyone."

"Ha, like that would happen." She turned on the hair dryer, and he went into the bathroom for his shower.

As he stood beneath the warm spray of water, his mind still worked to make sense of what had happened. But there was no way he could reason through it. And that worried him. This all worried him a lot.

The investigation had come to a grinding halt as no new clues had come to the surface. It was difficult to figure out who was behind a crime when nobody knew why it was happening.

Who was after Eva and why? That was the question that needed to be answered. If they could figure out the why, then maybe they'd be able to figure out the who. But right now there were just simply no answers.

He finished with his shower and pulled on a fresh pair of boxers and then returned to the living room, where

Eva was brushing out her hair. He sat next to her. "Let me," he said and took the brush from her hand.

She turned her back toward him, and he stroked the brush through her long hair, loving the feel of the silky strands against the back of his hand. "I always loved to brush your hair," he murmured.

She dropped her head back. "I always loved it when you brushed my hair."

Initially he'd felt the tension radiating from her, but the longer he brushed, the more relaxed she became. They didn't speak. No words were necessary.

She finally released a big yawn. "You'd better stop now, or I'll fall asleep right here." She stood and took the brush from him.

"Are you going to force me to sleep on this lumpy, uncomfortable sofa tonight?" he asked.

She narrowed her eyes. "You told me the sofa was surprisingly comfortable."

"Your bed would be far more comfortable," he replied. "I know it would just be for this one time, Eva. Let me go to sleep tonight with you in my arms."

She held his gaze for a long moment and then nodded. "As long as you understand this is a onetime thing."

Together they went into the bedroom and got into bed. He placed his gun on the nightstand and then turned out the bedside lamp, plunging the room into darkness.

He pulled her into his arms, spooning her against him. She snuggled in, and his love for her beat full in his heart. Tonight filled him with hope that there really was a future for them, that they could be the family he'd always wanted.

All he had to do was keep Eva alive.

Chapter Eleven

It had been almost a week since Eva had made love with Jake, and in the last week, she had tried to distance herself from him. However, it was difficult when she watched him interacting with Andy. He was so patient and loving with him, and she'd seen Andy blossom even more beneath Jake's attention.

He was the father she had always wanted for her son, the kind of man she would want in their lives forever. But it could and would all explode if he ever found out Andy was really his son.

He would hate her for the lies of omission, for the secret she had kept not only for the past nine years but had continued to keep from him when he'd arrived back in town. There was no way they could have a future together. Still, that didn't stop her from needing him now.

"It's nice that the weather hasn't been as hot the last couple of days," he now said.

They had just seen Andy off on the school bus and were now walking back to the house. "I'm just glad it's been another quiet week. No dead cows in the pasture and no cow hearts showing up anywhere. Isn't it crazy that the absence of those things makes it a good week?"

"It isn't crazy, it's tragic," he replied.

They had just reached the house when Wayne's car pulled up into the driveway. They waited for him to park and get out of the car.

"Morning," he said. "I've finally got some information for you." He carried a handful of papers with him.

"Come on in," Eva said. There was nothing about Wayne's demeanor that got her excited about whatever information he might have. All she really wanted to hear from the lawman was that the person terrorizing her was behind bars.

She wanted an end to her fear. Once the perp was in jail, then she'd be able to send Jake home and get the real distance from him she knew she desperately needed. She suspected she was only clinging to him right now because she was still afraid. And that wasn't fair to him or to her.

Eva poured Wayne a cup of coffee and then joined the two men at the table. "What have you got for us?" She gestured to the paperwork in front of Wayne.

"I finally got the names of people who charged the purchase of a Kincaid knife from all three of the convenience stores that sell them." He scooted the papers in front of Eva. "I thought you'd want to take a look at them and see if anyone looks suspicious. I did find one purchase a little telling."

"Which one?" she asked.

"I'd rather you find it for yourself," Wayne replied and then leaned back in the chair and took a sip of his coffee. "I had the stores go back a full year."

Eva picked up the first sheet of paper and began to read down the list of names. "I recognize several people, but nobody I know well," she said when she'd finished with the first page. She handed the list to Jake and then began to read the second page.

Her heart stopped on one particular name. "Wilma Ainsley? Griff's mother bought a Kincaid knife? Was this the one Griff supposedly lost in my barn?" She looked up at Wayne.

"Look at the date on that purchase," Wayne said.

A small gasp escaped her. "Two days after we confronted Griff about his lost knife." She looked from Wayne to Jake.

Jake's jaw tightened. "So, his mother was attempting to muddy the water by being able to show that Griff had his Kincaid knife."

"Either that or Griff used his mother's credit card, which is entirely possible," Wayne replied. "In any case, it makes him look damned suspicious."

"So, what are you thinking?" Jake asked Wayne.

"I'm really beginning to think this has all been the work of Griff and a couple of his friends. It wouldn't be a difficult task for a few big, burly teenagers to kill a cow or hang that cow heart on your porch. The peeping incident sounds more like a teenage stunt than an adult who wants to kill you."

"What about the attack in the barn?" Eva asked. Although her wounds had healed up, she certainly hadn't forgotten the terror she'd felt in the moment.

"I still think it's possible you were attacked because you interrupted the person who was going to set a fire," Wayne replied.

"So, if you think Griff and some of his friends are responsible for all this, then what do you intend to do about it?" Jake asked.

"Now I need to prove it," Wayne replied. "This afternoon I'm going to interview several of Griff's closest friends. I think if I lean on them hard enough, one of them will break and confess to everything."

"Let's hope that happens," Eva replied. It gave her a little relief to think that everything that had happened to her had been at the hands of a bunch of teenagers causing mischief, albeit terrifying mischief.

"I'll let you know how it goes later this evening," Wayne said and stood. "I'll definitely be talking to Griff again about the purchase of another knife."

"Makes him look guilty as hell in my mind," Jake said as they walked Wayne to the door.

"What are you thinking?" Jake asked once Wayne had left and the two were back in the kitchen.

She leaned with her back against the counter that held the remnants of the pancakes she'd made earlier for breakfast. "I'm thinking that if this all really was the work of teenagers, then I'm not quite as afraid as I've been."

She turned around and began to clean up the dishes. If what Wayne now believed was true, then she didn't think the teenagers would actually follow through to murder her. She finished with the dishes and then turned to look at Jake, who was seated at the table.

"Maybe I'm not in as much danger as I thought I was in and it would be okay if you went back to your home now," she said.

"But what if Wayne is wrong?"

His words hung in the air, and Eva frowned as she considered what he'd said. What if Wayne was wrong about Griff and his friends and she sent Jake home? As much as she wanted to distance herself from Jake, ultimately she was afraid to send him home until this horrifying mystery was solved.

"You told me you were sure that the person in the barn wanted to kill you," he continued. "Does it really matter whether it was a teenager or not? Whoever was in the barn that night is still out there somewhere."

"Point taken," she finally replied.

The truth was she wouldn't feel completely safe until somebody was behind bars. If nothing else, she had to think of her son. If anything happened to her, what would become of Andy? It was a question she didn't even want to entertain at the moment.

"If you have any dirty clothes, I'm going to do laundry this morning." She needed to keep herself busy and out of her own head. She needed the mundane of her life right now. She was mentally and emotionally exhausted from being afraid. "In fact, I'm going to spend the day doing some major housework."

"What can I do to help?" he asked.

"Nothing, just stay out of my way and let me do my thing."

"Then I'll just sit here and make some phone calls. I'll check in with David and then talk to Enrique to make sure there are no problems with the winery. I'm also talking to several people who might be interested in buying the winery if we decide to sell."

"That's great—now, dirty clothes?"

"I do have some things, but you shouldn't have to do my laundry all the time."

"Nonsense," she replied.

Minutes later she loaded the washer and got it running, then went back into Andy's room. Once there she stripped the sheets off his twin bed and tossed them into a pile in the doorway for the next load of laundry and then went to work polishing nightstands and the bookcase.

A smile curved her lips as she moved Andy's treasures that he kept on the shelves. There was the special rock shaped like a dragon and a large feather from an eagle. There was also a collection of arrowheads he had found around the ranch and a handful of drawings he'd accomplished in the last week or two.

Andy was a talented little artist, and she grabbed the handful of drawings and sank down on the edge of the bed to look at his latest creations.

Her smile widened at the first drawing, which depicted a boy and a dog—beneath it was written the caption Please, Mom. She could only assume eventually the drawing would make its way to her bedroom, where she would be sure to see it.

Maybe it was time to really think about a puppy for her son. When Jake went back home, it would be the perfect opportunity to get a dog that would hopefully take Andy's thoughts off the absence of Jake in their lives.

There were several more drawings of horses and wildlife, and then she gazed at the last one, and her heart constricted tight. It was a depiction of the backs of two people…a boy and a man. They walked side by side and had fishing poles over their shoulders.

It wasn't how the boy leaned into the man that squeezed her heart, nor was it the way the man had his arm around the boy's shoulders. It was the caption beneath that nearly gutted her. The man I want for a dad and me.

She quickly put the drawings back in order and placed them back on the shelf. As she dusted the rest of the furniture in the room, her heart held a deep sadness for her son.

He was going to be devastated when Eva finally shoved Jake out of their lives forever. There was no way she could fix the decisions she'd made so long ago so now they could all have a happily-ever-after ending. And somehow she didn't think a new puppy was going to help.

JAKE HUNG UP the phone after talking to David for some time. He was glad David was on board with the sale of the winery and had indicated Jake should go ahead with talking to any prospective buyers. They had agreed on a price that was way above what their father had paid for the winery fifteen years ago. Their conversation had then moved on to the ranch business. Jake was staying in touch with the ranch foreman, Bailey Turrel, who had been taking care of things for the past ten years.

Jake told his brother he intended to get more involved with the ranch once the issues at Eva's place were resolved. David once again told Jake how much he worried about Eva playing games with Jake's heart, and Jake assured his brother he had a handle on things where Eva was concerned.

He knew his brother meant well, but Jake didn't want to hear anything negative about being around Eva again, and so he cut that particular subject short.

This time with Eva and Andy had been wonderful. He felt like he'd finally found his home. Of course he would have loved to be sleeping with Eva in her bed every night, but currently he was just trying to prove he was the right man for her and that he belonged here forever.

But first they needed to catch a predator and put him behind bars. If that person was Griff, then he and whoever had helped him in terrorizing Eva needed to be in jail for a very long time. Jake was hoping that once the danger element was removed from her life, she'd realize she was in love with him again and that they deserved to live the future they had once dreamed about together.

As she started vacuuming the living room, he stepped outside the front door. His gaze shot in all directions, always looking for potential trouble.

In the distance Harley and Jimmy were on horseback in the pasture. Jake had come to like and trust Harley, who seemed to look at Eva like a daughter and wanted only the best for her. He was certainly less trustful of Jimmy, especially since the barn incident. Still, his money was on Griff. It was damning that he had gone out to buy another knife after being questioned about the one he'd owned.

What he hoped for was that by the time evening fell that night, the guilty party would be behind bars. He hated the whisper of fear that never quite left Eva's eyes. He hated that she was never able to completely relax.

One thing he did believe, even though she hadn't accepted it herself, was that she loved him. He saw it in the gazes she shot his way when she thought he wasn't looking. He felt it in the way she touched him. They felt like lingering caresses when she took the dirty dishes from him or whenever they inadvertently touched.

Yes, he truly believed she was in love with him, but she couldn't move forward because of the danger that filled her head and heart. He recognized there just wasn't room in her heart for him right now. He'd spent the last ten years loving Eva, and he could be very patient in waiting for her now.

As he watched Harley and Jimmy disappear from

sight, he was grateful that once again there had been no dead cows to contend with this morning. In fact, nothing had happened since the man in the ski mask had peeped through the bedroom window. Was it because Griff knew they were on to him?

The weather had been pleasant earlier, but now there was a building heat and an uncomfortable thick humidity. He turned and went back into the house, where Eva had stopped vacuuming and had disappeared into her bedroom. He walked down the hallway and saw her preparing to put clean sheets on her king-size bed.

"Let me help you," he said and moved to the opposite side of the bed from her.

"Thanks. This is the one job I always hate doing by myself." She threw him half of the fitted bottom sheet.

"I can make it so you never, ever have to do this job alone again," he replied, keeping his tone light and teasing.

"Just fit the sheet on, buddy," she replied.

He laughed. "You know I can be as handy as a pocket in a shirt to have around. You'd never need a back scratcher again or a stepladder for those high shelves in the kitchen."

"My back rarely itches, and I like my stepladder," she countered as she threw half of the top sheet toward him.

He laughed again. "You get a special price at the café for a family-style meal. Speaking of…why don't we get out of here and have dinner at the café this evening?"

She tucked in the sheet and straightened. "Oh, I don't know…"

"Come on, Eva. We've been cooped up here in the house for a couple of weeks now. A change of scenery for a little while would be good for us all." He'd love to take her out and display her proudly on his arm.

She grabbed the peach-colored bedspread off the nearby chair and threw it onto the bed, then straightened once again and blew a strand of her hair out of her eyes.

"Actually, dinner out sounds good. Andy always likes to eat at the café." A trace of fear darted into her eyes.

"Maybe it will be a celebration dinner if Wayne manages to break down Griff and his friends and they all confess they've been behind everything."

"That would really be wonderful."

"Why don't we plan on heading out of here around five," he said as they finished straightening the bedspread.

"Sounds good. That will give me time to finish with my cleaning and then get ready to go out."

"Ah, yet another reason to keep me around. I can cut your workload in half."

"Jake, I'm warning you." She picked up one of the pillows from the bed, her eyes suddenly filled with a teasing glint.

"If I was here all the time, you'd never get cold in the winter, because I'd be your snuggle mate."

The pillow flew across the bed and smacked him in the face. "I warned you," she said with a laugh.

"Ah, this means war," he said. He walked around the bed and then threw the pillow back at her, hitting her in the chest.

Within seconds they were in an all-out pillow fight. Their laughter filled the room, and laughing with Eva felt so damned good. They laughed even louder when one of the pillows split open and feathers flew everywhere.

He finally grabbed her around the waist and pulled her down to the bed.

For a long moment they simply gazed at each other as they tried to catch their breaths. He plucked several feathers from her hair and grinned. "I win," he finally said.

She returned his smile. "You won by breaking my pillow."

He laughed. "I'll help you clean up the mess, but first I want my prize for winning the battle."

One of her dark eyebrows crooked upward. "And what prize do you think you deserve?"

"At the very least, my prize should be a kiss." He half expected her to buck him off her, but instead her eyes darkened and her breath once again quickened.

"Okay, one simple kiss," she said.

He covered her mouth with his. There was nothing simple about kissing Eva. As his tongue sought entry, every part of his body was engaged in the kiss. His heartbeat accelerated, and his arms ached to wrap her up and pull her closer. He was instantly aroused as he deepened the kiss.

She allowed it for only a couple of seconds and then turned her head and shoved at his chest. "Okay, winner, your prize has been paid." He immediately stood and then pulled her up to her feet.

"I need to get this mess all cleaned up," she said.

"I'll help," he replied. "As handy as a pocket in a shirt."

"Start picking up feathers," she replied with a laugh.

Jake's heart squeezed with love. If this didn't end the way he wanted, then he would never be the same again.

At ten till five, Andy and Jake sat in the living room,

waiting for Eva to be ready to go out to dinner. "You think maybe I could get a piece of chocolate cake for dessert tonight?" Andy asked.

"You can have whatever you want," Jake replied with a smile to the boy who had crept so deeply into his heart. "If you want two pieces of chocolate cake, then you can have them after you eat your vegetables."

"That's okay. I don't mind eating some vegetables, but I hate brussels sprouts."

Jake laughed. "I hate them, too."

"Mr. Jake, is the bad man that hurt Mom going to get caught and put in jail?"

"I really hope so, buddy. I know Sheriff Black is working real hard to make that happen." Once again Jake was angered by the fear he saw in Andy's eyes. Damn the person doing all this to Eva and making Andy collateral damage.

"We're going to get him, Andy," he assured the boy. "You just need to stay strong for your mother until that happens."

At that moment Eva came into the room. She looked absolutely stunning in a pair of jeans and a violet blouse that showcased her slender waist and full breasts and perfectly matched her eyes. God, he was so proud to be the man by her side.

"You look very pretty," he said.

"Yeah, Mom, you look really good," Andy echoed.

"Thank you," she replied. "I don't know about you two, but I'm starving."

"Me, too," Andy replied.

They left the house, and the heavy humidity pressed tight. It felt like storm weather, and in fact the forecast was for thunderstorms to make an appearance later on in the night.

Minutes later the three of them were in Jake's truck and talking about what they intended to order to eat. For Jake, it was just another wonderful glimpse into what could be if he and Eva were together again.

"I think I'm in the mood for a big, juicy steak," Jake said.

"Me, too," Andy replied. "What are you going to get, Mom?"

"I'm not sure, but I'm leaning toward the chicken-fried steak with mashed potatoes and gravy," she replied.

"You always get that," Andy protested.

Eva laughed. "I just know what I like."

The Dusty Gulch Café was a popular place to eat. The food was good, the prices were reasonable, but more importantly, it was a great place for the gossipers in town to gather.

Jake felt the stares that followed the three of them as they made their way to an empty booth toward the back of the café. This was really the first time he and Eva had made an appearance together. The grocery store didn't count. The café appearance made it more official.

Jake took the side of the booth where he could see who came into the café and who might approach them. He definitely didn't want any surprises. Andy sat next to him and across from his mother.

They placed their orders, and then while they waited Andy kept them entertained with stories about what had happened at school that day. "Jeffrey brought his pet frog today and it jumped out of the box he had it in." Andy's eyes sparkled with merriment. "The girls all screamed and got up on their chairs, and the boys were all running around the room and trying to catch it."

"Who finally caught it?" Eva asked.

"Jeffrey did and Mrs. Roberts told him to never bring the frog again, but then she had us all write a story about Mr. Frog's adventures."

"And what did you write about?" Jake asked.

"My frog was a cowboy who lived in the pond and rode the range during the days on his favorite dog." Andy slid a sly look at his mother. "Frog took good care of his dog without his mother's help and they were best friends."

Eva smiled at her son. "I got the point, Andy," she said with a small laugh. "I might see a dog in your future, but first we have to decide what kind of a dog you want."

At that time their meals arrived, and the conversation turned to different kinds of dogs. They discussed the pros and cons of different breeds and whether Andy wanted a big dog or a smaller one, an indoor dog or an outdoor one.

They were almost finished eating when Robert Stephenson and his son walked through the door. Andy immediately spied his friend and waved to him.

Robert guided his son back to their booth. "Jake… Eva," he greeted them. "Eva, I'm glad to see somebody can get you to take a break and get a meal out," he said. Where before Jake had seen warmth in Robert's eyes when he looked at Eva, tonight Jake swore he detected a hint of coolness there.

Jake was also beginning to wonder if Robert had been stalking Eva. He and his son seemed to show up wherever Eva went.

Eva's cheeks warmed with color. "Jake twisted my arm to come out this evening," she replied.

"Bobby and I are doing takeout. I suggest you all finish up pretty quickly—the weather is looking pretty nasty out there," Robert said. "We're now under a tornado watch until three in the morning."

Storms in Kansas weren't anything to take lightly. A tornado could level a town in a matter of minutes. "Maybe we should take Robert's advice and get done and get home," Eva said as a worried frown slid across her forehead.

The three of them finished up quickly and then stepped out of the café. The air was sultry and still and there was no sign of the moon or the stars in the dark, cloudy sky.

"I don't mind storms, but I really hate bad storms," Eva said softly enough that Andy wouldn't hear her in the back seat.

"We'll keep an eye on it, and if we have to go to your storm cellar then we'll go," he replied.

He knew she had a storm cellar right outside the back door. The last time he'd been in the small space, it had contained shelving holding canned goods and a cot. If necessary, the three of them could escape a storm's wrath by going there and hunkering down for the duration of the weather event.

They arrived back home and turned on the television, where the tornado-watch box was at the bottom of the screen. The details of the watches and warnings scrolled across.

The three of them played a card game until it was time for Andy to shower and call it a night. When he'd been sent off to bed and had been tucked in, Eva and Jake sank down on the sofa.

The television station had now canceled all regular programming, and the local weatherman had taken over the screen. There were tornadoes spinning up all around the area. Storm chasers were active and checking in on a regular basis with reports of damage on the ground.

"I'm not going to sleep until all this weather has settled down for the night. We haven't seen this kind of active weather pattern for a long time," she said. "If you want to go ahead and go to sleep, I'll move to the chair and turn down the volume on the TV and try to be as quiet as possible."

"You can sit right here. I'll stay up with you. Another reason to have me around all the time—I would always be your storm-watch buddy."

She shot him a whisper of a smile and then turned a worried look back to the television. The minutes turned into hours as they talked and watched the weather reports. Occasionally he got up and went to the front door to peer outside.

Thunder clapped and lightning slashed through the dark sky. The wind whipped tree branches into a frenzy. It felt like a night of evil, and Jake wasn't only looking at the weather elements but also keeping watch for trouble of the human sort. Under the cover of a storm, a lot of madness could occur.

There had been no word from Wayne, and so he suspected the teenagers had remained strong through his interviews. That left a lot of uncertainty. Either that or the teenagers truly weren't guilty, which was even more troubling.

It was two thirty in the morning when the weather finally cleared up. Eva released a big yawn and struggled to her feet. "I'm totally exhausted," she said.

"Yeah, I'm pretty tired myself," he admitted. "I can't remember the last time I was up this late."

"Me, neither. Good night, Jake. Thank you for seeing me through the storm." She offered him a sleepy smile.

"Anytime," he replied.

He watched until she disappeared into her room, and then he went to the front door, opened it and stepped out on the porch. The air smelled fresh and clean after the rain they had received. Stars had begun to show back up in the sky, an indication that the dark clouds had finally moved away.

He looked around and, seeing nothing that disturbed him, he turned and went back into the house. *Thank you for seeing me through the storm.* Her words echoed in his mind as he stretched out on the sofa.

He'd seen her through this particular storm, but there was another one coming. A storm of a different kind, and he could only pray that he would see her through that one, too.

Chapter Twelve

Eva awoke slowly, her brain begging for just a little more sleep. She hadn't been up so late since Andy was born. Sleepiness kept her eyelids closed for several more long minutes.

She finally opened her eyes. With the shades pulled at the windows, no morning sun filled the room to help her wake up or know exactly what time it might be.

She rolled over and eyed the clock on her nightstand. Alarm pulled her upright. She'd overslept, and if she didn't get up and get moving right now, Andy was going to be late for school. And he was a boy who absolutely hated being late.

There was no scent of coffee in the air, which let her know Jake had overslept as well. She got out of bed and raced into the living room, which was also semidark because of the shades all being pulled.

He was still sound asleep. "Jake," she said urgently.

He shot up and fumbled on the side table for his gun. "What's up?"

"We've overslept. Andy is going to be late for school if we don't get moving."

He immediately got up from the sofa. "What do you

need for me to do?" he asked and raked a hand through his unruly hair.

"If I can get Andy ready in time for him to catch his bus, then you don't need to do anything. But if he misses the bus, could you drive him to school?"

He frowned, and she knew what he was thinking. "Jake, it's seven thirty in the morning—I'm sure I'll be fine here for the twenty minutes or so you would be gone. And now I need to get Andy up and moving," she said, aware of the time ticking by.

She hurried down the hallway and into Andy's bedroom. "Andy…honey, we're late. I overslept. You need to get up and dressed as quickly as you can so you aren't late for school."

"Okay," he said and sat up.

"I'll make you something for breakfast, but you'll have to eat fast." She left his room and hurried into the kitchen, where Jake was starting coffee.

"Andy hates to be late to school," she said as she pulled a skillet out from the cabinet.

"Calm down, Eva. Right now it's possible he might miss his bus, but if we leave here in the next fifteen minutes or so, I can get him to school without him being tardy." He turned to look at her. "You know I don't like the idea of leaving you here alone."

She sprayed the skillet, turned on the burner and then cracked an egg into it. "I'm sure I'll be fine for no longer than you'll be gone. There's no way I can get myself ready to leave this house and still have Andy make it to school on time."

She flipped the egg over.

"I can't believe I overslept so much," Jake said. He

got a to-go cup from the cabinet along with a regular coffee cup.

"We both had a really late night," she replied. "And it doesn't help that all the blinds are pulled and it feels like twilight in here."

Andy came into the kitchen just as Eva finished putting together an egg sandwich for him. "Jake is going to take you to school. You can eat this on the way."

She wrapped the sandwich in a paper towel, and Andy took it from her. Jake grabbed the to-go cup of coffee he'd prepared, and then the three of them headed for the front door.

She kissed Andy's forehead. "Sorry for the rush this morning. Just have a great day at school."

"I will, Mom," he replied with a bright smile. "I'll see you later."

She watched from the front door as Jake and Andy got into Jake's truck and then it disappeared down the lane. She closed and locked the door behind them and then released a deep sigh.

She'd been in frantic mode since the moment she had opened her eyes and seen the clock on the nightstand. She shoved a hand through her messy hair and headed back into the kitchen.

She hadn't even managed to get out of her nightgown, but all she wanted now was to relax for a few minutes and drink a cup of coffee. She'd clean up and get dressed after she had her coffee.

She sank down at the table with the cup that Jake had fixed for her before he'd left. She took a sip and leaned back in the chair.

Last night while she and Jake had been weather watching, they had talked about a lot of things. He'd told her about his brother, David, whom Eva remembered from high school, and his wife, Stephanie, whom Eva had seen around town but had never officially met.

He talked about how much he liked his sister-in-law and how he hoped to foster a good relationship with his nephew. Eva knew how important family was to Jake. Now with his father gone, she hoped he'd really be able to build those family bonds with his brother and his wife and children that would feed his soul.

The one thing they hadn't talked about was the past, for which she was grateful. Besides, they had built a new relationship now, one as adults instead of teenagers filled with nothing but youthful hopes and dreams.

She finished drinking the cup of coffee and then decided it was time to get up and get cleaned up for the day. She was about to get out of the chair when a shadow of a person moved across her back door.

Maybe it was Harley ready for their daily check-in. God, she hoped he hadn't found any more mutilated cattle this morning. She got up and went to the door. With the blinds pulled across the window, she couldn't see who stood on the other side. She wasn't about to open the door until she knew who it was. Before she opened it, she grabbed the cord and pulled up the blinds.

She gasped in horror at the sight of a man wearing a ski mask on the other side. She stumbled backward as the man picked up an ax and slammed it into the door, shattering the glass and cracking the wood.

For a long moment, she stood frozen in horror. When he raised the ax and hit the door once again, she screamed and sprang into action. She whirled around and raced for her room.

The crack of wood splintering sounded again, and

she knew she only had seconds before the man would be in her house. She flew down the dark hallway and into her bedroom, frantic to get to her shotgun, which was locked up in a gun case in her closet.

The continuing sound of cracking wood let her know the man wouldn't stop attacking the door until he got inside. Terrified tears raced down her cheeks as she fumbled to get the gun. She finally got the case open and grabbed the shotgun. Once she had it in her hands, she gripped it tightly and peeked out of her bedroom.

Silence.

It pressed in and made her chest tighten and her heart race so quickly she thought she might have a heart attack. The silence meant the man was now in the house.

At the moment she didn't care who he was—she was going to shoot first and ask questions later. He was in here to hurt her…to potentially kill her. She didn't intend to give him the chance.

He'd apparently been watching her house. He must have seen Jake and Andy leave and knew she'd be in here alone and vulnerable. Once again she tightened her grip on the gun. Using it to lead the way, she took a step out of her bedroom.

She stopped and tried to listen to any noise she might hear that would indicate where the man was now. It was difficult to hear over the pounding of her heart and the frantic gasps of fear that escaped her mouth.

Nothing. She heard nothing, and not knowing where he was made her fear ratchet up even higher. She tried to silence her own gasps and frantic breaths, knowing he would be able to track her by the sounds she made.

She took another step and then another. She was

about to peek into the bathroom when he reached out of the darkness of that room and, despite her tight grip, snatched her gun away from her. He threw the gun behind him in the bathroom as she screamed.

"Who are you? What do you want?" she shrieked. "Why? Why are you doing this to me?"

There was no way to run around him in the narrow hallway, and before she could turn to run back into her bedroom, he grabbed her around the neck. He pushed until her back was against the wall next to the bathroom doorway.

His eyes were dark, glittering orbs of evil as he began to squeeze her throat. Tighter…tighter he squeezed. Her fingers scrabbled at his hands in an effort to dislodge them as her oxygen was slowly cut off.

Stars flickered, and then her vision dimmed as no more air reached her lungs…her brain. She was going to die. Jake would come home and find her dead body. And what would happen to Andy?

It was the thought of her son that gave her the strength for one more effort to survive. As her beloved son's face filled her head, she drew up a knee and slammed it between his legs as hard as she could.

Instantly he groaned, released his grip on her and fell to his knees. She ran into the living room, knowing her best option was to try to hide until Jake got back.

A roar of rage sounded from the hallway. "I'm going to kill you, bitch," he cried.

The voice was unfamiliar to her. Who was the man and why was he doing this to her? Knowing the house would be a death trap to remain in, Eva flew out the front door, hoping and praying she could somehow survive until Jake got home.

As Jake drove toward town, evidence of storm damage from the night before was visible in the amount of tree limbs and branches that were down around the area.

"Wow, look at that one," Andy said and pointed to a big limb on the ground almost encroaching onto the other lane in the road. "Must have been a big storm, and I didn't even know it was happening."

"It was mostly just a lot of wind and rain," Jake replied. "Trust me, it was worth sleeping through."

"But you stayed awake with Mom?" he asked.

"I did. She wanted to keep an eye on the weather so she could keep you safe and sound."

"We had to go to the storm cellar one time when I was seven," Andy said. "But nothing happened and we were only down there for a little while."

"That's good," Jake replied.

"You like my mom, don't you, Mr. Jake?"

Jake felt the boy's attention riveted to him. "Of course I like your mom," Jake replied. "What's not to like? She's beautiful and smart and funny."

"But you *like* like her, don't you?"

"Yes, I *like* like her."

"I thought so," Andy replied with a look of self-satisfaction.

Jake was grateful to pull up in front of the school to stop any more questions Andy might have about him and his mother's relationship. It wasn't his place to talk about these things with Andy.

Jake found a parking place, and the two of them got out. He walked Andy to the school's front door. "Have a great day, Andy."

"I will, and thanks for bringing me, Mr. Jake." Andy quickly headed for the door and disappeared into the building, and Jake turned around to head back to his truck.

Before he got there, he ran into Benny, who carried a colorful lunchbox in his hand. "Hey, Jake," Benny greeted him. "I'm here because boy child left his lunch at home. What are you doing here?"

"I brought Eva's son to school," Jake replied.

"I heard that you were spending a lot of time with her. I've also heard there's some messed-up stuff going on at her ranch."

"Yeah, there is," Jake admitted.

"We still need to plan that dinner. I'd love to have not only you, but Eva and her son as well."

"That would be great, and we'll plan something soon, but right now I've got to get back to Eva's."

"I'm definitely going to call you soon to set up a dinner at our house," Benny said.

"I look forward to it. I'll talk to you later, Benny." Jake hurried back to his truck and headed for home.

He was eager to get back to Eva. Last night he'd felt a new emotional connection growing between them. They had talked about so many things that had nothing to do with who they had been as teenagers and everything to do with who they were as adults. He'd never felt as close to her as he did right now after the long night they had shared.

He couldn't believe how he'd overslept. He hadn't slept that late since he'd been a kid. He frowned as he looked ahead. The road was blocked by a city truck removing the large tree limb that Andy had pointed out earlier.

He came to a stop behind several other cars. There was no other route to get to Eva's ranch, and so he was stuck. Hopefully they'd get the big branch moved quickly and he could be on his way.

Already he was aware of the time ticking by. He told himself Eva would be fine. It was a morning filled with sunshine, surely not the time for any evil to take place.

Sometimes bad things happen in the light of day, a little voice whispered in the back of his head. He mentally shook his head to dislodge the thought.

There was no way anyone could have known that he and Eva would oversleep this morning and he'd end up taking Andy to school, leaving Eva alone in her house. Besides, she had good locks on the doors and windows and a gun she could get to if necessary.

He tapped his fingers impatiently on the steering wheel as he continued to be held up. He glanced in his rearview mirror and saw a line of cars now behind him.

He pulled out his phone and dialed Eva's number. He needed to tell her he was held up so she wouldn't worry. The phone rang three times and then went to voice mail.

He hung up without leaving a message. Maybe she was in the shower or her phone was still in the bedroom and she was in the kitchen and couldn't hear it. He waited five minutes and then tried to call her again. Same result…the call went to voice mail.

He tried to ignore the small bell of alarm that began to ring in his head. There could be all kinds of reasons she wasn't answering her phone. It didn't mean that she was in any kind of trouble.

Still, he needed to get back to her as soon as possible, if nothing else to still the faint alarm still ringing in his head. Finally the branch was removed, and the traffic began to move again. He stepped on the gas and drove as quickly as possible.

When he reached Eva's place, he was relieved to see nothing amiss. He parked and then hurried to the front door. It was locked. "Eva," he yelled and banged on the door. He waited a moment, and when she didn't reply, he took out the key she had given him a week before and unlocked the door.

He walked in and called her name once again. She didn't answer. He yelled her name louder, and the alarm bell in his head rang a little louder when she still didn't reply. The shower wasn't running, so she wasn't in the bathroom unable to hear him.

He flipped on the light and stared down the hallway but stopped and froze. Just inside the doorway of the bathroom, Eva's shotgun was on the floor. Immediately every muscle in his body tightened, and adrenaline fired through his veins. Where was Eva now? Why was her shotgun on the floor? Oh God, what had happened here while he'd been gone?

He hurried into the kitchen and stopped short as he stared at what was left of the back door. Shattered glass littered the floor, and the wood of the door had been completely splintered apart, making a hole large enough for somebody to enter the house.

He ran to the door and peered outside. His heart iced as he saw the ax that had apparently been used to break in. Where was Eva? At least he hadn't found her dead body lying on the floor…at least not in the kitchen.

With his heart in his throat, he turned back and raced toward Andy's room. *Please, please don't let me find her dead*, he prayed. He released a small sigh of relief when he didn't find her in her son's room. He then ran toward her room and once again prayed that he wouldn't find her lifeless in the bed or on the floor.

She wasn't on the floor on this side of the king-size bed, but what about the other side? He hurried around the foot of the bed. A gasp of relief swept over him when she wasn't there.

Not finding her anywhere in the house, he returned to the kitchen. Stepping outside, his heart thundered a million miles a minute, and he pulled his gun from his holster. He gazed around and listened, hoping to hear something…anything that would let him know where she was and that she was still alive.

Nothing. All he heard were birds singing in the trees and a cow mooing in the pasture. They were normal sounds, daytime noises, but the lack of any other noises scared him half to death.

His heart squeezed so tight he could scarcely draw a breath. Was he too late? Had he taken so long to get home that Eva had been killed? Was her body right now lying someplace in a pasture? Hidden in one of the outbuildings?

"Eva?" he yelled as loud as he could. Nothing. There was nothing to let him know whether she was dead or alive, but the silence cut deeply into his heart.

He had to do something to find her. If she'd run from the house, then maybe she was in one of the outbuildings. Maybe she'd somehow locked herself inside and now was afraid to come out.

With his gun still tightly gripped in his hand, he took off running toward the shed in the distance. He could only hope and pray that he would find her alive somewhere, because the alternative was too horrendous to consider.

EVA LEFT THE HOUSE and ran hell-bent toward the barn, hoping she could hide in there until Jake got home, hoping she could get inside before the man who was after her saw where she went.

She raced as fast as she could, her heart beating so hard…so fast…it felt as if it might explode out of her chest. She couldn't believe this was happening. Her nightmares were coming true, and she knew if the man caught her, he intended to kill her.

Why? The question screamed over and over again in her brain. Why was this happening? Why was a monster breaking into her home and trying to kill her? Who was the monster behind the ski mask?

She reached the barn, threw the door open and raced across the floor. When she came to the ladder, she climbed up as quickly as she could into the loft. She wanted to hide in the farthest corner of the building.

She found a stack of hay with a small space between it and the wall, and she quickly crawled in. She shoved her hand in her mouth to stop the hysterical cries that escaped her. Terrified tears chased fast and furious down her cheeks.

It was only when she was hunkered down that she realized she had put herself in a place without an exit. If he found her here, there was now positively nowhere for her to run. She could throw herself out the loft door, but the fall would probably kill her.

Quiet as a mouse. That's what she needed to be right now. *Quiet as a mouse*, she told herself over and over again. She nearly screamed as the barn door flew open.

"I know you're in here, Eva. Come on out now." He

laughed, the sound holding a maniacal glee that caused arctic chills to race up and down Eva's back.

She didn't recognize the low, raspy voice and suspected he was intentionally trying to disguise it from her. Did he really know for a fact she was in here hiding, or was he bluffing?

Once again she placed her hand over her mouth, fear welling up in the back of her throat and begging to be released on a hysterical scream.

Quiet as a mouse, she thought again. If he wasn't sure that she was in here, maybe if he heard nothing he'd go check out someplace else. *Please, go away*, she begged in her mind. *Please, please just go away.*

"Come on, Eva. You might as well give it up now. I'm going to search every inch of this barn, and I will find you and then I'm going to kill you." She heard what sounded like a stack of hay bales falling over and hitting the ground.

Where was Jake? What was taking him so long to get back from the school? Surely he should be home by now. It felt as if he'd been gone for hours. If he didn't get back soon, the man was going to find her, and even though she'd fight with all her heart and soul, she knew eventually he would be able to overpower her.

Again a question shot through her mind. Not the why of what was happening, but rather what would become of Andy if she was killed.

As it stood right now, he'd probably wind up in foster care, and the very idea of that happening was excruciating. She should have told Jake the truth. She should have told him that Andy was his son the minute he'd arrived back in Dusty Gulch. If she somehow survived this, she would tell Jake and take whatever consequences might happen.

Of course what she hoped was, even without Jake knowing the truth, he would petition the courts to have Andy in his custody. At least she'd know Andy would be raised with Jake's love. She no longer worried about Jake being tainted by his family's wealth and power. Jake's heart was as pure as it had been when he'd been a teenager, and she couldn't imagine that ever changing. But first, she had to survive.

"Eva, are you up here?"

She heard him take a heavy step on the ladder leading to the loft. "You must be up here, because I saw you run into the barn and I've checked all around down here. The longer I have to look for you, the angrier I'm becoming."

Another footstep sounded on the loft stairs. Terror tensed every muscle in her body with a fight-or-flight adrenaline. There was no place for her to take flight to, but she intended to fight until there was no more fight left in her body.

"You should have just left town, Eva. Things would have been so much better for you if you had just picked up and moved to another state when I first warned you."

She only hoped before she died, she saw the face of the monster beneath the ski mask. Maybe it would help her understand why, exactly, he wanted her dead.

She knew when he had reached the loft, because she could now hear his excited, rapid breathing. Could he hear her? Oh God, where on earth was Jake?

Hay bales began to topple down on the other side of the hayloft. If he was on the other side of the loft, then maybe she could get to the loft stairway before he could and she could get away. She had to do something or he would find her. Backed against the wall, there would be no way for her to get away from him.

She drew in several silent deep breaths and then sprang up and ran for the stairs. She almost made it, but he caught her by the ends of her long hair. He spun her around and to the floor as she screamed…and screamed…and screamed.

He was on top of her in an instant, his hands encircling her neck. "Who are you?" she gasped as his thumbs began pressing hard into her throat.

"You'll never know," he replied.

Her hands reached up in a frantic effort to dislodge his, but he was too strong. He was on top of her in a way that trapped her legs so there was no way she could bring up a knee in order to hit him where it might count.

This was it. She was going to die in this place where she had once found love. She would never see Jake again. Worse, she would never see Andy's smile again or hear his laughter.

Tears wept from the sides of her eyes as her air disappeared. Her lungs began to burn. Stars exploded in her brain. Her vision dimmed.

She was just about to lose total consciousness when she heard a distant roar and the man on top of her was suddenly gone. She rolled over to her side, gasping and coughing for air.

She opened her eyes just in time to see Jake hit the man once…twice…three times so hard in the jaw, the man fell backward and onto the floor. Jake immediately leaned down and held his gun at the man's temple. He pulled back on the hammer.

"No, Jake," she said between coughs. "Don't kill him."

"I want to." Jake's voice shook with his rage. "I want

to kill him for hurting you, but I won't." He released the hammer without shooting but kept his gun pointed at the intruder.

"Get up before I change my mind." He reached down and yanked the man up by the front of his black shirt.

Jake pulled his phone out of his back pocket and slid it across the floor to where Eva had sat up. "Eva, honey, call Wayne. We need to get this scum arrested and put away."

As Jake continued to hold the man at gunpoint, Eva called Wayne. "Sheriff Black," he answered on the second ring.

"Wayne, it's Eva. We have him." A sob of deep relief choked out of her. "He tried to kill me, but Jake has him and we need you to come out. We're in the barn loft."

"I'm on my way," Wayne replied.

Eva hung up the phone and stared at the masked man who had just tried to take her life. There was no doubt that he was the same man who had mutilated her cattle and hung the bloody heart on her railing. He was the same man who had attacked her in the barn and had put fear in her son's eyes.

"I need to know… I need to know who he is," Eva said. "Pull his mask off."

Jake reached out for the bottom of the ski mask, but the man pulled back from him. "I'll pull that off you dead or alive," Jake said angrily. He reached out once again and this time yanked off the ski mask.

Eva gasped in stunned surprise as she finally saw the face of her monster.

Chapter Thirteen

"David?" The very earth seemed to move beneath Jake's feet as he stared at his brother. Confusion weighed heavy in Jake's mind. Of all the people he'd expected to see, his brother was the very last. It didn't make sense. "You? It's been you behind all this?"

"I did it for you, Jake," David said. "Come on, man. She's nothing. She's nobody. I was just trying to protect you."

"Protect me?" Jake continued to stare at his brother in stunned shock. "Protect me from what?"

David looked down at his feet and then back at Jake. "I guess I haven't been thinking clearly since Dad's death."

"You mutilated the first cow weeks before your father's death," Eva said.

David frowned and didn't even acknowledge Eva's presence with a glance in her direction. His dark gaze bored into Jake's. "Jake, why don't you just let me walk away from all this and we all can just forget what has happened?"

"Forget that you terrorized me for over two months?" Eva got to her feet and moved to stand next to Jake. Her voice was husky and her throat was red and bruised, threatening to make Jake's anger rise up once again.

"Forget that you just tried to kill me?" Eva's voice shook with emotion. "That if Jake hadn't gotten here in time you would have succeeded?"

"Jake, just shoot her and let's get out of here," David said. "Come on, brother. Do the right thing. I'm your family."

"Do the right thing? What in the hell is wrong with you?" Jake pulled Eva close against his side. "The right thing is you are going to be arrested, and you're going to prison for a very long time."

David's eyes narrowed. "I gave her a chance to leave town. She should have heeded my warnings. She's bad, Jake. She's always been bad. She's ruinous for you, and you should have nothing to do with her. She's poison."

"Is that why you did all this?" Jake was still trying to wrap his head around the fact that his brother was behind all the attacks, that his brother had just tried to kill Eva.

David's face grew red with rage. "Don't you get it, Jake? Even Dad knew she was no good for you, that she didn't deserve to be anywhere around an Albright. And speaking of dear old Dad, while you were whooping it up in Italy, I was the one who had to suffer his foul moods and coldness. I was the one he mentally and verbally abused on a daily basis."

"I'm sorry for that, David," Jake replied. "But that doesn't excuse what you've done."

"You always defended Dad. You always tried to brownnose him, but he hated you as much as he hated me. He should have been sterile and never allowed to have children."

David's eyes glittered with utter hatred, and Jake

couldn't believe the kind of vitriol that had been inside his brother. "But you loved dear old Dad," he continued. "Maybe you wouldn't have loved him so much if you'd known that he was behind Eva breaking up with you all those years ago."

Jake frowned and looked at Eva just in time to see all the color leave her face. "What's he talking about, Eva?"

"We can talk about it later," she replied. "Wayne should be here anytime. Maybe we should get down from the loft."

Although Jake wanted to ask her about what David had said, he knew there would be time to talk to her after David was officially arrested.

"Eva, you go on down and then we'll follow," Jake instructed. He was still in shock that the person behind everything wasn't Griff or Robert, but rather his own brother. And he still didn't understand David's reasoning for wanting Eva dead. There had to be more to it than David somehow trying to protect Jake from her.

"Just let me go before Wayne gets here," David said as soon as Eva had left the loft. "You can tell him the man escaped and you never pulled off his ski mask. You can tell Wayne you still don't know who the perp is."

"And what about Eva?"

"Tell Wayne she's lying about me. It would be your word against hers, and Wayne would believe an Albright over a poor piece of trash like Eva."

Once again Jake looked at David as if he were a stranger—a very disturbed stranger. When he thought of David cutting the heart out of a cow, his brain threatened to explode. Who would have thought David had such evil inside him?

"Head downstairs," he said. "And David, if you try

to get away, I'll shoot you in the leg. Don't test me, because I promise you I'll shoot."

When they reached the main level of the barn, Eva waited for them, her face still pale and her throat a livid red that already had taken on shades of deep purple.

Jake's chest tightened with a rage of his own. How dare David put a finger on the woman Jake loved? How dare he fill her life with the kind of fear Eva had experienced?

David must think Jake was totally crazy if he thought Jake was going to just let him go and forget all this. As much as he loved his brother, David had to go to jail and pay the consequences for what he had done.

At that moment Wayne and a couple of his deputies walked through the barn door. Wayne looked as surprised as anyone to see David.

"What's going on here?" he asked.

"David tried to kill me," Eva said, and a hand went to her throat. "He...he tried to strangle me." Tears filled her eyes, along with a look of residual fear. "He's behind it all, Wayne. He did it all. He killed my cattle and hung the heart, and this morning he broke through my back door with an ax and...and I managed to escape him, but I ran to the loft and then he tried to kill me by strangling me to death."

The words rushed out of her as tears chased down her cheeks. Once again Jake pulled her against his side.

"Whoa," Wayne said. "We need to slow things down."

"I just want him arrested. I... I don't ever want to see him again." Eva turned her face into Jake's chest.

"Wayne, they're both crazy," David said. "You know me. I'm an Albright, and if you put me under arrest, I can promise you that you'll be sorry."

"David, we've always gotten along, but I'm the law. I really don't give a damn if you're an Albright or the governor of this state. If you broke the law, then you have to pay the consequences." He nodded at the two deputies with him.

They placed David in handcuffs, and David exploded in rage. "Why didn't you just die?" he screamed at Eva. "My son is a real Albright, and he's not going to share his inheritance with your bastard son or any children you might have. You aren't Albright material—you're nothing but trash."

Jake frowned. Bastard son? What was he talking about? He looked at Eva. He hadn't thought it was possible, but her face was now even whiter than it had been. Shock tried to work through him, but he fought against it. Surely David was mistaken in his thinking. He looked back at his brother. "Share an inheritance? So this was all about money?"

"Of course that's what it was about," David screamed, his face red and spittle flying. "It's about money and power and keeping it where it belongs, with the rightful Albrights. Dad knew she was trash, and that's why he got her to break up with you. But the minute you got back to town, you ran back to her like a dog in heat. I had to do something… I had to protect you from yourself."

"Take him away," Jake said in disgust. He couldn't trust anything David was telling him. It was obvious his brother was deeply disturbed.

"I'll need full statements from the two of you," Wayne said once David had been led out of the barn by the two deputies. "Are you up to giving them to me now?"

"I want to get this behind me as soon as possible," Eva said wearily. "So, let's do it and get it done."

They walked back to her house in silence. Jake's brain tried to sort out everything that had happened, everything that had been said, but he was still in a numbing shock that it had been David who had committed all the crimes.

A glance at Eva let him know she was probably in the same mental space. Her face was still pale, and as she reached up to shove a strand of hair behind her ear, her fingers trembled.

They went through the front door, and Eva led Wayne into the kitchen. "I'll be right back." She left the room.

The sight of what was left of the splintered back door still shocked Jake. He couldn't imagine the kind of terror that had to have filled Eva while David was breaking in with an ax.

"Hell of a mess," Wayne said when Eva had left the kitchen. "I would have never suspected David."

"I'm still in complete shock," Jake admitted. "He was behind it all, Wayne. My own brother was killing cattle and tormenting Eva. My own brother tried to kill her."

Eva came back into the kitchen wearing a robe over the thin nightgown she'd had on. She grabbed a broom from the pantry and began sweeping up the broken glass that littered the floor.

Wayne and Jake watched her for a minute or two. "Eva, come sit down," Wayne finally said. "I need your full attention while you're giving me your statement."

"I'll help you clean up later," Jake said gently. "Come sit down and let's get this over with." She hesitated a moment and then returned the broom to the pantry and joined them at the table.

"Do either of you mind if I tape this?" Wayne asked. They both said no, and Wayne pulled a small tape recorder out of his pocket. He set it on the table, spoke into it with the time and date, and then looked at Eva. "Tell me what happened this morning from the very beginning."

Her voice shook as she explained to Wayne about them oversleeping and Jake taking Andy to school. "When they were gone, I sat right here at the table and drank a cup of coffee, and then I started to leave the kitchen to get dressed for the day. I saw a person's shadow at the back door, and I assumed it must be Harley. I wasn't going to open the door until I was sure. So, I pulled up the blinds, and that's when I saw him."

The color that had crept back into her face faded once again. Jake reached over and captured her hand with his. Her fingers tightly squeezed his. "He had an ax, and he started hitting the door."

Her voice became breathless as she told them about running for her gun and then David knocking the weapon out of her hands. She recounted him choking her in the hallway and her hitting him to get away.

"I ran to the barn and climbed into the loft, hoping and praying I could hide from him until Jake got back home. He almost killed me… I was about to lose consciousness when Jake showed up."

"I got home and couldn't find her," Jake said. "When I saw the back door and didn't find her anywhere in the house, I knew she must have run outside, but I had no idea where she might be."

This time it was his fingers that squeezed hers. "I heard her scream and ran into the barn and realized she was up in the loft. I got up there and saw a man on top of her and strangling her." Even now, knowing she was safe, his chest still tightened as he remembered that moment.

"I pulled him off her and punched him and then pulled my gun. I wanted to shoot him, Wayne. I wanted to kill him for what he'd done to Eva. I can't believe it was David the whole time. I still can't believe it."

"He wasn't even on a long list of suspects," Wayne replied. "If he hadn't been caught in the act, we probably would have never caught him."

As Wayne and Eva continued to talk, Jake still tried to process that his brother had been behind everything, that David had actually tried to kill Eva. It was still difficult for him to comprehend.

It was just after noon when Wayne and his men finished photographing and collecting evidence both in the house and in the barn.

While Eva went into the bedroom to get out of her robe and nightgown and into clothes, Jake sat on the sofa to wait for her.

They still needed to clean up the kitchen where the door had been broken down, and they would need to contact somebody about a replacement door. But before any of that could happen, Jake needed some answers from her.

More than anything, he needed to know once and for all exactly what had happened ten years ago.

EVEN THOUGH EVA knew Jake was waiting for her, she took a hot shower before she got dressed. She needed to wash away the feel of David's hands on her, the abject evil she felt had touched her.

She had already had a showdown with a killer, and she suspected she was about to have one with Jake even though she didn't physically or mentally feel like having any more conflict for the day.

But David had opened up a whole can of worms, and she knew the time had come to pay for her past sins. When this was all over, she'd be alone, and she tried to tell herself that was what she'd wanted all along, but she couldn't help the weight of sadness that rode her shoulders as she went back into the living room.

She eased down on the sofa next to him. Her throat still burned and hurt, and now that the adrenaline of the moment had worn off, she had aches and pains in other areas of her body from the fight for her life.

"Eva." Jake reached out and took her hands in his, his beautiful eyes radiating pain. "I'm so sorry."

She looked at him in surprise. "What are you sorry about?"

The pain in his eyes deepened. "It was my own brother who did all these things to you. My brother…" He shook his head.

"Jake, you aren't responsible for your brother's actions," she replied softly.

He released her hands and instead raced his hands through his thick hair. "I know, but somehow I should have sensed something was off with him. I should have seen this coming."

"How could you? Why would either one of us even consider David wanting to harm me? I didn't even know your brother personally. This had nothing to do with you, Jake, so don't try to take any responsibility for it."

"Thank God I got here in time," he said.

She raised a hand to her throat, remembering that moment when she'd been positive she was going to die. "If you'd been one minute longer, I would have been gone. He would have succeeded in killing me."

He held her gaze for a long moment. "Eva, tell me

what happened ten years ago. Why did you break up with me and what part did my father play in all of it?"

She'd never expected this moment to come, when she'd have to talk to him about all this. He'd just had his brother exposed as a killer, and she hated to tell him now anything about his father that would destroy Jake's image of the man.

But it was time for truth telling. Before he left here today, he would know all her secrets, and she feared the consequences that would affect the rest of her life.

"Eva, it's time for us to talk about the past," he said.

"I know." She broke eye contact with him and instead looked down at the coffee table. "The night before I broke up with you, I was in the barn feeding the horses some treats when your father showed up."

She remembered how shocked she'd been to see Justin Albright parked in front of her home. He had been a tall, imposing man with cold, dark eyes. "I invited him inside, but he refused to come in and told me he just wanted to talk to me."

"What did he have to say?" Jake's voice was filled with tension, the same kind of tension that now twisted her stomach as she looked at him once again.

"He told me if I didn't stop seeing you, then he'd destroy my father. He would see to it that he lost the ranch and wound up with nothing." Jake's eyes filled with a new pain.

"Jake, if he'd threatened me, I probably wouldn't have broken up with you, but I couldn't risk him hurting my father. I knew he had the power to do what he threatened, and I was so afraid, so the next night I broke up with you. It was the most difficult thing I've ever done in my life. I'm sorry, Jake."

A new pain slashed across his features. "Don't apologize. I think somehow in the back of my mind I always wondered if he'd been involved in your decision to not see me anymore."

He leaned forward and raked his hands through his hair once again. "My family has caused nothing but pain in your life, Eva." He straightened up. "Why didn't you tell me at the time what my father had done?"

"Oh Jake, I knew how much you loved your father. The last thing I wanted to do was take that away from you. In any case, even if I told you, your father still held all the power."

"It all just makes me so sad." His gaze softened as he looked at her. "I was so in love with you, Eva. If my father hadn't interfered, I believe we would have gotten married and been happy for the rest of our lives."

"I believe the same thing, but he did interfere and that didn't happen," she replied softly.

They were silent for a moment, and all Eva could think about was the bombshell secret she still had to confess to him. She was vaguely surprised he hadn't already figured it out from what David had said about inheritances. However, the shock of finding out it was his own brother behind her terror might have made him miss a lot of what David had actually said.

She suddenly realized how much she wanted Jake to love her as he had before his father had gotten involved. She wanted him to love her for the rest of his life, as she knew she would love him. But she feared her final confession would send him out of her life, and he would leave behind utter devastation.

"Let me tell you what happened after I broke up with you and you went to Italy." She got up from the sofa, unable to sit next to him and tell him the depth of her deception.

She pulled the shade on the window, letting in the sunshine, and then turned to face him. "You'd been gone about two and a half weeks when my father died. Needless to say, I was devastated, and that's when Andrew stepped up as a comfort to me. I was overwhelmed with so many things, and he's the one who taught me what I needed to do to keep the ranch running smoothly."

"I wish it had been me, Eva," Jake said softly.

She nodded and smiled. "I know." Her smile lasted only a moment. "Anyway, Andrew came to me with the idea of an arrangement. He already knew he was dying. He hadn't been given that long to live, but he didn't want to die alone in a hospital surrounded by strangers. So, I agreed to marry him and take care of him to the end."

Jake frowned. "But if it was an arrangement, then what was in it for you? Were you in love with Andrew?"

"I came to love him in the three years we had together, but no, I didn't marry him for love. I agreed to marry him because he would give my unborn baby a name. I was pregnant, Jake. I was pregnant with your baby when I broke up with you."

"Andy is my son?"

She nodded and held her breath as he stared at her. The softness she'd seen shining from his eyes cooled and then hardened. "You should have told me, Eva. If you really wanted to, you could have figured out a way to get in touch with me in Italy."

"I was afraid, Jake. I was so afraid that if your father found out I was pregnant with your child, he would figure out a way to get the baby taken away from me and he'd follow through on his threat to destroy my father," she replied.

He stood, his eyes dark and unfathomable. "Why didn't you tell me when I got back here? My father was dead. Why didn't you tell me then?"

He didn't wait for a response from her. "You had no right, Eva. You had no right to keep him away from me. Nine years… I've lost nine years of his life, Eva." Anger tightened his features. "I've got to get out of here." He headed for the front door.

"Jake…wait," she protested. "Please, let's talk."

"Right now I'm too angry to talk." He opened the door and stalked outside.

Eva fought the impulse to run after him, to throw her arms around his neck and beg him to forgive her. But she didn't. Instead she sank down on the sofa and began to weep.

It had been her cowardice that had kept her silent when she'd first realized she was pregnant. She'd been a coward again when she hadn't told him about his son when he'd shown back up in town.

Jake had been betrayed today first by his brother, then by his father and finally by the woman he loved. While her heart ached for him, her tears were also for herself.

She'd been devastated when she'd lost Jake's love the first time, and she realized it was very possible she'd just lost it for a second time.

She'd survived the attack by David, but she wasn't at all sure she'd survive what might happen in her future where Jake and Andy were concerned.

Chapter Fourteen

Jake felt as if his very heart had been ripped out of his chest. He drove aimlessly as his chaotic thoughts tried to find some sense of order in his brain.

He'd thought David was just spewing out some kind of delusional nonsense when he'd talked about his son sharing his inheritance. He'd believed David was worried that he and Eva might have a child together in the future. He hadn't thought about Andy.

He was thrilled that the bright, loving boy was his own, but right now his heart was too bruised and battered by the fact that he'd lost so many years with Andy.

He'd missed not only the birth, but the first word… first step…a million other firsts that had already occurred. It was all time he could never get back.

She should have contacted him the minute she'd realized she was pregnant. Somehow, someway, they would have figured something out. But she obviously hadn't trusted him enough to be able to stand up to his father. He would have stood up to the devil himself if it meant staying with Eva and his son.

He wasn't sure whether he wanted to rage or to weep at all the overwhelming events of the day. He drove back country roads for the next hour or so and finally wound up at the Albright mansion.

His head was no clearer, but he was exhausted by all the emotional turmoil. It wasn't until he parked out front that he suddenly thought about his sister-in-law. Oh God, had Stephanie heard about what had happened?

Had she known what her husband was up to? No, there was no way Jake believed Stephanie would have any part in harming another human being. There was no way anything like that was in her DNA.

He walked into the hallway and called her name. She came out of the sitting room and stood frozen in the doorway. Her eyes were swollen and red-rimmed, and he instantly knew that she had heard what had happened.

"Ah, Steph," he said softly and opened his arms to her. She walked into his embrace and cried into his shoulder for several minutes. She finally stepped back from him and swiped her cheeks.

He took her by the hand and led her to the sofa in the sitting room where he pulled her down to sit next to him. "How did you hear?"

"Wayne stopped by to question me. I… Jake… I had no idea." Tears once again filled her eyes. "I knew something was going on with him. David was gone almost all the time. He left here early in the morning and didn't return until the middle of the night.

"He told me he was working on some new contracts, that it was business that had him staying gone all the time. But normally he did his work here in the office. He told me he was spending his time in his office in town, but I drove by there one night and he wasn't there."

She released a short, half-hysterical laugh as more tears spilled from her eyes. "He'd become so secretive and distant, I suspected he was having an affair. God, I wish it had been an affair. What he did…what he tried to do was absolutely unspeakable."

Her eyes became haunted. "I knew there were times David could be ruthless in his business dealings. I also knew he could have a cruel streak with the way he sometimes spoke to me, but even I wasn't aware of the utter evil he had inside him. I'm so sorry, Jake. And please tell Eva how sorry I am."

"I'm not sure how long it will be before I'm ready to speak to Eva again," he replied, his heart aching once again.

"What do you mean?"

Jake told Stephanie about everything he'd learned from Eva…about his father's machinations to keep the young lovers apart and about Jake being Andy's father.

"Nine years, Stephanie. I've missed nine years of Andy's life because Eva kept this secret from me." Anger swept through him once again.

"I'm so sorry, Jake," Stephanie said. "So, what are you going to do now?"

"To be honest, I don't know," he confessed. "I'm too angry right now to make any kind of a decision."

"I hope whatever you decide to do, you'll be kind to Eva. She must have been so afraid that your father would find out, and in any case, hasn't the Albright family done enough damage to her?" Stephanie stood. "And now I've got some packing to do. If you could give me just a couple of days, then I'll be out of here."

Jake looked at her in surprise. "Out of here? Stephanie, this is your home. Why would you pack up and leave?"

Her eyes became red and glassy with impending tears.

"I was here because I was married to your brother, and now I intend to seek a divorce from him and he'll be in prison for years to come. I have no place here anymore."

"That's nonsense. You are still my sister-in-law, and Richard is still my nephew. You're my family, and you're welcome to live here for as long as you want."

"Are you sure?" Tears filled her eyes once again and escaped down her cheeks.

"I'm very sure," Jake replied firmly.

"Thank you, Jake. I was feeling so lost. I was feeling like I'd not only lost my husband but also my home. I've been in a haze since Wayne left."

"Well, you don't have to worry about losing your home. You and Richard will always have a place here." Jake stood and so did Steph.

She hugged Jake and then stepped back, tears chasing down her cheeks once again. "I still can't believe what David did. I wish I could have someway stopped him, but I just didn't see the evil and hatred he had in his heart for Eva."

"Don't beat yourself up, Steph. None of us saw this coming."

She nodded. "Richard is taking a nap. I think maybe I'll rest a bit."

"That's exactly what I plan on doing right now."

Together they walked up the staircase. "Jake, I hope you find forgiveness in your heart for Eva. She's been a victim in this for a long time." She didn't wait for his reply, but instead turned and headed down the hallway toward her suite of rooms.

Jake released a deep sigh and headed for his own rooms. He couldn't imagine what Stephanie was going through right now. Her entire world had been destroyed by the man she'd loved and trusted, by the man who was the father of her son.

He slumped down on the sofa in his sitting room, his thoughts still in chaos where Eva was concerned. He wanted to hate her for what she'd done. He wanted to despise her for keeping Andy a secret for so many years.

But there was a more rational part of his brain that understood the choices she'd made. Certainly he now understood why she had broken up with him on that night so long ago.

Eva would have done anything to protect her father, and Jake knew how frightening his father could be. Eva had loved her father, and the threat against him must have been terrifying for her. Jake had adored his father, but now he realized he'd adored a man who didn't exist.

Justin Albright had been a bully who used his power and money to bend people to his will. God knew how many victims Justin had left behind when he'd died. He'd used his power and money against his own son, to destroy Jake's dream of marrying Eva and living the life of a simple rancher.

He tried to imagine how Eva must have felt when she'd been eighteen years old. Her father had died unexpectedly, and she'd discovered she was pregnant by a man who lived in Italy and at that time had hated her for breaking up with him.

She must have been absolutely terrified. She could have decided not to have the baby. Thankfully she hadn't made that choice. She'd chosen to have his baby despite the odds stacked against her.

He also wanted to hate Andrew Martin, but he couldn't hate the man who had helped Eva survive, the man who had agreed to give his son his name. He couldn't hate the man who had loved Andy for three years before his death. In fact, he thanked God that Andrew had been there for Eva.

Jake got up and began to pace, trying to untangle his emotions. There was no question that he now wanted plenty of quality time with his son.

Andy should be home from school now. Had Eva told him? If she hadn't yet, then when did she intend to tell him the truth? He had a feeling Andy would be thrilled to have a real, living and breathing father to add to his life. And Jake was positive Andy would be happy to discover that man was Jake.

In the time Jake had spent at Eva's, he and Andy had completely bonded. Jake had fallen in love with Andy even when he'd believed he wasn't Andy's father.

All he had to figure out now was exactly how or if he intended to coparent with Eva.

EVA SANK DOWN on her sofa and listened to the silence around her. It was the first time in weeks she didn't have the simmering fear as a companion. David Albright was in jail, and her back door had been repaired.

There would be no more dead cattle or chilling notes. She didn't have to worry about anyone wanting to kill her anymore. The danger was gone, and she should feel deliriously happy.

But she didn't. All she felt was a deep sadness and a new kind of fear. She hadn't told Andy the truth about Jake yet. Andy was now sleeping peacefully in bed, unaware of how his life was going to change.

And it was that change that now frightened her. She had no idea what Jake was going to do about Andy.

Would he fight her for full custody because she had had Andy to herself for the past nine years?

She couldn't imagine not tucking her son into bed at night or seeing his bright morning smile. It was torturous to think that she wouldn't hear about Andy's school adventures the minute he got off the bus, or they wouldn't deliver his eggs together.

And the worst thing of all was that without the danger, without the fear, she was left with only her love for Jake. It had always been him in her heart.

The teenage boy who had sat barefoot on the dock next to her had become the man she wished to spend the rest of her life with. But she didn't believe that would happen now.

In the end Justin Albright had won and the two young lovers would never, ever find happily-ever-after with each other.

Tears filled her eyes, but she quickly swiped them away. Maybe she'd cry later. What had happened with Jake was her own fault. She'd kept the secret of Andy too long, and now she could only wonder what price she'd have to pay.

Maybe she should just go to bed. She'd already put on her nightgown, and exhaustion weighed heavily on her. She could escape all her worry, escape the utter heartache of knowing the man she loved probably hated her now for a little while, if she'd just go to sleep.

But she remained where she was on the sofa, and even though she told herself she'd cry later, tears seeped from her eyes and ran down her cheeks faster and faster.

She felt as alone now as she had years ago when her father had suddenly died and she'd just realized she was pregnant. She'd find her strength tomorrow, and somehow or other she'd weather the storm that she feared was coming. Tomorrow she'd be strong for Andy, but tonight she had no more strength left. She just felt sad and anxious about what would happen next.

She was just about to head to her bedroom when she heard a soft knock on her door. Instantly her stomach clenched into a million knots. It could only be one person.

She opened the door to Jake. He looked tense and imposing and incredibly handsome dressed in a navy polo shirt and jeans. "Can I come in?" he asked.

Nodding, she opened the door wider to allow him entry. He took a seat on the sofa, his features unreadable. She closed the door and took a seat in the chair opposite him, her heart beating fast and furiously as she faced him.

"Needless to say, we need to talk," he said.

"I know," she replied.

"How are you feeling?" He frowned. "Your throat is really bruised."

She reached a hand up and touched her tender neck. "It's sore, and to be honest, I kind of feel like I was run over by a big truck this morning. But it will be fine." The last thing she wanted was any pity from him.

"Is Andy sleeping?"

"Yes."

"Did you tell him about me?" he asked.

"No. I thought that was a conversation we needed to have with him together," she replied.

Was he prolonging what he was here to discuss with her on purpose? She couldn't stand the tension any longer. "Jake, have you decided what you intend to do concerning Andy?"

"I have." His gaze held hers intently. "I want full custody of Andy."

Eva's world crashed down around her. She could hear nothing but the explosion of her heart. It was her worst nightmare come true. She would never be able to stop him. He had all the money, and she had none to fight him in a court of law.

He got up from the sofa and approached where she sat. "Eva, I also want full custody of you," he continued. "I want to marry you and live here with you and my son. I want to ranch with you here on your land. I want to make more babies with you and live the life we once dreamed about, but I don't know what you want, and I don't want you to choose me because of Andy. If you don't want me, then we'll work out a reasonable co-parenting relationship."

She gazed up at him as she slowly digested his words. "Oh Jake, I want you. You've always been in my heart and soul. I want that love we pledged to each other in the hayloft. I love you, Jake."

He grabbed her up from the chair and pulled her into his arms. His lips captured hers in a kiss that spoke of breathtaking passion and enduring love.

When the kiss ended, she smiled at him. "We'll tell Andy when he gets home from school tomorrow. He's going to be so happy, Jake."

"I loved Andy when I didn't know he was mine, and I love him now as my son. I loved you years ago, and I never stopped loving you, Eva." His eyes glowed with his happiness. "Can I spend the night with you?"

"You can spend all your nights with me," she replied.

"Do I have to sleep on that lumpy, uncomfortable sofa?"

She laughed. "You never have to sleep on that sofa again."

He kissed her once again, and Eva felt as if her life was finally complete. She would continue to raise her son with Jake as a partner.

There was nothing and nobody who could stop them from building the life they had once dreamed of, and it was going to be a life filled with laughter and happiness and love.

Epilogue

"Andy, slow down," Eva yelled to her son, who was running ahead of them to the pond.

Running at his heels was Princess, a black schnauzer who not only slept in Andy's room each night but also went almost everywhere her son went.

Princess was the first addition to the family, but there was also another addition coming in four months. Eva was pregnant, and both Andy and Jake were over the moon about it.

David was still in jail, facing a multitude of charges, but that hadn't stopped Jake and Eva from moving on with their lives.

They had gotten married two months after the attack on Eva. It had been an intimate affair with only the preacher and Stephanie as a witness. They had exchanged vows in the hayloft, making real the teenage vows they had once spoken to each other.

Jake now grabbed her hand as they headed toward the pond for a family outing of fishing. They reached the dock, where Eva and Jake sat side by side and Andy settled in next to them with Princess next to him.

"Happy?" Jake asked.

"Happier than I could ever imagine," she replied. "What about you?"

"I'm living my very best dream," he replied. He gazed at her with the light in his eyes that warmed her from head to toe.

"I'm living my very best dream, too," Andy said. "I've got a dad and a dog. What more could I want?"

Eva laughed. "You'd better want a little sister, because it won't be long and you'll have one. And we need to pick out a name for her."

"I'll be the best big brother you ever saw," Andy said.

"There's no doubt in my mind that you'll be a great big brother to little Posie," Jake said.

Andy laughed. "We can't call her Posie," he protested.

Jake continued to throw out names, making Andy laugh over and over again. Eva's heart filled with such love it nearly brought her to tears.

Finally, she had the happiness she'd wanted with the man she had always loved. Their love had survived family betrayals and death threats. Their relationship was built on forgiveness and passion and a love that had endured through space and time.

As the laughter of their son and Jake rode the breeze, and with the stir of new life inside her, Eva knew her future was going to be wonderful.

* * * * *

COLTON STORM WARNING

JUSTINE DAVIS

Chapter One

"It's your own fault."

Ty Colton gave his colleague a sour look. Mitch was a good friend, but he was also a sarcastic son of a gun. At least to his colleagues he was. He managed to rein it in with clients. Or maybe he was sarcastic to them because he had to rein it in with clients.

"How did getting stuck babysitting get to be my fault?" Ty asked, letting some of his irritation into his voice.

"If you hadn't gone all heroic and saved that Sawyer kid last year, you'd still be flying under the radar, dude."

"If I was heroic," he pointed out, "I should be getting rewarded, not punished."

"Would that life were that way," a deep yet quiet voice came from behind them. They both turned to see Eric King, the founder of Elite Security, the man who was technically Ty's partner but whom he most times deferred to as his boss, walking toward them with his ever-present tablet in his hand. "But then again," Eric went on, "a true hero doesn't ask for any reward."

Ty studied the older man for a moment, judged

he wasn't really angry and said deferentially, "You would know."

He meant it. He admired Eric King more than any man he knew. Including—perhaps especially—his own father. Fitz Colton was many things, but a loving, involved parent was not one of them. From the first day he'd met him, Eric seemed to care more about the path Ty was on than his father ever had. Once he'd decided the family business wasn't for him, that seemed to be the end of his father's interest in his eldest son.

And unlike his father, Eric didn't bark out orders gruffly. He didn't have to. Ty's sister Jordana, a police detective, had once told him his boss reeked of command presence, and he supposed that was a good description. He reminded Ty more of his Uncle Shep—newly returned to their hometown of Braxville—than anyone. Not surprising since Shepherd Colton had spent even longer in the Navy than Eric had in the Marines. Not, Eric pointed out, that anyone ever really left the Marines.

"Buttering me up won't get you out of this, Colton," the man said, although his eyes warmed enough that Ty knew the compliment had registered. "They asked for you specifically, so you're locked in. Mitch, you'll be his backup."

"Damned social media," Ty muttered, knowing that was probably how this family had discovered him, in that photo that had gone viral of him carrying little Samantha Sawyer from the warehouse where she'd been held for ransom. The rescue operation had been kept under the radar, but these days everyone with a phone fancied themselves a journalist, and one of them had caught that moment. When he'd first seen it, he'd simply been glad the terrified little girl's face had been hidden as she sobbed into his shirt. By the fiftieth time he'd seen it, he'd been well and truly annoyed.

Jordana had teased him, pointing out every time the shot turned up somewhere, and telling him to enjoy his fame. His brother Brooks, on the other hand, understood. "I wouldn't want it," he'd said. "It'd be hard to stay a *private* investigator when your face is all over every public domain in the country."

Of course, Brooks had been a lot more understanding about many things lately. Especially since he and Gwen Harrison had gotten engaged.

Ty barely stopped a grimace. He was happy for them. He was happy for Jordana, too, whose growing happiness with businessman Clint Broderick was obvious. Even Bridgette, the girl of the Colton triplets, had settled into a happy reunion with her high school sweetheart.

So the Colton kids are three for six on the happy-ever-after front. Too bad the oldest can't get it in gear.

He shook off the fruitless thoughts—he'd about decided that kind of happy wasn't in the cards for him—and focused on the matter at hand. He didn't like the idea of being pulled off the case his family had been sucked into after the grim discovery of two bodies sealed in the walls of an old Colton Construction building. He was getting close, really close, to unraveling that decades-old case.

But Elite Security had first call on his time, and the police—including his sister the detective—had warned him about jurisdiction issues, and not contaminating the case. Not that that had stopped him from doing a little digging of his own. But that was going to have to go on hold, at least for now.

"So what's the deal?" he asked.

"Parents worried about their daughter, who's been threatened. They've got a lot of clout, and this could be a good thing for the company." Eric grinned at him. "Almost as good as your heroics."

Ty grimaced. Dealing with bigwigs was never his favorite thing. "Is it a credible threat, or are we just keeping them happy?"

"Research is working on that."

"Who threatened the kid, and why?"

"Some guy named Sanderson, out of Kansas City. Another reason they came to us."

Ty frowned. "Name sounds familiar, but I can't place it."

"Research is working up a profile now."

"Research is busy," Mitch put in with a lazy smile. "What do they have on the parents?"

For the first time in this discussion—perhaps the first time since he'd known him—Eric looked…not uneasy, Ty didn't think he even could, but wary. And that alone made the hair on the back of Ty's neck stand up. "Research didn't need to find out who they are. I'm guessing we all know."

Uh-oh. "Drop the bomb," Ty suggested, already not liking it.

"Her name's Ashley Hart."

Ty frowned as he discarded the first thought that had come to him. Mitch let out a low whistle, indicating he hadn't discarded the seemingly impossible idea. And another look at Eric's face told Ty he shouldn't have been so hasty.

"Not… Andrew Hart? The Westport Harts?" In wealth and prominence, the Connecticut family ranked right up there with the likes of the Rockefellers. Although by Hart standards, the Rockefellers might still be considered new upstarts; the Harts had been American aristocracy as long as, say, the DuPonts.

"The very same," Eric said.

Ty groaned. "Great. So I get to not just babysit, but babysit some spoiled rich kid?"

Mitch snorted. Ty looked at him. "Like you weren't one, *Colton*?" his friend said, but he was grinning.

"Yeah, yeah," he retorted, his own grin a bit wry. "Hardly on that level."

"Speaking of babysitting," Eric said rather pointedly, "if you two are through?"

"Sorry," Ty muttered. "So where do I connect with the little darling? Westport?" *Hartford airport*, he thought. It was about twenty miles farther than La Guardia or JFK in New York, but a lot less hassle. He'd make up the time just getting out of the airport. Then he—

"No," Eric said. "She's in McPherson."

Ty blinked. "Our McPherson? McPherson, Kansas?" The town of some thirteen thousand just east of his hometown of Braxville hardly seemed like a place someone from Westport would likely be visiting, let alone a Hart.

"Yes, our McPherson."

"Why?"

"She was there for some meeting about the Lake Inman wetlands expansion."

Ty drew back. "Wait, I thought you said she was a kid."

"She is." Eric grinned at him. "But I'm old. To me, you're a kid."

Ty scowled at Eric. The man might be pushing sixty, but he looked a decade younger and was fit enough to put both him and Mitch on the floor. Probably at the same time. But before he could say anything, Eric's tablet chimed, and he waited as the man scanned the message. Then Eric tapped the screen a few times as he spoke. "Details on where you're meeting up and the threat report. I'll send it to your phone. Mitch, liaison with Research and send whatever they turn up on to Ty when it's ready."

"You mean I don't get to help wrangle?" Mitch's disappointment was clearly mock.

Eric finished sending the details before looking up at them. "Ty can handle it. McPherson's close enough you can get there in a hurry if need be. I'll be tied up with the loose ends of the Rivera case, but I'll be on our comms."

Ty nodded. The high-end private communication system was one of the things that made Elite work so well. They didn't have to rely on easily hackable cell networks or internet to connect with each other while on a job. Mitch, meanwhile, just looked relieved at escaping. "Anything else?"

"Nothing that's not in the report. Obviously, handle with care."

Ty sighed. He was not looking forward to dealing with some East Coast high-society type. But he said only, "Yes, sir."

He looked at Mitch, who was grinning at him, his relief obvious now. Eric turned to go, then turned back. "Mitch, make sure you look at the file now, too. You'll need to know who he's watching, in case you have to back him up. There's a photo up front."

Ty's brow furrowed as Eric walked away. There had been something a little too pointed in that look he'd given Mitch, who was pulling out his phone to follow the order.

"Damn," Mitch said. And it was heartfelt.

"What?" he asked.

"You have all the luck."

"Luck? Aren't you the guy who was just—"

He stopped dead when Mitch held out his phone. And Ty found himself looking at one of the loveliest women he'd ever seen. The picture had clearly been taken at some formal occasion. She was wearing an off-the-shoulder dress, white trimmed in black, but he barely noticed. Not with those lovely slender shoulders and delicate throat on display. Her face was…refined, his mother would call it. Delicate features. Dark bottomless brown eyes. Her dark brown hair was pulled back into some loose sort of knot, and small gold earrings her only jewelry. Not that she needed any adornment with all that luscious skin showing.

He sucked in some air, only then aware he'd stopped breathing for a moment.

Damn, indeed.

Chapter Two

Ashley Hart paced her small suite, focusing on the patterned carpet rather intensely so she didn't look up and glare at her innocent phone again. She'd barely stopped herself from blasting her irritation to the skies via a social media post, but she'd vowed long ago to keep her family, especially her parents, out of all her timelines. She didn't want to be listened to because she was a Hart of the Westport Harts, but because she was right.

Because she was telling the truth.

She stopped at the window that looked out toward the small town. She knew it was half the size of Westport, but that was probably the smallest difference between it and the oceanfront community she'd grown up in. Yet, in a way, looking out over the vast flat of the Kansas prairie was sort of like looking out over the vastness of the Atlantic. It was an interesting comparison, in any case.

She turned and paced back, this time waving her hand over the silent phone to light the lock screen and check the time.

Ten minutes. This guy had ten minutes to show up or she was leaving. She was already fuming over this whole thing, anyway. Her parents were overreacting.

This was hardly the first time she'd made someone angry with her. When she'd been overseas, in an especially rural area, she'd had an entire community angry with her for helping their long-time enemies set up a medical clinic. And back home, she'd had other communities—for that's how she sometimes thought of them—here in the US calling her names she hadn't even known the meaning of. Sometimes her social media feeds held as much anger and threats as accolades and appreciation, almost always hidden behind the cutesy names and the general anonymity of the internet.

Why this threat was so different, she didn't know. Except that it had been sent to her parents instead of her. She loved them, adored them in fact, but she was twenty-seven now, and while she always listened to them, they did not tell her what to do.

Except when they did.

What they'd told her this morning was to stay in her hotel room until the security they'd arranged arrived. A top-ranked firm, they'd said, as if the Harts would settle for anything less. She wondered, somewhat idly as she paced, what need there was for something called Elite Security here in Kansas, in the middle of—

She caught herself. She hated when she fell into the trap so many in her circle did, dismissing everything between the coasts as flyover country. It was called the heartland for a reason, she reminded herself. And hadn't the size of the group that had shown up to meet with her and discuss their concerns told her they cared as much as she did about what happened here?

And yet, even with the awareness she worked so hard at, she still had almost slipped into that dismissive mindset. No wonder many people here disliked people like her.

Enough to make threats to her parents? Apparently.

But if she'd been going to let threats stop her, she would have given up her various causes long ago. Because whether she was trying to preserve something or change something, it seemed there was always someone who was against it. Sometimes they came around. Sometimes they did not. The times she liked best were when she and the opposing interest were able to reach a compromise that both found acceptable, if not perfect. Then she felt as if she'd truly accomplished something.

Unlike now, stuck here in this room.

That was it. She was done with this. She needed to get moving. She wanted to spend some time researching. One of the people at the meeting had worked at the local library and mentioned there were extensive references there about the very thing she was here for. The library wasn't that far away, according to her map app. She could easily walk it. And she'd like a nice walk outside, some fresh air.

She liked doing that in different places, seeing how different the air smelled. From the salt-tinged air of her home turf to the cool, exotic scent of a rain forest to the air here that seemed impossibly tinged with both dust and damp at the same time, she loved it all. She thought that maybe she would come back here in the spring, when the vast fields were green and growing. She wanted to see where so much of the food the nation ate was actually produced. And perhaps one day, she might write a paper on the subject of how each region of the world, probably each microclimate, had its own distinct scent. It would be interesting to visit places scientists said had the same climate and see if they smelled the same.

She laughed at herself, but also promised her curious mind that someday she would take time for such esoteric projects.

Decided now, she glanced in the mirror over the large dresser. The black jeans and mock turtleneck sweater would do, she decided, and her hair still had a little wave at the ends that brushed her shoulders, from having been in a bun to keep it out of her way while she traveled. She picked up the black hoop earrings from the top of the dresser and slipped them back in place, then grabbed up her jacket and the rather oversized bag she carried while traveling. She liked having her tablet at hand to make notes with as various ideas came to her. And she would need it at the library, anyway.

She would stop at the desk and leave a message for this security person, saying where she'd gone and to meet her at the library. *Or not*, she added to herself with an inward smile.

It was a pleasant ride down, and as the elevator doors opened at the bottom, she stood back to let the older couple she'd been chatting with on the way exit first. As she waited, she glanced around the lobby, her gaze snagging on a man coming in through the glass front doors. *Nice*, she thought. *No, better than nice*, she amended, as she watched him stride across the lobby. Dark hair, short and a little tousled looking, tall—very tall, a couple of inches over six feet, she guessed, and… well, built. Or well-built. Lord, she was grinning at her own silly mental jokes now.

"Don't blame you, honey," the woman who had introduced herself as Ella Roth whispered, looking back over her shoulder. “That’s a fine hunk of man.”

Ashley felt herself flush slightly. She wasn’t in the habit of being so obvious. But that was indeed a fine hunk of man. She wondered where he was visiting from. He didn’t have the air of a big city guy, but of someone used to the wide-open spaces. She couldn’t quite picture him walking between towering skyscrapers.

They matched, she realized suddenly. Beneath a lightweight jacket, he was also in black jeans and a black-knit shirt, although his was a crew style. Which was nice, because it would be a shame to hide that very muscled male neck. And the way he moved, making her all too aware of what was obviously a powerful body beneath the clothes…

There she was, flushing again. She needed to get outside in cooler air. Her weather app said it was about fifty-six outside, not much warmer than it likely would be at home. That would do it.

Maybe she should wait until he was gone before approaching the desk to leave her message. She didn’t want to be caught blushing at the sight of a total stranger. But the idea of dodging said stranger didn’t sit well with her. And he was headed toward her.

Toward the elevators, idiot. Not you.

But then his gaze locked on her. There was no other word for it. And he did, in fact, head directly toward her. As if he’d recognized her. Knew her.

Belatedly it hit her. Oh, surely not. This couldn’t be the guy, could it?

Of course it could. Look at him. Isn’t he the living

image of what every woman would want as a...protector? A bodyguard?

She sighed inwardly. Kansas might not be the first place people thought of for top-notch security firms, but if this guy was any example, they obviously could grow them right.

"Ms. Hart," he said, as he came to a halt before her, holding out a photo ID. He had a voice that sent a ripple through her. Deep, and the tiniest bit rough. "I'm with Elite Security."

Of course you are.

She saw Mrs. Roth, walking toward the lobby, look back at her and smile, giving her a thumbs-up gesture. She resisted rolling her eyes.

"You going to check my ID?" he asked, and her gaze snapped back to his face. He looked just as good up close. Better, in fact, with those dark blue eyes and annoyingly thick eyelashes. And that jaw.

"Don't need to," she said with a barely suppressed sigh.

"You always need to," he said, rather sternly.

It didn't seem wise to explain that she didn't have to because all of this was just her luck. Not only having to worry about her parents' fears, and tolerate the only thing that would ease them, but end up with a guy who looked like he'd walked off the cover of a men's fitness magazine. She would have said some Hollywood tabloid, except he looked too tough for that make-believe world.

But then she laughed silently at herself, knowing anyone and everyone would laugh in turn at the idea of Ashley Hart moaning about her luck. She'd won life's lottery when she was born not only into the Hart family but to two people who adored her as much as they adored each other, which was saying something.

"Yes, you're quite right," she said. "I was…thinking of something else."

She looked at the ID card with the logo of an encircled globe in the upper left corner. Were they that big that they covered the world? Then she hit the photo, a typical ID card picture with no expression, just that chiseled face and those eyes, looking…annoyed. At having to stay still long enough to have his picture taken? At having it taken at all? Or was annoyance just his default mode? She imagined he could get away with a lot of it, with those looks.

She looked back at the living man before her, not that she really needed to compare him to the image; there was no mistaking him. Something in the way he was looking at her made her want to look away again. And in fact she did, ashamed of herself even as she did so.

This was going to be a definite pain.

"And," he added, "you're forgetting to ask for your code word."

Her gaze shot back to his face. Now she was thoroughly annoyed. Not at him, but at herself. How often had her parents lectured her never to trust anyone who came to her claiming to be from them who didn't have the code word? It had been part of her life since she'd been old enough to understand, but somehow this man had blown it right out of her mind.

She stiffened her spine. "You're quite right. What is it?" The moment she asked, she knew this would be amusing.

"Fluffy." She'd been right. Even the look on his face as he said it was amusing.

"My childhood pet," she said, unable to resist grinning at him. "I was seven."

"I've got no room to talk. My dog was Ripper."

"How very male of you."

"Says the girl who named her…cat? Dog? Fluffy."

"Actually, she was a turtle."

He blinked. "You named a turtle Fluffy?"

She nodded, still grinning. "Because she wasn't."

She saw his lips start to curve, actually saw him fight it. "At seven, how did you even know it was a she?"

"My dad and I worked it out. He made me look everything up and go through it step by step, length of shell, shape of plastron, length of front claws, that kind of thing."

"Don't they live a very long time?"

"They can, yes. Fluffy's still going strong, although she's teaching at my old elementary school now."

He didn't fight the smile this time, and she felt like she'd been given an award, which sent up a red flag in the back of her mind. But before she really recognized the warning for what it was, the name printed on the card, with the bold signature above it, very belatedly registered. Tyler Colton.

Jolted, she looked back at him.

"Colton?"

"That's what it says," he said flatly, his amusement and his smile vanishing.

Her first thought was the former president, and without much thought—a rarity for her—the question poured out. "Any relation to the—"

"Yes." He said it bluntly, and with obvious irritation. "But I'm not in the family business."

She gave yet another inward sigh. No wonder her parents had decided upon this company. Nothing like having someone connected to a former president looking out for your, as her father put it, strong-willed daughter.

Chapter Three

Ty was having a little trouble. One of his strengths, one that Eric had helped him hone and believe in, was reading people. He was good at telling when they were diverting, avoiding or downright lying. But at the moment, he couldn't seem to focus on those aspects of the exquisite woman before him.

He estimated she was about five-seven, and slender. Not skinny but lanky, like a spring foal who'd figured out her legs at last. Unlike in the photo, her hair was down, and it gleamed as if catching what light there was in the elevator alcove. And her eyes were the kind of deep rich brown that seemed so mysterious, and yet they held a sharp, observing intelligence only a fool would overlook. Her features were delicate—except for that luscious mouth.

The mouth he was staring at. He slammed back to reality and cursed at himself silently. *Some security expert you are.*

"—good friend of my father," she was saying.

He'd entirely missed the first part of that. "Your father," he said, trying to cover.

She nodded. "They met when he was considering running and going around the country, assessing support. My father was the one who urged him to do so. They've stayed good friends, even now that he's out of office." She smiled. "He was a good president, I think."

Joe Colton. She was talking about Joe Colton. That was why she'd reacted to the name. He'd thought she'd heard about the lawsuit and all the problems Colton Construction was having these days. Problems he would much prefer to be digging into, despite being warned off by Jordana and her partner, Reese Carpenter. He should have known better. Why would their little—relative to her life, anyway—problems matter to the likes of her?

"He's a pretty distant connection," he said, his voice rather gruff as he tried to cover his discomfiture at having so completely blown this initial contact. "I don't have anything to do with that branch, really." *It's enough dealing with my own.*

"Yet you felt defensive about it?" she asked with one elegant brow arched at him.

Okay, now she had him thoroughly embarrassed. Because he had kind of snapped at her. "No. I mean… I was referring to my family, not him. My father's company is…in kind of a mess at the moment."

Her brow furrowed. "I saw some reports about… Colton Construction, right?"

He grimaced. "Yes. It's kind of the main topic around here lately."

"I'm sorry." She sounded like she meant it.

"No need." He tried to get a grip. "But where were you going? You were supposed to stay in your hotel room until I got there."

"I felt trapped in that room."

"You'd have really felt trapped if that guy who threatened you had been on that elevator."

Her chin came up. "But he wasn't. And Mr. and Mrs. Roth were delightful. Besides, I was only headed to the library."

"Without protection."

"It's not that far. I wanted the walk."

"It's not that close. Two, two and a half miles. And you were going to walk. Alone." She shrugged. He studied her for a moment. "You're not taking this at all seriously, are you." It wasn't really a question, because he knew she wasn't, he could feel it.

"My parents are…protective."

"You'd make quite a target under normal circumstances. Doing what you do just raises your profile. It's understandable they feel protective."

"Too protective."

"From what I gathered, I doubt they believe there is such a thing."

She gave him a look that seemed nothing more than curious. "Is that how your parents are?"

"No."

She let out a short breath that verged on disgusted. "Why? Because you're a big strong man?"

He couldn't help it, the corners of his mouth twitched. "I am. But it's more because we don't hold a huge chunk of the world's wealth, tempting slimeballs who want to get rich the easy way."

"That has nothing to do with this," she said, sounding rather offended. "This is strictly me."

"You can attract your own threats, is that what you're saying?"

She blinked. Looked as if she were winding up for

a fierce retort. But then suddenly, unexpectedly, she smiled. Widely. And it was devastating.

"Touché, Mr. Colton. It's been known to happen," she said. "I seem to have a tendency to anger certain kinds of people."

"The kind who would like you to mind your own business?"

"But what I get involved in is my own business. Mine and everyone who gives a damn." A crusader. Dear God, Eric had stuck him with a crusader. "Now, if you don't mind, I'd like to get to the library. I have some research to do."

"Research?"

"Yes." She gave him a sideways look. "I don't rush into these things blind, Mr. Colton, nor jump on any passing bandwagon. My name bears weight, so I make sure I do my homework."

"A responsible do-gooder, huh?"

She drew up sharply. "You say that as if you think those two terms are mutually exclusive."

"Sometimes they are. And I know that from personal experience."

She looked about to say something else, then stopped. "I need to be on my way," she said, and he knew that wasn't what she'd been going to say. He wondered what had made her change her mind.

"My car's out front."

"I told you, I want the walk."

"You'll be safer in the car."

She smiled at him sweetly. Too sweetly. "Isn't that your job, to keep me safe wherever I am?"

The expression, and that syrupy tone that matched it, grated on him. But he kept his voice level. "And your job is not to make that impossible by being stubborn about it."

"Not the most diplomatic approach I've ever seen."

"You want a diplomat, you'd better head back home." *And someone else can take over this job I didn't want in the first place.* "I understand your family hangs out with that bunch."

She looked, finally, perturbed. "I see why you avoid the presidential branch," she said coolly. "They'd likely throw you out."

"Likely," he agreed. "I don't have the Machiavellian instinct needed for that crowd. The question is, is that a point for or against me?"

She studied him for a moment. He saw…something in those dark brown eyes change, as if she'd reached some sort of conclusion. "Well," she said, her tone quite different now, lighter, "since that's something I lack as well, I suppose I'll have to say it's in your favor."

He couldn't help it, her words made him smile. He hadn't expected that. "I have trouble believing you couldn't swim in that world, if you wanted to."

Her eyes widened, and he wondered why. He hadn't meant it as a criticism, except maybe of that world of politics, which he loathed. It was part of the reason he'd walked away from the family business; there was too much of that involved for his taste.

Then, quickly, she recovered. "I could swim with sharks, too, but I'd expect consequences."

And this time he laughed, almost unwillingly. And apparently surprised her, since she nearly gaped at him. But he pointed out, "In one sense, that's what you do, anyway. And right now there's one circling, so to ignore it would be foolhardy."

She looked strangely pleased, then thoughtful. And finally she sighed audibly. "All right. The car it is."

So she could see reason. He felt suddenly better about this whole thing. "Good. I'm out front."

She only nodded and started walking that way. He instinctively scanned the lobby, but there was no sign of anyone suspicious. Of anyone watching her, other than the desk clerk who was simply looking with obvious male appreciation. And he couldn't blame the guy for that. She was as beautiful as that photograph showed, in a big city sort of way.

But for an uber-rich East Coast sort, he found it interesting that her clothing was so simple. Even her jeans weren't some fancy designer-label type, but instead the classic brand that he himself wore.

To determine this, he realized he'd been looking at what was admittedly a nice trim but curved backside, which was not someplace he wanted to go. This was a job, she was a client—or rather her parents who owned half the world were clients—and so unattainable to an average guy like him, it was incalculable.

But, he thought as he followed, that didn't mean he couldn't appreciate.

Chapter Four

Ashley was glad he was a half step behind her. She was having trouble keeping her expression even as she analyzed two very unsettling facts. No, three. One, he was entirely too attractive for her to maintain her usual buffer with men she was forced by circumstance to be around. Two, her heart had nearly stopped when he'd smiled. And three, when she'd made him laugh, she'd felt a rush of pleasure that had completely startled and disconcerted her.

Maybe it was just because he had a great laugh. It had the same rough edge as his voice did, which somehow made it even more special. And he'd looked surprised, as if it had been a long time since he'd laughed.

My father's company is...in kind of a mess at the moment. It's kind of the main topic around here lately.

It seemed there was reason for him not to laugh easily just now. She made a mental note to do a little research on that, too. Only in the interest of knowing whom she was dealing with, of course. And because she felt a bit foolish in assuming that since he was a Colton, and related, even distantly, to *that* branch of the family, that the presidential connection would be front and center.

His vehicle was a black SUV of the sort her parents—and probably that presidential branch of his family—often used when attending official functions. He stopped to talk with the valet, and Ashley thought she heard the words, "No one went anywhere near it, Ty." She knew she hadn't mistaken the admiring look the young woman gave him. Understandable.

When he gave her the option of front seat or back, she gave him a sideways look, wondering if he expected her to assume she'd be driven around as if he were a glorified chauffeur.

"Back windows are tinted dark enough that you wouldn't be seen."

She raised a brow at him. "Are you saying a threat is imminent and I should hide myself?"

"Not yet, although that may change. And if it does, you'll need to follow orders without question."

She gave him a slightly sour look. "I've never done that very well."

"So your father said."

"Did he?" She'd have a word with Dad when she got back home. The last thing she wanted or needed was him spreading the idea she was hard to deal with, which was how that would be interpreted by many. Her goals depended on cooperation, which was hard enough to get. Starting with a distorted perception of herself made it that much harder.

Without addressing his follow-orders comment, she merely said, "I'll sit in front, then." She smiled at him, again too sweetly. "Until I'm ordered otherwise, that is."

"Up to you," was all he said. He opened the door

for her, but since it was his vehicle and he was standing there anyway, she didn't quibble.

"What if I wanted to drive?" she asked once they were inside the car, as much out of curiosity as out of an uncharacteristic need to prod this man.

"Sure. Just show me your defensive and tactical driving certificates and it's all yours. Seat belt," he added.

She frowned as she reached for the belt and fastened it. "Tactical driving? Is that like offensive driving?" She knew what that meant. Her parents' actual chauffeur, Charlie Drake, had explained it to her a decade ago. She'd just passed her first defensive driving test, at the behest of her father, and joked that she was now ready to learn offensive driving, being completely unaware there really was such a thing until Charlie explained it.

"It's more specific."

"Like?"

"Threat assessment. Motorcade tactics. Attack recognition and avoidance. Escape and evasion. High speed in reverse. PIT and counter PIT maneuvers. TVI, if you prefer. Want me to go on?"

Her brow furrowed as she dug for a memory. "PIT… pursuit intervention technique. I've read that. But not TVI."

He'd been reaching to start the vehicle, but now drew back slightly and turned to look at her. "Tactical vehicle intervention. Almost the same thing, with a little more flourish and some different approaches."

She nodded. "I'll remember."

"Why?" He looked genuinely curious at her interest.

"Because I always do," she said simply.

She could almost feel his interest sharpen. “Always?”

“Pretty much. Sometimes it takes longer to call it up, but it’s almost always there.”

“Just verbal or images, too?”

Definitely interest, Ashley thought, as she studied him in turn. “Both. And to a certain extent, video.”

“So if you’ve seen someone before, you’ll remember them later?”

If you mean you, then yes, I’ll remember you. Probably a lot longer and more clearly than I’d like to. Then again...

“Ms. Hart?”

She snapped out of the uncharacteristic meandering of her mind into odd places. Belatedly remembered who—or rather, what—this man was. A bodyguard. Of course, he’d be interested in her ability to remember people she’d seen or met. And no doubt would care less if she remembered him. This was a job to him, and if she were guessing right—and she was fairly sure she was, from a couple of his comments—one he wasn’t really happy about.

“Yes, I remember people. Places I’ve seen. Things I’ve seen done.”

“Accurately?”

“Quite.”

He gave her a slow nod. “Good to know.”

Watching as he finally started the car, she could almost see him filing that bit of knowledge away, as if it were something he might need to reference later. Or in the manner of a man who wanted to know all the tools at hand.

She was seized with an uncharacteristic attack of nerves as the silence spun out in the car. He drove, as she'd expected, with a quiet competence. And smoothness. She had a tendency toward motion sickness when not driving herself, another reason she'd chosen the front seat. But she had the feeling she could probably read a book with him at the wheel, he was that smooth.

"You'd be a great chauffeur," she said before she thought. She wondered if he'd take offense.

"A connoisseur of chauffeurs, are you?"

"Not by choice." She now felt compelled to explain. "I tend to get queasy as a passenger." He gave her a slightly alarmed look, as if he were wondering if she was about to demonstrate here in his car. "I'm fine," she added hastily, wondering how on earth he was able to rattle her when she was usually *the queen of keeping her cool*, as her best friend Kate said. "You're very smooth."

"So I've been told."

She nearly gaped at him. But then she caught the slightest twitch at the corner of his mouth she could see. And suddenly she was laughing. And relaxed.

"I love this library," she said, feeling better now. "I had my meeting there yesterday. It's just beautiful. They remodeled it a few years back. There are stained glass windows that are a wonderful touch. I want to get a closer look at them. I didn't have time yesterday."

He didn't answer until they were pulling into the parking area of the long, low white building. He parked, shut off the motor and turned to look at her.

"So this is a...personal visit? We're not walking into some kind of protest rally?"

She laughed, gestured at the nearly empty lot. "Does this look like a rally to you? Let alone a protest?"

"Just checking. I saw video of that group out in Inman."

"I actually had nothing to do with that."

"Except to stir them up."

Her laughing mood vanished. "If you followed my media feeds, you'd know I repudiated what they did. It was far too early for that kind of response."

"Seems like they went off the moment your name was attached to the wetlands issue."

"I can't help that."

"Like I said, you stir them up. That's what activists do."

"I'm not an activist, I'm an advocate."

"Po-tay-to, po-tah-to."

She was frowning now, feeling a bit beleaguered. "Is that all you think I do?"

"Isn't it?"

"If any of the causes I espouse devolve into screaming protests, it's only after I have spent considerable time and effort under the radar to avoid it. I meet, negotiate, offer solutions, work toward compromise long before I ever turn to garnering public support and protest. That is my utter last resort. And I consider it a failure on my part."

She'd had to explain herself and her approach often before, but she usually managed it without the irritation even she could hear snapping in her voice. Something about this particular man truly set her off. With an effort, she got control of emotions she didn't usually have to rein in, and set herself to what she called her pleasant chat mode. She was not going to let this man divert her. He was doing a job and to keep her father from ordering her straight back home, which would mean she would have to defy him to get her goals accomplished, thereby causing more tension at home, she had to let him do it. So she would, and otherwise she would ignore the guy.

Too bad he was also the sexiest guy she'd come across in a very long time.

Chapter Five

"This library has some very forward thinking ideas," she was saying as they reached the entrance, which was shaded by a large awning-style overhang. "I especially like their Automatic Advance Reserve program, where you can sign up for your favorite authors and they'll notify you when they release a new book and hold it for you to check out."

"Not bad for flyover country, huh?" he said, irked at her apparent surprise that small-town Kansas could actually be, if not ahead of the curve, at least even with it.

She gave him a sideways look. "Not bad for anywhere. I'm going to suggest it to several places."

"Don't you just buy a book if you want it?" He was genuinely curious, not for the first time.

"Yes," she admitted easily. "But not everyone is as fortunate as I am."

Well, that's the understatement of the century... But he supposed he had to give her credit for even being aware of that. Many in her position weren't.

Once inside, he looked around with interest. It had been a while since he'd been in a library, and he was a little surprised she was so enthusiastic about it. But he had to admit this was nice. The equipment was modern, and it ran from communal areas with comfortable chairs that could fit in a living room to computer stations to a magazine section, with more print magazines than he'd seen in quite a while in a space with windows that showed the outside.

But it was the stained glass windows she'd mentioned that really caught his attention. The train in the window to the children's area was fun. A pair of windows farther on represented the sunrise and moonrise. Then there was one that was almost a mural and, according to the title, showed the progress of knowledge. That was a bit esoteric for him, but he did like the one with the big tree, appropriately named Under the Reading Tree.

"That's my favorite," she whispered. He glanced at her, expecting her to be pointing at the mural one. But instead, she was smiling in delight at the unexpected image of a dragon, no fire-breathing in sight, as he sat happily reading.

"Why?" he asked, a little surprised.

"Because that's what it's all about, isn't it? Flights of the imagination?"

He was totally disarmed by that smile. That this woman of all people, the daughter of a family who could buy this whole town, took such joy in a simple thing amazed him. He'd like to meet her parents someday, because obviously they hadn't lost sight of what was important if they'd been able to raise a daughter who could still react like this.

Then he nearly laughed at himself. Yeah, that was likely, him hanging around with the likes of the Harts of Westport, Connecticut. That he was with one of them now didn't count; this was business, and he'd better stick to it.

"You mentioned you wanted to do some research?"

"Yes. One of the staff told me before the meeting yesterday that they have thousands of historic photographs, a history archive, including newspapers from the 1870s forward, and historical local and state plat maps covering the county. I want to see those, track the changes to the McPherson Valley Wetlands, and how and when they happened."

"Too bad they don't show the real cost." He thought he'd kept his voice fairly neutral, but she gave him a narrow glance, anyway.

"What's that supposed to mean?"

"There was a man who'd been farming around here for sixty years, on land his family had owned for well over a century, when someone decided half of it should be protected. That *willing surrender of property* to the state you…advocates talk about? Not so willing. He just couldn't fight the government anymore and took his own life the day after they took it over."

"That's horrible. But hardly my fault." She turned then, facing him head-on. She might be more than half a foot shorter than him, but there was a gleam in her eye that warned him he'd gone a step too far. "You make a lot of assumptions, Mr. Colton. Including, obviously, that I don't care about people."

"Maybe you do. Maybe it's just the fallout after your mission is accomplished that you don't care about."

"Are you always so rude to clients?"

In fact, he wasn't. Ever. And he wasn't sure what it was about her that prodded him so. Other than her looks, of course. But he'd worked with beautiful women before and never had a problem keeping a leash on his words.

He'd never had one send him into overdrive just from a photograph, though. Because those beautiful women he'd worked with before had, for the most part, proved to him that there wasn't all that much behind the beauty. But Ashley Hart, a woman he'd half expected to be the worst of that sort, had turned out to be a different kettle of fish entirely.

And he'd better keep himself in line or he was going to blow this job, a job that could catapult Elite Security to an entirely new level.

"My apologies, Ms. Hart. I was out of line." He gave her a contrite nod. "Please, proceed with your research. I will stay out of your way unless there's a need for me to interfere."

She looked, oddly, almost disappointed—and as if she had some further retort on the tip of her tongue and he'd spiked her guns. But in the end, she said nothing, just turned and headed for the separate room where a sign indicated all the historic documents were stored in a controlled environment. A woman from the library staff greeted her, they chatted a moment—Ashley was quite cordial and warm, he noticed—then went into the room. Ty took a look to be sure they were the only ones inside, and that there was no other way in, then settled down to wait.

He took out his phone and texted their location to the office via the encrypted connection. They could find him easily enough with the tracker on the car, but this was protocol. Eric himself responded—a good reminder of how important this case was, and Ty gave himself another silent lecture on behaving himself.

He grabbed one of the desk chairs a couple of rows of bookshelves down and brought it back to sit just outside the door to the room. Anybody after her would have to go through him, and that wasn't going to happen.

Except for a group of school kids, apparently arriving for a story hour, the place was as quiet as a library traditionally was. He got up now and then to stretch and move around, although he was constantly scanning the area that had access to the door to the document vault.

He was starting to wonder just how long she planned on being in there when his phone signaled an incoming text. Thinking maybe he should have muted it—library, after all—he pulled it out. The incoming was from Mitch, so he opened the app. When he saw what it was about, he stared for a moment, sure he was gaping at the screen.

Then he was on his feet and moving fast. He burst into the archive room, startling the women who were standing by a table that held what looked like a very old map. But he was focused only on one, the woman who stood there with her phone in her hands.

"Are you crazy or just stupid?" he snapped, grabbing the phone out of her hands.

For an instant, she looked actually frightened, which made him wish he'd toned it down a little. He didn't like scaring people—unless they were the bad guys—but especially women. Not that that made the question any less valid.

But she recovered quickly, and drew herself up with a haughtiness that he suspected Harts learned from the cradle. "Give me back my phone."

"No," he said bluntly. He slid the phone—a very high-end one, of course—into a pocket.

"No?" She looked stunned.

Nobody ever say no to you? He nearly laughed at the thought, because he guessed it was quite possibly true. And he could almost feel her anger growing. It practically vibrated the air around her. Ms. Ashley Hart of the Westport Harts was rapidly building toward an eruption.

He decided a change in tactics was called for. He shifted his focus to the still-startled librarian and said with an almost courtly politeness, "My apologies, Mrs. Washington. Ms. Hart may have failed to mention to you that her life has been threatened, and now she has broadcast to the world *exactly* where she is by posting the photograph she just took of your map."

The woman's eyes widened, and she paled slightly. She turned to stare at Ashley, who was gaping at him. "That's absurd!" she almost yelped. "How dare you barge in here and—"

Ty cut her off and continued speaking to the older woman. "I'm sure Mr. Washington would appreciate it if you made it home this evening, so we'll ensure your safety by leaving immediately."

Ashley opened her mouth, he even heard her intake of breath, as if she were readying a barrage of angry retorts. He imagined she was quite capable of that. It seemed to be intrinsic among those who ruled the world—or fancied they did. But suddenly she stopped. She looked at the librarian's horrified expression and shut her mouth again.

Well, well...maybe she's not quite as self-absorbed as I thought.

"My own apologies, Mrs. Washington," she said with exquisite grace and warmth. "It's not a true threat, you're not really in any danger, but perhaps caution is wisest. I'll come back at a better time for all concerned," she added with a sideways glare at Ty.

She waited until they were back in his car before she held out her hand. "My phone," she said icily.

"No," he said again.

"I don't know what authority you think you have over me, Mr. Colton, but I assure you it does not include stealing my personal property."

"My authority includes doing whatever is necessary to keep you safe. Including saving you from yourself. What were you thinking?"

"That your fellow Kansans needed to know what they risk losing."

"And to do that, your parents have to risk losing you?"

She gave a dismissive wave of one slender hand. "It's just talk. People bluster when they're able to hide behind the anonymity of the internet. I get threats all the time. They're not real."

"So you've said. But your family's own security staff's analysis deemed this one more valid. Elite agrees."

She blinked. "My family's security staff? They have nothing to do with me. I told my parents long ago I didn't want them trailing after me." Her chin came up. "And I don't want you."

He couldn't help it, he grinned at her. "I've been told that before."

"I'm sure you have," she said tartly.

"Not usually by a beautiful woman, though."

She ignored the compliment and stared at him a moment before saying, as if she were merely pondering the question, “At what point, do you suppose, does self-confidence become arrogance?”

He smothered another grin. He was starting to like the way she talked. But he answered her with dead seriousness, “At about the same point someone decides that just because she says so, her loving parents will stop worrying and looking after her.”

Her eyes widened slightly, and something flickered in the dark brown. They really were amazing, those eyes. Deep. Endless.

She let out a long audible sigh. “Point taken, Mr. Colton.”

She’d surprised him now. Apparently, the loving in the Hart family went both ways. He filed away the knowledge that he was already certain would be a key weapon in the battle to keep her safe.

That the battle would mostly be with Ashley herself, he already knew.

Chapter Six

"I should have known they wouldn't leave it alone," Ashley said rather glumly, staring out the windshield as they pulled away from the library. "What exactly constitutes a threat analysis, beyond looking at the person making the threat?" *And going over this vehicle with a fine-tooth comb and a couple of electronic devices I don't even recognize, even though it was parked in a nearly empty lot at a library, of all places?*

"Do you mean generally or in this case specifically?"

She gave the man in the driver's seat—in more ways than one, since he still had her phone—a sideways look.

"Yes?" she suggested.

He smiled at that. It wasn't quite as heart-stopping as that unexpected grin had been, but it was a close thing.

And you need to stay focused or he really is going to end up running your life the entire time you're here.

"In a case like this, where we're not certain of the identity of the person behind the threat, it involves analyzing the reason for the threat, the specificity of it, studying the language used, the method of conveyance, what history we have of possible prior threats. And in cases like this, we work on tracking location through ISP or carrier identification, although that's not particularly reliable without further data."

"My parents are certain," she said. "They're convinced it's William Sanderson, that man who wants to build his tract of luxury homes, and thinks I stopped him from getting his permit."

"Didn't you?"

"I hope so," she said proudly.

"So you're proud of stopping someone from pursuing their livelihood?"

"I'm proud of stopping him from destroying an important wetland for migratory birds."

"So birds take precedence over humans?"

She'd heard variations of this often since she'd found her calling a few years ago. Although she had to admit, he was calmer about it than most. "They can coexist, with some care. That's all I ask for."

"What you're asking for," he said quietly, "is control over what someone does with their own legally purchased private property."

"No, I'm asking him to understand and control what he does with it." They'd reached a stoplight and he looked at her, so she turned in the passenger seat to meet his gaze. She spoke earnestly now, warmed to her beloved subject. "People just need to understand, to know what effect their choices will have. Then they almost always do the right thing."

"The over-optimism of that assumption is boggling," he said, as he glanced back at the traffic light. His words were laced with a cynicism that surprised her. "But even if that were true, there's still the biggest question."

"What question?" she demanded, stung a little by his optimism comment, given she'd often heard it, especially from her parents.

He looked back at her and said flatly, "The *right* thing according to who?"

She blinked. "Well it's obvious what the right thing is, isn't it?"

"Not to me. The right thing according to who? You? What gives you the right to decide that?"

He was surprising her. She hadn't expected to have to defend her beliefs with the man hired to protect her.

Then why are you?

Speaking of obvious questions… "I don't have to explain myself to you."

"No, you don't. I'm just the hired help, after all. And worse, from flyover country. So I couldn't possibly be as smart as you. We hicks need elites around to tell us what we're doing wrong."

She wanted to retort sharply, but had so many things tumbling through her mind she couldn't pick one to start with. This conversation was sliding downhill rapidly, which bothered her. She thought about that for a moment. Wondered if it was because she'd gotten out of the habit of actually arguing her case. So often now she went places, gave a speech and left. If there were questions, they were generally from people who already agreed with her. And more recently, the discussions took place on social media, where she had time to think and lay out her best and most persuasive arguments. She actually hadn't engaged in this kind of rapid give-and-take in a while, and it showed. She was rusty. And how odd that it was this man of all people who made her realize that.

Or maybe it was just him. This man, who had quite literally stopped her breath the first moment she'd seen him.

We hicks...

She grimaced inwardly. She didn't think that way, truly she didn't, but she also couldn't deny that many of those she associated with did. She'd warned them time and again that not only were they wrong, that kind of attitude only antagonized people they were trying to persuade, but it seemed innate in so many. No wonder he assumed she was the same.

It was a moment before she responded, with every stereotype she could think of. "Yes, you hicks, in your bib overalls, chewing tobacco and spitting, smoking corncob pipes, speaking with a drawl and dropping g's all over the place." He was gaping at her now. "Yes, you seem just like that. And by the way, you've got the green."

As she said it, the faintest of polite honks sounded behind them. Unlike the blare you got in a big city when you missed the instant response to the signal changing, she acknowledged.

His head snapped back forward, and they started moving again. And, she noticed, he gave a wave of apology to the driver behind them. As opposed to the rude gesture she was more used to in the city.

When they were clear of the intersection, he said, in a musing sort of tone, "Just like you coastal elites are all arrogant, presumptuous, look down your nose at everyone not from there unless they're from an acceptable place on the opposite coast, and carry your Ivy League college degrees around with you to show off?"

"Exactly," she said pointedly.

He smiled. It looked somewhat rueful. “Point taken, Ms. Hart,” he said, echoing her earlier words.

“So can we agree to drop the assumptions?”

“And just get along? A city girl from the upper crust and a guy from farm country?” He lifted one hand and rubbed at his chin as if deep in thought about her question. It was so perfect, so exaggerated. She knew he was being as mocking as she had been. And a smile played around the corners of her mouth.

“Sounds like the tagline for a fish out of water movie,” she said. *Or a romantic comedy.*

That thought rattled her completely, as did the realization that for all the mockery, even that chin he was rubbing was attractive. And his hands, hands that were strong, capable…

He laughed, and it sent that little ripple through her that she’d felt at the first sound of his deep rough voice. She again had to yank her mind off a path she had no intention of traveling.

When she finally spoke again, she did it quietly. “You may have that backward, Mr. Colton. In 1648, one of my ancestors, along with four others, settled on land purchased from the Pequot people. They had to get permission from the town of Fairfield to do so. They were all farmers, Mr. Colton. I’m descended from farmers who worked as hard as the farmers of Kansas. Harder, most likely, given the advances in modern equipment and methods.”

“And I live in Wichita, about fifteen times the size of your Westport,” he admitted.

She wasn’t surprised he knew that. Her parents wouldn’t hire a firm who didn’t do their homework.

"So in truth, I'm the small-town girl, and you're the city boy."

"Consider the assumptions overturned," he said.

"Agreed," she said, smiling. But then what she'd just thought about them doing their homework went through her mind again. "What about this threat made you—your company decide that this one among all the threats I get is serious?"

"The specificity in part," he said. "And timing. The responses to your posts are always quick enough that we can surmise he follows you on several platforms." He gave her a sideways look. "And the posts he made about your talk at the library last night were almost simultaneous with your remarks."

It took her a moment to realize the implication. "You… You're saying you think he was there?"

"It's a definite possibility. And why your parents are so adamant you lie low until the threat is identified and eliminated."

She lapsed into silence. She had to admit the thought of someone who wished her ill—even dead—sitting in that room within feet of her was unnerving. Perhaps she did need to take this a little more seriously.

They were pulling up to her hotel before he spoke again. "Let's get you packed and checked out of here."

She blinked. "What?"

"You should do it in person at the desk, and mention that you're heading home."

"What?" she said again. She was not used to feeling behind, but this man was annoyingly short on explanations for his rather dictatorial orders.

"Just in case. Since we don't know for certain who

this person is, or where he might have contacts, it can't hurt to plant a false trail."

That did make sense, but she still felt a step behind. It was not a sensation she liked; she was usually the one in the lead. "But why am I checking out? I still have—"

"You're checking out because you announced to the world that you're staying at this location," he said. Then, with that sideways look again, he added, "You know, that post about your *surprisingly well-appointed* room?"

She felt herself flush. She wasn't easily flustered, but somehow this man catching her expressing something that fairly reeked of those assumptions they'd agreed to discard did it. Her mind raced as they crossed the lobby, trying to remember if she'd posted anything else that could be interpreted that way. Looking at her timeline through that lens, she was afraid she had. She needed to look, assess and determine if she needed to make a post explaining and apologizing. She needed to—

She'd been digging into the outside pocket of her leather bag, where her phone lived, without even thinking about it. Without remembering it was no longer there. And why.

"May I have my phone back, please?" she asked, very politely to contrast with her earlier imperious demand.

"When we get to the safe house."

She drew back sharply. "The what?"

"You're not familiar with the term *safe house*?"

"Of course I am. That's ridiculous."

"It will only be until the threat is neutralized."

"I have a hearing in front of the county planning

commission in three weeks about this, and I have organizing to do. Supporters I need to mobilize. I will not stay locked away—"

"You will if I say so."

Talk about imperious demands! "I will not."

She heard him let out a long sigh. "Your parents told me you were exceptionally bright, with a killer memory, but a bit naive. They failed to mention the stubborn."

"A bit naive?" she repeated, taken aback.

"They take the blame for that themselves, by the way. Said they probably sheltered you too much."

She was gaping at him now. "They…actually said that?"

"They did."

She was going to have to have a word with them. She was not naive. She just chose to think the best of people. And that if given the choice, they would do the right thing. Most of the time.

She consciously unclenched her jaw. "Because I love my parents, I will go," she conceded, but added firmly, "for now. But don't expect me to be happy about it."

"Not my job to keep you happy. Just alive."

For some reason that set her off even more. A reason she didn't care to analyze just now. "Two weeks," she said warningly, as they reached the elevator alcove. "I'll tolerate it for two weeks."

He hit the up-arrow button. "We'll start with that," he said mildly.

She bit back a retort that it wasn't a negotiation. They stepped into the elevator and she turned to face the front. And as the doors slid shut, she couldn't help thinking about the moment just this morning when it had been reversed, when those same doors had slid open and she'd seen a tall, built, gorgeous man coming into the hotel.

She hadn't realized that moment would end up being something that would disrupt her entire life.

Chapter Seven

She packed with much less care than Ty would have expected of a Hart. She simply tossed everything from the small closet onto the bed and then loosely rolled each thing up. But the carry-on-sized bag had a designer label, and he was guessing the clothes did, too.

"Want some help?" he asked, more out of reflex than anything.

She paused with a sweater nearly the same color as her eyes in her hands. And those eyes were fastened on him in a rather intent way. Then she gestured toward the dresser near where he was standing and very sweetly asked, "Want to get my underwear out of the drawer?"

For an instant, he was taken aback. But only an instant. She was testing him, of that he was sure. He just wasn't sure what she was testing for. So he merely reached out and tugged open the top drawer. He was met with a froth of lace and silky-looking fabric, in about three different colors. He gathered the whole lot and walked the two steps to set it all on the foot of the bed. And if he noticed the size and shape of the lacy bras in the process, well, what did she expect?

She was looking at him as if waiting for…something.

"Was I supposed to recoil? Or maybe start drooling?"

"No. I just expected you to tell me to do it myself."

He shrugged and said easily, "I've got three sisters. I've done their laundry. Doesn't faze me."

Now she was staring at him in an entirely different way. "You've done your sisters' laundry?"

"And they've done mine. My mom's kind of equal opportunity that way."

Suddenly she smiled, and it hit him like a runaway freight train all over again just how beautiful Ashley Hart was. "I like the way she thinks."

"She's the best," he said succinctly.

"What does she do?"

"She's a nurse, at the hospital in Braxville." Ashley looked surprised. "What? You expected a socialite who dabbles because she's a Colton?"

She gave him that too-sweet smile he was already learning to be wary of. "As you expected of me? No, I try to be more open than that."

"Sorry," he muttered. "I didn't mean to break the truce."

"I'll forgive it, since it was in defense of your mother. And by the way, the reason I reacted was that my mother was a nurse when she and my father met."

He blinked. "Oh." He hadn't expected that. Realized he should have read the family background part of the file Eric had sent him a little more closely instead of focusing mainly on the subject of this operation.

"It's one reason medical causes are so important to us," Ashley added. "She's seen firsthand the difference donations in certain areas and fields can make."

He tried to think of something to say that would make up for him blowing their agreement to drop the assumptions. "That's admirable. She must be happy to be in a position to do that."

"It's a calling, for her."

He studied her for a moment. Tried not to notice how lovely she was, and focused on those eyes, and the intelligence gleaming there so obviously once you knew what to look for. "And for you?"

"Absolutely. There are many things I support, but spreading good medical care and practices is chief among them."

So she wasn't solely some environmental crusader, what some would likely call a tree hugger. He was always wary of people so sucked up into a single cause that they were incapable of seeing anything else and put everything into that basket, as his mother said.

They were passing the city limits when she asked with a frown, "Where is this safe house?"

She said it with a bit too much emphasis on the last two words, and he knew she was still none too pleased about this. He was glad he'd cleared this with the family earlier. It was easier to present it as a done deal than having to explain he was spiriting her off to a place he, in part, owned.

"It's actually a fishing cabin." He gave her a sideways look as he got on I-135 and headed north. They'd actually be within spitting distance of Braxville when they got off and headed west. "And the exact location you'll keep to yourself. Please." He only added the last because he'd seen her stiffen at the order.

She didn't speak again, but her jaw was set. Ashley Hart clearly wasn't used to being ordered around. And why would she be? She'd inherited billions upon millions from her grandparents and was the only child of her equally wealthy parents. Nobody told that kind of money what to do, unless she let them.

He thought about trying a softer sell, convincing her to just let him do his job, since the goal was to keep her safe. But at the moment, he didn't think she was in any mood to listen. At the same time, he didn't want her sitting there stewing, maybe thinking of ways to make this more difficult than it was already going to be. Because he had a feeling when she discovered one particular aspect of the Colton family fishing cabin, she was very much not going to be happy.

They were off the interstate, almost halfway there, and it had been done in silence. He glanced at her again. "Tell me something. If Sanderson had been going to build, say, affordable housing instead of luxury homes, would your reaction be different?"

"Making assumptions yet again?"

"No. Asking an honest question."

She didn't speak for a moment, but he'd swear he could feel her eyes on him as he drove. Then she said, "In the same place? No. The type of housing doesn't matter, the destruction of habitat does." His peripheral vision caught her tapping a slender finger on her knee. "Looking for hypocrisy, are you?"

"Just trying to understand."

"What's hard to understand?"

He shrugged. "Since most of your efforts in this kind of situation seems to be toward making people stop doing things, I can't help wondering…who, exactly, are you saving the world for?"

"Everyone," she said, sounding puzzled.

He could risk a glance on this smaller road and looked at her. "But you don't want them to do anything with it? Kind of like having a beautiful piece of jewelry and never wearing it, isn't it?"

Her brow furrowed. It seemed she was considering it, at least. "I gather you're not an environmentalist," she said, her mouth quirking.

He looked back at the road, traffic lessening the farther they got from the interstate. "Not an answer to my question, but I'll bite. I think we should protect what we have on this planet, but not worship it."

He'd probably really ticked her off now. But at least she wasn't stewing about the safe house.

To his surprise, after a moment she said, "I understand that. There are many who cross that line into thinking humans should be removed altogether."

"Excluding themselves, of course," he said dryly.

"I'm not sure some I know wouldn't include themselves."

"Now that's scary."

"On that, we agree."

"Hey, miracles happen," he quipped. And when he heard her laugh, it was much more gratifying than it should have been. And he couldn't help smiling.

MR. TYLER COLTON WAS... Ashley wasn't sure what he was. All she was sure of was that, aside from being armed—she'd caught a glimpse of a handgun on his belt beneath the jacket—he wasn't what she had expected. She'd seen flashes of the kind of authoritative demeanor she'd never liked in her family's personal security people, although there she had long ago resigned herself to the necessity. Her family was prominent and wealthy enough to be targets for all kinds of unsavory people.

She'd had to accept it there, so she supposed she might as well accept it here. Besides, this man was a lot more intriguing than brusque and rather crusty Mr. Patrick who led the home team, as it were.

Not to mention gorgeous.

Yeah, that, too.

But he'd surprised her with the jewelry comment. In one sentence, he'd presented his viewpoint in a way that made more sense than most of the arguments she heard. And she couldn't deny there was validity to it. She wasn't one of those rabid sorts who placed people at the bottom of the hierarchy of things to care about. She just happened to believe people should be more careful, that they could be more careful and do a lot less damage.

She studied him while he was focused on driving. She told herself it was because she needed the distraction from being a passenger, and almost believed it. But he really was very smooth, as smooth as their driver back home. And from what he'd said, he'd obviously been well trained.

He was also the first man in a very long time to spark this kind—or almost any kind—of interest in her. She was all too aware that in her position, as the only child of very wealthy parents, and the heiress to her grandparents' vast fortune, she was an obvious target for fortune-hunting males. Because of this, she very rarely let anyone past the gates, as it were. So rarely that it startled her that the thought had even formed. Then again, looking at that profile—those chiseled features, that jaw, the slightly tousled hair that somehow made her fingers itch—it was no surprise. Obviously, they would be spending some time in close proximity, so she supposed she'd be better off admitting his appeal so she could steal herself against it.

"Is this what you usually do?" she asked in a very impersonal tone.

He didn't look at her, but he did answer. "Personal protection? It's a lot of what we do. But not all."

We, she thought. She didn't guess he was short on ego—how could he be, all six feet two of him, broad shouldered and solid muscle, with that hair and those amazing dark blue eyes?—so he clearly felt a part of a team, not a solo act. That was telling. "What else?"

"Risk assessment. Corporate security. Event security. On occasion, we work a support role for a bigger operation, coordinating with government agents for an official visit."

"You sound like a sales brochure." She made sure it didn't sound like a dig.

"We're good at what we do. My boss has built a good thing. We're not as big as Pinkerton, but we're as good."

She shouldn't, she supposed, be surprised he knew who handled their security at home. Her father had gone with the storied company not solely because of their long and famous history, but because he knew several of their people and trusted them.

"Speaking of that, Pinkerton's got offices in Omaha, St. Louis and Oklahoma City. So why us?"

"If you're laboring under the misapprehension that my parents discussed this with me, I'm sorry. They didn't bother."

He gave her a sideways glance. "They probably didn't want the fight."

She drew up straight. “Are you saying I’m stubborn again?”

“Are you saying you’re not?”

“No. I happen to think stubborn is just a facet of persistence, which is a very useful quality.”

One corner of his mouth—he really did have a rather lovely mouth—twitched. “Well, that’s a nice way to pretty it up. Doesn’t make it any easier to deal with, though.” She started to say something about that being his job but before she could, he added, very quietly, “Especially when it’s someone you love and you’re afraid for them.”

Her parents. He’d been talking about—and apparently thinking about—her parents. The instant he put it that way, the moment he planted the image of her parents afraid for her, her retort died unspoken. And the stubborn faded away.

“I’ll try to remember that.”

“I thought you said you always remember.”

“I do.” *It only gets foggy when emotion gets in the way.*

She was feeling emotions—and other things—around this man that she would do well to ignore.

Chapter Eight

Ty saw her looking around the inside of the SUV as if she were only now noticing some things that were out of the ordinary. The extra mirrors that gave him a wide visual range. The two fire extinguishers, one on each side. She reached up and rapped a knuckle lightly against the window beside her. Then she looked at him.

"Bulletproof?" she asked.

He didn't bother to deny it. He already knew she was too smart to fool. Besides, maybe it would stir her to taking this more seriously.

"We prefer the term ballistic glass," he said easily. "This is level five. Will stop handgun fire and many rifle rounds. My boss had to pull some strings to get it, military has first call." She barely winced. Points for cool.

"What else?" she asked.

"Body is lightly armored. Special gas tank. Run flat tires."

She looked over her shoulder toward the back of the big SUV. "Do I even want to know what you've no doubt got stored back there?"

He gave her a sideways glance. Thought of running down the list of weaponry in the equipment lockers that took up about half the wayback of the vehicle. Decided that would be both unwise and unprofessional—something he was not used to feeling but had been poking at him ever since he'd spotted her across the hotel lobby. Instead, he just lifted a brow at her. "I don't know. Do you?"

She sighed audibly. "No. Probably not."

"Just let me do what I'm trained to do, Ms. Hart."

"Two weeks suddenly seems like a very long time," she muttered.

He wondered what she thought would happen if the threat hadn't been rounded up by her self-selected two-week deadline. Did she really think her parents would simply go along, let her go back to her regular life and pretend there was no danger? From what he'd picked up in his brief video call with them, that wasn't just unlikely, it was guaranteed not to happen.

But he'd deal with that if and when it happened. Right now, he just wanted as little hassle as possible. *Sure. You're only dealing with one of the three richest heiresses in the country, if not the world. No hassle at all.*

He kept his eyes on the road, but one of his assets was excellent peripheral vision so he saw more than she probably realized. And he saw her tugging at her bag, the big brown leather satchel-type thing he'd noticed before if only for the lack of some blatant designer label. She wasn't looking at it, just reaching with long slender fingers into a side pocket. Then in rapid succession, she stopped, frowned, then let out an exasperated breath.

"I'd like my phone back now."

So you can post exactly where you are? "When we get there."

Just by the way she moved her head, he sensed her irritation. And he knew he was right. She was going to explode when they arrived and she saw all the facets of the Colton family fishing cabin.

Tough. Live with it. The words went through his mind, but he had to admit he grimaced inwardly at the idea of saying them to her.

It wasn't five minutes later when she repeated the motion of reaching for her absent phone. Again, she only seemed to remember when it wasn't there. Another fifteen minutes, when they were getting close to the lake, she did it yet again. And he couldn't stop himself.

"You're really addicted to that thing, aren't you?"

"It connects me to my platform," she said, sounding irritated.

"Because the world must know what you're thinking all the time?" He was poking an already aggravated woman, but his guardrails seemed to be out of whack around her.

"I notice you have one," she pointed out.

"Yes. And it's good at its function, which is communication."

"That's all you use it for? This tiny device that has more power than the computers that helped put men on the moon?"

He didn't know what was wrong with him, but the inappropriate words were out before he could stop them. Something he rarely did anyway, but never with a client. "Maybe it's the difference between being an impressionable teenager and an adult when the first smartphone came out."

That did it. "Are you purposely trying to be offensive?" There was more than just an edge in her voice now. "The people who follow me care about the same things I do, but I sometimes have access to information they do not. And that phone is one of the main tools of my work. As much as whatever you have stored back there—" she gestured toward the back of the SUV "—are the tools of yours."

The passion in her voice echoed in the confines of the vehicle. He wondered—even more inappropriately—if she was that passionate about other things.

You have lost your mind, Colton.

"You're right. That was unacceptable. I apologize."

"Give me back my phone and I'll accept your apology."

"I will. We're almost there." He lifted a finger from the wheel and pointed to the right. Kanopolis Lake gleamed in the winter sun.

"Oh!" She hadn't even noticed, he guessed. "It's pretty."

She sounded so astounded he couldn't help saying, "Shocking, isn't it?"

She had the grace to apologize in turn for her tone. "I'm sorry. I just didn't realize it was there." She gave him a sideways look. "I was apparently too obsessed with my missing phone."

He almost laughed, and finally found his tact. "No comment."

But he couldn't help the twitch at one corner of his mouth as he slowed coming into the small community on the west side of the lake. He'd always had a fondness for the place called Yankee Run, if only for the great name. But he liked the peace and the surroundings and the view, and had often thought if he ever left his modern high-tech house in Wichita, he'd move into the cabin for good.

They passed the first couple of small houses. She was looking around with interest now. He wondered if she'd ever spent any time in a place as small as this unincorporated community. He was glad of the status and size, because it meant there wasn't much to indicate exactly where they were, which he'd still prefer she didn't know, just in case.

"This is lovely," she said, surprising him. "The lake, and I'll bet the trees are beautiful and green when they leaf out."

"They are. We've got one beside the cabin that gives us a great shady spot to hang out in the summer. And the property is on a rise, so it was fun in winter if we got enough snow to sled down to the lake."

She looked at him as he made the last turn that would take them to the cabin's driveway. "You spend a lot of time here?"

"Not so much anymore," he said, "but most of the summer when we were kids."

"We?"

"Two brothers, three sisters."

Her eyes widened. "Big family."

"Wasn't planned," he said with a wry smile. "They were just going for number three and were going to stop, but fate apparently misinterpreted and thought they wanted three at once."

She blinked. "Triplets?"

He nodded. "Two boys and a girl."

"Wow. Do they run in the family?"

"Not that we could find."

He slowed, then hit the button on the remote he'd brought and the gate rumbled open. He made the turn onto the long driveway that wound through cottonwood trees to the cabin that was on a small point projecting into the lake. He'd told her they owned nearly fifty acres around the place, and if it weren't for the fact you could see the lake and the waterfront houses to the south, you'd never know there was anyone else around. If that kind of isolation bothered her, it didn't show.

He heard the crunch of their tires on gravel, to him a sound both welcoming and welcome. Dad had wanted to pave it but he'd argued him out of it. On the occasions when he had to bring someone here for work, he wanted that sound because it was a warning someone was coming, at least from this direction. That a pro would likely be coming silently through the trees or up from the lake would be dealt with in other ways.

"What about number six?" she asked, still apparently intrigued by the size of his family.

"Baby sister," he said, with an affectionate smile. "She surprised everybody five years later."

"Let me guess… You're the oldest?"

Something in the way she said it made him ask, "Why would you think that?"

"Oh, maybe your authoritarian manner?"

"That's my job right now. And I prefer to think of it as being a natural born leader."

"How about the bossy attitude?"

"You left out organized and prompt."

"I'll bet you were ordering your younger siblings around as soon as you could talk."

"You read a list somewhere, didn't you? Since we're back to assuming, that's better than being a spoiled, self-absorbed, demanding, I'm-so-special only child."

To his surprise, she burst out laughing. "Touché, Mr. Colton. I did read a list, years ago. And apparently you read the same list."

Driving slowly down the private drive, he could risk looking at her. Which may not have been wise. He appreciated her beauty, but her laugh made him want to make sure she laughed every day, which was the craziest thought he'd ever had about a woman.

"Years ago?" he asked.

"Yes. When a girl at my elementary school threw those same charges at me, I looked it up."

He drew back slightly. "What, twenty years ago?"

"Eighteen, actually. I was nine."

They were into the small grove of cottonwoods now, healthy trees so happy here that even their bare branches were thick enough to provide some shade. And in their shade, he was quickly reminded it was November. With the winter sun pouring in through the windows, it had been deceptively warm in the car.

"So you really do remember everything," he said, thinking this could be both a good and bad thing, for him and the job he had to do.

"Yes." She didn't sound happy about it.

"Even things you'd rather forget?" he asked quietly.

She gave him a rather startled look. "Yes." Her mouth—that mouth—curved into a smile that was both appreciative and sad at the same time. "And points to you. Most people don't think of that side of it."

"I will take," he said carefully, "all the points I can get."

He had the feeling that, with this woman, he was going to need them.

Chapter Nine

"This," Ashley said, "is not what I'd pictured when you said cabin."

"What did you picture?"

He'd lifted her bags out of the back of the vehicle while she stood there looking at the long, low dark brown building. Somehow, she'd had in her mind a building like, maybe her parents' carriage house. Small, with a high pointed roof. A fairy-tale kind of building. This wasn't that.

She turned to go back and pick up her bag. Glanced into the back of the vehicle and saw, as she'd guessed, a storage locker. Two, actually—one along each side of the cargo space.

She looked back at the building that seemed more small house than cabin. "No secure garage to lock it up in?"

She meant it archly, but he just shrugged. "It has a custom-built alarm system that will go off if a rabbit sneezes within ten feet of it. And," he added with a gesture up to the side of the building, "there's 24/7 video surveillance."

She drew back. "Then why the detailed check of it when we came out of the library?"

"Because some humans, the craziest ones, can be sneakier than a rabbit."

"That," she said, "I won't argue with."

He gave her a sideways glance. "I'm sure you could if you tried."

His tone was amused, not nasty, so she didn't rise to it. "I can argue most sides of most things," she said as she picked up her bag. She noted that he let her, then remembered how her parents' security people never carried anything, so their hands were free at all times.

"Even sides that oppose what you want?" he asked. He sounded as if he seriously wanted to know, and so she answered accordingly.

"Especially those. That's why I like having both sides of an issue angry with me at one time or another. I take it as proof I'm doing the right thing, not a one-sided thing."

He looked surprised, then thoughtful. "Points to you, then," he said, and went to open the door.

She walked down a rather dark but short hallway with paneling that matched the outside and a wood plank floor. And then the space opened up, and she set down her bag in amazement.

The room was like nothing she'd ever seen. The inland side of the cabin might be all solid walls, but this large space was nearly all windows—except for one wall that was almost entirely a large and quite full bookcase—with a glorious view over a spacious deck down to the lake glistening in the near-winter sun. There was a huge stone fireplace with a heavy wood mantel at one end of the oblong room, and a kitchen with somewhat-dated tile but sleek new appliances at the other.

It was furnished with comfortable-looking, rather mismatched furniture. It would drive her meticulous mother crazy. Clearly, there had been no professional decorator in charge here. And she wasn't sure she didn't like the place better for it.

But what completely caught her attention was, of all things, the ceiling. It was made of what looked like metal tiles, or a single sheet of metal crafted to look like individual tiles, each perfectly square with a raised hammered ridge on the edges and a circular decorative medallion in the middle. The golden expanse should have been out of place, she supposed, but it wasn't. The color blended perfectly with the lighter wood of the walls, and it warmed up the entire large room.

She hadn't even noticed he'd come up behind her when he spoke. "It came from an old bank building in Braxville, our hometown. When they tore down the building, Mom bought it and had it installed here."

"It's beautiful. And unique."

"I'll give you unique," he said with a wry grin and lift of his eyebrows.

She found herself smiling at him. "Had to explain that a lot, have you?"

"How could you tell?"

"The explanation did sound fairly well practiced."

"It was easier when I was a kid. I'd bring a friend out here, he'd look up and say *weird.* And I'd say *yeah.* And that was it."

She laughed. When he wasn't being dictatorial, she quite liked him.

She walked over to the windows and looked out. "That's the tree you mentioned?" she asked, pointing at the big cottonwood to the right.

"Yep. My mom again. And my Uncle Shep. They planted it as a sapling when I was about three."

She stared at the towering tree. "A sapling?"

"Yeah. It wasn't much taller than Uncle Shep at the time. They grow really fast at first, like about six feet in a year. Only took until I was seven to be tall enough for me to fall out of and break my arm."

She turned quickly to look at him. He was smiling. "I'll bet your parents loved that."

"Mom kind of freaked. Funny, considering she's a nurse. Dad was in the middle of some project, so he didn't find out for a couple of days."

For a moment, she said nothing. She tried to imagine her father, even as busy as he always was, not finding out that she had broken an arm at seven. The image wouldn't form. He'd talked to her practically every day of her life, asking her not just about her day but her life, her dreams.

"My father would probably have wanted to cut the tree down for daring to be complicit."

He tilted his head as he looked at her, as if he were studying her. "And I'll bet you would have stopped him, saying it wasn't the tree's fault."

It unsettled her a little that he was exactly right. "Of course."

He didn't say any more about it, only, "Let's get you settled in."

This time he did pick up her bag and started up the stairs that led up off the entry hall, directly opposite a closed door to either a closet or a room behind the expansive great room. She followed him up, brow furrowed as she tried to remember from the outside. It had seemed to her there wasn't much of an upstairs, that it had only covered about a third of the lower story.

When they reached the top, she realized that the entire space was a rather grand, spacious master suite, with a large picture window that looked out at the lake. He set her bag down on the foot of the bed while she looked around. The four-poster bed seemed huge and was covered with a blue-and-gray comforter. The blue matched the color of the lake today, and she guessed the gray matched it on cloudy days. There were coordinating drapes at the big window—the only window, she noticed—but she couldn't imagine ever wanting to close them.

"Guest closet," he said, jabbing a thumb toward a door on the back wall. "Bathroom," he added, now pointing toward a door to her left.

Curious, she went to look. "Lovely," she said, meaning it. The bathroom was worthy of the spa her mother adored to frequent. She could soak in that tub—which also had a view out to the lake, carefully angled so it didn't go both ways—up to her neck. And she stood there, staring out the carefully placed window, fighting down the ridiculous flush that had begun to rise at the thought of being naked in that tub under the same roof with this man. The realization that it was plenty big enough for two.

"Should be towels and whatever else in the tall cabinet," he said, clearly not bothered by such fevered imaginings. "My mom keeps it pretty well stocked."

She steadied herself and then turned to face him. "Shouldn't this be your room?"

He shrugged. "There's another bedroom downstairs."

"Like this?"

He smiled. "No. A lot smaller."

"Then I'll take that one and you—"

"No."

And there he was, back again, Mr. Authority. "I've slept in mud huts, Mr. Colton. As long as I sleep, it doesn't matter where."

"Noble of you. But in this case, it does matter."

The jibe stung. She hadn't said it to sound noble, just to make a point. But he seemed insistent on putting the worst spin on…everything. She'd dealt with village elders who were less cranky. With an effort, she kept her voice level. "Why does it matter here?"

"Because there's only one way to get to this room. And they'll have to go by me to do it."

She stared at him. Now she guessed she knew that door at the bottom of the stairs led to the other bedroom. "You say that as if you expect armed troops to show up."

"I don't expect them. That doesn't mean I don't prepare for them." She couldn't argue the logic of that, so didn't try. Instead, after yet again reaching for her bag before remembering the special pocket for her phone was empty, she held out her hand. "My phone now, please?"

"Oh. Yeah." He sounded rather odd, but started to reach into his pocket. He also nodded toward her bag. "No fancy designer label?"

"I thought we swore off assumptions."

"Just asking," he said. "It looks like something my sister would use, if she needed to carry but couldn't wear a holster."

She glanced at the bag, startled. "I had it made," she

said briefly, managing not to frown in impatience as he pulled out her phone yet didn't hand it to her.

"Ah. Custom job."

He made it sound like that was somehow worse than carrying a big-name designer bag around. "Hard though it may be for you to believe, I actually prefer the low-key look of this bag, and I've had it for years. My phone?"

At last, he handed it over. Then he said briskly, "Get settled in. I'll go see what my partner's idea of stocking the kitchen was."

He was gone before she could answer, and she had the strangest feeling he hadn't just left, he'd escaped.

Chapter Ten

Ty glanced at his watch. If he were a betting man, he'd give her five, maybe ten minutes before she erupted.

He walked to the other end of the hall and went into the room he'd set up as an office—among other things—after he'd gone to work for Elite. He checked the comms equipment connected to their private system, sent the message that they were here and safe, then left it in monitor mode with the notification signal on. They'd agreed on periodic check-ins, but if they turned up something he needed to know, he didn't want to miss it. It was also powerful enough to send a notification to his phone, as long as he was on the property.

Then he headed back to the kitchen, wondering how far afield Mitch's idea of supplies wandered from Ashley Hart's. Since the guy's taste ran more to burgers and fries than caviar, he could only imagine. He was perusing the stack of steaks in the freezer, grinning at the addition of some bags of frozen veggies as a token, when what he'd been waiting for happened. He heard the sound of footsteps on the stairs, coming down.

What he hadn't heard was the shriek he'd almost been expecting. But then, she didn't really know. Yet.

He surreptitiously watched as she walked around the

great room, with her phone held up in front of her. Ah. Checking to see if there was a signal elsewhere in the house. So she didn't immediately jump off a cliff when cut off. That seemed significant somehow.

Then she headed for the door out onto the deck, still staring at the uncooperative screen of her phone. She reached for the door handle, clearly intending on heading outside.

"Ms. Hart."

She stopped. For the first time, the phone came down. She looked back at him over her shoulder. And his heart nearly stopped. Damn, why did she have to look like…that? It wasn't just that she was beautiful, or so obviously smart, she was…she was so alive it fairly crackled around her.

"What?" she finally asked when he couldn't seem to find his voice.

He made himself focus. "Don't go outside alone."

She frowned. "I thought you said your family owned the surrounding fifty acres and the house is protected with alarms?"

"And the lake with open access is twenty-five yards away. That's an easy pistol shot." He pointed back toward the grove of cottonwoods they'd driven through. "A pro could do it from back there. Throw a rifle into the mix, and the shooter could be outside the property line and still take you out."

"If you think I'm going to sit inside for two weeks—"

She stopped when he held up a hand. "Just don't go out alone."

She turned around to face him, then. Her brow was furrowed as she looked at him. "If it is that professional you mentioned, and that someone is not even on your property to set off any of your alarms, why would you being with me make a difference?"

He hesitated for a moment, then decided on the truth. Maybe it would jolt her into taking this more seriously.

"Because he'll likely go for the bigger threat first."

"You."

"Yes."

A little to his surprise, she didn't argue the assessment. She merely looked at him consideringly. "And you accept that?"

"It's part of the job."

"Then tell me, Mr. Colton, once you're dead, what, exactly, am I supposed to do?"

Her voice was cool and calm. A little too much so for his comfort. But she did have a point. He'd planned to do this later, when she'd settled in, but the subject had come up now so there didn't seem much point in delaying it. Besides, it would postpone the inevitable blow up a little longer.

"Come with me," he said. Then added a careful, "Please."

He started back down the hall toward the office. She did follow without arguing, to his relief. He opened the office door, and nodded at her to step inside. She looked around, clearly surprised, no doubt by the rather stark utilitarian room and equipment.

"What is this?"

"Three things," he said briskly. "This room is bulletproofed and sealable from the inside. If you have to, you head for here and hit that pad beside the door."

"So it's like a panic room?"

"Yes," he said, realizing the Harts probably had something similar. You didn't have the kind of wealth they did and not be aware you were a target for those who wanted to take it, not earn it. And somehow inheriting it seemed even worse to that sort of person, no matter that Ty knew Ashley's father had doubled the family fortune through his own efforts.

"Okay."

"Secondly—" he turned to the comms setup, pointed to a large red switch "—you flip that, push down that button and yell for help."

She seemed to consider that, as well. "What if no one answers?"

"They will. 24/7. They'll know where you are, so all you need to do is tell them what happened."

"You mean that you're dead?" she asked sweetly.

She was either the coolest customer he'd ever dealt with, or the coldest. And when he found himself thinking he'd like to have the discussion about the difference between those two with her, he knew he was in trouble. He was going to have to stay seriously on his guard.

"Exactly," he said, doing his best to sound unruffled. "You're under threat, and that's real. I didn't bring you here because it's unfailingly safe. No place is, and you need to be aware of that. I brought you because it will be harder for anyone to get to you here."

He saw her look around the office, saw her gaze snag on the first-aid locker on the wall beside the door. It was, as was everything Elite, stocked with the latest and greatest, and included a smaller portable case that held lesser amounts of everything in the main locker. Just about any kind of situation was covered, although if pressed he'd have to admit he'd only learned the minimum on some of the newer stuff. The injuries he encountered tended to be pretty basic, and if it was anything more complicated than a broken bone or a minor knife or gunshot wound, he was out of his depth, anyway.

Her gaze shifted to the locker on the other side of the door. The one with the actual lock on it. And for the first time some tension crept into her voice. He was glad to hear it. "I'm guessing the things in there are what make the things in there—" she gestured back at the locker marked with the red cross "—necessary?"

He smiled inwardly at her correct guess; there was a weapon in there to handle nearly anything. "Mostly they stop them from being necessary." Her gaze shifted to his face. He didn't remember from his admittedly somewhat hasty research that this had ever been one of her issues, but he asked anyway. "Don't care for weaponry?" His tone was just a hair too polite, but she answered evenly, with a glance at his side, where his jacket concealed his holster, that told him she was fully aware he was armed.

"It has its purpose and function." Her voice was cool again. She was back in control. "And given my family has had full-time armed security for years, it would be very hypocritical for me to crusade against their tools."

"Points to you again, then."

She met his gaze, and he didn't think he'd mistaken the amusement in her eyes. "As someone once said to me, I'll take all the points I can get."

He couldn't help it—he let out a chuckle. "I think you're ahead at the moment."

"I shall endeavor to stay there."

She said it so snootily he knew she was putting

it on. And a moment later, she was grinning at him, proving it. She was quite an unexpected package, was Ashley Hart.

Ashley Hart, richest heiress in the civilized—or uncivilized—world, Colton. Remember that.

"What's the third thing?"

He blinked, yanking his mind out of what was threatening to become a groove. "What?"

"You said this room was three things. You gave me two."

"Oh. Yeah. You already guessed." He walked over and pressed his thumb to the scanner on the weapons locker. A moment later, it clicked and disengaged. He pulled open the double doors, wondering if she'd freak at the sight of the rather impressive array. He looked back over his shoulder at her. Those delicately arched brows were lowered, but she didn't look intimidated, or particularly worried. Not worried enough for him, anyway. He didn't want her scared, but he didn't want her relaxing her guard, either.

Knowing the likely answer, he said, "I'll leave out something simple, just in case. A revolver, so no chance of a jam."

She came closer, scanned the racks that held everything from the mentioned revolver to a semi-auto rifle.

"Actually," she said casually, pointing at the single shotgun there, "I'd be more comfortable with the Mossberg." He blinked. She smiled at him. "Assumptions again, Mr. Colton?"

"Apparently. When and how did you pick up that particular bit of know-how?"

"My father took up trap and skeet shooting when I

pitched a fit at age eight over him hunting live birds. I learned along with him."

"You any good?"

"Quite."

He studied her for a moment before he asked quietly, "Could you shoot a human being if you had to?"

To her credit, she didn't give him a snappy comeback. And after a moment, she nodded. "Under certain circumstances, I could."

"But you won't shoot a bird? A bit illogical, don't you think?"

"It's perfectly logical. The bird is innocent, being hunted while unaware, just trying to go about its life. A human has made a conscious choice."

For a moment, he just looked at her. She was surprising him on every hand. "Okay, now you're really ahead on points." He reached up and lifted the Mossberg 500 Tactical from the rack. "Twelve-gauge, five plus one, you know?" She nodded. "Want the pistol grip?"

"No. I'm not used to it, so it would just distract me."

"Good call."

When she took the weapon he held out to her, she took it with a familiarity that told him she hadn't been lying. Not that he thought she was. So far, she'd been honest to a fault. She studied it for a moment, and he pointed out a couple of things he guessed were different from the version of the weapon she was used to, for their tactical purposes.

"It fires pretty true," he said, "but we can take it out in the morning for you to fire a few so you can be sure." He gave her a wry smile. "No shooting range gear, I'm afraid. But I can throw something for you."

"That will do," she said.

"What's the difference between trap and skeet, anyway?"

She gave him a sideways look. "Testing me or do you really want to know?"

He held up his hands innocently. "I want to know. I've never done either."

"Skeet, the targets come across your field from the sides, and always at the same speed and height. Trap, they come from all directions and are moving away, not across."

"Trap sounds like it would be trickier."

"They both have their challenges." She took the box of shells he held out then and quite proficiently loaded the weapon. Then she looked at him. "Are we leaving it in here?"

He shook his head. "You might need quicker access. There's a rack in the great room."

She nodded, and soon the weapon was settled securely on the rack next to the door leading out onto the deck. It was already getting dark, the days growing ever shorter this time of year. It was also getting colder, so he set about building a fire in the fireplace. With the limited wood in the rack.

"What was that look for?"

She'd startled him. Again. He hadn't realized he'd been grimacing. "Just acknowledging that the last person here was my father."

"Meaning?"

He nodded toward the half-empty firewood rack beside the hearth. "It's sort of an unspoken rule you refill that when you leave. He never thinks about the next person who'll be here."

"Sounds...annoying."

"Yeah, well, that's my father."

"Rude or just thoughtless?"

"Oh, he's quite capable of being both. If it's not business-related, he doesn't much care. He—never mind," Ty cut himself off, wondering how on earth he'd let his father become a topic of conversation with this virtual stranger. Especially now, when Colton Construction was facing mounting problems, both personal and legal. Problems no one would appreciate him blabbing about to that stranger.

Except...she didn't feel like a stranger. He felt as if he already knew more about her, in these few hours, than he'd expected to.

Thankfully, she didn't press. Instead, she pulled her phone out once more and again started wandering the house. He knew perfectly well what she was looking for, what she wouldn't find. Finally, she made a swipe and a couple of taps on the screen, studied it for a moment and her brow furrowed in that now familiar way.

Here it comes...

"Okay, this is ridiculous. I can't get any kind of a carrier signal. And it's telling me there's no Wi-Fi in range."

He braced himself. Straightened up from where the fire was starting to take off. Then turned to face her.

"That's because there isn't any."

For the first time, she looked blank. Which told him a lot. "Any what?"

"Of either."

She stared at him. "You don't get a cell signal here?"

He pointed to the wall in the kitchen, where an old,

rather nauseatingly yellow phone hung. "That's not there because it's pretty."

She blinked. "A landline? Seriously?"

"Very seriously. It's that or nothing out here."

"Wow." She looked back at her phone.

"Might want to turn the phone off, save the battery."

She looked as if he'd suggested she cut off a finger. "I'll turn off the carrier function, so it's not searching for a signal," she said, and did so. "But why is there no—" She stopped abruptly, and her eyes grew wider as she stared at him. "You don't have Wi-Fi, either?"

"Nope."

She was starting to look as if she were sliding into shock. "Tell me you at least have broadband?"

"I try never to lie."

She muttered something he was pretty sure there was a rude internet acronym for. "I haven't had to deal with dial-up since I was…what, seven?"

"You still won't have to."

She brightened. "Oh, that was mean. What, you have a satellite connection or something?"

"Nope. No satellite."

"Then what?"

He sighed. Loudly. Then, bracing himself for the blast, he very carefully said, "You, Ms. Hart, are offline. Completely. For the duration."

Chapter Eleven

He was kidding. He was just ragging on her about her social media time again, that was all. Just kidding.

He had to be kidding.

Now she was gaping at him. While he was simply looking at her. Looking at her almost expectantly. She closed her mouth, almost embarrassed. She prided herself on her ability to keep an equanimous exterior no matter what she was thinking, but she was having trouble with that at the moment. In fact, if she were honest with herself, she'd been having trouble with it since this man had strode into her life and taken over.

"Are you saying," she enunciated carefully, "that this place does not have internet access at all? Or are you saying it does but I can't use it?"

"I believe the phrase is off-the-grid, internet-wise."

She supposed, of the two options, that was the better. Not that either was acceptable, but she had the feeling that had he been refusing her access, she would have…

She would have given him the explosion he'd been expecting. That was why he'd looked as if he were braced. The idea that he thought her so predictable was irksome. Or worse.

So she simply asked, "Why?"

"Choice."

"To be out of touch?"

He gestured with a thumb toward that indeed unpretty yellow wall phone. "Landline."

"Yet, you have that radio set up in there," she said, gesturing toward the room with the communications equipment.

"Precaution."

"Because you're remote out here? Or is it because you use this as a safe house?"

"Yes."

She'd had about enough of the one-word answers. "What, exactly, do you expect me to do?"

"Have a tantrum? Pitch a fit, as my grandmother used to say? Addicts tend to do that."

She blinked. Maybe the one-word answers were better. "Addicts?"

"A person who is addicted—driven to use compulsively—to a habit, activity, substance…or device or platform."

She drew back slightly. "My, aren't we proficient at quoting—and editing—the dictionary."

He ignored the jab. "I'm a security expert. I don't have much patience for people under threat who insist on increasing their risk by refusing to stay off social media. Which is a dangerous thing to begin with."

"Not that you have an opinion or anything."

"It's more than an opinion. It's based in fact. Would you like a list of the victims who were injured or even killed after being unable to resist making a post that betrayed where they were?"

She didn't doubt that—she'd seen too many stories

about just that. The problem was she couldn't believe this was that kind of threat. She'd grown up knowing she could be a kidnapping target, because of her family's wealth and standing, but for someone to come after her not for money but when she was trying to help, to benefit everyone?

Somehow, though, his words had taken some of the wind out of her sails. Because if she thought past her irritation, he had a point. A very valid point. Her mouth quirked, almost unwillingly. "Not to mention those who have managed to kill themselves trying to take a unique selfie?"

He looked startled, and she took no small amount of pleasure in that. And then he smiled, slowly, a slight dimple flashing in his right cheek, and that thought of pleasure shifted into an entirely different realm. She froze, inwardly. This was so not happening. Absolutely not.

"Yes," he said. "Thankfully, you're very much not stupid."

That pleasure expanded in a new direction now. Which unsettled her. What did she care if he thought her smart? Or stupid, for that matter? "Or hungry for fame?" she said hastily.

His smile turned wry. "You were born with that, Ms. Hart."

Before she really thought about it, she said, "Could you dispense with the formality? Two weeks of *Ms. Hart* is going to be very wearing."

The smile faded altogether. "I'm not sure that would be wise."

Something knotted up in her stomach. Why would he say that? Why would he think it? The pleasure she'd gotten from his smile and his compliment had rattled her. The thought that maybe, just maybe he was feeling something similar shook her down deep.

"Why?"

It came out as barely above a whisper, and to her own ears betrayed everything she was thinking. But he answered as if it were a routine question. As if there had been none of her inner turmoil in her voice.

"You're a client, Ms. Hart. And Elite has protocols. Rules."

His businesslike tone, without a touch of regret, or anything other than a cool professionalism, chilled her emotions enough for her to say evenly, "Using my first name is against one of those rules?"

Something flickered in those dark blue eyes, and then he lowered his gaze as if he'd suddenly seen something of interest on the floor. His lack of an answer made her prod further. And she chose her words very purposefully.

"And do you never, ever break the rules, Tyler?"

His gaze shot back to her face, as if he were again startled. "Ty," he corrected, as if it were automatic. But then his voice changed. "I've been known to," he said, and there was a slight roughness in his voice that sent a shiver down her spine. She saw him take in a rather deep breath. Then, in his normal voice, he added, "And I've almost always regretted it."

"Only almost?"

"I still say that pursuing a child abductor off a roof was worth it, sprained ankle and all." This time his smile was practiced, and thus more distant. She didn't like that.

And she didn't like that she didn't like it.

Damn. Get a grip, Colton.

There was no reason in hell her just saying his name should have had that effect. None at all.

But it had.

He popped the tab on the caffeine-laden soda, not worrying about it because he needed to be sleeping light, anyway.

Right. Like you're going to be sleeping at all, with her right upstairs.

He took a long swig of the soda while staring out the kitchen window. It faced toward the cottonwoods, their winter-bare branches looking a little eerie against the night sky. He glanced at the clock on the oven, saw it was nearly an hour until moonrise. Not that it would matter much; the waning quarter moon stage they were at wouldn't put out much of that silvery light he loved.

"That's a nice smile. What brought it on?"

She'd come quietly up behind him and the smile vanished. On some level, he'd been aware, but he hadn't turned to look. Afraid to? Better not be. He was her bodyguard—damn, there had to be a better word than that—after all.

"I was thinking about the moon."

"Going to howl?" There was such a teasing tone in her voice that he couldn't help but smile again.

"Not full," he pointed out. "And it's waning, not waxing, so it'll be the end of the month before it's howlable."

She laughed. "Then what were you thinking?"

"More remembering."

"What?"

He was certain it was stupid, wouldn't be surprised if the sophisticated woman she was laughed, but he wanted to share the memory with her anyway. And he wasn't nearly as scared by that as he probably should have been.

"My mom took us all to the Flint Hills, to the Tallgrass Prairie Preserve when I was ten. It had only been established a couple of years before, and she wanted us to see what Kansas used to be. On the way back home, we had to pull over because the triplets started squabbling. I got out and walked over to look down the road, and it was just as a full moon was rising. It was huge, too big to be real, and it came up exactly where the road went over the last hill I could see, like it was leading the way, like the road was there just to take you to it. It was the most amazing thing I'd ever seen. And I think of it every time I look at the moon."

She was staring at him. Probably thinking he was the biggest goofball farm boy she'd ever imagined, far, far removed from her elite East Coast life.

"Thank you," she whispered.

He drew back. "For what?"

"Sharing that."

He was embarrassed now. Shrugged. "It's just something I remember."

"Don't belittle it. It's a memory to be cherished."

It was, to him. He'd just never expected someone like her to get it. It struck him that he was still making assumptions.

"Where was your father on that trip to the preserve?"

He managed to keep his expression even. "Working. Like always."

"Too bad. He missed something special."

Like always.

He quashed the sour thought as she moved, and he realized she was reaching for one of the back pockets of her jeans. She frowned, started to look around, then let out a sigh.

The phone again. She'd been reaching for her now useless phone. When she noticed he was watching, she seemed to feel compelled to explain. "I wanted to look up that preserve. I remember seeing the name when I was researching the wetlands, but I didn't follow it up then."

"Why would you?" He was trying to figure out how she thought.

"Because I like to know about things as a whole. And the tallgrass appellation was intriguing. Made me wonder if there were short-grass prairies."

"Yes. More, actually, wider-spread."

"Obviously I need to up my study of the Plains."

His mouth quirked. "Don't look at me. I think everybody should. For too many people, when they think of Kansas the only thing that comes to mind is *The Wizard of Oz*."

"I think he's been supplanted as the wizard of record," she said.

"You mean that kid with the round glasses? Yeah, I think so."

They both laughed. Hers was light, genuine, and Ty felt… He wasn't sure how to describe how he felt.

Because he'd never felt it before.

Chapter Twelve

"That was some really good spaghetti sauce," Ashley said. She was looking at him across the table. The meal hadn't been fancy, but it had been warm and filling, and the sauce had indeed been delicious.

"Thank my mother. It's her specialty."

That surprised her. "Was she just here?"

He shook his head. "She makes it at home, a huge batch, and bottles it up."

"That's quite a process."

"She learned it from her mother, so she sees it as a sort of tribute to her to keep doing it."

"That's lovely." She gestured at the bread. "And that's one of the few times I've actually had garlic bread with enough garlic. Is that hers, too?"

One corner of his mouth went up. "No, you can blame me for that."

"Ah. A fellow garlic lover."

He nodded. "In my view, many foods are improved by a suitable application of garlic. Usually I'd tone it down for a guest, but your mom said you loved it."

Ashley drew back, startled. "You talked to my mother about my taste in food?"

He shrugged. "Of course. So besides the basics,

there are bagels and cream cheese—" he gave her a smile "—peanut butter, green tea and a few other things. The purpose here is to keep you safe, not miserable." He paused, gave her a sideways look. "She did mention something about you using the garlic as an excuse to keep from kissing boys in high school, though."

Ashley felt her cheeks heat. Her mother had told him about that long-ago discussion they'd had? But she lifted her chin and shrugged in turn. "If they didn't want to kiss me badly enough to overlook the garlic, then I didn't want to be kissing them."

"Sounds like a good operational plan," he said, as if they were discussing the weather. "At least, until you run into a garlic lover."

Like you?

Had he done that intentionally? Made such a comment after acknowledging he was just that? Because that would imply—

She broke off her own ridiculous train of thought. What was wrong with her? She'd met this man mere hours ago. There was no way her mind should be careening off in *that* direction. She'd spent a great deal of time and energy fighting stereotypes, and she wasn't about to become one—the helpless female who falls for her bodyguard.

Bodyguard. What a ridiculous word, as if a person's body was all that mattered. But somehow protector seemed…too intimate. Or too close to another kind of protection that only came up during preludes to the kind of encounter she had been wary of ever since that flirt Aiden Schmidt had proven himself the worst kind of liar.

This man would not lie. She wasn't sure why she

was so certain, but she was. He might dissemble or postpone—like not telling her until they were here that there was no internet—or he might not answer at all, but if he did answer, it would be the truth. There would be no little fibs, no outright lies, no sweet nothings coming from this man. And no false flattery.

Again, she caught herself reaching for her phone. She stopped the motion with no small amount of irritation. She should have done what had occurred to her on the way to the library and run a check on Ty Colton. She'd done so on his agency, Elite Security, the moment her father had told her they'd called in the local firm. But the only person profiled on their website was the founder, Eric King, a retired Marine and full colonel with an almost staggering résumé. Which was only to be expected, she supposed.

So now all she knew was he was a partner in a private and well-respected security company—which, if it had passed her father's vetting, was no doubt top-notch, despite the troubles his family's business was having—and was distantly related to the former president. She stifled a grimace at the connection. Her parents would have had the Secret Service looking after her if they could have. For all she knew, Dad had gotten the recommendation from Joe Colton personally. She should call Dad and—

Yet again, she found herself reaching for a phone that wasn't working. Her jaw tightened.

"Dependency is a tough thing to shake," Ty said, his tone neutral.

She started to give him a glare, but it wouldn't form. Because she was starting to realize there was more than a little truth to his assessment. She enjoyed and depended on devices and the internet to stay in touch, and more importantly for her work to get out the word. She had built a large platform over the past five years, ever since she had sat down with her father and told him what she wanted to do.

But she didn't like that she had apparently become the stereotype of her generation, someone incapable of surviving without those admittedly multiple-times-removed connections. The majority of them people she didn't personally know and likely never would.

She'd never kidded herself about that. At least she thought she hadn't. But she also hadn't really realized until now just how much those distant connections, many of them hiding behind screen names they thought cute or cutting-edge, had filled her life. How often they had crowded out other things, how often she had chosen composing an important—or so she thought—post over other things she could be doing. Things involving actual human contact.

And she had to admit, she didn't like the thought.

"You really don't like social media, do you?" she asked him, even though he'd already made his feelings quite clear.

"I don't like that it allows people to hide who and what they are, which gives them the comfort of anonymity as much as wearing a mask while rioting in the streets and beating up people you disagree with, or robbing a bank."

Since she'd just been thinking something quite similar, she couldn't argue with that. "But you use the internet," she said instead.

"It's a useful, powerful tool, with proper precautions. But it's only that, a tool. Just like a vehicle or weapon." He leaned back in his chair. "Which do you think is more effective, your online interactions or the meeting you had at the library last night?"

Had it only been last night? It felt longer. Probably because her entire life had been upended by this man. But she had to admit, he'd asked an important question. "They're both important. The internet gives me a much broader reach, but the personal interaction is crucial. It makes people feel personally involved, makes them feel like they themselves can actually do something."

"What's your measure of success?"

Her brow furrowed. "Action taken?"

"Does that mean the compromise you mentioned or protests organized?"

He was making her think about things she hadn't in a while. And she found, to her surprise, she liked it. "Protests have their place. Sometimes they are the only thing that will catch the attention of those ignoring the problem. But those assaults you mentioned do not. We gain nothing by resorting to violence, except turning many who might support an acceptable compromise against us."

"What about those who find no compromise acceptable? The ones who do that assaulting?"

"Those people," she said flatly, "are living in a fantasy. And I suspect many of those who turn to violence do so because that's what they wanted to do all along."

"Well, well. Reality." His brows had risen in surprise. She counted that as a win, since he'd kept his expression so detached throughout this conversation, as if he were merely curious.

And why would he be anything more than that? He's

just trying to pass the time. This is a job to him, nothing more. You're a job to him, nothing more.

She didn't like the fact that she had to continually remind herself of that. It made her voice a little sharp as she retorted to his reality crack.

"I do live there."

"Apparently. More than I expected." He held up a hand before she could speak. "Yes, I admit, another assumption. Don't shoot me."

Suddenly she found herself fighting a smile. Her oddly tangled reaction to him aside, she had quite enjoyed this conversation. It was always good to have to state her beliefs, if only because it kept them clear in her own mind. It was too easy to slide into the surface stuff, thinking that making a post made a difference. It might lead to that, but in itself it meant nothing without that action taken.

Later, after they'd cleaned up, she walked over to peruse the large bookcase she'd seen. She saw on a lower shelf the wizard books they'd talked about earlier and looked over her shoulder at him. "Yours?"

"Started out as mine, but all of us read them." His mouth quirked. "My mother had quite the battle to ration them out when the triplets all wanted to read them at once."

She laughed. "How did she resolve it?"

He rolled his eyes. "She made me choose. Since they were mine first."

"Oh, nice dodge!" She had the thought that she would probably quite like his mother.

"She thought so. I wasn't so happy about it."

"So what did you do?"

"I wanted to let them fight it out, but that didn't go

over well with Mom. Then I thought Bridgette because she was the fastest reader so the others would get them sooner, but the guys didn't like that. So I went with a double coin flip."

"Sounds fair. Who won?"

"Bridgette."

She laughed. "So you got your second idea anyway."

"Much to her glee."

Still smiling, she turned back to the bookcase, scanning the shelves. Everything from nonfiction on one to a wide expanse of novels on the other. She saw a couple of titles that appeared to be Kansas history, but also a novel she'd been meaning to read for ages.

"No checkout required," he said from close behind her. She imagined she could feel his breath against the nape of her neck and had to suppress a shiver of response.

"Thank you," she said, hating that she sounded a bit unsteady. "I'd like something to read tonight."

She didn't hear him move, but when he spoke again, it seemed he'd backed up a step or two. And it was in that level, professional voice.

"When you go up, don't close the door."

"That seems…counterproductive."

He shook his head. "I told you, they'll have to get past me. And I need to hear, just in case somebody decides to try and scale that outside wall to your window."

She blinked. "That wall is straight up-and-down."

"Doesn't mean it can't be done. Or that a drone couldn't blast out a window and get in."

She gaped at him. "A drone? Really, Mr. Colton, don't you think that's—"

"A possibility. A distant one, admittedly, but we

didn't build our reputation on overlooking even distant possibilities."

She stopped her retort before it was spoken. She'd agreed to this for her parents' sake, and she would gain nothing by arguing every little point. So she merely said, "Fine," and grabbed up the novel, thinking she would have trouble focusing on history at the moment. Then, too sweetly, she asked, "Do I have your permission to go upstairs?"

For an instant, he looked weary, and she regretted the jab. "Good night, Ms. Hart."

She was five steps up when she looked back at him. "And when do you sleep, Mr. Colton?"

"Not your problem."

"It is if you're too tired to react."

He crossed his arms and leaned one shoulder against the stairway wall, looking up at her. He was backlit by the light from the great room, and the near silhouette just emphasized how tall and broad shouldered he was. The man truly was built. She could only faintly see his face when he answered her. It didn't matter—she remembered all too well exactly what he looked like with that chiseled jaw and those blue eyes.

"I've done this job for a decade, Ms. Hart. I haven't lost anyone yet, and I don't intend to start with you. Go to bed. And keep that door open."

It was a measure of her state of mind that the thing that irritated her was that continuing *Ms. Hart.*

Chapter Thirteen

He'd expected her to be restless, most people were the first night in a strange place. He hadn't expected her to be up pacing the floor quite this much. She had at least done as he'd asked and left the door at the top of the stairs open. He appreciated that. But it didn't answer the question of why she was still awake at nearly 2:00 a.m.

Maybe that was her normal schedule. Maybe she was always up until the wee hours. If so, she'd probably laughed to herself when he'd told her to go to bed before eleven o'clock.

Or maybe she was still missing her phone. Maybe she really was an addict.

Maybe she's missing something else... Someone else.

And that was enough maybes. He got up out of the chair, an old not-too-comfortable recliner he'd pulled up close to the door of the downstairs bedroom—close so he could hear, and not-too-comfortable so he wouldn't sleep too soundly to wake up at the slightest noise—and stepped out into the dark hallway. He slid the Dan Wesson TCP he'd had on the small table beside the chair into the clip-on holster on his belt. The maker of the tactical compact pistol was a subsidiary of a Kansas City company, and he liked to keep his business local when he could. Besides, even though the 1911 model handgun had its detractors, he liked the idea of the care that went into making only a thousand or so a year.

He grimaced inwardly at the feeble trick of thinking about his everyday carry weapon in an effort not to think about what had been on his mind. Which pretty well exemplified the merry-go-round his brain seemed to be on. He made himself focus. There hadn't been anything in the file Eric had given them about a current boyfriend. A brief mention of an ex, a professor at some upscale northeast school, including the information that the breakup had apparently been mutual when the man had relocated to take a position at an even more upscale European school.

He remembered his first reaction upon reading that had been steeped in those assumptions he was trying to shake. Of course she'd dated someone like that. He'd studied the photograph of the man more out of curiosity than anything. He looked younger than he was—nearly two decades older than Ashley—with curly hair and big-rimmed glasses. He had that look Ty had always associated with the type, almost soft features and that air of superiority that seemed inbred. Assumptions again.

His second reaction—which should have been the first—was to check that they'd confirmed the man was where he said he was, and had been in the nearly a year since the split. Not that things couldn't easily be arranged from halfway around the globe, but there were no signs. There had been a few contacts between them at first, but that had faded away after about three months. And the thorough report indicated the man was now semi-attached to some distant connection to a royal family from somewhere.

But his reaction now, upon remembering that file, was different. Now he found it somehow significant that she'd chosen to stay here rather than follow the guy. He wondered if it was a sign of her love for her home or not enough love for the man.

His second thought, as he stood there listening to her moving around, was to wonder how on earth she'd managed to stay, if the Elite report was accurate—and they were almost never wrong—unattached for nearly a year. She was smart, beautiful, rich and… He fought against letting the word sound even in his mind, but it was already there. Again. Passionate.

He had about as much luck as he'd had the first time it had popped, utterly unwelcome, into his head stopping himself from wondering if that passion for her causes spilled over into her personal life.

Into her sex life. Because, surely, she had one.

He heard the creak of the third step. The one that had never been fixed, because he'd insisted it remain as noisy as possible. The family knew to avoid it if they wanted stealth, but for his purposes, it served as a makeshift alarm. His father had grumbled, but then he'd never liked the idea of using the place as a safe house, anyway. His mother had told Ty to ignore him, that the real problem was still that Ty had chosen not to go into the family business. Fitzpatrick Colton had been stunned that none of his children had made the choice he'd assumed they all would. And, of course, it never occurred to him that the reason why was his own lack of interest in them in any other way.

He dragged his mind off that well-worn path. He

waited, not wanting to startle her while she was negotiating the stairs in the dark. But when she took the last step, he spoke.

"Need something, Ms. Hart?"

He heard her smothered gasp, saw her shadow spin around toward him.

"God, you startled me!"

"Why I waited until you were off the steps," he pointed out.

"Oh." He heard her take a deep breath, as if to regain what he'd startled out of her. "Thank you. I think."

He reached for the switch beside his door and flipped it. Light flooded the hallway. She squinted at the sudden flare. And then her eyes widened again, and she was staring at him so stunned that he looked at himself, wondering if he'd inadvertently grabbed a guest's left-behind T-shirt with a rude graphic without realizing it, something that might offend her. But it was, as he'd thought, his old University of Kansas shirt with the bright blue Jayhawk character on it. It was a bit small after years of washing, but there was nothing on it to make her stare like that.

Maybe it's too flyover for her. If it were Yale or Harvard, she'd be smiling, not gaping at me.

He, on the other hand, was having to fight gaping at her. He was sure the rather simple knit pajamas she had on weren't intended to be sexy, but on her long almost lanky, yet entirely female shape, they were. The soft cloth flowed over her, especially the soft curves of her breasts, in a way that made his fingers itch oddly.

"Did you need something?" he repeated, his voice rather harsh because he was fighting an inner battle he was quite rusty at.

"I… No," she said, dragging her gaze away from his shirt. "I just…couldn't sleep."

"Strange place."

"No, it's not that, I'm used to that, I just… I couldn't…"

"Couldn't find the off switch?" he suggested.

Her mouth shifted into a small smile. "Exactly that," she said, although something in her voice suggested to him that she meant it in a different way than he was thinking.

"I've always wondered if you turn off that switch, who turns it back on again?"

The smile widened. Damn, he liked that smile. "I've always assumed it's on a timer, and will come back on in the morning in time to start thinking about whatever it is again."

"Sort of an automated Scarlett O'Hara approach?"

The smile became a laugh. An appreciative laugh that warmed him far more than it should have. "I wouldn't have thought that was on your reading list."

"More that it was my grandmother's movie. She was born on the day it came out, so it was a big deal to her. She and my mom watch it on her birthday every year."

"That's a lovely tradition."

"Better than Oz. I can only handle so much 'If I Only Had a Brain.'" He got the laugh again. And the same burst of warmth. He put on his best glum face. "Easy for you to laugh. You didn't have your uncle whistling that at you as a kid, any time he thought you were doing something dumb."

"Actually, that sounds like a rather sweet way of guiding you."

He couldn't hang on to the glum, and his own smile

broke through. "It was, in retrospect. At least he cared." He winced inwardly. He hadn't meant to let that out. So he quickly asked, "What do you usually do when this happens?" He wondered if she relied on medication, smoked pot or what.

"What I was about to do. Find a book to read until I can fall asleep."

Well, that was about as benign as it gets. "I thought you had one."

"I did, but it was too engrossing."

"So you need something boring?"

"No, because then I'll just sit there, thinking how boring this is and not get any closer to sleeping. It's better if it's something that hooks me just enough so I fall asleep almost without realizing it. Best is something I'm familiar with but still like enough to get into, just enough to turn the rest of the brain off." She grimaced. "Sorry, more than you asked. I'm tired. And frustrated."

Quickly deciding that thinking about her and frustration was something best to avoid, Ty shoved off from the doorjamb and walked into the great room and over to the bookshelves. He bent down, grabbed a hardcover volume and held it out to her. She immediately recognized the colorful dust jacket of the first book in the wizard series they'd talked about, and the grin she gave him was like a punch to the gut. And all he could think was that it was a good thing he'd kept his jeans on instead of pulling on the pajama bottoms that were much more comfortable, but much less able to hide what was currently happening south of his beltline.

"Perfect," she said as she reached out and took the book from him. He fought the urge to hang on to it—

to make her ask or pull, anything to draw out the moment. He wanted more than anything to slide his hand forward just enough to brush her fingers with his, but fought down that very unprofessional urge, too.

Book in hand, she headed for the couch. She turned on the light at the end closest to the fireplace and sat. And he blurted out, “You’re not going back to bed to read?”

She shook her head without looking at him, already seated and opening the cover of the tale. “If I do that, my brain knows what I’m trying to do and fights back.” There was such a rueful note in her voice the corners of his mouth twitched. But at the same time, he smothered a sigh, because now there would be no sleep at all for him.

As if he could have anyway, after the sight of her in those pajamas that weren’t in the least sexy.

Not in the least.

Chapter Fourteen

Ashley stared down at the first inside page of the book, at the name written there in a bold yet childlike hand. The combination didn't surprise her in the least. Fighting the image of the man this child had become standing there in the sudden flare of light, the T-shirt with that silly bird caricature on it tight across his chest and short enough to give her a peek at an impressive set of abs, she tried to keep her voice even.

"How old were you when this came out?" she asked, still not looking at him.

"Exactly eleven," he answered.

She smiled, the same age as the intrepid hero. She turned to the title page just as he turned to walk away, and instinctively she looked up. Immediately her gaze fastened on the back pockets of his jeans. She didn't think she'd ever seen a pair of jeans filled out better, front and back.

Heat shot through her, and her eyes widened as she forced her gaze back to the title page. What was wrong with her? She did not—ever—react to a man like this, especially a man she'd just met less than twelve hours ago. She didn't understand, and so instead of reading as she'd planned, her sometimes-riotous brain tackled the question.

It wasn't just that he was good-looking in a very masculine way, but he was bigger, more confident, to the edge of swagger. She supposed it took a very confident man to do the kind of work he did, but it was more than just that.

She heard him moving around in the kitchen and wondered what he was doing. Surely not coffee this late? He didn't seem the sort who would go for decaf. Then again, if he planned on staying awake all night, on guard, maybe caffeine was the method. But he had to sleep sometime, didn't he? Had she awakened him, or had he been still awake when she'd come downstairs?

Maybe the key was that he was so different from the men she was used to. He dared to order her around—which was, she had to admit, his job just now—when most men who knew who she was tended to defer to her, sometimes to the point of obsequiousness. Ty Colton did not. Nor could she imagine him acting in any sort of sycophantic way. She would be willing to bet he would stand up to her father in a way no one, even Simon—or maybe especially Simon—ever had.

No, Simon Karlan had turned into that sycophant, kowtowing to her father in a way that had made Andrew Hart's lip curl and her own stomach churn. In fact, if anything, it had been that memory that had been the main factor when she'd decided she was much better off without him when he left for Europe.

No, she couldn't see this man fawning over her father or anyone else. Not even the former president he was distantly related to.

She heard footsteps coming back and hastily turned a page so that at least she was looking at text and not the title page she'd never gotten past. He stopped in front of her, and she tried to mentally brace herself to look up, chanting the order not to end up gaping at that flat, toned stomach of his, or the breadth of his chest and shoulders.

When she did look up, her gaze snagged instead on what he was holding out to her. A steaming mug. Her brow furrowed. Why would you offer coffee to someone already having trouble sleeping?

"Hot chocolate," he said.

She stared at the mug for a moment, then at the strong, steady hand that held it. Managed not to let her gaze slide from there up that powerfully muscled arm. She gave herself a mental shake.

"Just how long did you and my mother talk?" she asked.

"Actually, it was your father who suggested we have this on hand in case you couldn't sleep."

She took the mug, for some reason feeling off balance by this. "I suppose you think that's silly, that my father would know that."

"Silly? Hardly. Enviable, maybe."

She took a sip and found the brew rich and sweet and soothing. And familiar. They hadn't just gotten hot chocolate—they'd gotten her favorite. He'd also made it with milk, not water, just as she liked it.

She studied him for a moment as he stood there, towering over her as she sat with her legs curled up under her. "I gather your father wouldn't be able to match that feat?"

He let out the barest breath of a chuckle. "I doubt my father could tell you what color my eyes are."

"That's hard to believe. They're rather striking."

He drew back slightly, as if she'd surprised him. She gave an exaggerated roll of her own eyes. "Oh, please. I'm sure you've had woman admire your eyes—" *among other things* "—before."

He seemed to recover quickly, and the corners of his mouth twitched. "Last client who did was old enough to be my grandmother."

She arched a brow at him. "Ageist, are you?"

"No. I don't hold yours against you."

What was that supposed to mean? Was that what all the ordering around was? He thought her a child? He couldn't possibly be that much older than she was. If her phone were working, she could find out in a moment. But it wasn't, so she had to guess, and put him at thirty to thirty-five until she could confirm. *If I ever see civilization again.*

"How gracious of you," she said, rather sourly.

"She, on the other hand, was vetting me like a stud horse, for her granddaughter."

She blinked. She felt the corners of her own mouth twitching. And then she couldn't stop it. She let out a laugh. "Well, at least she has good taste." He blinked in turn. Went very still. She felt the pressure to say something else, to make what she'd said less of a blatant compliment. Perversely, the words that came out only made it worse. "Assuming she was going for good looks and a striking eye color."

His expression didn't change. He didn't move. He stood there, towering. And finally he said, his voice oddly quiet, "What makes you think it wasn't brain-power she was after?"

She felt herself flush. But she held her head up as she answered, purposefully making it not a question, "Then she would have hit the jackpot on all counts, wouldn't she."

For a moment, he didn't react. But then a slow smile curved his mouth—that mouth—and she saw a gleam come into his eyes that made her oddly twitchy. "Your professor," he said with slow emphasis, "was a fool."

She should have been stunned that he knew about Simon at all.

Instead, she was sitting here with alternating chills and heat rippling through her as she watched him walk away.

THIS WAS CRAZY. It was crazy and it had to stop. Right now. The loaded conversations, the utterly unveiled compliments, the whole back-and-forth thing had to stop.

Ty drummed his fingers on the kitchen counter as he waited for the coffee machine to kick out enough to even half fill his mug. He'd tasted the hot chocolate and immediately rejected it. The soporific effect would likely do what he'd hoped it would for her, put him to sleep. But for now, if she was awake, he was awake.

But when they were both awake, it seemed they couldn't stop veering into those byways he didn't want—couldn't want—to go down.

Even waiting for the coffee was too much. He walked out of the kitchen and over to the coat rack by the door and grabbed his heavier jacket and his keys. "Going out for a quick recon," he said when he saw her look at him, even as he wondered why he felt compelled to explain when he was simply doing his job. As she no doubt knew, having grown up with security around her.

He didn't wait for her to respond but pulled the door open. Caught the sturdy stock of the Mossberg shotgun she'd handled with familiarity out of the corner of his eye. She was a bundle of contradictions, was Ashley Hart.

He stepped outside before he could change his mind. The cold air would do him good, chase the tiredness. Because he was tired, much more tired than he should have been.

Keeping up with her wearing you down, Colton?

He nearly laughed at his own thoughts. He took in a deep breath, watched his breath form a cloud in the light through the window from inside. If it wasn't freezing tonight, it was close.

He didn't really need to do this. All the alarms and cameras were functioning fine and would warn him if anything outside the house turned up. Outside the immediate perimeter, he'd check with the drone tomorrow. What he needed was to be a little farther from her, for a few minutes at least, and this was the only way he could do it and not slack on his job.

Then she would have hit the jackpot on all counts...

He felt an odd thump in his chest he would have called his heart skipping a beat if it weren't so ridiculous. He had to get his mind off this path before it became a rut he had to fight his way out of.

So put it to work on the two dead bodies from the warehouse.

The mystery of who they were had been solved fairly quickly, thanks to his brother Brooks. Sadly, the female had been identified as Olivia Harrison, the mother of Brooks's now-fiancée, Gwen, and the male Fenton Crane, a PI her grandmother had hired to try to find Gwen's mother who had vanished years ago. But who the killer was, or even if it was the same person—although the methodology certainly suggested it was—remained a mystery.

He'd been hoping to dig into the case, to get to the bottom of what was turning into a scandal for Colton Construction, but instead here he was, making freaking hot chocolate for a spoiled rich kid.

Even as he thought it, his sense of fairness kicked in. She was rich, all right, beyond most people's wildest imaginings. But to his own surprise, she wasn't spoiled.

And she's not a kid.

Oh, yeah, don't forget that one. She was not a kid, no matter that it would be easier for him if he could think of her that way. But no, Ashley Hart was all woman. Slender curves, luscious mouth, glossy dark hair, bottomless brown eyes—yes, every inch female.

And a few male inches of his liked every bit of her. Too much.

It took two rounds of the house before the chill of the air was able to take the edge off the heat from being in the same room with her. When he finally went back, he eased the door open as quietly as he could and locked it before he even turned around.

Apparently, the combination of chocolate and book had worked. She was still on the couch but half lying down now, her head on the cushioned arm, clearly asleep. The book, while still in her hands, had fallen shut.

He stood there for a moment, simply looking at her

while silently delivering a barn burner of a lecture to himself. To stop noticing how lovely she was, to stop enjoying their bantering conversations so much, to stop wondering what it would be like to stop one of those conversations with a kiss. The Colton family might be a big deal in Braxville, in Kansas, in mid-America for that matter, but they were nowhere near the thin-air territory of the Harts of Westport. She wasn't just out of his league; she was another game altogether.

Not to mention forbidden.

She stirred slightly, stretching out more comfortably but not waking. Ty sucked in a deep breath, then walked over to his mother's favorite chair, where there was a thick knitted throw over the back. He brought it and gently spread it over Ashley. And when she smiled slightly in her sleep, released the book and snuggled into the soft wool, he took a hasty step back as an unfamiliar sensation of longing rocketed through him.

He stared a moment longer, then reached down and took the book before it fell to the floor and woke her. He turned out the light above her and walked back to his mother's chair, where there was a small lamp she could angle onto a book or the frequent needlework projects she took on. Like the throw he'd just tucked around Ashley.

He sat down, took a last look at the woman across the room, then turned on the reading light and opened the book himself. He wouldn't look at her that way again, he vowed. This woman was his to protect, but nothing more.

Chapter Fifteen

Ashley opened her eyes slowly, vaguely aware she was not in a bed. With her travels, she was used to not waking up in her own bed—sometimes she hardly remembered which place she technically called home—but she did usually make it to a bed. She blinked blurry eyes, feeling as if she'd slept more soundly than she had in weeks. Which seemed strange, since she remembered pacing the floor into the wee hours.

And then her gaze focused on the reason for her restlessness last night. The man who had plunged her into a situation she'd never found herself in before. Not being under threat. That happened occasionally. But she'd never found herself walking the floor, unable to sleep because she couldn't get a man out of her mind. Worse, a man she'd just met.

He sat in the big chair across the room, a reading lamp aimed at the book on his lap, the only light in the room. The book she'd been reading last night, the loved but familiar story just enough to distract her whirling mind and allow her to sleep. Why he had it now, she had no idea. Perhaps he'd meant to stay awake reading. If so, it hadn't worked, because his eyes were closed and his head lolled back against the chair.

Which gave her far too much of a chance to study the strong, corded muscles of his neck and the long, powerful length of his legs, stretched out and crossed at the ankles some distance from the chair itself.

It was a very pleasant sight. And she was glad he'd at least gotten some sleep.

Don't want your bodyguard too tired to function.

That strange jolt of heat shot through her again as she realized other ways those words could be interpreted. Thank goodness she'd only thought them, not spoken them.

She made a note of how warm and comfy she was beneath this soft thick throw. Her pulse skipped a beat as she remembered she'd seen it before, folded across the very chair he was in now. Had she truly slept through him tucking it around her? That was hardly part of his bodyguard duties, to see to not only her safety but her comfort. So had he done it simply because beneath the tough, competent exterior he was a nice guy? Because this was, despite the use he was putting it to now, a family place? Or because—

She cut off her own thoughts before they could careen into silly territory. Telling herself not to be stupid, she raised up on one elbow to look out the window. The instant she moved, his head came up. She didn't think she'd made any sound at all, and yet he was suddenly as awake as if she'd shouted.

"Morning," he said.

Okay, that voice, that low, deep rumble shouldn't be allowed first thing in the morning. She wasn't awake enough to deal with it.

"Is it?" she muttered, glancing at the still dark windows.

To her annoyance, when she looked back, he was

grinning. “Not a morning person? Although I’ll grant you it is early.”

“Define early.”

He glanced at the windows she’d just looked at. “I’d say we’re well into astronomical twilight, headed for nautical twilight.”

Okay, now she was really annoyed. She sat up. “Translation, please?”

“Nautical twilight is when the center of the sun is between six and twelve degrees below the horizon and—”

She put a hand to her forehead, rubbed. “Stop. Please stop.”

He relented. “I’m guessing it’s between 5:30 and 6:00 a.m. Past time to get up and get to work around here.”

Her first thought was to find her phone and confirm the actual time, her second was to wonder if the phone had enough charge left to keep time, since it had no network to read it from, and her third thought was a sneaky little wish that he be way wrong.

“Don’t trust me?” he asked lightly.

She disentangled herself from the throw and stood up, stretching. “Did no one ever tell you it’s not nice to poke at a non-morning person at…whatever hour this is?”

“Must have missed that lesson.”

“We’ll see how you like it when I wake you up at midnight.”

Something flickered in his eyes, but he only said, “You already did.”

He had a point there. But she was cranky enough not to concede it just yet. She walked over to the kitchen to where she could see the clock on the oven. And grimaced.

"How close was I?"

"Congratulations, Mister Astronomer, it's 5:52."

"Good to know."

He glanced back at the window again. "Get dressed and put your jacket back on."

She blinked. "What?"

"We're going outside."

"What?"

"Not far," he said. "Just over there."

He gestured rather vaguely toward the waterside of the house. "Why?"

"I just want to show you something."

What was this? Some kind of escape hatch or something he wanted her to know about? Someplace he wanted her to run to if something happened? With a smothered sigh and a yawn, she went back upstairs and dressed, sat and pulled her ankle boots back on, wishing she hadn't vowed last night to not be a hindrance when the man was only trying to do the job he'd been hired to do.

She went back down to find him standing there, holding out her jacket for her to slip on. "Thanks," she muttered. *For that, at least.*

She'd known it would be cold, but it was nothing she wasn't used to this time of year. Before she'd packed for this trip, she'd compared the temperature averages of her destination with her home ground, and somewhat to her surprise, they were rather similar. Wichita might have Westport beat on the record high and low ends by over ten degrees, but the average lows were within a couple of degrees.

But stepping out into the night—or early morning, apparently—chill accomplished one thing. Ten feet out, she was thoroughly awake. She would have grumbled that this better be worth it if it hadn't felt rather good. She could see the faint glint of light reflecting off the lake. She could see stars, lots of them, but also dark patches of cloud that masked them. There was just enough light to see a wide expanse of water, but without a trace of a breeze only the faintest of ripples. No city lights reflected here, and even the other buildings she could see farther south were still dark in this…astronomical twilight. She fought a smile as she drew in a deep breath of the chilly air.

"What?" he asked, and she realized she'd let out a "Hmm."

"Just thinking how, even at the same time of day—" she shot him a glance "—or night, and at the same temperature, places can smell and feel so different."

"Missing your salt air?"

"More noticing than missing," she said. "But this feels more like home than, say, Santiago's salt air, so it's not that, per se."

"How about the Amazon?"

She wasn't surprised. She already knew he—or Elite—had done their homework. His knowing about Simon had proved that. "Whole different kind of smell and feel."

They walked a little farther, then he stopped. "This'll do. Have a seat."

She wondered if this was some sort of test. Did he think her too finicky to sit on the ground? Hadn't his homework on her time in the Amazon included that she'd lived in a native hut for nearly six months?

She quickly sat to prove her point. Fortunately, the ground was dry. He dropped down beside her. And said…nothing. And she was wondering again what this was all about, this sitting here in the dark, waiting for…what?

She did noticed the sky seemed to be getting lighter. *When the center of the sun is between six and twelve degrees below the horizon…*

Maybe she should be wondering about where his job as a security expert took him instead of assuming she was the more well traveled one. She had made some assumptions of her own. Again.

"Here we go," he murmured.

She glanced at him to see what he was looking at, but he seemed to be simply staring out toward the lake. Or toward the other side of the lake. The east side, unless she'd gotten her directions seriously turned around. Which told her, belatedly, what to look for. As she thought it, she saw it, the slight demarcation between land and sky. He was staring out toward the horizon, and—

East. The faint line slowly became more definite. And then she saw the first distant change in color, from black to near black, then even lighter. The world seemed impossibly silent, as if everyone and everything was holding its breath, waiting.

And then the sky was a deep dark blue. Almost the color of his eyes. She suppressed an unwelcome imagining of what his reaction would be if she said that, that his eyes were the color of the sky just before sunrise.

The blue got lighter, the clouds more visible. "Welcome to dawn," he said, his voice so soft it seemed part of the quiet around them. The way he said it, with quiet appreciation, made the simple words sound almost… poetic. And that was something she never would have expected. “And we’re not alone,” he added.

She felt a jolt over his words. And then she felt an entirely different kind of jolt over the warm touch of his hand to her face as he gently turned her head toward the trees to their left.

“Down low,” he whispered.

She looked and saw movement. A low slinking trot and the flick of a thick bushy tail as the creature disappeared into the trees.

“A fox?” she asked.

“Yes. An armadillo would be shinier.”

He’d said it in a completely neutral tone of helpful instruction. But she was learning about him already, and knew he was teasing her. “And have a skinnier tail,” she said seriously.

She saw his grin even in the faint light and felt crazily as if she’d won some prize.

Your professor was a fool…

His words, practically a declaration, echoed in her mind. *Stop. Don’t be a fool yourself. Just enjoy the thought of Simon’s face at being called a fool.*

And then everything changed again. The undersides of the clouds seemed to catch and reflect the growing light. Suddenly there was color, orange, yellow, pink, painting the clouds with the surest of hands. The horizon became a physical thing, accented by the silhouettes of trees made ebony by the brightness behind them. And then, between two of the tallest trees, the edge of the sun cleared the horizon and light arrowed across the lake, streaking it with fire.

She'd seen sunrises around the world, in some beautiful places, but somehow none had moved her more than this welcome to morning in a place she'd never thought to be. She felt a burst of understanding as sudden as that rush of light: this was what they meant by heartland.

Past time to get up and get to work around here.

He hadn't been teasing about that. This was the world he'd grown up in, where by dawn many had already been long at work.

And that he had wanted her to see this meant…she wasn't sure what.

"Somebody else late getting home for the day," he said, pointing now that it was light enough to see. Not allowing herself to admit she preferred the touch of his hand on her cheek, she looked. It took her a moment, so perfectly matched was the creature to the surroundings, but again it was the movement that let her focus in time to see a large bird winging silently into the trees as if that arrow of sunlight were its only predator.

"Owl?" she asked, having just gotten a glimpse of its head.

"Great horned one," he said. "There's a pair that's nested in those trees for at least three years."

"Shades of that wizard book again."

She got the grin again. And felt that same rush of pleasure that made her beyond nervous. This was ridiculous. She was here because she had work to do, work that had indirectly brought this man into her life. And when it was done, when the situation was resolved, he would be out of her life again. So becoming infatuated with the man's grin—never mind his touch—was a fool's errand.

That she would never do.

Chapter Sixteen

Ashley Hart was a puzzlement. Or a wonder, Ty wasn't sure which. He never would have expected a woman with her background would be so taken with a simple Kansas sunrise. In fact, he'd brought her out here as much to show himself that she wouldn't be, that she wouldn't react with the wonder he always felt, as to show it to her.

She'd reacted with all the appreciation he could have wished.

Why the hell does it matter to you? She's a client. And she'll be back on her unending world tour as soon as this threat is resolved.

And yet, from that sound of excitement she'd made when she'd spotted the fox, the smile when she'd seen the owl, you'd think she'd never before strayed out of her own backyard. How did a woman like her, who had lived a life of old-money-style wealth, hang on to such a simple thing?

"Can we look around later?" She sounded like a little girl, excited about a wonderful new place. He hadn't expected that, either. "I mean," she added, with a touch of mockery back in her voice, "if I'm allowed outside in the daylight."

"Not alone," he said, rather gruffly at her tone.

"I assumed." The mockery was still there but vanished when she went on. "Besides, who else will show me everything, good and bad?"

"Good and bad?"

"You know, good like the fox and the owl, and bad like… Do you have snakes?"

His brow furrowed. "Of course we do." When she shuddered, he added, "Only five of the almost forty kinds are venomous. And nobody's died from a snakebite here in about half a century."

She gave him a wry smile, which he could see clearly now that there was enough light. "Thanks for the facts, but it's not my logic that reacts to them."

"Ah. Lizard brain, huh?"

"Did you have to use another reptile analogy?" she asked sourly.

He laughed. She managed a more genuine smile, but he could tell she was serious. And it would probably be wise to know more. So he asked, "How do you react? Freeze or run?"

"Both, in that order. The length of the freeze depends on how close and how big."

He wondered if she'd had to answer that before, then remembered where she'd been. "Let me guess, your least favorite part of your sojourn in the Amazon?"

The shudder was more pronounced. "Oh, yes. Do you know they have ten varieties of coral snakes alone?"

"What about the famous anaconda?"

"Oddly, they didn't bother me. When faced with that size of snake, my brain just shuts down and refuses to admit it's real."

He laughed again, admiring her honesty and that despite her fears she'd gone ahead with her venture. "Don't worry. We've mostly got prairie ringnecks, which are small, and very shy. The bluish ones are even kind of pretty. We had a big gopher snake around, although I haven't seen him in a while. But I think he's still here because the rats and voles haven't gotten out of control."

"Oh, I freely admit they have their purpose. I'm not one of those who wants them killed on sight. They're a crucial part of the system. I just don't ever, ever want to be around them. I can't even go into the reptile section of a zoo."

"Fair enough," he said. Then, not certain why, he added, "For me it's spiders. Hate those suckers."

She looked startled, but then she gave him the broadest smile yet. "How gallant of you to admit that."

Her tone was teasing again, and it made him grin yet again. He thought he'd done more of that this morning with her than he had in a month. She was surprising him, which in turn intrigued him, which in turn—

No. Not going there. So very not going there.

They headed back to the cabin, and Ashley went into the kitchen to fix her breakfast. He went back to the comms room—he called it that because it bothered his mother to call it a panic room—and made contact with Mitch.

"How'd the first night with her highness go?"

"Not as bad as I expected," Ty said. *And then some.*

"We'll see how you feel after catering to her for a few days."

Ty knew his buddy was just jabbing at him but felt compelled to correct his assumption. "Not sure that's going to be really necessary. She's actually fairly normal, once you get past the surface."

There was enough of a pause that he knew he'd surprised Mitch. "Whoa. Didn't expect that."

And I didn't expect a woman who'd go all soft over a fox, an owl and a Kansas sunrise.

"Neither did I," he said. And changed the subject before he said something stupid. "Anything new?"

"I've been keeping an eye on Sanderson," he said, naming the developer who had the most to lose if Ashley succeeded, and who had blurted out the threats against her. "Nothing unusual. He's not giving up on his project, but he's keeping his head down, too."

"No more threats?"

"No. But a little news on that front. Tech guys found out that several of the social media accounts used were from the same IP and via the same provider."

"So fake?"

"Probably like hundreds of other noisy ones, trying to make the protest against her seem bigger than it is. Or that he has more support than he does. I know social media's useful on occasion, but…"

"The usefulness comes with built-in opportunity for fakery," Ty finished.

"Yeah. You know, if it is Sanderson, I kind of feel for him. He bought that land decades ago, with these plans in mind. But then the government comes in and tells him he can't build, so it's now useless to him."

"While he's still paying taxes on it and has been all this time. I get it. But she's not the one he should be going after."

"She's the one with the big megaphone, who called

attention to it in the first place and got the hold put on his permit."

"It's what she does."

"Well, at least they didn't declare those puddles a navigable waterway," Mitch quipped.

As Ty shut down the connection a moment later, he rubbed at the back of his neck. He'd been having that sensation of being watched for at least thirty seconds.

He spun around. Ashley was there and, judging by her expression, had heard at least some of the conversation. He swiftly ran it back in his head, spared a moment of thanks that she hadn't been there when Mitch called her "her highness." He'd have to remind Mitch she could be within earshot. Of course, Mitch would just tell him to shut the damn door, but he had the feeling that would just rouse her curiosity, and what he was communicating wasn't what he wanted Ashley curious about.

Put a lid on it, Colton. And nail the sucker down.

"Your partner doesn't seem to like me much."

"He's never met you."

"That doesn't seem to stop him from having an opinion."

"Does it stop anyone?"

She sighed. "I suppose not. By the way, I did not agree with that previous interpretation of wetlands. Which I've made clear in the past."

"Declaring a mud puddle in someone's backyard a wetland does not make it one?" he quoted.

She drew back slightly. "You really did do your homework. That was a long time ago."

"The more I know, the better I can do my job."

She studied him for a moment. He didn't know what

she was thinking. But he supposed a woman who ran in her circles, and who gave testimony in front of government committees, was probably fairly skilled at hiding her thoughts. Her emotions, not so much. Something about what he'd said hadn't pleased her.

But whatever it was, she shook it off and said only, "Can we go outside now?"

He looked at her, considering. Which he knew irked her. The whole permission thing was obviously bothering her. "I was about to do a drone check of the property, but a personal one wouldn't hurt."

"Drone?"

He nodded. We've got a small one, with a good camera. Actually belongs to my Uncle Shep, but he lets us play with it."

"The uncle of the tree planting?"

"Yes. He just moved back to Braxville recently, so he's spent some time here." He looked her up and down. "Got any sturdier shoes?"

She looked down at the ankle boots she'd had on yesterday and had pulled back on this morning because they were handy. "Don't like them?" she asked, that edge of sweetness back in her voice that he was learning didn't bode well.

"Whether I like them isn't the point. Whether you can walk on uneven ground with them and they'll hold up to mud and rocks is. And if you want to risk...whatever those cost doing it."

"They weren't that expensive," she protested.

"Honey, I don't even want to know what you consider expensive. Do you have other shoes or not?"

She didn't say a word, but turned and went back down the hall, her every step declaring she was once more not happy with him. She disappeared up the stairs, and he let out a long audible breath.

He glanced at the weather station on the wall above the radio. Still in the low forties. He walked into the bedroom he was using and picked up the extra magazine for his TCP. He clipped it on his belt and shifted the weapon itself slightly. Tried not to think about needing it, but knew there was no guarantee, even out here. They were isolated, yet not unreachable. Not to someone angry enough.

Back out in the great room, he took his jacket off the rack by the door and pulled it on. After a moment's thought, he grabbed one of the knitted wool hats from the basket below the rack.

And the entire time tried not to think about what had seemed to flash in her eyes when he'd called her *honey.*

Chapter Seventeen

"Better?" Ashley asked sweetly.

The irritating man glanced down at her hiking boots. If he was surprised by how heavy-duty and well-worn they were, he didn't say so. Which irritated her in turn, because she had a sharp answer about more assumptions ready to fire at him. Her work often required her to walk through wilder places, and she'd learned early on to be always prepared.

"They'll do," he said. Then he held out a heavy knit hat. "Here. This'll help until it warms up more."

She glanced pointedly at his bare head. Tried not to notice the way his hair still managed to look tousled even though it was fairly short. She liked the way it kicked forward, thick and dark. But then she liked a lot about this man. In looks, anyway. Any woman would, she consoled herself.

Just like any woman's heart would have kicked up the pace if he called her honey?

He noted her look, reached down to a basket and pulled out another similar hat. "Happy now?"

"No, but that's not your job, is it?" For an instant, the briefest flash of…something flared in those dark blue eyes. The first, totally insane thought that hit her was that he was wishing that it were his job. Making her happy. Rattled at her own reactions more than anything, she looked down at the hat she held. It felt indeed warm. And soft, almost luxurious. "This is luscious. What's it made of?"

"You'd have to ask my mother. She's the knitter."

"Oh? She made this?"

"And that blanket thing."

The throw he'd tucked so carefully around her. She shoved aside the memory and said only, "She does beautiful work."

"She's a beautiful woman. Inside and out."

He said it without the slightest bit of hesitation or male embarrassment, and since there was absolutely no sign he was a mamma's boy, she liked that. A lot. She let that show in her smile. "I hope you tell her that."

"Often. We all do."

They stepped outside. It was still chilly, and she tugged on the hat. So did he, and she noticed he gave it an extra pat when he had it down over the top of his ears. Because his mother had made it? She found that sweet, as well. Mr. Ty Colton—cool, competent, slightly bossy security expert—had a soft spot, after all. That it was for his mother, she found charming.

If you want to know how a man will treat his wife, watch how he treats his mother.

The old saying popped into her head out of nowhere. And nearly stunned her. What on earth was she doing thinking about *that?* She scrambled for something else to say, before she let something inescapably stupid out.

"What about your father?"

How quickly the very male shrug came back. "He is who he is."

"And from what you've said, not the warm and fuzzy type," she said, recovered now as they went down the steps of the deck.

He let out a short sharp laugh. "Not unless you've got a great lot or building he wants for sale. He's all business, all the time."

"My father used to be like that."

"Used to? I'd have thought with an empire to run, he still would be."

She gave him a sideways look at his use of the word *empire*, but decided to let it go since he was smiling. Also she quashed the unexpected thought that she would forgive a lot for that smile. She suddenly remembered the conversation with her mother when she'd called to tell her that her father had hired a security firm.

Eric King is a solid, honest contractor, and he's promised he'll put the man your father asked for on it. Cooperate, Ashley.

His best man. She glanced up at the man beside her, all too aware of his size and obvious strength. Too aware of the way he moved with that easy grace and power. Too aware of those dark blue eyes framed by thick dark lashes.

Too aware of how his freaking hair grows.

Somehow she didn't think that was the kind of cooperation her mother had meant. But then her mother hadn't seen Ty Colton. And Ashley couldn't even imagine a woman who wouldn't be hyperaware of this man.

It was just that she never was. She never reacted this way to a man. She might be intrigued, or curious, even admiring. At least she could learn something from a man—that had been what had lured her into the relationship with Simon—but her on-all-levels awareness and fascination and, she had to admit, physical response had never happened before.

She'd been so lost in her thoughts she hadn't really noticed they'd walked out onto the small dock on the lake. The lake that was much larger than she'd thought, although she'd only glanced at a map since her goal was miles away from here.

"What kind of fish are there?"

He looked a little surprised but answered without comment. "Walleye, few kinds of bass—we usually have luck with whites right out front here—crappie, and catfish, of course." He gave her a sideways look, then. "If you're into bottom-feeders."

"One of the most amazing fishes I've ever seen is a catfish. From Thailand. A glass catfish."

"Okay, you got me."

"It's tiny, two or three inches. And it's completely transparent. All the organs are clustered up near its head, so the entire body is just skeleton-like. It's quite remarkable. And even more interesting, they only settled its true taxonomy fairly recently. They thought it was the same as another larger species—are you laughing at me?"

"No," he said instantly. "Just admiring—okay, maybe envying—your recall."

He said it so easily, with no hint of the jab she often got when people accused her of being a walking encyclopedia of useless trivia. "Sometimes I wish I could shut it off," she answered honestly.

"And the rest of the time?"

"I rely on it."

He nodded as if he'd expected that answer. She

looked out at the water again, thinking that this was the easiest exchange she'd ever had about her ability to remember even the most minor facts.

"Lots of boats out there."

"Trout season opened last Sunday. Lot of folks headed toward the seep stream, since they stocked it at the end of last month."

"There's a dam, right? It's not a natural lake?"

"Dam's about five miles down." He nodded, toward the north. "Smoky Hills River comes in right up there."

She glanced in the direction he'd indicated. "Could we walk there? To where the river comes in?"

"It's about a mile and a half, to the start of the delta flats."

"So not that far, then."

He glanced down at her well-worn boots again. "Guess not," he said with a grin.

She smiled back at him. "Then can we?"

"Are you actually asking me permission?"

"I'm asking the man who knows the way," she pointed out.

To her surprise, he laughed. And once more it seemed her every nerve tingled in response. "Good—and practical—point." He seemed thoughtful for a moment. "Let me scout it out first, after the rain we had last week. There's no real trail, and I haven't seen it in a while."

"I don't need a trail. I've hiked in many places without one." She frowned. "I don't have my compass with me, though."

"I have one. But I'm thinking more about any threat."

For a moment, she'd actually forgotten. Why she

was here, why she was with this man at all. "You really think…somebody might be out there, lying in wait or something?"

She hated how small her voice sounded. But being so completely out of touch had apparently affected her more than she would have expected. When she went to places where she knew ahead of time there would be no internet or phone communications, she mentally prepared for it. But she hadn't expected that here, so she was having a little trouble adapting.

You're really addicted to that thing, aren't you?

Maybe he was more right than she wanted to admit.

"I was thinking more about snakes," Ty answered her, giving her a look too innocent to be true. Quickly her mood shifted and she laughed.

"In that case, have at it."

"I'll be back in under an hour. Lock the door and keep the shotgun handy until I do."

She purposefully fluttered her eyelashes at him. "Oh, dear, how will I know it's you?"

He grinned. Damn him. "You mean besides the wall of windows?"

"I wouldn't want to shoot you by mistake."

He gave her a long look. "I have the feeling if you ever shot someone, it would not be by mistake."

She didn't know why that pleased her. Why she was feeling pleased at all during a conversation about shooting someone. But she was. It unsettled her enough that she questioned just how much she wanted to do this.

"If this is too much trouble—"

"It's fine. I need to do a wider recon, anyway." He walked into the kitchen and grabbed a couple of bottles of drinking water. Then he went to a small cabinet on the other side of the door out onto the deck and opened it. He reached in and pulled out a small loaded backpack, tucked the water into side pockets, and slung it over one shoulder. When he saw her looking at it, he shrugged. "Better to lug it and not need it than the other way around."

She wondered what was in it. First-aid things, she supposed. Survival gear, although why he would need it here, and this close to the cabin…unless he got hurt. A slip and fall was always possible, and if he broke an arm or leg out there, he'd be screwed with no phone service. Of course, the likelihood of big tough Ty Colton needing help was silly, she supposed. But still…

Even as she thought it, he reached back into the cabinet and brought out two hand-sized walkie-talkies. He turned knobs on both, then handed her one.

"It gets a little spotty at the river because of the terrain, but up until then it should be clear."

She let out a relieved sigh. "Good, so you can call for help if you need it."

He looked utterly startled. With a bemused smile he said, "It's for you to call for help if you need it."

She watched him go, feeling a bit bemused herself at the fact that they had each been thinking of the other. Of course, it was his job just now to worry about her.

But that didn't explain why her first reaction had been to worry about him.

Chapter Eighteen

Upon getting back to the cabin, Ty was surprised to find that she'd set out snacks for them. "How long are you planning on being out there?" he asked, masking his amusement at the array. More water was good, but she'd found his stash of energy bars, grabbed a couple of apples from the bowl on the counter and thrown in a couple of candy bars she must have had herself. She'd also apparently had a small folding backpack in her luggage, because it was also on the counter.

"Better to lug it and not need it, I believe someone said?"

He smiled at that. And noticed yet again he'd done more smiling in the last twenty-four hours—almost—than he had in weeks. There hadn't been much to smile about with all the chaos going on around Colton Construction. Nothing like finding a couple of bodies sealed up in one of your old buildings to put the blight on your outlook.

"Sounds like a smart guy," he said, glad to see that she took it as he'd meant it, jokingly.

"So, we're clear to go?"

He nodded. "Nothing out there but some wildlife. Didn't see a single snake, by the way."

"Thank goodness."

He walked into the kitchen, over to the erasable note board on the fridge. He unclipped the marker and scrawled a note.

"Tree down?" Ashley asked, having followed him in and read past his shoulder.

He nodded as he put the marker back in place after noting the location. "First one of us with the time and energy will cut it up for firewood. Which is good, because we'll need more by next year. If we spend much time up here this winter, we'll go through what we've got."

"Can't you buy more?"

"If we can find some local wood, but out here most people use up their own. The motto is buy it where you burn it. So people don't bring in new invasive species or transport new pests." He gave her a sideways look. "But you probably know that."

"I knew about the federal policy, but I confess, not the motto. Sounds effective."

"Personally, I think the photos of forests peppered with dying trees are more so, but the words do stick in your head."

She seemed to hesitate, then said, "You don't disagree with my goals, then."

Uh-oh. He resorted to his usual response in tricky areas like this. A shrug. "Doesn't matter if I disagree. Nothing to do with my job."

"But you follow the policy?"

"It makes sense."

"And if it didn't?" Another shrug. "So you do disagree?"

"Doesn't matter," he repeated.

"I'm curious."

"Then you'll have to stay curious," he said firmly. He was *not* going to get into a debate with a client. If he made her mad, she'd be less likely to cooperate and that could be dangerous. "You ready for this hike?"

To his relief, she let it drop, although something in her expression had him thinking the reprieve was only temporary. She hadn't gotten to where she was today, an advocate with a reputation for getting things done, by letting things slide. And he doubted many people told her no, anyway.

He tucked the snacks into an outside pocket on his backpack, and she did the same. She also slid her phone into the back pocket of her snug jeans. The pocket that curved over her delightful backside.

Lucky phone.

The errant thought put an edge in his voice when he said, "If you're hoping for reception out there, don't count on it."

Her chin came up. "I was thinking about photos. Do you have a problem with that?"

"Not as long as none of them see the light of day before the threat has passed." He hesitated, then added, "You do realize this is a risk, going out like this?"

She met his gaze. Then she sighed. "This is selfish of me, isn't it? Putting you in a position where it will be harder to do your job?"

Her sudden, unexpected admission wiped away the rest of his warning. "Worry about the risk to you, not my job."

Her mouth quirked. "Kind of entwined, aren't they?"

He shrugged. "You're in danger. But you shouldn't have to be a prisoner. So be aware but let me do…what

I do. Oh, and about those pictures, I'd prefer you didn't advertise the exact location to the world. We'd like to keep this little corner as it is."

"So you do believe in preservation? Or only of what you yourself own?"

"I do believe in preservation, and right now that means self-preservation, so we're not having this discussion."

"Coward."

He didn't rise to the obvious bait. "You'd better hope not."

"Point taken," she admitted. And she didn't quibble about him leading the way. But then he already knew she wasn't foolish, just determined. And maybe the tiniest bit spoiled. Nothing like he would have expected, of course. Those assumptions again.

Once they'd crossed the cleared area around the house and got into the trees and underbrush, the walking grew harder. But she didn't comment and got through easily enough. He was hyper-attuned to their surroundings, on guard, but he still noticed she often turned sideways to avoid breaking branches and managed to avoid stepping in places that were more muddy and neatly dodged rocks. She obviously hadn't lied; she was used to this.

And she was smiling. Constantly, although it widened whenever they encountered wildlife, and turned to a delighted grin when he stopped her and pointed out a couple of black-tailed prairie dogs, which she'd never seen before.

"They don't hibernate?" she asked, watching the two small creatures in the distance.

"Not fully. There's a stage in between they go into at night in the winter, to lower their metabolism."

"Torpor," she said. And then laughed as the animals called out to each other. "They really do bark!"

"Hence the name," he said.

"What else have you seen out here?" she asked as they walked on.

"Year-round? The usual. Lots of squirrels, gophers and rabbits. Raccoons, we've got a ton of those. Foxes, as you saw. Badgers. Coyotes occasionally. And last summer I swear I saw those last two working together."

"Working together?"

He jerked a thumb back toward the prairie dogs. "Hunting those guys." She winced, just slightly. "Don't like the laws of nature?" he asked.

"I try not to dwell on things I can't change and focus on things that I can," she said, "and I understand the food chain and its necessity in the natural world."

"Harder when the prey is little and cute, though." Her gaze sharpened. "At least, it is for me," he added.

And again, quickly, she went from the edge of offense to laughter. "I thought you were jabbing at me again."

He shook his head. "Hey, I'm as big a sucker for a cute, furry face as anyone."

She looked back toward the prairie dogs, or rather where they had been. They'd vanished now—maybe those barks had been a warning. He made a mental note of that. There was nothing here that would be truly dangerous to humans, but a hungry coyote was always something to be aware of.

"How did they work together, the coyote and the badger?"

He kept it as bloodless as he could. "The prairie dog's instinct is to burrow away from the fast coyote, who can't really dig deep, and run from the slower badger, who can. The badger scared one into running, then the coyote pounced."

She looked thoughtful. "That makes sense. Each using their particular skills." Her brow furrowed. "But did the coyote share? That seems unlikely."

"No. But I assume it works in reverse, that the coyote scares the prey into the burrow for the badger to dig out, often enough to make the partnership worthwhile for both."

"So even though they're competitors…"

"Yep. We could learn from them, I think."

"I wish we would," she said with a sigh. Maybe she wasn't quite as innocently optimistic as her parents feared, because that hadn't sounded at all confident.

They were some distance farther on when she stopped again. He turned back and saw her tilt her head as if listening intently. He smiled. "Meadowlark. Our state bird."

"It's a beautiful call. Your favorite bird?"

"Well, as a born and bred Kansan, I should say yes, but I'm more of a raptor guy."

She smiled. He was really getting to like that smile. "Why am I not surprised?"

"Of course, I do have a soft spot for roadrunners, ever since I saw one once, down near Coffeyville."

"Too many cartoons as a child, perhaps?" she asked innocently. Too innocently.

"Don't tell me you watched cartoons?" He said it with as much feigned shock as he could manage. "A woman with your upbringing?"

He got the laugh again. "We're just shattering assumptions all over the place, aren't we?"

"Well, there's the little fact they feed on spiders, too. Oh," he added, giving her a raised brow, "and snakes."

"My new favorite bird." She was still laughing, and as they started to walk again, he had the craziest wish that she wasn't a client, that they just…were. Together. Under other circumstances.

But they weren't. She was a client. A job.

And even if she weren't, she was way, way beyond his reach.

Chapter Nineteen

This was not fair.

This was so not fair.

She'd spent her entire life from the time she was old enough to understand assumptions and clichés, fighting against becoming either. Besides teaching her to beware of those who would pursue her for her name, wealth and of late fame, her parents had taught her early on that people would assume things about her because of that wealth. That many would have a picture in their mind, a clichéd perception of who she must be without having ever met her.

That was why she had built some very sturdy walls around her heart and emotions, why she didn't trust easily. Why she had worked so hard, studying, learning, so she could never be written off as one of those famous sorts who mouthed off and revealed a lack of knowledge about most things. The biggest cliché of the social media age, she often thought.

And now she was turning into a living, breathing cliché herself. The woman in danger who fell for her bodyguard.

She'd met a lot of people in her travels. Many kinds of people. A lot of them had been men.

But she'd never ever met a man like Ty Colton. And she wasn't sure if that spoke more to the circles she'd been running in or the man himself. She had a feeling it was some of both. Simon, for instance, had always looked upon men who focused on fitness of body with a certain disdain. It did not matter, he'd often said, usually with a sniff through his elevated nose, if the body was fit when the brain was not. Because she'd been flattered by the brilliant man's attentions, she had stopped herself from asking if that meant the reverse was also true. Funny, she'd never quite thought about Simon this way before. Never realized that in his own way, he had quite limited his own life.

She tried to picture the professor out here, striding so confidently yet carefully through thick underbrush and sometimes muddy terrain. The image that formed was laughable. She had never done that, laughed at Simon, even though his lack of stature and solidity had earned that from many of his students—behind his back, of course, which had only made her rise to his defense.

Ty didn't need any defense. He had muscles her ex could only dream of, shoulders broad enough to be a cliché in themselves. And the sight of his butt in those jeans explained completely why Simon had never worn them.

Ty was so hyper-alert and aware. He seemed utterly focused on their surroundings yet at the same time he was aware every time she stopped to look at something, or slipped slightly, or even turned her head. Simon would be oblivious, except perhaps to complain about the lack of a paved trail, which was about where his adventures into anything outside city skyscrapers ended.

To be fair, because she always endeavored to be, she tried to picture Ty among those city skyscrapers. She had the feeling he would be just as confident there, although perhaps not quite as comfortable in a stylish suit. For some reason, the image of him in formal wear, a tux even, formed in her mind, and for a moment it was so vivid she forgot how to breathe.

His head snapped around, and she realized she'd gasped aloud. "You okay?"

He stopped, and she nearly ran into him. Spent a moment wishing she had kept going. Wondered how it would feel to go into his arms willingly.

"Fine," she said, embarrassed now.

"Need to rest?"

"No, I'm good. Really. I was just…thinking."

His mouth—speaking of things that made her forget how to breathe—quirked upward at one corner. "Are you ever not?"

"Rarely," she admitted.

He gave her that look that told her she wasn't the only one thinking. But she doubted very much he was wrestling with the same kinds of thoughts she was. The same kind of revelations. How had just being with him, pried by force from her phone and other connections, so rattled her mindset? She had the oddest feeling, something almost bedrock—or that she'd thought was bedrock—was shifting, changing. And it was because of him.

Which made her edgy, because to him she was just a client, and likely one he found problematic, given his reaction to a simple social media post. Although in retrospect, if she worked off the assumption the threat was real, she could see his point.

And she hadn't liked how twitchy she'd gotten since access had been removed. Hadn't liked the thought that perhaps she really was addicted. She vowed then and there to cut back. To enforce personal restrictions, to have times when she put the phone away.

He was indulging her with this hike, however. Although he didn't seem to be minding it much. Even though he'd made the same trek once already today. *To make sure I'd be safe. The man is a professional. And part of that job is probably making clients feel comfortable, at ease. Remember that.*

He led her up a mild but rather rocky slope, and they came out on an outcropping of the orangish rock that she'd seen in the area. And below them was the spread of the area where the river met the lake, water running to the lake here, marshy flats there. An ideal place for the plant growth so crucial to migrating wildlife.

They sat on that outcropping, and she had to admit she was ready for the break. He seemed unaffected, and she wondered if he did this regularly, or if his fitness came from gym workouts.

They'd been sitting quietly, looking out over the view for a few minutes when he spoke again. "Do you ever change your mind about something?"

Her brow furrowed. "Of course. If the circumstances or the information I have changes, or is proved wrong."

"What if it's something you've…taken a stand on? Publicly."

"Then I have to admit I was wrong, or misinformed, as publicly as I took that stand, and explain why I changed my mind."

"You *have* to?"

"Well, yes. To be fair."

"And that's important to you. Being fair."

She almost snapped out a rather peevish "Of course," but something about the way he was looking at her made her pause. The answer she finally gave him was much more than she usually said.

"Life itself is so often unfair—especially to the smaller among us, like those prairie dogs—so I feel it's up to us humans to at least try to even it out."

He nodded back the way they had come. "Those prairie dogs build entire cities underground, a network of burrows with rooms at different depths for different purposes. They've got fine-tuned hearing so they can hear a predator's approach even while underground. They've got those warning barks. Nature equipped them pretty well for survival."

She knew she was staring at him. She hadn't expected him to reel off all that…knowledge. "If you care enough to learn all that, how can you think it's wrong to protect their habitat?"

"I don't. But I also think that while we humans may be at the top of the food chain—unless we do something stupid—we're just as much a part of the system as any other animal. And I don't appreciate those who believe we should be completely removed from it, as if we have less right to be here than those below us on that chain."

"I've never believed that. But I do believe that with that status at the top comes responsibility."

"I wouldn't disagree with that." He shrugged again, that very male gesture she was coming to envy. "I guess I'm just more of a conservationist. For all of the planet's inhabitants."

"And I wouldn't disagree with that," she said quietly. That got a smile that did crazy things to her insides.

After a moment, he pointed across the river to a clear area on the other side. "If this was spring, you'd be looking at a field of sunflowers."

"So they really do grow wild here?"

"And cultivated."

"Before I started researching," she said, as she took out her water bottle for a sip, "I would have been among those who assumed Kansas was completely flat."

He gave her that sideways look. "Sure you want to admit that to a native Kansas boy?"

"I'm not embarrassed to admit my ignorance, as long as I'm working to alleviate it."

"Why does that sound like something you'd say in one of your speeches?"

She couldn't stop her laugh. "Because it is?" It got her another smile. And she wished she could stop feeling like she'd won some kind of prize every time that happened.

"We're used to it, even though we're only the twenty-third flattest state. But most people's idea of Kansas comes from *The Wizard of Oz*, or *Little House on the Prairie.* Personally, I prefer being Superman's home state."

She found herself laughing yet again. "I don't blame you."

They sat quietly for a while, just looking. Which he seemed content to do. She was vaguely aware that the warmth built by the hike was seeping away and the ground was cold beneath her, but it wasn't yet uncomfortable.

"Well, well," Ty murmured, "hello there."

He was looking upriver, and she shifted her gaze that direction. She didn't say anything, but once more he was obviously aware of her movement, because without looking at her, he added, "Find the tallest tree on the left bank, then look straight right to the one jutting out over the river."

It took her a moment, but then she spotted the large bird perched on a branch. Had it not been barren of leaves she never would have seen the distinctive white head and tail.

"A bald eagle?"

He nodded. "We have a nesting pair in the area. They're usually at the seep stream about now. They figured out trout season long ago."

She laughed. He smiled. And for a split second, she wondered if he felt the same way when she laughed as she did when he did. *That sounded silly even unspoken.* Searching for something to say that wouldn't betray that silliness, she asked, "Do you usually go fishing when you're here?"

He kept his gaze on the regal bird. "Not my first thought this time of year. But I keep the license updated. And I heard a rumor there are a lot of white bass right out in front of the point just now."

"Do you want to go?"

He looked at her then. "This isn't a vacation trip."

She sighed. "I know that. But I like fishing."

He blinked. "You do?"

"Must you always sound so surprised?"

"That was nothing personal. Well, except that you're female. I don't know that many who like fishing."

"Maybe you need to meet more females," she said

rather sourly as she lifted her bottle for another drink of water.

"Now you sound like my mother."

That caught her off guard, and the laugh that burst from her, then caused a spew of water. He gave her a look she could only describe as that of a rather mischievous little boy.

And another of her inner walls melted away.

Chapter Twenty

"Do I need a fishing license?" Ashley asked. She shifted the pole she was carrying as they walked toward the lake, a much shorter distance than yesterday's trek.

Ty raised a brow at her. She still wasn't taking this threat seriously enough for his taste. And he was a little edgy—again—after a second restless night. Not because of her being restless, because this time she'd gone to bed and stayed there, but because… Hell, he didn't know why he hadn't been able to settle. He'd learned to gauge his limits, and figured he had another night like that in him. But after that he was going to need some serious sleep or he was going to be tired enough to possibly miss something.

Unless something happened, of course. Then adrenaline would kick in and carry the day. At least, it always had.

But she was looking at him in honest inquiry, as if she'd never thought of the ramifications. Which was another surprise. He would have thought, her parents being who they were, she would have had security precautions hammered into her practically from birth.

"And how long do you suppose it would take for

word to get out that Ashley Hart of the Westport Harts bought a fishing license in tiny Yankee Run? You might as well post our coordinates to the world."

She grimaced. "Just trying to obey the law, Mr. Colton."

"I told you, I've got one," he said. "And this is a unique situation." *Not to mention I can't see even the state government seriously going after the sole Hart offspring.* "But we'll take the heat and pay the fine if you get caught. Or catch anything," he added, in an exaggeratedly teasing tone.

"If? Humph," she retorted, her nose so far in the air he knew it had to be intentional. She had a sense of humor, did Ms. Ashley Hart of the Westport Harts. And wasn't afraid to poke at her own image. He liked that.

He liked a lot about her.

And he hoped he didn't regret this. But while going out on the water in the small runabout in the boathouse would have been akin to stepping out onto a sunlit stage with a target on them, they were fairly sheltered here on the point. Visible from certain angles on the lake but masked to a great extent from others, and almost completely hidden from anyone who might be trespassing on Colton land. They'd have to get really close before they could see them, and if they managed that without Ty hearing them coming, he deserved what he got.

But she didn't.

He'd never failed on a protection job, even in a couple of near-miss circumstances, once when he'd spotted the threat in time and gotten the protectee to safety, and once when he'd taken out the armed suspect. He'd earned Eric's pleased approval, something he treasured because of his respect for the man. But somehow this time was different.

The thought of failing to protect Ashley made him feel crazy tense. If he did fail, and if because of that she was hurt or worse, he somehow knew that would be a shift of the ground under his feet so large he wasn't sure he could withstand it. He'd never felt this before, and it made him nervous, edgy, and complicated things even further.

And he'd known her exactly twenty-four hours. How the hell had this happened in twenty-four hours?

How the hell had it happened at all?

He tried to focus on what they were here for. "We're lucky it hasn't gotten too cold yet, or they'd be really sluggish, and clustered in deep water."

"So they're prepping for winter?"

"Feeding up," he said with a nod. "Just in different places. Springtime, you can catch them as fast as you can reel in and recast just about anywhere. It's like a frenzy." As they reached the lake's edge, he scanned the water. There were several boats off the point, so the fish must still be striking.

"Is that a problem?" Ashley asked, looking at the other anglers.

At least she'd thought about it. That was progress, he supposed. "No. I know who they are."

She blinked and turned to look at him. "All of them?"

He nodded. "They're all locals or regulars I've seen before. Typical, this time of year." At her expression, he couldn't help chuckling. "You hang out in big cities too much," he teased.

"There are advantages," she said, "but disadvantages, too. I like the idea of knowing all the people around you."

Yet again, she surprised him. But he kept it to himself as he pointed at a spot a few yards out in the water. "There's some brush right around here that ends up underwater when the lake's full, like now."

"Good hiding place," she said.

"It's a little tough to cast out that far from here onshore, but it can be done."

"Shall I take that as a challenge?"

He gave her a sideways look. "Not from me. I don't generally fish from here. I'm too lazy when there's a perfectly good boat around."

Something shifted in her expression, and he couldn't read it at all. "Sorry to disrupt your routine."

His words could have been taken as a complaint, although he couldn't see why she'd think something like that would be important to him now, on the job. But something in the dark depths of those chocolate-brown eyes had him grabbing for a response. And the moment it came out, he regretted both the words and the rough note that had come into his voice.

"There's nothing about you that's routine."

To his relief, she didn't reply to his ill-advised admission. She just gave him a curious look, as if she weren't quite sure how to interpret what he'd said. He couldn't believe that. Hell, she was probably more than used to guys hitting on her. She probably—

Damn.

Hitting on her?

Client. Protocol. Rules of conduct.

The warnings pealed out in his mind. And once he'd led her to the spot where she could cast out a lure and still be mostly hidden, he backed away from her. Again, she gave him that curious but unrevealing look.

He scanned the area behind them, listening carefully. There was a slight breeze today, but nothing that would have masked the approach of anything the size of a human being.

He turned back in time to see her finish rigging the pole and the bright spinner lure he'd suggested she try first. She'd done it competently. More than competently.

"Who taught you to fish?"

"My father, first. He likes sport fishing, although he's more of a salt water guy."

Of course he was. Probably prize marlin fishing or something.

But she'd said first. "And second?"

"A tribal member in Alaska was generous enough to share some of their knowledge with me. Once I proved I was up to it, of course."

She flicked a glance at him with those last words, and he suspected she thought she was having to prove herself again. And he supposed, in a way, she was. She was certainly shattering most of those assumptions of his.

"Why were you in Alaska?"

"I spent a couple of months visiting an isolated area that needed a medical clinic built, so the one doctor they had would have a central location and facilities." She smiled then, as if that memory were a special one. And that made him want to know more. As if what was special to this woman was important to him.

"You spent two months there?"

"I hadn't planned to, but Dr. Kallik changed that.

She's brilliant. In those two months, she taught me a lot about rough-and-ready medicine." She gave him another sideways glance. "I even assisted her on a couple of operations, when she needed more hands."

He nearly gaped at her. Yet he could see it—she was cool, calm and brilliant herself. What other unexpected skills did she have?

His mind immediately careened into the gutter and he clamped his jaw tightly to keep from letting something beyond foolish tumble out of his mouth. He watched her silently. She was obviously familiar with the equipment, and while her first cast was off a bit, the next was better. But she still wasn't happy with the location. He saw her studying the top of the brush that stuck up out of the water, and the next thing he knew she startled him completely by wading hip deep out into the water.

"If I'd known you were going to do that, I would have brought waders."

"I'll dry," she said briefly, clearly unconcerned.

Chalk another one up in the surprise category. Ashley Hart was just full of them. She didn't look at him but was completely intent on her next cast. This one she apparently put where she wanted for she let it drop. He would have, too, if he'd hit that spot.

There was something about her intensity, her focus, that had him thinking odd things. Like about the amount of research she must do to be as knowledgeable as she appeared. About her apparent ability to see both sides of an issue, even one where she had strong feelings or convictions. About the love in her voice when she spoke of her parents, as if they were an ordinary, loving mother and father instead of one of the richest couples in the world. Although that, he supposed, said as much about them as her.

He nearly laughed at himself when he felt a jab of envy. His own father had been far too busy and involved with the business to take his son, or any of his kids, fishing. His mother told him he'd always had plans to teach him, but after the triplets had been born his dad had, understandably Ty supposed, focused utterly and entirely on making enough money to support a family that had suddenly numbered seven.

Then he slid into simply watching her. He didn't know how much time had passed when a faint rustle behind them snapped him out of his fascinated scrutiny, of her focus, her concentration, the grace of her movements, the curves of her slender body. His head snapped around toward the sound, and a moment later, he saw a pair of gray squirrels busily foraging for the nearing winter. He scanned farther, saw nothing, went back to the squirrels. He heard the same sound again, as one of the animals dug through some downed leaves.

Breathing easily again, he turned back. He glanced at his watch as he did so, startled to see well over an hour had gone by. He looked up as Ashley let out a whoop of triumph. In short order, she reeled in a respectably sized white bass. His instinct was to help her unhook it, but he quashed it. He had the feeling she wouldn't appreciate help she didn't need. He did dig a stringer out of the fishing gear bag he'd brought along.

"Move fast," he suggested. "If they're striking, they're hungry."

"So am I." She was grinning so widely he couldn't help but grin back at her.

She did as he'd suggested while he put the fish on the

string and dropped it back into the water. She caught three more in short order, while Ty stood there marveling at the pleasure she took in the simple act. And she never even blinked at handling the fish. Clearly, she wasn't afraid to get her hands dirty. Or her feet wet.

"Nice work," he said as they packed up the gear. "We'll eat well tonight."

Her brow furrowed. "I don't know much about bass, but I've heard…"

"People who don't like the taste don't know how to fix it. More exactly, they don't know how to trim it." She arched those delicate brows at him. He grinned at her. "You caught 'em, I'll cook 'em."

"You cook?"

"Only things I've hunted down myself, like any good caveman," he said, deadpan.

She burst out laughing. Yeah, he liked that. Too damned much.

"Then the real question is, who gets to clean them?" she asked.

"We'll split them up."

"Before we split them up?"

It was his turn to laugh, and she looked just as pleased as he'd felt when she had. With the feeling that he was wading into water much deeper than the thirty-five feet of the lake, he turned and led the way back to the cabin.

Chapter Twenty-One

"Any reason not to use this?"

Ashley blinked. She'd been watching with fascination as Ty worked. He seemed at home in the kitchen—this one, at least—and it was a pleasure to watch. Of course, he was a pleasure to watch anyway, doing anything.

Except ordering you around, she reminded herself sternly. And, if she were honest, it also bothered her when he left the cabin periodically, with his usual cautions and reminders about how to contact Elite in case of emergency. He was doing regular reconnaissance, which reminded her of why she was here. Why that was upsetting, beyond the obvious, she didn't want to think about.

What, you want to pretend you're just off on a vacation with him?

But now he'd stopped in the middle of prepping what would apparently be a sauce for the fish, holding up a bottle of white wine. It took her a moment to realize he was asking if she had any problem with alcohol.

"Oh. No." She wondered why he'd asked, if it was routine or if he suspected she had a problem. She did not. She almost had, when she'd been at college and it had been rampant, but she hated the aftermath so much she rarely drank more than a couple of drinks in an occasional evening.

She'd watched with interest as, after they'd cleaned, scaled and filleted the fish, he'd shown her the reddish flesh along one edge. "That's what gives it the taste some people don't like," he'd explained, and trimmed it away.

Now he poured about a cup of the wine into the pan and raised the heat. He'd sautéed the salted and floured fish in the skillet and then covered it while he peeled and cut up garlic and a lemon, half of which he squeezed for juice, the other half he cut into thin slices. He didn't consult a recipe, so he'd clearly done this before.

"Have to settle for dry oregano, since it wasn't on the stocking list," he said, as he added butter to the pan, then the seasonings.

"It already smells wonderful," she said.

And when she took her first bite, her eyes widened. "Oh. My, that's good."

"Must you sound so surprised?"

It was such a perfect imitation of her own intonation earlier that she nearly burst out laughing. "Touché," she said, and took another bite. The flavors were an amazing blend, and the fish light and flaky. "Except for my mom's swordfish, this may be the best fish dinner I've ever eaten."

"Considering where you've likely eaten, I'll take that as a great compliment." Then, with a warm smile, as if he'd liked that she'd given her mother the exception, he added, "And I'm sure your mother's swordfish is amazing."

"You—" She cut herself off in more than a little shock when she'd been about to say, *You'll have to try it sometime.* She never ever broached that subject with a man. Never brought up the possibility of taking him home to meet them. It was part of her vetting process. If a guy asked to meet her parents within the first three months, she knew he was after something.

But that was a guy she was dating. Not a guy her parents had hired to protect her.

"She loves to cook," she said instead, rather inanely. "I think she looks forward to their cook's vacation more than he does."

She was watching his face to see if he reacted to the fact that her parents had a full-time chef. He didn't. Normally she would have thought he'd developed an excellent poker face for his work, but she'd seen him surprised—and annoyed.

The real question was, if he did have that poker face, why was he letting her see that surprise, that annoyance…that humor? He wasn't at all the stiff-lipped sort she was used to on her parents' security staff. Yet he seemed no less trained, and certainly no less capable. Perhaps the more personable, more human approach was part of his style, to put clients at ease.

That he was always on the job was pounded home when, after the kitchen was cleaned up in a quick joint effort and he'd started a fire in the fireplace, he left again, this time stepping out into the fading light of dusk. She wondered if he really expected to find something—or someone—or if it was just part of the routine. Part of being thorough.

When she heard him coming back, she quickly sat down near the crackling fire, so he wouldn't come in and notice she'd been pacing the floor the entire time he'd been gone.

"Ever thought about a guard dog?" she asked when he came in.

"Often," he said as he shed his jacket. She looked away from the weapon on his belt. She wasn't repelled, it was a tool of his trade, nothing more, but once again it reminded her of why they were here. Why they were together at all. "My boss is thinking of adding one or two to the staff."

"My parents have a pair at home. They're wonderful."

He walked over and laid another log on the fire, then sat in the chair opposite her nearest the hearth, probably for the warmth after his trek outside. "What are they?"

She quashed the silly wish that he would have sat next to her on the couch and answered evenly, "Malinois."

He nodded. "Good dogs. Smart, strong, quick and if need be, lethal."

"You forgot beautiful and intense."

He smiled. "That, too."

"It always amazes me how they can go from playing to on duty in a split second." *Kind of like you.*

She inwardly rolled her eyes at herself as she compared him to a dog. Then again, every adjective they'd applied to the animals applied to him, too. And she didn't know which unsettled her more, the lethal if need be part or the beautiful part.

Of course, what unsettled her most was the thought that the lethality might be necessary. She wasn't used to walking around worrying about everything around her, watching constantly for anything out of the ordinary, looking for threats. And she didn't like it. But she also knew the fact that nothing had happened was no guarantee nothing would. There were times when, as much as she had come to like this place, she understood that isolation wasn't always a good thing. Because the only targets out walking around were her, and Ty.

"What's Wichita like?" she asked abruptly, before she said something seriously stupid.

"Biggest city in the state. Started as a trading post on the Chisolm Trail. Incorporated in 1870. Nicknamed Cowtown, and Wyatt Earp was the law there for a while."

She blinked at the four-sentence history lesson. "Wow."

"But now," he went on, stretching out those long strong legs, "it's the Air Capital of the World."

"Air capital?"

"Beechcraft, Cessna, Stearman all started production there in the early days. Learjet, Airbus and a few others followed."

"I had no idea." She studied him for a moment. "I suppose that doesn't surprise you."

He shrugged. "I only know it because I live there, and was born in Kansas. Ask me about, say, Cleveland, which is about the same size, and all I'd know is it's on Lake Erie and home of the Rock & Roll Hall of Fame."

"More than some would," she said with a smile.

For a brief moment, he stared at her, and she wondered why. Then she saw a muscle in his jaw jump and he looked away, into the fire.

Into the fire.

She'd heard the phrase countless times, in various

contexts. But at this moment, sitting here with him, so close and yet so distant, she could only think of one. She'd been raised to have the courage of her convictions, but also to be beyond cautious about people who would mask their true goals behind a facade of friendship or caring. She'd been burned more than once, but she'd learned. Every time she'd learned, become even more cautious, until her walls were high and solid.

Yet here she was now, part of her wanting to leap right into the fire she sensed between them, the fire hotter even than the one he was staring into. She'd been attracted to men before, but she rarely allowed it to take root because so many times it went sour, or she found out they'd had a plan all along, that usually involved access to Hart money.

It had never been as powerful as this. So powerful all her usual walls and defenses seemed useless. All her self-lecturing, all her telling herself it was the circumstances, the imposed isolation that was causing these feelings were failing miserably.

"What was it like, growing up an only child?"

She gave a start, both because of the abrupt and unexpected question and because his voice had sounded just like hers had when she'd asked about Wichita to keep herself from saying something she'd regret. It took her a moment to formulate a reply, which in itself felt odd. She usually had quick answers to almost everything. This man truly did discombobulate her.

"Good and bad," she finally said. "Good because you got all the attention, bad because you got all the attention."

He smiled at that, and the odd tension eased a little. "I get that. Being one of six gave me a lot of cover."

"It was hard," she confessed, "being the sole focus of all their hopes and expectations. At least, until I realized that their biggest hope trumped all the rest."

"Which was?"

"For me to be happy." She was a little stunned. She almost never talked about that with anyone.

He looked at her steadily then, one corner of his mouth curving upward. "Consider another assumption blasted. Your parents sound great."

"They are." That, at least, she could say with full faith and force.

"And they must be incredibly proud of you."

"They are," she repeated. "Even if this isn't the path they would have chosen."

His mouth quirked higher. "I know that feeling. But my old man wasn't as understanding. Which may be why none of us went into the family business."

Her mouth quirked in turn. "Our family business seems to be being the Harts of Westport."

He laughed, and Ashley felt that quick jolt of pleasure yet again.

If this kept up, she wasn't going to have any guardrails left.

TY WASN'T SURE what he'd expected. He didn't really think she had exaggerated her skill, but he was having trouble reconciling his image of Ashley Hart, heiress, with the woman he was watching now. The woman who was consistently hitting the blocks of wood he was tossing, no matter what direction or height he threw them.

The sound of the shotgun echoed through the bare trees, and he could only imagine every living creature within a mile taking cover. They didn't hunt much out here, but the sheer volume alone would send him running to hide if he were, say, one of those little prairie dogs.

He waited while she reloaded. Then she nodded, and he started tossing again. And as before, she didn't miss. In fact, the only time she'd missed at all was in the beginning, when a bird had broken for cover just as he tossed the second block. She'd yanked the shotgun off target, he guessed, to be sure she didn't hit the bird by accident.

He had a sudden vision of an eight-year-old Ashley fearlessly confronting her father, demanding he stop hunting living birds. He could just see her looking at him, the pain of what he was doing reflected in those deep brown eyes. And he wondered how many people around the world would never believe that Andrew Hart, head of the global Hart empire, would give in. To a little girl, even if she was his daughter and his only child.

He believed it. Because he already knew that when determined, Ashley Hart could be a nearly unstoppable force.

He also knew, with wry acceptance, that his own father would never give in like that, unless it was something he wanted to do anyway.

This time when she had emptied the weapon, she stopped, took out the ear protection he'd retrieved from the locker in the SUV and turned to look at him.

"You're as good as you said you were," he said, figuring she'd earned it.

She smiled so widely it made his chest tighten a little. "Your turn," she said.

He laughed. "Not my thing."

"Do you hunt?"

"Not much anymore, unless there's another reason."

Her brow furrowed. "Like what?"

"Renegade coyote. Rabid skunk. That kind of thing."

"Oh." She looked down at the Mossberg, then back at him. "Not birds?"

He gave her a rather sheepish look. "Nah. I like them too much. So I'm a hypocrite who eats them, but I don't want to be part of the process."

To his surprise, she smiled. "I'm afraid I'm with you on that. You sure you don't want to try?"

"I'd embarrass myself."

"I could teach you."

His entire perception shifted in that moment. An image formed in his mind of Ashley standing close behind him as she showed him how to aim, to fire… things he already knew but had never done in this particular exercise.

And he knew from his own instant, fierce response to just that imaginary vision that the answer had to be no.

And he spent a good portion of the hours of darkness regretting that.

"WHY DO I get the feeling you didn't call just to say hello?"

Ty grinned despite the fact that his brother Neil couldn't see him over the old landline. "Come on, what's the good of having a high-power attorney for a brother if he can't give you a little helpful advice now and then?"

"You know what I make per hour to dispense helpful advice?"

"You want to charge the brother who saved you from drowning when you were five?"

"Yeah, yeah. One of these days I'm going to call that paid back."

"I'll consider it a big installment if you can tell me how we can put this jerk who's after Ashley away for a long time."

There was a split-second pause before Neil said, "Ashley?"

Uh-oh. He knew instantly that he should have kept it professional, referred to her simply as a client or protectee. Neil was just too damned good at reading people, even if he only had a voice to work with. He scrambled to cover.

"We decided it would be wiser not to throw around that particular last name," he said.

"Hmm." The non-word fairly echoed with his brother's lack of acceptance of the excuse. But to Ty's relief, he let it go. "You do realize I'm not a prosecutor?"

"Please. Who would know better how to destroy the perfect defense than the guy who builds them?"

That got him a laugh. "Are you sure it's who you thought it was?"

"It's not confirmed," Ty had to admit. "He's been lying low since we pulled her off stage." He'd talked to Mitch early this morning, before Ashley had come downstairs. Wearing that damned silky-looking robe thing that made her look like some forties movie star or something. And he'd waited until she'd gone back upstairs to dress to call Neil, denying even to himself it was so he wouldn't think about that sleek fabric sliding off her sleek body.

"Maybe he thinks he won when she went quiet."

"Maybe. But she won't stay quiet, so we need to be ready."

"Stubborn, huh?"

"Determined. And dedicated."

"Was that actual admiration I heard in my hard-to-impress big brother's voice?"

He opened his mouth to refute it, but the words wouldn't come. "She's…not what I expected."

"And I gather in a good way? Sounds like it's getting personal, bro."

No. It can't. I'm not that stupid. Am I?

"Can we dispense with the analysis and get to an answer?"

"All I can say is that where it stands right now, if it is him, at most he'd likely get off with a fine and probation. He's done nothing but mouth off, so far."

"So far," Ty said grimly. "If he gets angry enough, he could follow through and come after her physically."

"If he does, you'll keep her safe," Neil said, with such certainty that Ty couldn't help but feel warmed by his brother's faith.

"Yeah," he said. "I will."

And it was a vow to her as much as to himself. He would keep her safe. The world needed more Ashley Harts, not less.

Chapter Twenty-Two

"You have to do it anyway, right?" Ashley asked as she stood looking at the downed tree he'd made note of when they'd first arrived.

Ty sat on the thick trunk and grinned at her. "I was thinking I'd leave it for my little brother Neil," he drawled lazily. "So he doesn't get soft sitting in that office all day, wearing those expensive suits."

She laughed, because she knew he was anything but lazy. And when looked at in the larger scheme of things, he was working very hard at making this as easy as possible on her. Including trekking out every day because she wanted to learn about this place she'd never been, when it would obviously be easier to do his job if she stayed safely inside the cabin. She studied him for a moment, trying to picture him here as a kid. She wondered if he'd ever had an awkward stage, or if he'd always been…

"What?" he asked at her look.

"Just pondering the sibling thing again," she said hastily, trying not to betray that she'd been mentally drooling over him. Again. "And what I missed, being an only."

"Maybe you gained just as much," he pointed out.

"Did you all compete?"

"Sometimes. Unless someone outside came at one of us."

"Came at?"

"You know what I mean, when—" He stopped, and his mouth twisted wryly. "No, I guess you don't." He looked thoughtful for a moment. "When she was thirteen, some older kid started harassing my little sister Bridgette. She's the girl of the triplets."

"Older kid?" Possibilities tumbled through her mind, none of them pleasant.

"Yeah." His lips quirked in that way she was coming to quite like. "He was thirteen and a half."

She smiled. "What happened?"

"I found her hiding and crying one day, and it seriously pissed me off. So I went after him."

"How old were you?"

"Sixteen." He gave her a sideways look. "And I'd already hit six feet tall. He wasn't much over five. I picked him up and took him behind a dumpster for a chat."

Her eyes widened at the image that made. "You must have scared him to death!"

"That was the intention. He made Bridgette cry."

Ashley felt a wave of something warm and almost wistful. "I… That's wonderful. You must have been a great big brother."

He shrugged. It seemed to be his reaction to compliments. "Anyway, that's what I meant. We might be at odds with each other, but to the outside, it was all for one and all that."

"Sometimes I do truly wish I hadn't missed out on that dynamic."

"It had its moments." His mouth quirked again. "Looking back, I think he probably had a crush on her, but I didn't recognize that then."

Do you now? Recognize crushes?

Her breath jammed up in her throat, and she quickly turned away, masking it as looking toward the sky, which was rather gray today, as if rain were on the way. She was not used to this, not at all, and it was very unsettling. She heard him move, looked back just in time to see him stand, that tall powerful body moving with a grace and ease that made her pulse kick up all over again.

"Are you sure you don't want to cut this up?" she said quickly.

"Not my job right now."

No, she was his job right now. Job, not…crush. "What if I stay here with you?" *Oh, now that sounded disinterested.*

"You'd end up being put to work."

She was startled at how much that idea appealed. "I'd like that. A lot. I need something physical to do." She nearly groaned aloud at that. But he didn't make any suggestive comment. Because it never occurred to him that *something physical* could mean…something else?

And so an hour later—after he made yet another check of the property—he was armed with a chain saw and an ax and, wearing a pair of goggles, attacking the dead tree. The moment he started trimming the smaller branches, she started gathering them up and piling them a few feet away. He looked over at her, then nodded. And before he went back to work, she thought she saw a trace of a smile.

They continued the process, and she had the silly thought that they worked well together. She guessed she was trying to focus on that rather than notice he'd pulled off his jacket as he worked. He was into the bigger limbs now and cutting them into smaller—fireplace-sized, she realized—lengths. She started stacking those, trying to keep it neat until he shut the chain saw off and spoke.

"They'll need to be split anyway, so don't worry about neatness yet."

She turned around to look at him. And nearly choked as he raised an arm to shove the goggles up to his forehead so he could wipe his face. In the process, his shirt lifted and gave her a full view of what she'd only suspected all along: a perfect set of abs.

She looked away quickly before he lowered his arm and caught her gaping at him. Went back to her stacking before her rattled mind recalled what he'd said to her. She tossed down the logs she'd been about to place neatly on top and turned to go get more. And ran smack into those abs as he brought over more wood.

"Whoa," he said, twisting to drop the logs to one side rather than have them hit her, then grabbing her as she wobbled forward. The motion pressed her harder against him, and suddenly she couldn't seem to remember how to move. Nor could she look away. She just stood there, looking up at him, barely capable of breathing, let alone moving.

The only saving grace was that he didn't move either, for a long silent moment. And when he did, it was to slowly, as if against his will, lower his head. Then his gaze shifted from her eyes to her mouth, and her pulse began to race and her lips parted and he was—

He jerked away. Took a swift step back. Started to speak but stopped, and she saw him swallow. Then, in a voice that had no intonation at all, he said, "Let's wrap this up. Rain coming in."

It took them another half hour to get everything he'd cut moved to the pile for splitting. And she spent every minute of it telling herself that he had *not* been about to kiss her.

ASHLEY TURNED A PAGE, listening to the rain that had started last night, just as he'd predicted as they left the half-finished tree yesterday. She was more than a little surprised at herself. And it wasn't just her unexpected reaction to Ty, although that was surprising enough. It was that she was actually enjoying this.

They'd been here five days now, isolated, in a place with no internet, no connection with the outside world except for seeing the occasional boat going by and that ancient landline phone. There were books to read and movies to watch—on DVDs—but no streaming, online research and no social media. And yet she wasn't climbing the walls. In fact, she was more relaxed than she could ever remember.

Well, except for the Ty-making-her-pulse-race thing. And that near kiss she kept telling herself hadn't been that at all.

She'd spent days quietly reading with Simon, but even that was different. Because he had seemed startled whenever he'd looked up and noticed she was there. With Ty, it seemed every time she looked up, he looked at her within seconds, as if he somehow knew when her attention had shifted. As if he was utterly, completely aware of her no matter what he was doing.

That's his job.

It had become a mantra, repeated to herself time after time as she tried to convince herself it was nothing more, that she was imagining that…something that seemed to flash in his gaze for an instant.

They'd spent the nicer days outside, and he'd seemed okay with letting her simply explore their property however she wanted, as long as he'd checked it first, either personally or with that little surveillance drone he handled with such skill. If she had questions about something she saw out there, be it wildlife or vegetation or terrain, he always had the answer.

She wondered if there was anything he wasn't good at.

And that gave rise to a flood of heated thoughts that made her consider walking out into that cold November rain just to cool off.

She stole a glance at him, certain she must have mistaken the times before just as she had mistaken what had happened out by the downed tree. He was once more in the chair opposite her favored place by the fire, reading a rather thick tome that he said belonged to his uncle—she presumed the uncle of the tree planting he'd told her about—on naval history. He seemed intent on it, and she was about to look away, convinced now her imagination had just been overactive, when he looked up at her.

"Sorry about the rain. Feeling antsy?" he asked.

Yes, but not because of the rain. "I'm fine."

"Sorry you can't talk to your folks."

He'd explained yesterday morning, with regret she didn't doubt was real, that while this line was secure, he couldn't guarantee the other end would be except for Elite, his police detective sister, Jordana, and his criminal attorney brother, Neil, who also had access to secure, monitored lines.

"They know you're okay," he had relayed from Mitch, who had spoken to her parents. Then, with a slightly puzzled look, he added, "And they said to tell you to remember Ashworth."

As it came back to her now, she sighed. She hadn't wanted to explain then, but it had been nagging at her ever since. She closed her book. "Ashworth," she said, "is the private school my parents sent me to when I was a kid."

He didn't even blink at the abruptness of it or the delay. "I know."

Of course he did.

He didn't push or pry, just waited silently, giving her the option to go on or end it. It occurred to her that he did that often, gave her the choice, whether it was where to explore outside, what movie to watch or this. Making up for the choices she didn't get to make? Interesting thought. But then she found many, many things about Ty Colton interesting.

"I didn't want to go. But it turned out to be the best thing in the end."

"Why didn't you want to go?"

Interesting, she thought, that that was his first question, not about the school or why it had turned out for the best. "I didn't want to be…different."

"You're Ashley Hart. You were always going to be different."

"I know that now. At aged ten, not so much." She gave him a curious look. "And you're a Colton. Everywhere there's a branch of your family, they're in the middle of things." Surely that meant he could understand what it was like? He was connected to the former president, even if it was distantly. "Didn't you find that difficult sometimes?"

"That's one thing about us heartland folks. We generally take people at their own worth—or lack of it—not their name."

She caught herself sighing again. "That sounds… wonderful. Hard to believe, but wonderful."

"Hard to believe in your world, maybe. That's one reason I stay right here. So I can just be myself."

"I envy you that," she said softly. The longing that filled her at that moment surprised her both by simply existing at all and by its power.

Then, with a rather crooked smile she found oddly endearing, he added, "I'm not saying the name isn't a factor, but I've always looked on it as something to overcome, not trade on."

And that, she thought, said a great deal about the kind of man he was. "Your parents must be very proud of you."

He looked a little startled, as if he weren't quite sure how to take that. "My mother is. My father…not so much."

She would have smiled at his echoing her own words if what he'd said hadn't been rather sad. She'd gathered his father irritated him, but how could any father not be proud to have a son like him?

"I'm sorry to hear that," she said, meaning it.

He shrugged. She wondered if it was because he didn't want to talk about it, or because it didn't really matter to him. She hoped it was the latter. And wondered if his father had any idea what he was missing.

Chapter Twenty-Three

Ty stood looking out the window, rubbing his unshaven jaw. The weather was still spotty, the weather-alert station was predicting it would get worse as a large front approached, and they were warily monitoring an unsettled jet stream. But he thought they could risk a walk outside, at least out to the point and back. She hadn't complained, but they hadn't been out in a couple of days, and to his surprise, he found he missed trekking around with her.

Of course, if she knew that what sleep he'd gotten last night had been decorated with dreams where he hadn't pulled back from her, where he'd gone ahead and kissed her and his world had gone up in flames, she likely wouldn't come anywhere near him.

"Cliché much?" he muttered under his breath.

"Problem?"

He nearly jumped as she spoke from right behind him. *Some bodyguard you are.* He didn't look at her. He didn't dare. Because he was afraid those dreams would somehow show in his eyes.

And when did you turn calf-eyed, Colton?

The self-lecturing wasn't working too well. He made himself answer casually. "Thinking about a walk out to the point, if you wanted to go. I think the rain will hold off for a while."

"I'd like that," she answered quickly.

"Gear up, then," he said. "I don't know how long it'll hold."

She was ready more quickly than he would have expected, but he'd already seen she wasn't one of those women who took hours to get ready to simply step out into the world.

As they walked, he updated her. "Elite has been watching Sanderson steadily. He's been relatively quiet. No more direct threats."

She seemed oddly troubled by what he'd thought would be good news for her. "Indirect ones, then?"

"Not really. He's changed tacks, it seems. Maybe he realized he went too far."

He half expected her to suggest that this was overkill then, that she didn't need to be tucked away here, didn't need to be protected. By him.

But she didn't. Instead, she merely asked, "What's he doing now?"

"Now he's touting the benefits of his development in the way of jobs, housing, bringing money into the economy."

He'd intentionally kept his tone neutral, but she reacted rather defensively. "And you agree with that?"

"I agree those are valid points and should be considered. Looking for a fight?"

To his surprise—again—she gave him an almost sheepish look. "I sounded that way, didn't I?"

"Pretty much."

"Sorry. I don't want to fight." She lowered her gaze to the narrow trail they were walking. "Not with you."

She said those last words so softly he wasn't sure he was supposed to hear them. But hear them he had, and it knotted him up inside. He didn't dare risk answering her. Because he was starting to realize just how much trouble he was in here.

Then they were at the point that jutted out into the lake north of the cabin. He showed her to his favorite spot, where the sandstone had been shaped by wind and water into a serviceable place to sit and look out over the lake.

"This is lovely," she said, as she sat on the stone, apparently not caring that it was wet in spots from the earlier rain.

"I did a lot of my teenage thinking here."

"I can see why." She gave him a sideways look and a smile. "Although some would say the terms *teenage* and *thinking* are mutually exclusive."

"Not me," he said, holding up his hands in mock defense. "I did a lot of thinking." He couldn't hold back a grin. "Of course, most of it was crazy wrong, but it was thinking."

She laughed, and he had the thought he'd rather hear that laugh than just about anything. And that had him remembering that moment again, when he'd nearly kissed her.

Talk about crazy wrong thinking...

"That's Kanopolis State Park over there," he said abruptly, pointing across the lake and not caring if he sounded like a tour guide. Not now, when he was trying not to look at her, at that luscious mouth that was too damned tempting. "It was the first state park in Kansas. They've got a full-on prairie dog town over there, makes ours look like an outpost." She smiled at that, and he went on. “And some serious hiking trails. About thirty miles' worth. Horsethief Canyon'll kill you on a hot day.”

“Sounds challenging.”

“The wildlife viewing area is a lot easier. And fun, really.”

“What kind of wildlife?”

“Anything from woodchucks to wild turkeys. Porcupines. Mule deer.”

She looked at him rather intently for a moment, he wasn't sure why. “What's your favorite?”

He had to think about that for a moment. “Bobcat, maybe. Or kestrels. I like the way they hover like oversized hummingbirds.”

She laughed at that. “So, the higher-ups on the food chain you were talking about, then?”

His brow furrowed. “I hadn't thought about it like that, but I guess so. I admire getting the job done.” He gave her a sideways look. “I suppose you're more for the prey than the hunters?”

“I think an eagle—or a bobcat—on the hunt is a beautiful thing. But I also think the mouse has his place.”

“Then we agree,” he said quietly.

She smiled at that. “I'd like to see this refuge sometime.”

And I'd like to take you there. He bit back the thought before it made it into words. “It's a great place. Two ponds, a marsh, a bunch of photo blinds and an observation deck.” He raised a brow at her. “But what I think you'd like best is what it used to be.”

“What did it used to be?”

“A motorcycle racetrack.”

She blinked. "What?"

He nodded. "It hadn't been in use in a while, so some area folks donated the money and it was converted to a natural sanctuary."

"That's wonderful!"

He'd known she'd like the idea, but he hadn't quite expected the delight that shone in her eyes.

And he couldn't quite stop the wish that he could put that look in her eyes in another, much more personal way.

USUALLY IN A place like this, Ashley would be more aware of her surroundings than anything else. She would be looking at everything, plants, animals, birds, smiling at the familiar while searching out those she didn't know, filing the image of them away in her brain to research later. Normally she would have pulled out her phone and done it right then, but to her surprise, she didn't miss it. She had belatedly realized that her prodigious brain gave her an advantage others might not have: the ability to remember exactly what she'd seen later and track it down.

Usually in a place like this, her focus would be on where she was, not who she was with.

But nothing with Ty Colton was usual. Not for her. And that was unsettling enough that it had her completely off balance. Which in turn was startling enough that she didn't quite know how to deal with it.

She tried to focus on other things. What he'd told her about the sanctuary they'd built over there in the state park. But that just made her think about how he'd known what that would mean to her. So she tried thinking about the fact that the creatures he admired most were the predators, and what that said about him.

I admire getting the job done.

So did she, didn't she? Her entire life was about getting the job done; it was merely a different sort of job. She—

"I wonder," he murmured, staring out over the lake as if he were seeing something else entirely.

"You wonder what?" she asked after a moment when he didn't go on.

He still didn't look at her, but he answered, in a tone that sounded like her father when he was thinking out loud. "If Sanderson would be willing to move his development back a little, and maybe put some effort into improving the wetlands, or maybe building a sanctuary of sorts, or a bird study center. Maybe the county would trade him some land to do that."

She nearly gaped at him. That was exactly the sort of compromise she always worked toward, and he'd come up with it just like that.

"He could make it a selling point," he murmured, even more quietly now, brow furrowed, still staring out over the water. "Give buyers a stake in preserving the wetland, maybe even put part of homeowner's association fees toward maintaining them. I'm sure there are people who would buy into it just for those reasons." For another long moment, he kept looking out over the lake. Then he gave his head a sharp shake. And glanced at her. "Sorry," he muttered. "Just thinking out loud."

She was certain she was still gaping at him but couldn't help it. "Don't apologize. It's a perfect solution. Exactly what I work toward." He smiled then, looking pleased, although there was a touch of surprise in it. "Do you think the county would do that? Could they afford it?"

"No idea," he answered. "There might be some Chickadee Checkoff funds available, since it's essentially to protect wildlife." She was familiar with the term in some states for the checkboxes on tax returns that sent taxpayer donations to specific causes. "Problem would be convincing them, since everyone thinks their cause is the most important."

She smiled at back at him. "I'm very good at convincing." She was looking right at him then and didn't—couldn't—miss the flare of something hot and almost intimate in his eyes.

"I know you are," he said, and his voice sounded as his gaze had looked. A strange combination of heat and chill swept over her, and feeling a shiver go down her spine at the same time, her cheeks flushed. It was an experience she'd never had before.

But she'd never met a man like this one before. And certainly never one who did such crazy things to her, when they'd never even kissed.

Yet.

The single short word echoed in her mind. And she knew that on some level her mind had already decided it would happen. She also realized that if left up to him, it would not. Because he wouldn't. He would see it as a violation of his duty. She almost blushed all over again at the thought, which seemed old-fashioned to her very modern mind, but she couldn't deny it was very appealing.

It also meant it would be up to her.

A challenge. She was always up for a challenge.

Chapter Twenty-Four

Ty was actually grateful for the new boat that cruised into sight off the point. As he'd told her, this time of year, there were more locals and regulars out than strangers, but this was a brand that was chiefly used by a boat-rental operation near the park.

He watched the small vessel for a moment, noticed the turn and the overcorrection as it tried to get closer. Unfamiliarity with the controls, or maybe boats in general.

It was enough.

"Time to head back," he said, still watching.

"What is it?"

"Time to head back," he repeated, turning and taking her elbow in case she wanted to argue. Even as he thought it, she denied it.

"I wasn't arguing, but why? That boat you were staring at?"

"It's a rental."

"Is that unusual?"

"Sort of. It's from a place that closes down to just a few boats this time of year, so they can repair and maintain the rest of their fleet." He glanced at her, then.

"I used to work there summers, and some of those renters brought boats back in sorry shape."

She looked out toward the newcomer. "Like this guy, who can't figure out the controls?" No, she didn't miss much. He'd just had the thought when he heard her breath catch. "You think he's here…because of me?"

"I think we don't gamble he's not."

To his relief, she didn't make a case out of it and started back the way they had come. He felt a little easier once they were out of sight from the water, knowing that if it had been someone intent on her, they'd been far enough out and the boat's driver awkward enough that they likely hadn't had a chance to verify it was her.

She seemed intent on the walk, but he knew all too well by now that that agile mind of hers never rested. She would be hell on wheels to try to keep up with.

Why he was even thinking that escaped him. It certainly wouldn't be his job to keep up with her, not after this was over. Since she'd only promised her parents two weeks, it soon would be. Although he had a feeling if Elite could show a valid actual threat, her parents would at least try to convince her to extend the situation. He didn't know whether to hope for that or not.

Of course not, you idiot. You want her in danger?

No, he didn't. But he wasn't looking forward to the end of this job, either. He'd gotten too much enjoyment—something rare enough for him to be notable—out of the quiet hours they'd spent reading, or the time spent hiking, fishing or just talking.

Of course, it would be entirely different on the outside. In her normal life, she'd be on the go all the time, jetting here and there, mostly glued to that phone of hers, or being interviewed or making speeches or giving talks on her favorite causes. There wouldn't be many quiet, peaceful hours of the sort they'd shared under these conditions. No, her life was not only different, it took place in a different world, and one he wanted no part of.

As if that were an issue. It's not like she—

He heard her let out a little cry in the same instant he saw her start to fall backward toward him as she apparently slipped or put her foot down wrong. He reacted instinctively, instantly grabbing her and stepping forward at the same time. She stayed upright but ended up pressed solidly against him.

"Oh," she said, rather breathlessly.

Yeah. Oh.

He thought it as his body went on full alert. The jolt of adrenaline when he'd thought she would fall had shifted to other purposes, and when he felt the taut, luscious curve of her backside pressed against him, there was no denying where it had gone.

He should let her go, step back, yet the simple act seemed beyond him at the moment. And so he held on, until she turned in his arms, obviously unaware of what the added friction was doing to him.

She stood there, looking up at him with the oddest expression. Warm yet cautious, shy yet intent. And that smile, that slight curve of those soft lips he just knew would be warm and pliant, was the sweetest damn thing he'd ever seen.

And then she was moving, still pressed against him but stretching up, her slender body sliding over him in a way that made newly awakened parts start demanding.

"Ash..."

He couldn't even finish her name, because he'd

known where she was headed. Again, he gave his body the order to step back, to get his hands off her. And again, it ignored him, far too enamored of the feel of her to give it up merely because he knew he should.

Then she was kissing him, and it was more than even his recently vivid imagination could ever have produced. Her mouth wasn't just warm and pliant. It was luscious, sweet and at the same time fierce and demanding. And when he felt the tip of her tongue brush over his lower lip, it sent a shudder of sensation through him and he was lost.

FOR A MOMENT, Ashley was afraid she'd miscalculated. Or else she'd stunned him, which was more acceptable than thinking he hadn't wanted this at all.

But that was her last coherent thought. In the instant after she had her first delicious taste of him on the tip of her tongue, he broke and was kissing her back. She knew he had wanted this, and if his intensity was anything to go by, he'd wanted it as much as she had. That made her want even more.

She hungrily deepened the kiss and savored the low groan that ripped from his throat. Her head spun, but she didn't care, as long as he didn't stop. The ground seemed to shift, until that slip and near fall she'd manufactured might become the real thing. It built and built as she probed, tasted, relished. Only a need for air, after longer than she would have thought possible, made her pull back enough to catch a breath.

His fingers tightened on her shoulders, as if he were afraid she would bolt, which made no sense since she'd started this. With full and aware intent. But without any idea what it would really be like, with no clue about the way it would erupt into a searing blaze. How could she have any idea, when she'd never felt anything like it in her life?

Her first thought, when friends told her of their own experiences, was that the accounts were exaggerations. That while you could feel attracted, even fiercely so, to someone, the tales of fire and soaring sensation were hyperbole. But then she would think of her parents, and their decades-long love affair, and the fact that despite their wealth, all they had ever told her to do was to find the kind of love they had and be happy. The more disconcerting fact was that they both insisted that they'd known their destiny before they'd even spoken, the moment they'd spotted each other across a college lecture hall.

That she was thinking that now, after a kiss that had shaken her from head to toe, was beyond unsettling. If Ty hadn't looked as stunned as she felt, she didn't know what she would have done.

He started to pull back, or at least tried to, but it seemed he was no more able to move away than she was. She caught a glimpse of his eyes, a darker blue than ever, heard him suck in a breath so deep it hinted that he'd needed it as badly as she had. Then his head came back down, his mouth captured hers, and she felt an entirely different kind of thrill, which made no sense to her either. Why would it be different? Why would him kissing her instead of the other way around be so very…special?

Then she was lost again in that flood of sensation, that rippling heat, until she was clutching at him almost wildly, wanting more, ever more. Right here, right now, on the cold ground, she didn't care. She had to have more. She had to have it all. With him, it had to be all.

When he broke the kiss, her head kept spinning for a moment. She heard a low, faint "Damn," and it took her a moment to register he'd actually said it. She felt a shudder go through him, ending with his hands tightening on her shoulders once more. And then he stepped firmly, purposefully back away from her. If she hadn't had the prominent evidence that he'd been as aroused as she had been pressing against her abdomen seconds ago, she might have felt hurt.

"That should never have happened," he said stiffly. "I'm sorry."

She, who had an answer for every situation, didn't seem to have one ready for this. It took her a moment to remember how to speak, anyway.

"I...believe I'm the one who started it."

"Doesn't matter. I should have stopped it."

She should have realized he would react this way. If she'd learned nothing else about Ty Colton this week, it was that he took his job—protecting her—very seriously. And obviously, in his mind, that included protecting her from him. Even if she didn't want that particular protection.

"I'm very glad you didn't," she said softly. "I wouldn't have missed that for the world."

He looked startled that she'd said it, but when he looked away, as if he couldn't meet her gaze any longer, she thought she saw the slightest curve of one corner of his mouth. As if he were pleased but didn't dare show it.

"It's getting late. We'd better get back." His voice was so rough she knew she'd been right. And that was enough.

For now.

Chapter Twenty-Five

Ty's jaw was getting tired of being clenched so much. This was ridiculous.

On their hike back to the cabin, they had reached the spot where the tree had gone down, and he thought that grabbing the splitting ax and tackling that big pile of logs would be just the thing to take the edge off. Too bad it was already getting dark. Besides, he couldn't leave her alone for as long as that job would take. Which of course compounded the problem.

Yeah, he'd made a mistake, a huge one, letting that kiss happen. He'd compounded it by initiating one himself. But that didn't mean he had to spend every minute obsessing about it. He could stop that. Use some of that stubborn he was known for. Hadn't his boss told him one of the reasons he took him on was that he was stubborn enough to stay out of the Colton family business?

And damn lucky you did, or you'd be a suspect in that mess instead of trying to unravel the truth about it.

Not that he'd gotten much unraveling done since Eric had dropped this job on him. He knew his sister Jordana was still digging, and that she wouldn't stop until she had the truth; she was nothing if not determined. Eric himself said she was the kind of determined he always looked for when recruiting. Ty had always admired the way she'd stood up to the old man, and when he'd told her that, she'd said she admired him for the same thing.

"I guess we did stand up to him, didn't we? He was about as happy about you joining the Navy as he was about me going with Elite."

And in the end, they respected each other for taking the harder path because it was the right thing for them.

But he kind of doubted Jordana envied anyone these days. She and Clint had worked things out and she was happier than he'd ever seen her. He'd always told her he thought the Chicago businessman was a good guy, and the way he'd handled the chaos that the current Colton mess had brought into his life had only proved that in Ty's book.

But that hadn't slowed down her dogged investigation in the least. Still, Ty was bothered by not being hands-on himself, despite the fact that technically he had no legal standing. Because he knew that in a private capacity, both he and Brooks could sometimes get people to open up in ways the police could not. Something about that lack of arrest powers made people more willing to talk.

But he wasn't out there working on it. He was stuck here. Stuck with the woman he'd thought would be the proverbial spoiled little rich girl but who instead had intrigued him at every turn. Including physically, he reluctantly admitted. It was a line he'd never crossed while working before, yet now he wanted not just cross it but obliterate it. And that shook him to the core.

"That's quite a frown."

A snap of adrenaline shot through him. That was

twice now she'd come up on him and he'd been unaware. Which meant he'd been unaware of their surroundings, too, out here in the open.

Idiot. Get your head in the game, Colton. You're supposed to be protecting that body, not lusting after it.

This had to stop. Both times she'd surprised him, it had been because he was so deep into thinking about her that he'd been oblivious. In this case, he'd been reliving that kiss, again and again in his mind. And that, obviously, was not something he could admit to her. He could barely admit it to himself.

Backtracking in his thoughts for an answer to her comment, he said, "Just thinking about a family problem."

She studied him for a moment. Not that he knew that from looking at her, since at the moment he didn't think he dared. But he'd swear he could feel her gaze on him as they started walking again.

"The bodies they found or the cancer cases?" she asked. He stopped dead, turning his head sharply. Stared at her. "I told you I saw something. Now I remember what it was. Researching the area, I saw some of the stories, about both," she explained.

"And the idea that those cancers are somehow connected to Colton Construction is right up your alley, isn't it?"

His voice was sharp, and he was a little surprised at himself. He'd sounded more than just edgy because he felt like he'd been slacking off on the job at hand. He'd been worried about the whole situation, yes, but he wasn't used to feeling defensive about the family business, and didn't know why he'd retorted like that. Except she got to him in many ways he wasn't used to.

"I have some knowledge and experience with such cases, yes," she said easily, as if he hadn't snapped. Then he realized she was probably used to dealing with upset or angry people about these things. "And the fact that in the study I saw, all the men who've become ill worked for the same company at the same time, at the same building site is highly suggestive."

"I'm sure." He'd thought the same thing, and again wondered why he was feeling edgy about her putting it into words. Sure, he'd always defend his family, but that she was saying what others had, what he himself had considered seemed different somehow.

"There could be many causes," she said. "Contaminated building materials, lack of careful workplace practices."

"Right."

She tilted her head as she looked at him. "I'm not making accusations. It's far too early for that, and it may well be your family's company has nothing to do with it. It could be something that had already been in place, nothing they were responsible for. For example, if something had once been built there using arsenic-treated wood before it was banned. The arsenic can leach into the soil and contaminate it, and there would be no way to have known without testing."

By now he wasn't surprised at her knowledge about similar situations. It had become clear she was no figurehead, no front or money supplier who talked big, spent money, but knew nothing. She did, as she'd said, her homework, and she learned and remembered.

What surprised him was her willingness to proffer an explanation where Colton Construction was absolved.

Someday maybe you'll get it through your head that she's not what you expected, in any way.

Someday? He was thinking as if it would matter on that future someday. As if when this was over she wouldn't simply go back to her world, and he would stay here in his.

He was calling himself all sorts of stupid when they finally cleared the trees. And he stopped dead again. Glanced at his watch, wondering if it was off. It was barely past sunset, so he'd thought the deeper darkness had been the trees. Even leafless, the big cottonwoods cast shadows.

But now, for the first time since they'd left the point he got a clear look at the sky to the west. The storm clouds had arrived and were piling up in a way that told him that the predicted strong frontal system was approaching. But it wasn't that that had the hair on the back of his neck prickling, it was the sky itself.

Green.

There was no mistaking the tint of green in more than one place.

"Come on," he said, "we need to get to the cabin."

"Why the rush?" she asked, although she picked up her pace to keep up with him. And she could do it, with those long legs of hers.

He gave himself a mental slap. Now of all times he needed to focus. "I don't like that sky," he said.

She looked. "It does look strange." Her brow furrowed. "Why does it look green?"

"We can have the science-versus-folklore argument about that inside, but for now just accept it doesn't mean anything good and keep moving."

He was thankful she didn't argue. They kept going,

and he kept giving the sky wary glances. They were halfway across the clearing the cabin stood in when the hail started. Sudden and hard, the frozen pellets came down like a vertical avalanche, bouncing as they hit the ground. And them.

"Now we run," he said. And grabbed her hand. He told himself it was simply to be sure she kept up, but he didn't even believe it himself.

They ran. The hail was getting larger, harder, and there was already enough on the ground to keep it from melting quickly.

"It's moving fast," she exclaimed, and he heard the first tinge of concern in her voice.

"Yes."

He left it at that, seeing no need to voice his particular thought yet. But by the time they reached the deck of the cabin, it was more than a thought, it was apprehension. The moment they were close enough, he heard it, the blaring sound from inside. He swore, low and harsh.

"What?" She sounded worried for the first time. Distracted, she slipped on the step up to the deck that was slick with the icy pellets.

He grabbed her, kept her upright as he said with angry disgust, "We get about one a year in November, and it has to be freaking here and now? Keep moving." His gut was yelling *run* but the deck was as slippery as the steps, and he didn't want to deal with a broken limb on either of them.

"What?" she repeated, her voice rising a little. He stalled until they got inside. He closed the door behind them. "Ty? Tell me what that sound is."

He tried to ignore how much he liked her using his

first name. And finally turned to face her, the alert ringing in his ears.

"It's a tornado warning."

Chapter Twenty-Six

A tornado. In Kansas. Ashley couldn't help it, she laughed. "Seriously?"

"Very." There was no denying the grim tone of his voice. He was already headed down the hall toward the panic room.

She could tell now that they were inside that that's where the whooping alert sound was coming from. She followed. This was one phenomenon she had zero experience with. She'd been through hurricanes, earthquakes, even a volcanic eruption once, but she'd somehow managed to never encounter an actual tornado. The closest she'd ever been was one of her mom's favorite old movies—and not the one involving the flying monkeys.

He looked at the weather station in the array of electronics. Swore again. The landline phone in the room rang. He grabbed it. The conversation was short.

"Looking at it. Yes, too close. Going now. Hope so."

He hung up and spun around. "Come on. We're heading for the cellar."

She blinked. What cellar? "But shouldn't we stay here in the safe room? It's solid and—"

"Aboveground. They're saying the one that touched

down in the area was an EF3 to EF4. This whole place could be gone."

Fear spiked in her at those words. She decided it would not be wise to argue with him, not over this. He was Kansas born and bred, and obviously knew what he was talking about.

"I'll just go grab my—"

"No! No time. Tornadoes this time of year tend to move faster. We have to take shelter now."

His urgency drove her fear higher. She was close on his heels as he ran back down the hall. They went through the kitchen, he grabbed up his keys from the counter, then yanked open a door she had assumed was some kind of cupboard or pantry. But it was a stairway going down to the cellar she hadn't known existed. It was, oddly, mostly underneath what had to be the deck area.

He insisted she go first, and he closed the door as she started down, casting them into pitch-black. But then he apparently hit a switch because light flared. As she reached the bottom, she looked around.

She didn't know what she'd expected, but this wasn't it. It was larger, maybe twenty by twenty, with walls of what appeared to be solid concrete, broken up only by a set of steps on the far wall, leading up to what looked like an exit hatch of some sort. The heavy metal hatch had a small window that looked like it had been made for an airplane and able to withstand just about anything. There were shelves with what looked like emergency supplies along one wall, in addition to a counter with a sink and a microwave. On another wall was a small television and what looked like a duplicate of the weather station upstairs. There was a small couch and some upholstered chairs in front of the TV, and a table with several chairs near the makeshift kitchen.

That was all she had time to notice before a movement Ty made drew her attention and she turned in time to see him swinging a door shut at the bottom of the stairs. This was no ordinary door; it was thick, solid and metal, not wood. And it closed with sliding bars from the inside of the door that entered openings in the wall itself. It looked as if it could withstand a direct hit from a bomb.

"Why do I feel as if we're going into lockdown at NORAD?" she said nervously.

Ty gave her a look that was at first startled but then, unexpectedly, he grinned. Suddenly her fear ebbed a little. "That's actually where my Uncle Shep got the idea," he said. "He had the chance to go on a tour there once when he was in the Navy."

"That hatch his idea, too? It looks like it could be on a submarine."

The grin widened. "Exactly. It was made by a company that does just that. He wanted the window so we could at least get a peek outside without having to go out there. And it lets a little light in when the power's out."

"Your uncle sounds like quite a guy."

"He's the best," Ty said simply. And he said it, she noticed, with much more warmth than he'd ever spoken of his father. Then he gestured toward the back corner of the room, where she saw now there was a second small room, rather grimly built of cinder block. "That's the bedroom and the last resort," he said. "If it gets really bad, that's where you go."

She walked over and looked into the corner room. It

looked like a jail cell with the narrow bunk, but there were bottles of drinking water lined up on the shelves opposite. And a large white case with the too-familiar red cross on it, which only added to her unease.

"Define really bad," she said, nerves kicking up again.

"If you feel the cabin lifting."

She stared at him. Was he serious? Dear God, he was. She looked at the very heavy beams above them. Then back at him as he walked over and turned on both the second weather station and the television, tuned to a twenty-four-hour weather channel.

"How far away?" she asked, staring at the map.

"The one that touched down was just west of the dam." Her breath jammed up in her throat. "That's four miles from here, which is a long way, in tornado terms. Bigger concern is where there's one…"

"There can be more," she finished, looking upward again.

"Yes."

As she looked up, she remembered what she'd noticed before. "Why is this mostly under the deck rather than the house?"

One corner of his mouth curved upward in that way that made her want to kiss him all over again. "Good catch. It's so that if it gets really bad up top, we don't end up with a refrigerator on our heads."

She blinked. Then she smiled back at him. "I am forever amazed at the power of the human survival instinct."

"That was my father. He does know the construction business."

There was respect in his tone, if not warmth. At

least not the kind of warmth that had been in his voice when he'd spoken of his uncle. The Coltons must have a complicated family dynamic. She supposed that with eight of them, it couldn't be any other way. She wondered if all of them had the same rather stiff relationship with their father.

She made a mental note to give her father a hug when this was over. Even if he had annoyed her with insisting on this protection measure. Then again, if her father hadn't insisted, she never would have met Ty. And that somehow seemed a much greater loss than having her life restricted for a while. Truly, she hadn't felt restricted since they'd gotten here. In fact, until this storm had begun, she had barely thought about being without her phone. Her thought had been to retrieve it before they came down here, but that had been habit as much as anything, since it wouldn't change the fact that there was no reception.

But now it occurred to her that she wished she did have it, just in case. She could write notes on it, to her parents, her friends. Or texts that could be found later if the worst happened.

"You're looking pretty grim."

She nearly jumped. She hadn't realized he'd come up beside her. "I…was just thinking."

"Well, there's a news flash," he said, and the way he said it made her smile again. "About what? Being stuck in a storm cellar?"

"A pretty nice storm cellar. I would have pictured something rather dark and dank."

"It'll be dark if—" he grimaced "—make that when the power goes out." He glanced around. "But it is nice. Dad built it, but furnished and stocked it to my mother's specifications. She's all about taking care of people."

Ashley's smile widened. "Good nurses are like that. My mother's the same."

"But that's not what you were thinking about."

She'd hoped to divert him, but she should have known better. This was not a man who would be diverted unless he wanted to be. "No. I was thinking about…leaving notes for my family and friends. Just in case."

For an instant, he simply looked at her, but then he took a step and wrapped her in his arms. "Hey, hey, don't be going there. We'll be fine."

She should pull herself together. She should tell him she was all right. She should stand on her own two feet as she always had.

But this felt too darned good to do any of that.

Just for a minute or two. I'm allowed that much, aren't I?

She felt a shiver ripple through her. She knew it was a reaction to him, to him holding her like this, but he tightened the embrace and murmured more reassurance. Which only intensified her response to the strength of him, the heat, the caring.

For a long moment, they stood there, and she felt his cheek come to rest atop her head. It felt strangely intimate, as intimate almost as that kiss. And then he went tense and his head lifted. She looked up, saw him staring at the television screen. She hadn't been paying much attention to what the meteorologist had been saying; it had become background noise as she explored the cellar. Now she turned her head to look, but before she could register what she was seeing, the screen—

and the cellar—went dark. She wasn't startled. She'd expected the power to go out after what he'd said, but…

"What is it?" she asked. "What did she say?"

"Another touchdown, just north of Yankee Run."

She felt a chill. It was such a cute little town. She'd hate to see it badly damaged. Did everyone have a cellar like this, or at least something? She hoped so. She'd hate to think—

It hit her then. North of Yankee Run.

They were north of Yankee Run.

Chapter Twenty-Seven

This time when she trembled, there was some genuine fear in it. She might not have been through a tornado before, but she'd certainly seen enough images of the aftermath and damage they could leave behind. She told herself to trust his word that they would be all right. And in fact she did trust him, more than she ever would have expected. But still…

A loud crash from outside made her jump, even though it hadn't sounded too close. He tightened his arms.

"I suppose you're not in the least afraid," she said rather wryly.

"Worried," he conceded. "Although come to think of it, it might do my father good to have to rebuild this place. Give him something else to think about."

She supposed he meant both the bodies found in the Colton building and the cancer cases link. She found it rather touching that despite the fact that they didn't have the close relationship she and her own father had, that this was what he thought of. "I'd hate to think of losing that amazing historic ceiling."

"That'd really bum out my mom. She loves that thing."

This time the crash was even louder, and much

closer, and a little yelp accompanied her jump. She heard the blare of what she guessed was the SUV's alarm faintly over the wind. Ty reached into his pocket and a moment later that noise amid all the rest stopped. But he didn't let go of her, and she gave up all pretense of not wanting or needing the comfort. She did need it, and she surely, surely wanted it.

"I think," he said, having to lean down to say it against her ear so she could hear him as the howl outside intensified, "we'd better hit the bunker."

She shivered again. She wondered for a moment if he would have retreated to that final shelter if she hadn't been here, but decided she didn't care. She'd feel better knowing they were as safe as possible. So she didn't resist and they headed across the cellar and into the bunker.

And then the already fierce howl became thunderous. She remembered hearing that tornados sounded like a freight train. What they hadn't said was it made you feel as if you were stuck on the tracks watching it bear down on you. It got, impossibly, even louder. Genuine fear plunged through her as he pulled her into the cinder block shelter. She held on to him, more like clinging to him, and she didn't care.

"It's okay, Ash. We'll be okay."

She heard the words, but it felt strange. She was certain he normally would have said them quietly, comfortingly, but he had to shout them for her to hear. And two things hit her simultaneously. One, that she would accept the usually hated shortening of her name from him, and second, that if he'd told her instead that they were going to die, the thing she'd regret most at this moment was that they'd never gone beyond those kisses.

An instant later, she felt it, that lifting he'd talked about. She bit back a little scream. And then startlingly, his mouth came down on hers. As if he'd read her thought, or as if he'd had a similar one himself, a regret that they'd never explored what lay beyond the amazing fire they'd kindled with just a kiss.

He plundered her mouth and she let him. Then she probed further herself, letting the thrill of the taste of him, the feel of him, the heat of him push back the fear. It was fierce, and fast, and held a sense of urgency she'd never felt in her life. She didn't just want, she simply had to have him. When his hands slid down from her shoulders to her waist, to pull her closer, she realized from the prod of rigid male flesh against her that he was as aroused as she was. And suddenly nothing, not who they were, not even the storm outside mattered more than having this man completely.

She became some wild thing she didn't recognize, pulling at his clothes, hastening to shed her own. Some part of her half expected him to stop her, to rebuild that wall he persisted in putting between them, but he never faltered. *Decision made*, she thought dizzily as his hands cupped her breasts and his fingers toyed with her nipples, sending fire shooting through her to pool low and deep.

And then she had his shirt off and she felt a new spike of heat at the sight of that broad strong chest and flat ridged belly. She was only vaguely aware of ridding herself of the remaining barriers of cloth, and they went down to the narrow bunk in a tumble. It didn't matter that it was narrow, because they were already so tightly together there seemed like more than enough room.

It was mad, it was wild, it was almost desperate. She couldn't reach enough, couldn't touch enough, couldn't stroke enough. And when he finally levered himself over her and paused, she arched her hips and reached to guide him, giving the answer to the question she couldn't have heard, anyway.

He drove home in a thrust as powerful as the storm outside, and she cried out with the sheer pleasure of it. Nothing mattered but this, and she vaguely realized that this was the human instinct that should amaze her, the human instinct she'd never completely understood until this moment, with this man.

Sex had been pleasurable for her before, but they'd surpassed that level with that first kiss. This was something much, much more, something bigger, something transcendent.

When he shifted to take one nipple into his mouth and suckle it, then flick it with his tongue, her body careened out of control. She felt as if she were headed for some crazed plunge into the unknown. Then came the explosion, and she knew what had come before had been only a prelude.

She let herself scream because she couldn't help it, but it was drowned out by the storm.

TY WONDERED IF he'd ever heard such silence in his life. He knew it technically wasn't silence. There were noises—mostly things falling, it seemed like. Creaking as things settled. He knew it just seemed like utter, total silence after the roaring sound last night that had come closer and closer until it was deafening. The total darkness of the storm cellar intensified the feeling, and had seemed to magnify the already deafening roar.

The sound, and the rumble he could actually feel, that had brought real, genuine and thankfully rare fear with it, fear that he and Ashley wouldn't survive the hit that sounded nearly direct.

But they had survived.

Oh, boy, had they survived.

His body was still feeling the aftershocks of that moment, a moment he would have sworn had come at the peak of the tornado strike that he knew had been far too close. The moment when she had moaned out his name as her nails dug into his back, and her sleek, hot body had clenched around him, driving him over the edge into some dizzying, swirling place he'd never been before. The pulsing throb had gone on and on, until he couldn't even hear the howl going on above them over the hammering of his pulse in his ears.

And now, in the silent darkness, his instinct should have been to emerge, to check the damage, but all he wanted to do was stay right here, buried in the heat of her, and start all over again.

It was dark out, anyway. Better to wait until morning, right?

Even as he silently admitted he was using the dark as an excuse, she arched up to him, wrapped her arms around his neck and pulled him down for yet another of those deep, lingering, luscious kisses. They proved just how long he'd neglected this aspect of his life by the way he responded to her instantly.

More quickly than he would have thought possible, they were soaring toward that peak again. And then in that utter and complete darkness, savoring the sweetness of holding her close, he finally slept.

It was still fairly dark when he awoke, but his inner clock was saying it was morning. Early, but morning. He'd taken off his watch for some reason—

Memory slammed home. He'd taken off the watch for fear it would scratch the beautiful, delicate silk of Ashley's skin. Ashley, who was curled up beside him, with seemingly every inch of that naked skin against his own.

Where was the damned watch? He needed to know what time it was, needed to know if it would be light out yet, needed to check in with Elite and let them know they were all right, needed to get topside and assess, needed to find out if there was anything left standing up there.

He also knew he was focusing on all of that to avoid the huge, looming and utterly beautiful mistake he had made.

Ashley stirred. He started to pull away, as he knew he needed to. But her arms were around him, holding him close, and he couldn't quite bring himself to detach. Not yet. Just one more sweet moment.

But the longer he stayed here, nestled against her, the more interested his rebellious body became in a rematch. And while someday, far in the future, he might be able to write off last night as an adrenaline-induced, fear-heightened lapse in judgment, doing it again now that the immediate threat was over would be something else again.

But damn, she felt good. In that instant when he'd first exploded inside her, he wouldn't have cared one bit if that twister had landed on top of them. He half felt like it had anyway, because it had been like nothing he'd ever experienced in his life. And no matter how he tried to chalk that up to a long dry spell when he'd had neither the time nor the inclination to go after no-strings sex, there was a small voice in the back of his head stupidly chanting that this was what it was supposed to be like.

"Hi," Ashley whispered, "and wow." And damned if her tone didn't match that stupid voice in his head.

"Yeah," he muttered. What he wanted to say was, *Last night was incredible, let's do it again. And again and again and again, endlessly.* And that realization shook him enough to finally make the move.

He lifted himself off her, trying not to look at her slender naked body in the faint light as he stood. Not that not looking helped. He was hard all over again, and under current circumstances, it wasn't something he could exactly hide. Then she reached for him, her slender fingers curling. The memory of the first touch of her hands on him, those fingers encircling, stroking, caressing his rigid flesh from tip to bottom, nearly made his knees buckle. Knowing her first touch would incinerate his willpower, he took a step back and away.

He saw her puzzled look. "Ty?"

She'd lifted up on her elbows, and the movement drew his eyes to the soft rounds of her breasts, where he had nuzzled and stoked, and to the rosy tips he had suckled and flicked with his tongue until she had cried out. He felt a surge of heat that nearly staggered him. He covered it by backing up another step, safely out of her reach.

She sat up, then. "Ty?" she repeated. "It's all right. I

mean…if you're worried, I'm on birth control. There are crazies out there, so my parents insisted, just in case."

He hadn't even thought of that. Stupidly, it had been the last thing on his mind.

For a long silent moment, he just stared at her. The faint light from the hatch window barely gave him enough light to see her outline. But he didn't need any light at all. He knew that limber, lanky shape intimately now, and it was etched into his memory with such depth he knew he'd carry it forever.

Along with the knowledge that this had been the biggest professional mistake of his career, probably his life. Because he already knew he was going to pay the price for this one forever.

"What's wrong?"

"This," he answered hoarsely. "This was wrong. A mistake."

She went very still. "A mistake," she said, sounding as if she were enunciating each word with exquisite care.

"Yes. It should never have happened. It was incredibly unprofessional of me, and I apologize."

She was on her feet in an instant. "You *apologize*? After…*that,* you apologize?"

"Yes. I'm sorry. You have every right to make a complaint to my boss and—"

For the first time since he'd known her she swore, rather colorfully. "The only thing I have to complain about is myself, apparently. For being stupid enough to become a living, breathing cliché, the poor little woman falling for her bodyguard."

Her bodyguard. That was what he was. All he was. But then the rest of what she'd said hit. Falling for?

She'd fallen for him? That was crazy. She was a Hart, and no matter the local standing of the Coltons, and the higher standing of other branches of the family, she was way out of his league. They weren't even on the same playing field.

Hell, they weren't even playing the same game.

Chapter Twenty-Eight

"My friends will laugh themselves silly," Ashley said, not caring how harsh she sounded as she gathered her scattered clothes.

"Ash—"

"Just shut up, will you please? I find I desperately need to get dressed." And as she did so she found she needed to revoke the permission she'd silently given him. "And don't call me that. It's Ashley to you." Deep down she knew she would never forget how he'd whispered it in the darkness, or how he'd groaned it out when he'd gone rigid as he pulsed fiercely inside her. "Or perhaps we should go back to Ms. Hart."

He went very still. She told herself she didn't care. When she wobbled pulling her right boot on, she saw from the corner of her eye him moving to help and she waved him off. If he touched her again she was afraid she might lose her resolve. And wouldn't the world just love to hear about the lofty Ashley Hart begging a man to…

She'd almost thought the words *love her.* And that made her angrier still. It wasn't that she'd never begged before, she had. But she'd begged for her causes, for people to see reason, to listen to each other, to understand. But a man? No. Never. When Simon had left, she hadn't asked him to reconsider, hadn't even asked him to take her with him. So why could she picture herself begging this man all too well?

"Ashley," he said, "please understand—"

She threw up a hand to stop him. "Oh, I do. I get it. It was…it was storm-induced madness and I was handy, right? Meaningless."

He let out a short, harsh laugh. "Meaningless? Is that what you call something I'll never ever forget? Something I'll torture myself about for the rest of my life?"

She stopped with the other boot in her hand, straightened to stare at his shadowy shape. She hated that she couldn't see his face clearly, his eyes. It was lighter than it had been even a couple of minutes ago, but his back was to it, casting his face in shadow.

"I've achieved greatness now, haven't I?" She hated the way she sounded, the way the pain echoed beneath the sarcasm. "I've become someone's greatest regret." She yanked on the other boot, then straightened again. "There are some people, some I even know, who would pride themselves on that. I've never been one of them."

She determinedly did not look at him as she tightened the laces and then tied them. She was aware he was getting dressed himself, and forced herself not to steal even a split-second glimpse. She didn't need to. Every line of his powerful body was etched into her brain, probably permanently. And whatever her future held, if ever there was another man in it, she doubted very much if he would ever measure up to this one.

He finished dressing, and out of the corner of her eye she saw him reach for the weapon that she only now realized he'd put on the floor within reach last night. Ever the bodyguard.

Then he stood looking at her for a silent moment. "Ash," he began, and his tone was full of so much regret it was the spark to her fury. If she were the type who resorted to physical violence, she would have slapped him. Hard.

"I told you not to call me that! You don't have the right anymore."

He went very still. And when, after a moment, he spoke, that cool, detached professional she'd first encountered in the hotel lobby was back. In force. "You're right, Ms. Hart. I need to go topside and assess damage. Please stay here and—"

"I'm not staying down here, wondering."

"I need to make sure there are no hazards, things that could fall—"

"The tornado hit some time ago." And what should have been terrifying had turned out to be the sweetest moments of her life. But what she had wanted more and more of, he apparently didn't want at all. Didn't want her. She hated the way even her thoughts sounded whiny. Made herself focus. "Wouldn't everything that's going to fall have done so already?"

"There could still be things that could be dislodged and cause injury. I'll take a quick look first."

"And if you get killed by a falling chimney, what am I supposed to do?" she asked, her voice dripping with false sweetness.

"Just stay put," he said, not even blinking at her snark about his possible death. "Elite will be out here soon if I don't report in."

He walked out into the main cellar. When she

stepped out behind him, she saw that he was headed not for the stairway up into the house but the hatch, where the morning light was getting brighter. This had the effect of making it look as if he'd stepped into a spotlight. Her breath caught as the light poured down over his tall, lean body, reminding her too, too vividly of that body naked in her arms, against her skin, driving into her with sweet, luscious force, driving her upward to an explosion she thought would likely ruin her for any other man.

She shoved the very thought out of her mind as he started up the steps. "Why *that* way?" she asked and was pleased to hear she'd managed an almost matter-of-fact tone.

"Because I can at least see this is clear. There could be anything piled up against the inside door."

Meaning the whole cabin could be in rubble. She felt a qualm at the thought of him losing this place that had clearly been a family refuge. The thought of that unique hammered-metal antique ceiling being scattered to the winds, lost forever, made her unaccountably sad. She had felt…not just safe here—and she knew that was more because of Ty than the place—but comfortable. At home. She liked the simplicity of it, the lack of flash and glamour and the focus on comfort and relaxing. She even had come to like—well, not like, but at least not mind—the being cut off part. It had taken her a while, but eventually she had stopped unconsciously reaching for her phone all the time. If nothing else, this had taught her just how truly addicted she was to the darn thing. She was going to have to work on that, when this was over.

Over.

If the cabin was gone, this part would certainly be over. She wondered what would happen next, but didn't give it a great deal of thought. It occurred to her that Simon would have insisted they stay here in the cellar, where they had food, water and were relatively safe, until the authorities rescued them. But Ashley had spent a lot of time in parts of the world where there were no authorities interested in rescue and had learned you needed to at least try to help yourself. She knew perfectly well she'd be doing exactly what Ty was doing, in that case.

She didn't dwell on that, either. She was too busy watching as Ty undid the rather aggressive-looking latches that held the hatch in place. The man was a pleasure to watch move, no matter what he was doing.

Right. And he regrets what he was doing with you last night. It was wrong, a mistake, it never should have happened. He couldn't make it any clearer.

Some reasoning part of her, the part she seemed to have trouble hanging on to around him, understood. He was a professional, he had a job here, and that job did not include getting involved with…the subject. The client. Her. But neither of them had asked for this. And she, at least, had certainly never expected to react to the man the way she had. As if he'd been what she'd been waiting for her entire life. Even if that was how she felt, it would be crazy, suicidal even, to show that so soon. She'd known the man less than…ten days. What was that, a fraction of a single percent of the days of her life?

She gave her head a shake before her brain could dart down that rabbit hole. She watched as he swung the heavy hatch open, and more light poured in. It seemed the calm after the storm had arrived, and with it clear, or at least bright, skies. But she felt no relief, no joy of survival. Because as he started up and out, as she watched that long, lean, powerful body move, all she could think of was what else he'd said, and the wrenching tone in which he'd said it.

Meaningless? Is that what you call something I'll never ever forget? Something I'll torture myself about for the rest of my life?

"Well, Mr. Ty Colton," she murmured when she knew he couldn't hear, "I may just have to make sure you really do never ever forget."

Chapter Twenty-Nine

Ty was a little surprised when he clambered out of the hatch and found the cabin still standing. Not undamaged, but still standing. A quick scan of the surroundings didn't show anything immediately threatening, so he called back down into the cellar, "It's okay, if you want to come up."

He was startled when she popped up beside him a split second later. Obviously she'd already been on her way up.

"Good," she said, with surprising cheer. "I didn't really want a chimney to fall on you. It would spoil all my plans for later."

His head snapped around and he stared at her. That sounded like… It couldn't mean what it sounded like. But she was smiling, a rather private, knowing smile that made him wonder if maybe it had meant exactly what his clearly overstimulated—and attracted—brain had provided, complete with full-color images.

He fought down the surge of heat that rocketed through him at the idea. The thought of having her again, the light of day gliding over that silken skin and lithe, limber body was enough to make him want to head back down to that bed right now.

Finally deciding anything he said in this moment would likely get him in trouble, he said nothing and tried to focus on inspecting the damage. The chimney was indeed still standing, although the roof around was missing a lot of shingles. The deck furniture was gone, except for the big table, that was dangling over the edge lopsidedly. One of the large front windows was a spiderweb of broken glass radiating from the probable impact point of the branch he saw lying on the deck. But a look through the unbroken window showed that, save for some things knocked over and another broken window in the kitchen, things appeared fairly stable. And the door to the cellar was clear.

"It looks good. Can we go in?" Ashley asked.

"I want to check the propane tank first. I don't smell anything, but I want to be sure. And look for any power lines down that might cause a problem when the power comes back on."

She nodded. "I'll do that."

She turned away, as she went pulling some sort of elastic band out of a pocket and tugging her dark brown hair back into a tail. Practical, but all it made him want to do was pull it back off again so he could thread his fingers through that soft silk. Which made him think of it trailing over his body as it had last night, stroking him in a way he'd never known could curl his toes.

Damn.

He headed for the big propane tank at a much faster pace than he'd intended, because he was sure if he didn't get away from her, he would say something stupid. Not that anything he'd say could be stupider than what he'd done, but at least he could avoid compounding the issue.

Once he was as certain as he could be that the tank and the lines to and from it were intact and no explosion was imminent, he just stood there for a moment, pondering the unpleasant fact that he didn't want to go back to the house. He didn't want to face her. He had no business even worrying about that when he needed to be assessing damage and reporting in.

Lecturing himself every step of the way, if only because it kept him from remembering last night, he went. Ashley appeared completely able, unlike himself, to focus on what should be first on the list.

"The structure looks fairly good. Besides the roof damage, there's some siding missing on the north side and another broken window in the kitchen. And that," she said, gesturing at the deck railing he'd already noticed was missing. "I haven't looked inside yet."

He nodded, not trusting himself to speak, and headed for the door to the cabin. Once inside, he was relieved to see that except for some debris in the living room near the broken window, and the same in the kitchen, things looked pretty intact.

Me, not so much.

He didn't look at her as she followed him into the kitchen. He picked up the landline phone. As he'd expected, it was dead.

"No flying refrigerator," she said.

"Not this time." He supposed he should be glad she could joke. Or not. He wasn't sure. He wasn't sure of anything right now, and that was a state he was unaccustomed enough with to be beyond unsettling.

"How long does it usually take for the power to come back on?"

He didn't look at her. Didn't dare. "Depends on how

much damage was done. There were likely places that got hit much worse than we did."

"Just wondering if we should keep it closed to retain the chill for a few hours, or give it up and eat everything."

He still didn't look at her. "Whatever you want."

"On the other hand, you could simply stand there and radiate chill," she said sweetly. "Everything would be frozen within an hour."

His head jerked around then, almost involuntarily. Just in time to see her turn on her heel and walk into the living room, where she began to pick up some things that had been knocked over.

"Don't mess with the broken glass." The words were out before he could stop them, and before he could think about the wisdom of speaking in the tone of an order to an already-pissed-off woman.

"Why?" she asked, and her voice was even more deadly sweet now. "Afraid I'll cut your throat with it?"

He let out a long breath. "I wouldn't blame you if you tried."

She straightened, indeed holding a shard of glass that would do the job. "I won't say it isn't tempting at the moment. But while I may have made a mistake about your feelings, I knew my own, and the decision I made last night was mine."

He stared at her. It was a moment before he could get any words past the tightness in his throat. "The only mistake last night was mine. I should never have let it go so far."

"It? *It?*"

He'd handled many things in his life, faced more than a few tough situations in his work, and yet he felt utterly incapable of dealing with a woman this angry. Especially since he deserved every bit of it.

"I need to check in," he said roughly, and headed down the hall. With his luck at the moment, the battery backup on the comms had failed along with everything else, or something else would go wrong.

But it hadn't, and there was an undertone in Mitch's voice that told him it was a good thing. "Man, the boss has been walking the floor since sunup. The chopper's just about in the air."

"Stand down, we're okay. A little damage to the cabin, but it's still standing. Power's out, so we'll need to relocate."

"I'll set up the secondary location," Mitch said. "How soon you figure on leaving?"

"Right now, but I don't know what shape the roads will be in."

"You had better," Ashley said from behind him, "think about what shape your car is in first."

He frowned and turned to look at her. Damn, that was stupid of him. He'd assumed it was the wind blowing things around that had set off the alarm. But if the car was actually damaged, that was going to make things trickier. They might need that helicopter evac after all. "Hang on, Mitch," he said, as his partner started to speak.

"I didn't get to that part of my outside look around," Ashley said.

Before what had happened last night had caused a different kind of heat between them.

"What part?"

"A tree came down, partly on your car." For a moment, sorrow seemed to show in her expression. Sorrow that they might be stuck here, together awhile longer? No doubt. Before he could speak, she added softly, "The tree."

It took him a moment to realize what she meant. That it was the big cottonwood, the one Uncle Shep had planted. And a whole new possibility for why she'd looked sad popped into his head. He was probably gaping at her, but he couldn't seem to help it.

"Ty?"

Mitch's voice snapped him out of his daze. "I'll get back to you," he said. "I need to see if we have transport or not."

A minute later, he was on the inland side of the cabin, staring at the mess the big tree had made coming down. The only good things he could see were that it hadn't come down on the cabin, because it would have likely destroyed the upper floor, and that the main trunk hadn't hit the SUV. As it was, several large limbs had. The windshield was cracked and the hood had a serious dent that ran from one fender to the other.

"I'm sorry," she said quietly. "I know that tree meant something to you, to your family."

He didn't know what to say to this woman who moments ago had been furious with him. This woman who had both frustrated and inflamed him. Who had both made him angry and sent him to physical heights he hadn't even known were possible.

The woman he never should have laid a hand on, let alone everything else he'd done to her and let her do to him.

Emotions he wasn't used to dealing with roiled inside him and needed an outlet. He walked over to the front of the car and grabbed a branch to test the weight.

It wasn't going to move easily. He went over to the main limb that was on the car and could barely budge it thanks to the resistance of the wide groove it had made in the hood of the vehicle.

"Maybe you should try starting it before you kill yourself trying to get that tree off of it."

He looked at her across the damaged hood, through the branches of the downed tree. Her expression was as neutral as her voice had been. His mouth quirked. "Good point," he conceded.

He didn't make the mistake of thinking she wasn't still angry with him, but for the moment they seemed to have a truce. He dug into his pocket for the keys as he walked toward the driver's door near where she stood.

He was nearly there when a sharp crack split the air. That was no tree limb breaking. He whirled as two more came in rapid succession. A metallic bang told him something had hit the vehicle.

No question.

Shots.

Chapter Thirty

It happened so fast Ashley was barely able to process it. Ty dived across the three feet between them. He took her down to the ground, the thud nearly knocking the wind out of her. Then, her mind still that half second behind, she realized he was shielding her with his own body.

He'd drawn his own weapon as he did so. He fired a couple of rounds in the direction the shots had come from. The shots were impossibly loud, and she couldn't help wincing. Ty's free arm tightened around her as if in reassurance. And then he all but forced her up to her knees, pushing her to crawl to the relative shelter of the SUV. She had to tug at her blouse, which seemed to have caught on something, the way it was oddly clinging. Then she winced again as Ty shot once more.

For a moment, nothing happened.

"Come on," Ty muttered from where he was crouched beside her. "Shoot back, jackass."

Ashley nearly gasped. "You want them to shoot again?"

"I need a read on exactly where he is."

So he'd been hoping to draw return fire. It made sense, but didn't make her any happier.

All the while, Ty's attention was fixed across the clearing. And stayed there when he asked, "You remember how to work the comms?"

"Of course. Do you want me to go call for help?" Her mind was already racing. She'd go around the side of the house, away from the shooter, and go in the side door she'd noticed. If it was unlocked, there was that. She—

"Not unless you have to," he said, cutting off her rampaging thoughts. He gave her an odd sort of smile, then, to her surprise, reached out to touch her cheek. But shortly after, he was all business again. "Keep the engine block between you and the clearing."

It was clearly an order, and while she understood the physics of it, she didn't understand why he—

He was moving, in an oddly fluid sort of crouch, toward the back of the big SUV. Away from her. The pistol he carried was in both hands, in a grip she was certain meant he was planning to shoot again. Surely he wasn't going to go out there? She nearly screamed at him not to be stupid.

"Ty!"

He glanced back. "Stay down!"

And then he stepped out from the cover of the vehicle, weapon raised. And in that instant it came to Ashley so clearly it was undeniable. This was not a man who would ever, in anything, sit and wait to be rescued. He would take action. In this case, he would take out the threat, or die trying. It was why he'd reminded her about the communications setup.

And that moment when he'd smiled and touched her had been a "just in case."

Another shot rang out. And in one smooth, practiced motion, Ty adjusted his aim and fired. Once, twice. She heard a yelp from the direction of the trees across the clearing. A moment later came the sound of something—someone—running through the trees and underbrush.

"Run, you bastard," she heard Ty mutter.

But he didn't move for a moment, and she understood he was waiting to see if there had been more than one shooter. Standing there in the open, a target. And again she wanted to scream at him. And when no further shots came, she breathed a sigh of relief.

But then she saw the way his shirt was clinging to his side, as if wet. And her thoughts started to tumble in rapid succession. She looked down at her blouse, where it had been oddly clinging. Saw the wet red smear. Touched it, but felt no pain. Looked back at Ty.

His blood. It was his blood. God, he'd been hit. Shot. And since there was blood on her, it hadn't been now, when he'd stepped out from behind the car.

He'd been shot when he'd thrown himself over her to protect her. He'd been shot then, but he'd just kept going.

Even as the pieces fell together for her, he swayed on his feet. He reached out and touched the back of the SUV for balance. She wondered if he even realized yet. He'd probably been running on pure adrenaline, and when the crash came, coupled with being wounded, it would be ugly.

She ran to him. "Let's go inside."

He looked at her, shook his head. "I should go after him."

"In what?" she asked, gesturing at the pinned, damaged vehicle. "We need to make contact, like you said.

They can look for him." He wasn't moving. Stubborn, stubborn man. So she pulled out the one tool she was certain of. "Please, I'd like to go inside. I'd feel safer."

"Oh. Sure."

He was starting to sound a little foggy, and she knew the crash was imminent. And yet he put an arm around her as if to support her, when at any moment he was going to go down like the proverbial ton of bricks. And when he did, he'd be stuck where he was, because there was no way she'd be able to move an unconscious six feet two inches of pure muscle.

She let out an inward sigh of relief when they made it back inside. She kicked the door closed behind them, very aware he was leaning more heavily on her with every step. It was then that he looked downward, touched his side with his free hand. Looked at his bloody fingers. Then he glanced at her, saw the blood on her blouse. His eyes widened, and there was pure distress in his voice when he said her name.

"Ash? You're hurt?"

Was it possible he still didn't realize? "It's not mine, hero."

She grabbed a towel within reach from the kitchen counter and folded it quickly, then pressed it against his side to at least slow the bleeding that seemed frighteningly severe to her. He swayed, and she abandoned any idea of getting him to the closest bed. The couch was only three feet away. It would have to do.

"You're all right? You're sure?"

She didn't know what to think. Was this just professional concern? It didn't seem like it. It seemed a lot more personal. Especially from a guy with morning-after regrets.

"I'm sure. Sit down—actually, lie down before you fall down."

"I need…to…"

"Down," she repeated firmly. He was getting so vague it was scaring her even more. Once he was on the couch, she was swamped by the realization it was all up to her now. She was aware on some level that this was not something that normally bothered her, and on an even deeper level why it was bothering her now. She really had let herself fall for this man, and angry as she'd been at him this morning, she couldn't just shut that off.

"Call," he began, but his voice was getting fainter.

"I will," she said. "Bleeding first. I'm going to go get the first-aid kit."

She ran down the hall to the safe room, grabbed the white box that was a duplicate of the one on the shelf in the bunker. The bunker…the bed. She fought off a flood of memories from last night. There was no time now, even if it had been the most amazing night of her life.

Back at his side, she opened the lid. The briefcase-sized kit was well organized and equipped.

"Pack it," he said, his voice fainter yet.

"I know." She'd never actually dealt with a gunshot wound, but she'd helped Alaskan Dr. Kallik with a knife wound and a deep accidental stab with a spear, and figured the principal would be similar.

Except for the bullet part.

She'd deal with that later, right now getting the bleeding stopped was paramount. The bullet, infection, all of that had to wait. She dug into the first-aid kit and spotted what she'd hoped would be there.

She should have known Elite—and Ty—would have the latest advances for emergencies; her father would settle for nothing less. She knew about the new purpose-specific packing gauze that held small specially designed sponges that expanded and put deep, solid pressure throughout a deep puncture wound. It was better at stopping bleeding than anything else she'd heard about. It was not a pleasant process, for either the person doing it or the victim, but it worked, and nothing else mattered.

And if he bled out and died, she would never get over it.

He groaned the moment she started, but bit it off and clenched his jaw.

"Hang on, Ty," she whispered, as she proceeded with the ugly job of stuffing gauze into a deep open wound. Damn, she could feel the bullet. It wasn't really that deep, and it felt…misshapen somehow. And she could feel a sharp edge, doing more damage even now.

She swore, something she rarely did. Even in his condition, Ty noticed. "What?"

"I can feel the bullet. It's… It feels mashed."

"Ricochet," he got out through gritted teeth. "I heard the smack when it hit the car."

"The edges are making it worse," she said. "Every time you breathe."

"Just as…soon…keep doing that," he said, and Ashley felt a wave of emotion for this man who could joke even now.

"I could get it out, if I just had something bigger than tweezers to grab it."

"The kit."

His voice wasn't nearly as strong as it had been just

a moment ago. Hastily Ashley dug into the first-aid kit. Found, amazingly, small forceps. When she turned back, his eyes were closed. And he looked ghastly pale.

"Stay with me." And she didn't even care about all the ways those words could be interpreted.

His eyes fluttered open. His right hand moved, and lightly grasped her wrist. Her gaze shot to his face. He held her eyes. "I trust you."

The words echoed in her head. *I trust you.* Even after this morning, when she'd been so furious with him, when just an hour ago she'd been yelling at him, he trusted her. Trusted her to do what was necessary, even if the task was ghastly.

Which told her he knew her better than she thought he did.

Then his fingers tightened a little. "Last night…still should never… But I'm not sorry."

He said it with more energy than she would have thought he had. And apparently it was the last he had, because the moment the words were out, his eyes rolled up a little and he passed out.

Chapter Thirty-One

It was way too bright in here.

Ty's first thought when he tried to open his eyes floated around in his head for a moment before things settled. He tried raising his eyelids again, wondered why they were resisting, and if he'd have to pry them open manually.

"Come on, honey, come back to us now."

The soft coaxing voice was loving, and familiar.

Mom.

He smiled before he managed to get his eyes open at last. There was another moment or two of blur before things swam into focus. She was right there, as she had always been, her blue eyes warm with love and concern. Her dark auburn hair, usually up in a tidy knot, had a few strands hanging loose, as if she'd been in a hurry. Which was odd, because she was usually fairly fastidious about that. It struck him belatedly, as he also noticed the furrow between her eyebrows, that she'd been anxious.

It all tumbled together now, the sounds, the smell, the rails on the bed… Hospital.

"Hi, Mom," he managed, although his mouth and throat were dry.

Relief changed her expression immediately. She leaned forward and, unable to deliver her usual hug, simply grabbed his hand and squeezed. And he saw tears starting to streak down her cheeks.

"I've been so worried about you, Tyler," she said, her voice as tight as her grip on his fingers.

"I'm…fine." His brain was kicking into gear now. Shot. He'd been shot. He tried to move, and pain shot upward from his side.

"Hold still," his mother ordered. "You nearly bled to death, and you've been out for two days. Thank goodness for Ashley Hart."

His eyes widened. "Two days? Wait, where is Ashley? I—"

"She's safe." The second voice came from the foot of the bed and his gaze shifted. Jordana. "Mitch said to tell you she's safe, at one of the Harts' other houses. Mitch wouldn't tell even me where."

"Need-to-know basis," Ty muttered. But damn it, *he* needed to know. He needed to know where she was and that she was safe.

"Right," Jordana said. When she went on, it was in the concise manner of her job as a detective, although Ty was pretty sure he heard in her voice the urge to read him the riot act for getting hurt and no doubt scaring them all. "Mitch also said they have no idea who the shooter is. Elite had Sanderson under observation, and there's been no variation in his routine."

"He's not stupid."

"Unlike your chosen career," his mother said, apparently deciding that now that he was awake and at least coherent she could let her upset out a little. "I do wish you'd reconsider that."

They'd had this discussion often, and Ty understood that it was his mother's fear for him driving her now. He squeezed her hand and didn't respond to her words.

"Your girl's pretty smart, though," Jordana said.

"I know," Ty said, not even caring what it might betray that he accepted his sister's assessment. Although he did wonder if she'd meant it generically or if she'd somehow guessed how he felt about Ashley. This was Jordana, and she was pretty darned smart, too.

She went on. "She not only saved your sorry butt with that field surgery of hers, she saved the bullet she pulled out of you. It's pretty messed up, being a ricochet, but Yvette's got what ballistics they could get, and is running it through every system known to man or she'd be here."

He tried not to think about what Ashley had had to do and just be glad she'd had the knowledge—and the guts—to do it. "Good," was all he said.

"And," his mother added, "she chewed your father out rather fiercely."

Ty blinked, wondering if he was on the verge of passing out again. "She…what?"

"He was quite taken aback. She told him he was a fool if he didn't see the amazing man you are. If he wasn't prouder of you than anything he'd done in his life."

Ashley had said…that?

"And that," Jordana said with a grin, "pretty much told us where you two stand."

"Indeed," said his mother with an approving smile.

There was a flurry of footsteps at the door to the room. Ty looked in time to see Fitz Colton stride in, with Brooks and Neil at his heels, and some steps behind them Uncle Shep. His father looked strained. Older. Worried. He rushed to the bedside.

"They said you were awake. You scared the hell out of us, son."

He sounded genuinely concerned. They'd been at odds so much about Ty's refusal to go into the family business that most of the time they maintained a sort of armed neutrality. Maybe Ashley—damn, she'd really gone after the old man?—had gotten to him.

"Amen to that, jerk," Brooks said, with a swipe at his arm.

"Ditto," Neil agreed, only his light smack hit Ty's left knee. And off to one side, Uncle Shep smiled warmly and nodded at him.

Ty was more than a little moved by the solid presence of his family. The only one here who hadn't spoken was Bridgette, and when he looked at her, he saw the shadow in her blue eyes. Not only had she buried one man she'd loved, she'd gone through her own life-threatening experience just last month, and he saw the understanding in her gaze. Later, they would talk. And as if she'd read his thought, his sister nodded.

He glanced back at his father, again noticed how worn and tired he looked. He would also have to ask Bridgette about how far she'd gotten in her own investigation, into the link between Colton Construction and the outbreak of cancer cases among the workers. But maybe not with his father right here. He shifted back to Jordana, and thought about asking what the status was on the investigation into the bodies. Damn, there was too much going on, when all he wanted to do was find Ashley and see for himself that she was all right.

But before he could do or say anything, a wave of weariness engulfed him and it all faded away again.

When he woke up again, the fogginess had lifted. And…he was moving. Not he himself, but the bed. Gurney. Whatever it was. Down a hallway.

"Hey, welcome back."

His gaze snapped to his right, and he smiled at the tall slim blonde walking alongside him. "Hey, sis. What's up? Find something?"

"Still old cut-to-the-chase Ty, huh?" Yvette wrinkled her nose at him in obviously mock irritation. "Much as I love my work, I wish my family would keep me a little less busy."

"Wouldn't want you to get bored," he said. He glanced up at the orderly pushing the gurney. "Where are we going?"

The man smiled at him. "Your own spacious, private suite."

Ty blinked, and his brow furrowed. Yvette laughed. "Guess you wore out your welcome in ICU, bro."

He looked back at the orderly. "What would it take to get you to steer this thing out the front door?"

The smile became a grin. "More than you got on you, dude."

Given that he had nothing but the damned hospital gown, Ty couldn't argue that. But that realization brought home something else. He looked back at Yvette. His little sister might not be a field officer, but she'd been with the Braxville PD for nearly a year now. She'd get it. "Speaking of that, where is my…stuff?"

"We've got your clothes and wallet," she said, "and Mitch has your gear."

She put the slightest of emphasis on the last word,

and he knew she'd understood he meant his weapon. He nodded, relieved.

The process of moving into the bed in the regular hospital room proved to him, much as he hated to admit it, that heading for the front door would have been a bad idea. When at last they were alone, his sister looked at him seriously. "You scared the heck out of us, Ty."

"Not my intent."

"I didn't get to meet your Ashley, but when I do, I'm giving her the biggest hug in history. She saved you. And had the smarts to preserve the bullet."

Your Ashley. Damn, he liked the sound of that. And he'd give just about anything to see her. Anything except her safety.

"Something you're not telling us, bro?" Yvette asked, one brow arched.

Guessing his thoughts must have shown in his face, he hastily said, "Nothing."

"Try that on somebody who didn't just see you go all soft."

"That's a pretty unscientific assumption," he said, hoping a teasing jab at her particular skill would divert her.

"You want the lecture on micro-expressions?" Yvette countered coolly. "Not to mention I have years of experience reading you."

"She's a client."

"Uh-huh."

"Just tell me what you came up with," he said, feeling a bit exasperated. And frustrated at being stuck here, when he should have been out looking for the shooter. And the person responsible for those two bodies sealed up in a Colton warehouse.

"The bullet was already deformed from the ricochet." She gave him a serious look. "Which is also why it cut you up inside so badly. But also why it didn't go as deep as it could have. And it took some doing to get a valid result on the characteristics."

"Which were?"

"Aside from the lands and grooves, it was a .45 ACP."

He winced. "Then I was damned lucky it wasn't a direct hit."

She nodded. "Bad enough as it was. But there's one more thing." She paused, as if for effect. "It had a left twist."

His brows shot upward. There was only one major US manufacturer whose weapons didn't use right-twist rifling in their barrels. "A Colt?"

"Looks that way. Unless it's a British import."

"Narrows it down." In fact, he had a Colt .45 himself, but it was a historic, collector-type weapon he rarely shot. "Couple that with the fact that he wasn't a great shot with it. Maybe he borrowed the gun."

"They find it, I'll match it," she vowed. "Nobody shoots my brother and walks away free."

It hurt to lift up enough to grab and hug her, but Ty did it anyway.

Chapter Thirty-Two

Ty threw a shirt into the duffel, paused, thought about where he was headed and added a heavy sweater and a pair of gloves. Every time he turned he could feel the tug on his injury, but he didn't let it slow him down. Just as he hadn't let the doctor's orders change his plans.

He'd been laid up in that damned hospital for nearly a week. He'd been up pacing the floor of his room since six this morning, but with typical efficiency, it had been nearly noon before his release orders had finally come through. He'd considered just walking out without the paperwork, but he didn't want his boss chewing him out for making Elite look bad.

It was enough that a shooter had gotten to them, although Eric had dryly stated he figured a tornado touchdown was a good enough excuse. Although that still didn't explain how the shooter had found them in the first place. Ty knew no one at Elite would have let that out, so somebody else had to have slipped up. The family should know better than to talk about his work when he was on a case, and his parents were the only ones who'd known why he wanted the cabin, anyway.

He didn't bring up the subject with his boss, knew

he didn't have to; he would be already on it. He spared a thought for how lucky he was, even though he'd gotten himself shot. Lucky to have work he loved and a boss he both admired and respected. Eric had not only driven to Braxville to check on him, he'd waited around so he could give him a ride home to Wichita. Ty guessed there weren't a lot of bosses who would go to that extreme. And after learning where Ashley was—at her parents' ski lodge in Beaver Creek, Colorado—in the interest of not having to defy him as well as the doctor, he hadn't mentioned his plans. Or much of anything else.

He'd let Eric talk, noticed he'd once more seemed impressed with Jordana after speaking with her outside the hospital room. He had found Ty's mother warm and charming, but was unimpressed with his father. And unsurprisingly, as former military himself, had liked Uncle Shep, although he'd also noticed the slight tension in the family when the former Navy man had been present.

But he'd underestimated his boss's perception, because the last thing he said to him after he dropped him off was, "Don't do anything stupid, Colton."

"Not today," he'd answered, unwilling to go any further.

"Good. There's nothing that won't keep until you get a decent night's sleep."

Only the knowledge that the man was right, he wasn't up to the task at the moment, had kept him home last night. But with his plans firmly in place, he'd slept well, awakened early and was almost ready to roll.

He was grabbing his winter jacket out of the closet when his doorbell rang. He pulled his phone out of his back pocket. The phone he'd been tethered to since he'd gotten it back from Jordana, searching for any mention of Ashley, since he hadn't heard one word except from Mitch through Elite, that she was all right. Her followers were questioning her absence on social media, although it appeared they were determined to follow through on the demonstration she'd organized at the wetlands near Lake Inman, where Sanderson was planning his development. But she herself hadn't posted, which surprised him a little. He'd thought once she had a signal again she wouldn't be able to resist making up for lost time.

Maybe she had taken his warning seriously. He'd like to believe that.

Right. If she took me—or what happened between us—so seriously, she'd have at least called.

He knew Elite would have hustled her off to another safe site, and apparently Eric had agreed the Colorado location was safe enough, so he'd never expected her to visit him in the hospital, but a call would have been possible. If she'd wanted to.

Which made his plans a bit problematic. But damn it, this was his job, no matter how tangled he'd let things get. Her safety was his responsibility. *She* was his responsibility.

Not to mention that she'd likely saved his life. Even the doctors had agreed on that, that it would have been a lot more touch and go if she hadn't had the knowledge and the nerve to do what she'd done.

The doorbell came again, and he shook his head sharply. Looked again at the phone he'd grabbed and then forgotten as his thoughts spiraled. Maybe it was whatever drugs they'd given him in the hospital that was making it hard to focus.

Even as he thought it, he knew better. It wasn't hard to focus. It was just hard to focus on anything but Ashley.

He tapped the screen and called up the cam at the front door. Was surprised to see Jordana standing there, looking worried. What was she doing here at six on a Saturday morning? He tapped for the speaker. "Come on in," he said, as he unlocked the door.

He started that way, hearing his sister's swift steps across the entryway floor. He made sure he was walking normally, and that the ache in his side didn't show on his face. She'd tell him to take a pain pill, and that wasn't in the game plan.

"You're a ways out of your jurisdiction," he said jokingly as he got to her, to further stave off any fussing over him. She did look him up and down, but apparently that he was upright and moving was enough.

Or that what she had to say took precedence, he realized as he looked at her expression.

"It's Dex," she said bluntly.

He blinked. "What's Dex? Besides the guy who insulted Gwen and who makes promises Dad has to keep."

"The gun's his."

Maybe the drugs they'd given him in the hospital were still in his system, because he was having trouble processing. "Wait…you're saying Dex shot at Ashley?"

"No. He shot *you.* Yvette matched the slug to his .45."

Ty drew back slightly. Too quickly, and the tug

on his wound made him wince. "Why the hell would he—"

"I think he's behind the bodies in the wall."

Ty stared at her. He knew his sister was good, very good, but he was going to need more to just buy this wholesale. "Give it to me," he ordered, his voice tight.

"He had access to the building from the beginning. He asked Dad if he could use the cabin, and Dad told him you were using it for work."

Ty winced again, mentally this time. "Damn. I really don't want that spread around, that we use the cabin as a safe house. I thought Dad realized that."

Jordana gave him a rather odd little smile. "He does. But he was bragging about you, and it slipped out."

Ty knew he was gaping at her now. "Bragging? About me? I don't believe it. The old man's never forgiven me for going with Elite."

"That doesn't mean he's not proud of what you do, bro," Jordana said quietly.

He was going to need time to process that particular revelation. He focused on the immediate problem. "Just because he wanted to use the cabin—"

He stopped when she held up a hand. "Dad also bragged that you were getting close to finding the truth about the bodies. That being private, you weren't hamstrung like we are sometimes. And that you'd never quit until you did."

If there'd been a chair handy, Ty would have collapsed into it by now. Not because of his injury but in shock. His father had never said anything like that to him. He'd never had the slightest idea he was proud of him, of his work, he'd only known that he was unhappy he hadn't gone to work for Colton Construction.

Jordana apparently read his expression. "Come on, firstborn, you know you're the favorite." She let out a sigh. "Which is a lot better than being the misfit."

"Who's the misfit?" he asked, mystified.

She grimaced at him. "Me, of course. Not the oldest, not one of the triplets, not the baby. I'm just…there."

Ty stared at her. "You're the best cop on the force, one of the best in the state. Even my boss is impressed with you. If Dad's not prouder of you than any of us, he's a bigger fool than I think he is."

To his surprise, his sister blushed. "That's what Clint says."

Ty smiled at that. "I knew I liked that guy." He had approved of Jordana's romance with the Chicago businessman from the beginning.

But he supposed it was a measure of how far he was off his game that he had to work to concentrate on the sense of what she'd said about the cold case that had thrown the family into chaos.

"So you think Dex killed Fenton Crane and Olivia Harrison, and tried to kill me because he thought I was getting close?"

She nodded, and looked at him even more intently. "And I think he would have killed your client, too, to make it look like she was the target and throw off suspicion."

The thought of Ashley dead chilled him. The thought of her dying because of this mess his family was in and his failure to protect her made the chill arctic. He was supposed to protect her, and instead she ended up saving him.

He shook it off. He had no time for even self-recrimination now. "How sure are you of this?"

"Very. For one final reason."

"Which is."

"Dex has dropped off the map."

"Damn. Damn, sis."

"Yes."

"Have you told Dad?"

"Not yet." Again, she gave him that assessing look. "I thought you'd want to let the Harts know right away."

Ty nearly groaned aloud. "That our family mess nearly got their daughter killed? Yeah, I can't wait to have that conversation."

"I got the feeling you were a bit more personally involved than that."

He looked into those blue eyes so like their mother's, and couldn't lie to her. "Yeah. Well. My mistake."

"Are you sure it was a mistake?"

"Geeze, Jord, she's Ashley freaking Hart of the Westport Harts. Yeah, I'm sure."

"I seem to remember you telling me to go for it with Clint," she said neutrally. "He may not be Hart-level rich, but it's the same principle. So I'll say the same to you, bro. Go for it. If you lose, you'll only be where you already think you are now."

His sister, Ty thought as he got behind the wheel of his own SUV this time, had a way of putting things that made sense. *You'll only be where you already think you are.*

A little over an hour later, he was through Salina and on I-70 heading west. Just over five hundred miles to go. He had grudgingly sworn to make himself stop now and then to rest a little and eat, although it took some self-convincing. He didn't want to end up in a ditch, or later off the side of a mountain, if he pushed too hard.

Or worse, take some innocent bystander with him. And he had to admit, after a week of hospital food, a little gorging on fast food was necessary.

He was crossing into Colorado before noon. He was sure now it had been the right decision to drive rather than hassle with flight schedules and rental cars. It probably would have taken him just as long either way, and this way at least he could decide when he needed to stop for a rest. He ignored the ache in his side as best he could, used the pain to keep himself alert. And pondered Jordana's news.

Dex? He'd always thought the man a little smarmy, a little too charming. Many women seemed taken by him, in any case. And he took advantage. Personally, he'd thought Dex's wife, Mary, was deserving of much better treatment by her non-prince of a husband. It had been one of those not-so-secret things that no one talked about because they didn't want to hurt her, since she was so nice.

But…a double-murderer?

Neither of the victims in the walls had been shot, but he didn't think Dex carried a weapon around; Ty would have noticed. That wasn't the sort of thing he missed. Then again, this had been three decades ago. He had no idea what Markus Dexter had been like then. At three years old, he'd only known he didn't like the guy much, but his wife was nice.

When he got back, he was damned well going to find answers. And he'd use whatever resources he had, whatever methods—some of which Dad had been right about when he'd said he wasn't as hamstrung as the police—to do it. The family's future depended on resolving that double murder.

But his future depended on reaching Ashley.

Chapter Thirty-Three

The lodge was a timber-frame-style building, large but managing to be unpretentious at the same time. There were balconies all around, no doubt giving great views down the valley one way, up the mountain on the other side. That was the focus—the location, not the home itself. It suited the Harts, because it seemed they were everything Ashley had said they were. Kind, loving, generous…and crazy, utterly in love. He'd learned a lot about body language and signals in his career. Everything about these two declared they were a unit, inseparable.

When he'd arrived, they were just getting out of a large luxury SUV, returning from a day in Roaring Springs, another resort town to the west. They had gone to look at a location for a resort catering to people with disabilities they were considering investing in. They'd invited him in, gushing out enough thanks to make him uncomfortable.

"We ran into the local sheriff there," Andrew Hart said, as they stepped inside. A quick glance around showed him the interior was fairly unpretentious, confirming the focus was on nature outside, and Ty was even more impressed than before. "Trey Colton. Any connection?"

"I… Yes. Distantly." He tried for a smile. "I think we're all over the place."

"Well, he was a very nice man," Angela Hart said.

"And tough enough for the job, I think," Mr. Hart added.

He could see Ashley in both of them. She had her mother's hair, the same rich shade of brown and sleekly straight. But she had her father's eyes, that deep dark brown, with the same quickness and intensity. The problem was they were embarrassing him a bit with their effusive thanks and praise. He wasn't real happy about how this whole thing had gone down—the fact that he had slept with their daughter aside—and wasn't sure he deserved any of it.

"Ashley insisted we go take the meeting," her mother said, as if feeling she needed to explain why they weren't here with her.

"Of course," Ty said.

"Our personal security detail is watching her," her father added. "They know the house and the area."

"Is she all right?" The words tumbled out of his mouth before he could stop them, and he wondered if his anxious tone would register. Wondered if—and what—Ashley had told them.

He'd had a long time to think while trapped in that hospital bed. One of the things he'd focused on was the discussion he'd had with his sister Jordana when she'd come back from Chicago, trying to hide her heartbreak over Clint. All because Clint had never really told her how he felt about her. Jordana had told him how that had made her feel. Which in turn had led him to picture that morning after in the cellar, from Ashley's point of view.

This was wrong. A mistake.

How would he have felt if Jordana had told him Clint had said that, the morning after their first time together? He would have wanted to shoot the guy.

Memories of harsh words spoken had tumbled through his mind in an endless loop.

It was...storm-induced madness and I was handy, right? Meaningless.

Meaningless? Is that what you call something I'll never ever forget? Something I'll torture myself about for the rest of my life?

But the phrase that tortured him was the one where Ashley had in essence done what Clint had not. She'd admitted to her feelings.

...falling for her bodyguard.

He didn't know how much damage he'd done. He didn't know if anything could be salvaged from the wreckage he'd caused. He only knew he had to try. He tried to pull himself together.

"I think I should ask are you all right?" Mrs. Hart asked, eyeing him with concern. "I can't believe you drove this far a week after being shot."

"You and my mother," Ty said wryly, then feeling a little explanation was required, added, "She was a nurse, too, although she mostly teaches now."

She seemed surprised for a moment, and Ty realized it was probably because he'd known about her work. Did Ashley never tell people things like that? He'd understand it if she didn't. They probably always had to be on guard about people using any information they could find against them.

Andrew Hart didn't appear surprised at all. But then he was focused on only one thing. "Is there any progress on identifying the shooter?"

Ty braced himself. He hadn't been looking forward to this. "Yes. And my family and I owe you an apology."

The man's brow furrowed. "Your family?"

"It appears the shooter wasn't after Ashley. He was after me."

Mrs. Hart gasped, but Ashley's father held his gaze levelly. This was the man who had built upon the fortune left to him, not merely lived high on it. "You'll pardon me for saying that the name Colton seems to attract..."

"Chaos? I wouldn't argue that," Ty said wearily. He could feel the cost of the exertion to get here creeping up on him. "And that's why the family apology."

He dreaded the next part, admitting that being with him had put Ashley in danger. That Dex likely would have killed her, too, to make it look as if she had been the target and he himself just collateral damage.

"I understand," Mr. Hart said, now with an edge in his voice as his gaze flicked to his wife and then back to Ty. "All of it. And let's leave it at that, shall we?"

Ty stared into eyes so like Ashley's, deep brown, alert and doing nothing to mask the intelligence behind them. The man did understand. And he didn't feel his wife needed to know how close their daughter had come. At least not now. But Ty had the feeling that if the mother was as smart as the daughter, she'd figure that out on her own.

"Yes, let's," Mrs. Hart said. "You didn't know at the time, and you acted to save Ashley, taking the bullet that could easily have struck her," her mother said briskly. "And for that, we will be eternally grateful."

"May I…see her?" God, thirty-three years old and he felt like an awkward teenager asking a girl's parents' permission to take her out. He was just thankful they had no idea of the extent of his unprofessionalism. Yet.

Of course, if Ashley was still furious with him, as she had every right to be, they would likely never know.

"I'm sure she'll want to see you. She hated leaving you in the hospital," her mother assured him, and led him over to what appeared to be the main stairway. She gestured upward. "Turn right at the top of the stairs. Her room is all the way at the end." She smiled. "Ashley likes to look out at the mountain. Says she sees more of the local wildlife from there."

"That…sounds like her," Ty said, his throat tight.

Something must have crept into his voice, because Mrs. Hart's expression changed, her eyebrows lowering slightly. "Do we need to talk, Mr. Colton?"

He thought of everything Ashley had said about her parents, how much she loved, admired and respected them. And he knew he couldn't lie.

"That," he said, "depends on Ashley."

"In that case," her father said, "you'd better go up and see her."

He wondered, on his way up, how much longer he could stay on his feet. It was catching up to him. He could feel it. But the thought of seeing Ashley kept him going. He could crawl across the Sahara if he knew she was on the other side.

Still, it took him a moment to work up the nerve to knock on the door when he got there. And the silence that followed made it worse.

Finally he heard through the door, "Who is it?"

He'd never expected the effect just hearing her voice would have on him. An odd combination of heat and chill.

"I… It's Ty."

"Oh."

Oh. That was it? Okay, that made it a little chillier. "Ashley?"

He thought he heard something else, another voice, he thought male but couldn't be sure through the thick door. The possibility that another man was with her, in her bedroom, hit him hard. Had she started seeing somebody else already, in a week? Had the prof maybe seen his mistake and come to try to get her back? Had she—

"I don't need the car after all, Ty," she said as if talking to the family chauffeur, and without opening the door. "But will you please feed my pet snake for me?"

Every instinct he had kicked to life. That chill he'd felt hadn't been his reaction to her, it had been to the undertone in her voice.

Fear.

He'd been so focused on what on earth he was going to say to her that it hadn't made it through to his conscious mind, but his instinct had picked up on it instantly.

Feed my pet snake. Like there was a single chance this side of hell that Ashley, his Ashley, would have a pet snake.

He'd been right about one thing. She wasn't alone in there. But he'd been completely wrong about the rest. There was a man in there all right. And he wasn't there by invitation.

Ashley was in trouble.

Chapter Thirty-Four

She'd been such a fool.

Ashley knew she'd brought this on herself. First, and most importantly, by getting so mad at Ty. Now that she was calmer, now that she'd had a chance to think about it rationally, she should have understood. He was a man with a personal code, one he lived by as few did these days. And falling for a client violated it. Maybe he hadn't been exactly tactful about it, but in retrospect she found she preferred his bluntness to Simon's dodging the issue, letting their relationship simply fade away because he was too much of a coward to face her and tell her he was leaving and it was over. Ty would never do that.

Not that she would ever let him slip away.

Secondly, she should never have left him. It had torn at her so fiercely to leave him lying there, helpless in a hospital bed. She should have known that no matter what he'd said on the proverbial morning after, her feelings for him hadn't really changed.

Not that her parents had given her much choice about leaving. They'd sent a team of their own security who had practically carried her to the airfield where the private jet sat waiting. Only when they'd threatened to fly her to Europe did she capitulate and agree to join her parents in Colorado.

Her most recent mistake had been today, insisting her parents' security leave her alone. Nothing had happened for days now, she'd told them, and there was no indication anyone knew she was even here. She'd promised she'd be staying in her room, catching up online and not leaving the premises. And in fact she'd done exactly that.

But after chivying her reluctant parents off to their previously scheduled meeting, she'd spent a few minutes with her afternoon latte out on the balcony, taking in the clean wonderful smell of the mountains. When she'd come back in, she hadn't locked the doors, intending to take breaks out there periodically. It was a private balcony after all, and in her mind, it was part of her room, so it never even occurred to her.

And then this lunatic with a handgun had landed on it, and found she'd practically welcomed him in with that unlocked door.

She'd wasted a few moments wondering how on earth he'd done it, gotten onto the balcony. A few more wondering how he'd found her in the first place. None of that mattered. He was here, had a gun pointed at her, and she had to figure out what to do.

She'd known why he was here the moment he told her to go to her laptop and make a post. She resisted, but he'd grabbed her and forced her into the chair at her desk. He quoted what she was to write, saying she'd been wrong about everything and was calling off the rally she'd set up.

All her self-defense training was useless in the face of that weapon. Her crazy, quirky mind called up an old saying, that God made man, but Sam Colt made them equal. That mind then leaped from Colt to Colton, and she thought that if the worst happened and she died here, without ever seeing Ty again, it would break her heart. Which was stupid, because she'd be dead.

She reeled in her careening thoughts. *Think!* she silently ordered.

She tried talking, telling the man that Sanderson was making a huge mistake, that coercion would get him nowhere but in trouble. But this guy didn't even know what it was all about—she suspected he wouldn't know a wetland from a bathtub—or care. He didn't even react to the name, and Ashley wondered if he even knew it. No, the man was just the hired gun, and couldn't care less what this was all about. All he cared about was getting paid.

It had occurred to her that if the man could be hired for something like this, perhaps he could be unhired with the same incentive: money. She certainly had access to enough of that.

She had been about to open her mouth again to try the bribe when there had come a knock on the door.

The man's order had come fast. "Don't open it, and get rid of whoever it is. Fast."

She'd gone, hoping against hope it was one of the security guys coming to check on her.

When she'd heard Ty's voice, she'd nearly gasped aloud.

She quickly made up something about the car, hoping he'd get that she wasn't going anywhere because she couldn't. But she doubted that was enough for anyone to make the jump to what was really happening. She tried desperately to think. She didn't think her vaunted mind had ever worked faster in her life. There had to be some way, some words she could say that would warn him. He was smart and quick and he knew her, he knew her so well, even after only ten days…

He knew her.

It had hit her, then. And the words about her nonexistent pet snake had come out easily.

There was barely a moment's pause before he answered. "Sure. I'll do that right now. That rat'll be dinner momentarily."

His words told her "message received" so clearly she felt joy surge within her. And crazily, it was as much because he'd understood as because she knew she now had help. Very real and very, very proficient help.

"Thank you," she said through the door.

She heard—as did her captor—his footsteps going back down the hall. She thought she even heard him starting down the stairs. She didn't know what he was going to do, but she knew he'd do something. All she had to do was stay alive long enough for him to do it.

"Now get back to it. Get this done, so I don't have to shoot you right here."

"And then try to escape past our security? Good luck with that." The man's eyes narrowed, and she realized belatedly that she was so buoyed by Ty's presence that she'd let it show.

"Your security won't be a problem," the man said, and a chill seized her. Had he killed them? She didn't know the two men they'd brought here, but that didn't mean she wanted them to be hurt—or worse—trying to protect her. As Ty had been.

Her optimism wobbled a little as what she should have thought of first hit her. Ty was just out of the hospital, and it was less than a week after he'd been shot and nearly bled to death. She should have been worried about him, not overjoyed that he was here to save her. God, she really was a spoiled child.

Use that brain you're so proud of and think! What could she do to help when Ty did whatever he was going to do?

The only thing she could think of was to keep the man occupied, try to give Ty the advantage of total surprise. But how?

She went back to her desk, slowly, making him hurry her along. "You'll have to tell me again what to say, I've forgotten."

The man gave a derisive snort. "Figures. Just say it's called off, tell them not to show up."

"And you think they'll do that?" she asked, trying to keep him focused on her.

"They'd better," he said, and she wondered if the snarl was supposed to be scarier than the pistol pointed at her head.

"And what about the other platforms?"

He looked startled. "What?"

That's it. She could tell by his reaction she'd found the key, that he didn't get the complexities of the various social media outlets. "I've organized this on multiple platforms. I have the most followers here—" she gestured at the screen "—but I have well over a hundred thousand or more on two or three others. Oh, and I can't post to the major one without a photo." He looked utterly blank. "That's what it's for, sharing pictures," she explained as if to a child. "They all have a different focus, and on this one it's photographs. That's why it was established. You can't really make a post without one."

"Then find one."

He was starting to sound even more impatient. This was going to be a fine line to walk. She put on her best dumb socialite demeanor. "But all I have are pictures for the protest, and that would only encourage them to come." She tried to sound worried, when in fact her pulse had kicked up fiercely as, in the middle of her social media explanation, she'd heard the faintest of sounds from the balcony. Her captor's back was to it and he hadn't reacted at all, so she didn't think he'd heard at all, or else he had and had dismissed it.

She saw movement on the balcony, glimpsed a shape past the man's left arm, knew, just knew it was Ty. Her mind was racing full speed now, searching for a way to distract the gunman even more. Just posting wouldn't do it she needed something else, something to keep his attention focused on her, so he wouldn't look behind him.

She suddenly remembered how furious Ty had been with her about that post from McPherson, betraying exactly where she was. An idea struck. She called up the thumbnail of an old picture of the mountains she'd taken from the overlook not far from here. She kept it in the thumbnail size and gestured to it.

"How about this, to show them I'm not even there, so there's no point in showing up?"

As she'd hoped, he had to lean in to see the tiny image. She suppressed a shudder as the cold metal of the handgun brushed her forehead.

"Yeah," he said. "Yeah, do that."

She tried not to wrinkle her nose at his breath that

smelled like an old gym bag. "Now what should I say again?" she asked.

"God, you're stupid, woman!"

"I'm sorry," she said, in a meek tone she had never used in her life.

But she was able to do it because while he was utterly focused on her, Ty had made it into the room. He was coming toward her, but so slowly… Why didn't he just pull his own gun? Why didn't he—finally, stupidly, it hit her. Ty wouldn't shoot if there was a chance she'd be hit, and the man was so close to her that if Ty drew his own weapon, it would be a standoff. She could just hear that crude voice saying something like out of a bad gangster movie, telling Ty to drop it or he'll blow her brains out. So for her sake, Ty—just-out-of-the-hospital Ty—was going to try to take the guy down physically.

This all raced through her mind in an instant, and she quickly went back to keeping the gunman focused on her.

"I'm sorry," she said again. "I'm just so scared."

"You should be, honey." The man practically caressed her with the barrel of the pistol, and it made her skin crawl. As she was sure he'd intended.

"Please, don't," she said, and now the tremor in her voice was real. But she reached out in a pleading manner toward him, as if begging. He started to smile, and her stomach turned nauseatingly.

On the edge of her vision, she saw Ty launch himself. The instant he moved she did, too. She slapped as hard as she could at the hand that held the handgun, pushing it sideways. In practically the same motion, she dove off her chair in the opposite direction. She heard the man start to swear but it changed to a startled shout as Ty hit him, low and hard.

They both crashed into the desk. Her laptop went spinning onto the floor. She didn't care. The man was grabbing for something. In the surprise attack, he'd dropped the gun. She scrambled around the grappling men, eyes searching the floor. She saw the barrel, just visible beneath the bottom drawer of her desk. She didn't want to risk getting down on her knees, so she merely kicked it out of reach.

And then it didn't matter because Ty was kneeling on the man's back, holding his arm—the one that had been reaching for the weapon—tight behind his back, wrenching it so hard the man yelped.

It was over.

"Hey, lighten up, I didn't hurt her."

"Shut up," Ty said shortly. "Nobody threatens my woman and gets away with it."

As male bluster went, Ashley supposed it was fairly mild.

As a declaration of his feelings, it was the most wonderful thing she'd ever heard.

She didn't even mind the possessiveness of it. Probably because she was so happy to hear it. Much better than declaring what had leaped to life between them a mistake. A sin she supposed she would have to forgive him for.

Well, after he'd atoned in a suitable manner, anyway.

Chapter Thirty-Five

Things had happened fast, once the threat was neutralized.

Ty had disarmed the man—with the wry knowledge that he'd have been better off if this had been the shooter at the cabin, since he was carrying a 9mm rather than Dex's more lethal .45—quickly. He'd called Elite the moment he had the guy contained and he was sure Ashley was all right, and told them what he had and to keep Sanderson from scarpering.

Her parents had been badly shaken, and Ty had been almost amused by the acquiescent way Ashley had endured her father's anger once he found out she'd not only left her balcony doors unlocked but had disabled the alarm on them so she could step in and out as she wanted.

"I was wrong, and stupid, Dad," she had said quietly. "Nothing had happened in so long I thought it would be okay now."

Ty wouldn't consider less than a week "so long" but he didn't say it, mainly because he didn't want to pile on. Her parents were having a sufficient effect on her. Besides, considering how he'd come to feel about her in about ten days, he didn't feel he had much room to talk about time spans. And he had already been feeling self-conscious because of her parents' outpouring of thanks yet again, her mother's delivered as she clung to her daughter with tears unashamedly spilling down her cheeks.

They had learned the two security men—suitably embarrassed and angry—had been dealing with a man they'd caught climbing over the outer wall, a man hired by the gunman to divert them while he came in from the opposite direction. Judging by the look in her father's eyes, Ty didn't envy them. But once all that was dealt with, her father had ushered them into his study, where he made a phone call of his own. Ty could only imagine what power Andrew Hart was bringing to bear.

Ashley gave her mother a final hug before stepping back. Then she turned to Ty, and her smile was the most warming thing he'd seen since he'd set foot in these chilly mountains.

"The minute I knew you were here, I wasn't afraid anymore. I mean, I never thought he'd really kill me, not when he needed something from me, but he made me so mad, thinking he could just coerce me like that."

"And you," Ty said dryly, "are too optimistic for your own good."

She simply grinned at him. Gestured at them both, standing upright. "Obviously not. Besides, I knew you'd get it when I said that about the snake, I just knew it!"

Then she threw her arms around him, and Ty finally started to breathe normally again. He hugged her back, but the fear-induced adrenaline that had flooded him was slow to ebb.

"What the hell were you thinking, taking that swing at him?" He knew he would never forget that moment when she'd moved, when she'd shoved the guy's gun arm.

She drew back, although she still hung on. "What?"

"If you hadn't made that dive to the right, the guy could have shot you right there."

"That's why I made the dive to the right, honey," she said, in that too-sweet tone he'd learned was a warning. He opened his mouth to retort when, belatedly, the last word registered.

Honey? Did that mean she wasn't still furious with him?

"I... If you'd been hurt, I..." It was all he could manage to say.

"Then you'd know exactly how I felt when I realized you were shot protecting me. When you nearly died protecting me. And," she added in a rather fierce tone, "if you tell me that you were only doing your job, I won't be responsible for my reaction."

Since he'd been about to say just that, he appreciated the warning. Just as he appreciated her nerve and her quick thinking.

And the feel of her in his arms again.

On second thought, appreciation was much too weak a word for what he was feeling. He looked down into her eyes and knew he loved everything about them. Especially when they were warm and loving, but also when they were sparking fire. This was not a woman who would make for a comfortable, easy life. A life he wanted more than anything else. That realization didn't even shake him. No, a life with Ashley wouldn't be typical.

But he would never be bored.

"It wasn't only a job from the first moment I saw you," he said. And he would have kissed her if they hadn't been standing in her father's study, with him on the phone and her mother just a few feet away. A mother who was already watching their embrace with a pointed interest that made Ty even more aware of what he had yet to face.

Ty's phone chimed an incoming text, and he was thankful for the momentary reprieve from a set of, at the moment, hovering parents watching him carefully.

"That's Mitch," he said to Ashley. Reluctantly, he released her to pull out the phone. She didn't protest, but stayed close. He glanced at the text and let out a long breath. He looked back at Ashley. "Elite found Sanderson. Called the police in and turned him over. And he's talking."

He heard a small sound from Ashley's mother, and a low heartfelt oath from her father. But all he could see was Ashley looking at him with those eyes…

"Dear?" It was her mother, and Ty looked up in time to see she was gesturing to Mr. Hart. "I think these two need a little time alone. And frankly, unusual though it is, I find I need a drink."

"I hear that," the man answered fervently, and came out from behind his desk. He stopped beside them and gave Ty an assessing look. "You'll be staying for dinner."

Ty swallowed, felt Ashley's gaze upon him. But he steeled himself and faced the freaking richest man in the hemisphere. The man whose daughter he'd fallen for like the proverbial ton of bricks, no matter how unprofessional it was.

"Yes, sir," he said respectfully.

"Thank you," Ashley said after they'd gone. "For not arguing with him. As you can imagine, my father is not used to it."

"Except maybe from you?"

She grinned at him. "Maybe."

He smiled back. "This wasn't the time, not after what nearly happened here." One corner of his mouth quirked. "Besides, the respect was for your father, not Andrew Hart."

She tightened her arms around him again, and he knew he'd somehow found the right words. They stood there for what seemed to him a long time, but he didn't care. He didn't want to move. It felt delicious, and he wanted to savor it. He was feeling a steady, rather fierce throb from his side, but he didn't care about that, either. In fact, it felt right, very, very right, to be standing here with the woman who had kept that from being a fatal wound.

"I won't stop my work," she said, almost in a warning tone.

"I wouldn't expect you to." He grimaced. "And now that my sister's convinced there's a connection between Dad's company and the cancer cases, I see your point. Things like that need to be investigated."

She looked more pleased than he would have expected. "And I need to be more aware of the unintended harm—like that poor man's suicide—that can be done."

He gave her a crooked smile, the best he could manage at the moment. "Compromise?"

"Deal," she agreed, smiling back.

He was only vaguely aware that he was feeling a bit fuzzy around the edges, as if the world around him was blurring. No, as if the world outside them was blurring. And that didn't seem wrong at all. As long as she was here and bright and alive with all her Ashley-like sharpness and wit, the rest of the world could just blur away and he wouldn't mind.

But he needed—desperately—to kiss her. It had been too long, and they were alone now, so there was no reason not to, was there? He leaned in, already anticipating the sweet feel and taste of her. But the blurring suddenly expanded, engulfing him.

"Whoa!" Her sudden yelp startled him. He felt her move, quickly, felt her hands on him as if propping him up. "Don't pass out on me again."

"I'm fine," he said, but even he didn't believe it. She was urging him to move, although he didn't know to where. Didn't care where. This was Ashley and he'd go wherever she wanted him to.

"Sit down before you fall down," she said. They were next to a long leather couch. When he didn't immediately move—his processing seemed to have slowed down—she urged him with some gentle pressure on his shoulder. "You'd better rest up, Mr. Bodyguard. I have detailed plans for that body of yours later."

"Oh, I hope so," he said, giving her a crooked grin.

Then he sat, rather lopsidedly as his side jabbed him with pain again.

"On second thought, lie down," Ashley urged, and he didn't feel like arguing with her. It was belatedly starting to register that his wound coupled with an adrenaline crash was not something that he was going to be able to slough off as nothing.

Ashley moved away. He frowned. He didn't like

that. He heard her quick footsteps, then, over what sounded like a weird sort of soft static in his ears, he heard her yell from the doorway.

"Mom! Mom, we need you in here!"

He liked that *we*.

It was all he had time to think before he went under.

Chapter Thirty-Six

Ashley hadn't expected to be spending Thanksgiving this way, but now that she was, she was delighted. After Ty had rested up for a day, he was talking about heading home. But then her mother had stepped in, at first simply offering the invitation to stay and join them on the holiday, but following up with her best nurse's orders that he needed to rest longer, anyway. Ty had clearly felt a little awkward about accepting, but when he'd found out it would only be the four of them, he'd given in.

"What did you expect, a formal dinner for a small glitzy group of fifty?" she'd asked him. And at his sheepish, guilty grimace, she'd teased him unmercifully about those assumptions again.

They spent the intervening days mostly together, although Ty had a lot of reports to file, which she was happy to loan him a computer for. "You'll notice," she said with an arched brow, "we have an excellent WiFi signal, even here in the mountains."

He'd merely grinned at her. "I noticed you're not living with your phone in your hand anymore."

"I had it surgically removed," she joked right back. And silently looked forward to endless days of this.

Not at all to her surprise, even over Thanksgiving dinner, her mother and Ty got along famously. Mom had said Ty had told her his mother was also a nurse, and she expressed a rather pointed desire that they meet soon. All Ashley could say to that, rather dryly, was that if her mother didn't mind, she'd like to meet Mrs. Colton first.

Her father had apparently done a little nosing around, as she should have expected. He had a couple of cogent questions about the information he'd gathered about both the discovery of the two bodies in the wall of a Colton building—which Ty had tactfully said he couldn't discuss—and the shutdown of Colton Construction due to the link to several cases of lung and esophageal cancer.

"My sister Bridgette works for the state in public health. She was the one on that case," Ty said flatly. "She's certain there's a connection to the renovations in the historic district. She had to recuse herself because of our father, and now she's as ticked off at him as I am about it. And he's upset because her investigation resulted in Colton Construction being shut down until it's resolved."

She was a little surprised at how honestly and openly he answered, but she smiled inwardly. It was just another level of that respect for her father he'd mentioned.

Ty had told her about the man Bridgette had fallen in love with—the man's father was one of those who had contracted cancer. His concern for his sister had warmed her, and she found herself eager to see his family. Except, perhaps, his father. She didn't care much for how he'd made his oldest son feel.

If Ty understood he was getting a subtle third degree from both her parents, he didn't let on. He simply continued answering honestly, as if he found nothing amiss in being practically interrogated over the traditional turkey and cranberry sauce. This, too, was an expression of that respect.

She couldn't deny that she took a secret pleasure in how openly he declared his long-term intentions, the plan of a life together, which they had discussed in the late-night hours when she'd slipped down to the guest room her mother had lodged him in. Ashley hadn't missed the glint in her mother's eyes. She knew her mother fully expected there would be some hall traffic between that room and Ashley's own. Ashley had agreed to be that traffic when Ty had, half-seriously, said he didn't want to be the one to make her father mad. Since she wasn't certain she was ready to try to sleep in the room that had been—albeit via her own slacking off—invaded by that lunatic, she'd been more than happy to snuggle up to him in the guest room.

When the meal was done, down to the pumpkin pie, Ty leaned back in his chair, thanked them for the meal—much of which she and her mother had prepared together, leaving only the turkey itself to the cook—and casually asked her father if he'd passed.

Ashley almost laughed aloud at her father's startled, then rueful look. "Lost a little subtlety, did I?"

"She's your daughter, sir. I'd expect nothing less."

Her father nodded approval at that. But they'd still been cautious. Her father had been, anyway. "Then you won't take offense if I ask Ashley—" he turned his gaze on her "—you're certain? This happened fairly quickly, under stressful circumstances."

She was ready for that. "I did the math. We spent

ten days together, round the clock. That's two hundred and forty hours. An average beginner date might last a couple of hours, a serious one four hours, so compromising on three hours, and assuming dates on both Friday and Saturday, plus an extra during the week, that works out in the end to nearly six months of normal dating. And we—"

She stopped herself before the next words came tumbling out. Out of the corner of her eye, she saw Ty gaping at her. She seized on that to escape what she'd nearly said, and turned to look at him. "Problem?"

"I just never thought of it quite that way. How very… Ashley of you."

He was grinning at her now. Somehow she sensed he knew exactly what she'd almost said. And she grinned back, wondering what her parents' reaction would have been had she gone ahead and finished with, *And we didn't have sex until the last day, so that's really waiting a long time.*

When she looked back at her parents again, they were both smiling. Ty looked at them, too, and told them yet again he didn't want their thanks. "I only want your acceptance. Because I am crazy in love with your daughter."

He said it easily, but her pulse kicked up anyway, as it always did when those words came from him. And she believed them, because the man hadn't just told her repeatedly, he'd proven it by risking his life yet again. So that was three times, she'd told him teasingly. Once at the cabin, and twice here in the mountains, first when he'd come over that balcony and then again when he'd faced her parents, the power couple who intimidated world leaders.

"And I'm crazy in love with him," Ashley echoed.

Her parents simply smiled more widely. "We noticed," her mother said. "You look at each other the same way we did at your age."

"Got news for you," Ty said fearlessly, "you still do."

And in that moment, at the look on their faces, Ashley knew he'd won them over completely.

"THIS IS YOUR PLACE?" Ashley asked as the headlights lit up the big modern house with the three-car garage to one side.

Ty gave her a sideways look as he pulled into the driveway and the garage door closest to the house began to rise. "You were expecting a farmhouse, perhaps?"

She laughed, and he smiled as the sound washed over him. "Have I told you I love it when you're a smartass?"

"Do you, now…" he drawled, giving her a suggestive slow smile.

The smile she gave him back was full of promise, and had him trying to remember how big a mess he'd left his bedroom. "It's half the reason I fell in love with you," she said. "You never cut me any slack because of who I am."

"You," he said pointedly, "do not need slack from anyone." The look she gave him then told him he'd found the right thing to say. He told himself he'd best remember that about her. Then he added, "And that's half the reason I fell in love with you."

"What's the other half?"

"Let's get inside, and I'll make you a list."

She grinned at him in that happy, silly way he was

coming to treasure. He'd seen it often on the drive, and that alone made it worth it. Her parents had offered their plane for the trip to Wichita, but that would have left Ty's car there. And he thought it might be as well that they had the long drive together to talk. They had things to settle. Maybe it was the chaos that had struck his family lately, but he'd about had it with uncertainty.

He had asked her, when they were beside the car but before they'd gotten in, if she was sure about what she wanted. She'd kissed him so fiercely it left him wanting to go back inside and head for the nearest bed.

And when he'd found out she often drove herself around when she was here at the lodge, he had no qualms about turning the wheel over to her when she suggested she drive. That earned him another kiss; he wasn't exactly sure why. She clearly had more experience with these mountain roads than he did.

He'd taken over once they were back in Kansas. It had felt good to be back.

It had felt better to be heading home with Ashley.

Are you sure you want to live in Kansas?

You know what I find amazing about Kansas? How kind and generous the people are. I'd always heard about the heartland, but never realized how accurate the name is.

That had made him smile. His Ashley was ever and always willing to learn and change. *Can I take that as a yes?*

I want to live with you. The rest is just details.

He'd asked it as they crossed the state line, and her answer had come quickly and decisively, easing his nerves about the idea of Ashley Hart of the Harts of Westport settling down in Middle America. He was still working on the idea of he himself being connected to them, although the warm welcome of her parents had done a lot to alleviate his concerns on that score.

She insisted on carrying her own bag inside, teasing him that when he was fully healed, she'd expect him to do it, along with a few other more athletic things, words that sent his mind racing all over again.

When they were inside, she looked around with great interest, while he watched her a little nervously. He'd called in his mother for help with the furnishings, while he focused on all the electronics and connected devices that made the house state of the art. Thankfully, his mother knew him well enough to know what he didn't like, and so he'd ended up with things he found comfortable and thought looked good.

"I love it!" Ashley exclaimed, standing in the middle of the great room. "It's not ornate, not starkly modern. It's just homey and welcoming."

"Thank my mom for that," he said. "She picked most of it out. I just told her what I needed function-wise and approved her choices."

"I want to thank her for more than that," Ashley said, coming over to him. "She raised a wonderful son. When do I get to see her?"

"I..." He stopped, suddenly uncertain, as he understood he was on the cusp of changing his entire life. What had happened in Colorado had been sort of connected to his job of protecting her, but this...this was just them. He saw something change in her expression, realized he was giving her agile mind too much time to think. "I hadn't thought about when, yet. I just wanted to get you here, then...organize everything."

"At least you said when, not if."

Her tone was a little dry, enough that it bothered him. Hastily he said, "Let me show you the rest of the place."

She was impressed by the media room and his well-equipped office. Glanced at the guest room, which he explained was purely his mother's taste since this is where his parents stayed when they came to the city.

"She has good taste," Ashley said.

He felt a little awkward when they reached the double doors leading to the master bedroom. It was plainer than the rest of the house, a little too uber-masculine his mother had said, but he'd wanted it that way. Then.

And he had left it in a bit of a mess. "Sorry," he muttered. "I was in a hurry."

She smiled at that and looked around. But said nothing.

"Uh…there's plenty of room in the closet," he began, then remembered who he was dealing with, and that she probably had a wardrobe that could fill the entire sizable walk-in closet that he himself only used about a third of.

She walked over and looked, but only nodded, still saying nothing. He was starting to get nervous.

"The bathroom's pretty nice," he said, sounding lame even to himself. "And there's a sitting room over there." He gestured toward the glass French doors that led into the space just big enough for the couch and small desk he had there for late-night ideas or contact with the office.

She nodded.

"Look, I know you'll want some changes." He was now thoroughly into uneasy at her lack of reaction. "If you want, we can gut the place and you can make it how you want. Or we can move, if you'd rather."

She turned to face him, then. "I was just…absorbing. This is a special place, the…lair of the man I love, if you will. It has meaning to me."

He blinked. Would she never stop surprising him? He felt a slow smile curve his mouth. No. No, she wouldn't.

"I mean," she added, glancing around, "I'd add a dash of brighter color here and there, but nothing more."

"Anything you want," he said fervently.

She looked back at him and arched a brow in that way that made him brace himself. "And that sitting room, private but easily accessible, would make a perfect nursery someday." Ty's eyes widened, and he swallowed tightly. "Scare you?" she asked.

"A little," he admitted.

"Good," she said, and at last she smiled. "That means you take the idea seriously."

"I want kids, someday. With you," he added pointedly, reassured by her smile. "I was more worried about…figuring out how to be a father. I haven't had the greatest example."

"Feel free to borrow mine," she said airily.

"Deal," he said instantly. It made her laugh, and he grinned back.

"One thing I definitely don't want to change in here is that." She gestured toward his big four-poster bed.

His pulse kicked up. "You sure?"

"Yes. I love the style."

"I don't know," he said, putting as much doubt as he could manage into his voice. Her brow furrowed as she looked at him, clearly puzzled. "I mean, how can you be sure until you've tried it?"

Her expression shifted instantly to that glinting, teasing one he loved. "Was that an invitation, Mr. Colton?"

"Why, I do believe it was, Ms. Hart."

"Accepted," she said, with that delighted laugh he loved even more.

Ty pulled her into his arms. In the moment before he kissed her, he wondered just how long would be reasonable to wait before he asked her to marry him.

Another ten days, maybe.

* * * * *